T0246657

Togetha

Togetha

KEITH F. MILLER, JR.

HARPER
An Imprint of HarperCollinsPublishers

Library of Congress Control Number: 2024944523
ISBN 978-0-06-326497-7

Typography by Alison Klapthor
Illustration by SogoArts
24 25 26 27 28 LBC 5 4 3 2 1
First Edition

This book is dedicated to you. May this story wrap its arms around you and remind you: Because you exist, hugs, hope, and healing are possible.

Part One
Homecoming

1

JAY

In the car on the way home from the hospital, I'm grateful to finally be leaving. In a couple of weeks, I should make a full recovery—at least that's what they say—but everything still hurts. Every time I close my eyes, I see fire, I smell smoke, and I feel the heat as I choke. If I don't remind myself of the truth—that we made it out, that I'm alive—I'm stuck in my memories on repeat.

The doctors gave me an inhaler to help with the symptoms from smoke inhalation, but what about the pain they can't see, that only I can feel? I clutch the inhaler, more aware than ever of what it can't do, and as our house comes into view, something catches my eye, a massive pot of flowers. We've received tons of them at the hospital, but this one is missing the "Get Well Soon" ribbon.

Momma pulls into the driveway, cautious. "Y'all stay in the car. I'll be right back."

"Huh? Ma . . . Ma?" Jacob asks as he opens his door. But when Momma threatens him with her eyes, my big brother, in all his muscular glory, stays seated, even though he refuses to close the door. "What's wrong?"

Momma walks closer to the flowerpot, brown bleeding into blue. Its flowers, white upside-down trumpets, are beautiful, but she looks at them like they're dangerous.

"They prolly from Jay's doctor who couldn't stop smilin' at you," Jacob says.

Momma takes the pastel yellow envelope from one of the stems and reads it with a blank face. Suddenly, she crumbles the card in her hand, then storms into the house.

She reappears, holding Dad's hatchet, and lets loose a fury that levels the plant down to its jagged stems.

We stare at her, surprised.

When she's done, heaving, she wipes her forehead and says, "Y'all come on out and head into the house. We'll clean it up later."

What just happened?

"What did the card say? Who is it from?" Jacob says just loud enough so Momma hears him from across the lawn as we walk over, but soft enough so she won't think he's yelling.

"Nothin' and nobody." Momma kicks one of the fallen trumpets. "Y'all wash up and get ready for dinner," she says, walking into the house.

Before Jacob can say anything else, I gently steer him inside by the reins of his T-shirt. Out of Momma's sight, we both hover just before the stairs, stealing a glance as we hear her throw the crumpled card into the kitchen trash.

"You think the flowers might be from Dad?" I ask as we climb.

"Doubt it."

"Then who?" I follow Jacob into his room, pushing for any clues, and close the door behind me. "You think it could be someone we don't know?"

Suddenly, the room spins, and it's as if I'm back with Leroy, both of us trapped in the back office of Rissa's diner, smoke filling the room. I try to close my eyes, anchor myself in the present, but it's a trap—the darkness only makes it worse.

Now I'm stuck, I can feel the heat seeping in from the other side of the locked door. There is no one to hear us but the crackling flames hissing and whoever started the fire.

I can't breathe. I can't see. I can't feel Leroy. We're going to die, if no one—

"You good?" Jacob says. I nod so I don't have to lie, focusing on the sound of his voice.

Jacob stretches back across the bed, pulls me back with him to the present.

No more flames, no more smoke.

"You're probably thinkin' the same thing I am," he says, holding on to me.

"We need to get that card." I finish his thought, safe.

"If you do the dishes, I can take out the trash and swipe it then."

"Unh-unh," I counter. "You can do the dishes, and I'll take out the trash and swipe it then."

We go back and forth until it erupts into a tickling contest Jacob inevitably wins. Soon the room is silent except for the purr of the box fan and the rhythmic rock of Jacob's leg on the bed, lulling us to sleep despite the questions still echoing in the back of our minds.

Long before Momma has to, the aroma from the kitchen begins to call to me from downstairs. I slide from beneath Jacob's arm, creeping toward the door to the hallway.

"Where you goin'?" Jacob says, as if he hadn't fallen asleep in the first ten minutes. I freeze, caught. I turn around and shine the brightest smile.

I make a run for it.

Only one thing can create such a clash between brothers: Momma's yock.

Pushing and shoving down the hall, I ignore the burning in my throat and chest, hold it in as much as I can. I don't want to go back to how things were after the shooting last spring, where I felt like a burden to Jacob.

I want the invisible space between us to disappear. Maybe then he'll tell me how he's able to call Leroy "Lee," and why Taj and Leroy call him "Jacobee."

I bolt down the stairs, but Jacob jumps over the banister. He lands right in front of me and holds me at a distance as we barrel into the kitchen. I try to block the pot, staking my claim, and fight back a dry cough tickling the back of my throat. When I can't talk, I shake my head, brave through it with a smile.

"Jacob, let Jay have first bowl—the chicken broth will do his throat some good," Momma says. I smile, victorious, but it doesn't last long.

As we both sit down with our plates, something feels off. The crumpled card may be in the trash and out of sight, but it's not out of mind.

"How does your throat feel?" Momma sips, holding her sweating glass of red Kool-Aid with both hands.

"Good. The warm broth helps."

"I put some extra yellow onions in there and boiled them down for you real good. That should help with any inflammation."

I nod, look over at Jacob, to see if he senses the tension.

She sips again, longer this time, a breath before diving into the deep end. Under the table, Jacob reaches for my hand, holds it.

"Lin and I been talking, and after the shooting at Leroy and Taj's house last spring, you being attacked by the DKs along with Will last summer, and now you and Leroy almost dying in the fire at Rissa's diner," Momma says, looking at me, "Jay, I think it's best you move to New York and spend the rest of your senior year there." She keeps talking, as if the world around us isn't crumbling to dust.

This isn't about the card at all—it's about *me*.

"I know this might be a lot to take in, and, Jacob, Lin said there's room, if you'd like to come as well, but it's just not safe here anymore, and I need to do everything I can to protect you. The arrangements should be made in the next couple of weeks."

I don't speak. I can't even breathe. I just stare at the swollen spaghetti noodles and the barely eaten chicken drumstick now drowning in yock sauce, heartbroken.

Then I do the only thing I can and walk upstairs to my room to cry myself to sleep.

Fully dressed for school an hour early, I tiptoe down the stairs. The doctors gave me a note for the rest of the week, but I can't spend another second in that room after last night, thinking about everything I'll lose. I reach for the door and—

"Where you goin' without breakfast?"

I turn around.

It's Jacob, wearing Momma's white apron with purple letters that say "Love."

"Ma left early," he announces, reading my mind like always.

I breathe a sigh of relief.

Jacob's eyes pull me to the kitchen table, where he sets my food—a bowl of cinnamon banana oatmeal and blueberries for me and the works for him: pancakes, sausages, bacon, and fried eggs.

"Mission accomplished." Jacob places the crumpled envelope and card on the table. My heart nearly leaps out of my chest. I was so thrown off by Momma's news last night, I forgot I was supposed to get it while taking out the trash.

I quickly open it and read the message written in sloppy cursive:

Best of luck on the growth of your business
—Louis B.

"Louis Bainbridge?" I look up at Jacob in shock. "Why would he send Momma flowers?" This isn't anything but a threat to say, *I'm watching you.*

"Well, it can't be to actually wish Ma luck wit her business," Jacob answers.

I stare at the envelope. Whatever Louis B is up to, we've sent him our own message.

Since discovering the Bainbridge family's plan to get rid of the Black Diamonds so they can push our and the rest of the Black neighborhoods out of K-Town and redevelop and extend downtown Savannah, it's been nonstop drama and danger.

Louis B won't stop, but neither will we, especially now that Leroy and I cracked the code to the jump drive containing the research Louis B sent hired guns like Frank and Myrrh to kill Faa over. It's his kryptonite: a donation list with names of everyone in his pockets, from politicians to community leaders.

We're getting close, and Louis B knows it—he's scared. But before I can tell Jacob so, there's a melodic knock at the front door.

"It's for you," Jacob says as a pancake and three sausage links disappear into his mouth in a matter of seconds.

I look at him, confused, and go to the door to open it. On the other side, Princeton stands in a black-and-white flannel shirt, white pants, and all-black Timberland boots.

Princeton hugs me before I can get a word out, smelling of Big Red gum and Old Spice. "You got it?" he calls out to Jacob.

"Yup." Jacob brings him a paper plate covered with aluminum foil, filled with strips of bacon and cheesy eggs.

How did Princeton know I was going to school today? I didn't even know until 2:00 a.m., after coughing and crying all night. A car beeps locked behind him, and me and Jacob almost lose our minds. That's because it's not just *any* car, it's an all-black everything 2005 BMW 3 Series.

"Nice lookin' out." Princeton peels a part of the foil back, then folds multiple strips of bacon into his mouth. "If I ain't get Jacob's text last night, I woulda neva thought to bring my whip so I could scoop you."

I glare at Jacob, who loudly crunches bacon bits while locking eyes with Princeton.

"Don't get mad, now," Jacob says to me before leaning on the doorframe to get a better look at the BMW.

"Wait, when did you get a car?" I ask, half-dumbfounded, half-impressed.

"I always had one, just neva used it since I always walk to school witchu."

"Why bring it today, then?"

"'Cuz I ain't want you walkin' with . . . you know . . ." Princeton tries to check with Jacob, but I lean to block his line of sight, so he stuffs his mouth and pleads the Fifth.

As we head out, as usual, Jacob guilts me into kissing him on the cheek. But things get hilarious when Princeton pretends to do the same, and Jacob nearly chases him around his car.

Soon enough, Princeton is whipping the car into the school parking lot. He turns off the engine but doesn't move to get out. I try to, but then he gently pulls me back.

"You mad at me?" Princeton looks as if my words could break him.

The question throws me. Mad? At Princeton? He's been the best friend I could ever hope for. "No, why would I be mad?"

"Then why you ain't call me?"

Oh, right. "At the hospital, I had a lot—"

"Nah, not then. Last night. Why Jacob have to be the one to tell me you plannin' on coming back to school today?"

I don't know what to say to make him feel better. If I tell him about Momma sending me to New York in a couple of weeks, it could—

"I thought we were boys. I mean, iono how you feel, but to me, you my best friend. I cried when I found out you was in the hospital. I thought you might . . ." He shakes his head, then reaches for something out of his bag in the back—a thermos. "Here, I had my moms make it."

"Thanks," I hold the thermos, as if it's a precious gift. "What is it?"

"Slippery elm tea. Helped back when I had strep throat." He reaches for his binder, then holds out his hand for mine.

Normally, I would resist, but I hand it over and watch as he stacks it on top of his own, silently proud. When he reaches for his door, I say what I've always felt, even if the words don't feel easy coming from my lips.

"I didn't mean to make you feel like we weren't close. It's just that this is all so new." I feel for the heat of the thermos in my palms, play with the top to steady my hands, my heart. "For so long, I've only had Jacob. I've never had a best friend before, so I'm sorry if I kinda suck at it. I don't mean to. I just want you to know, I care about you, too."

"We official, then? Best friends?" He steals a glance at me and grins. "That'll make the surprise even better."

"What?" I wait for him to explain, nervous all over again.

Princeton gets out of the car, gestures for me to follow him, draping his arm around my shoulders as we walk toward the double doors.

"Welcome back, Jay!"

"Hey, Jay!"

"Whaddup, Jay?"

Different people call out as we pass them in the halls. I don't know who is prouder to hear the words, me or Princeton, as he smiles wider, watching my face. He stops in front of the announcement bulletin board.

In big bubble letters, it lists the names of everyone nominated for homecoming king and queen. Under queen is Christina's name and another name I don't recognize. And under king are a few familiar names. I keep reading until I see it—my name is in the center. I look at Princeton, half-confused, half-scared. It can't be real, can it?

"Why? How?" Is this a prank?

"You sure you okay?" Princeton places the back of his hand on my forehead. "Maybe you got a fever."

"I'm fine." I roll my eyes at his dramatic response, hiding the warmth growing in my chest. "It's just kind of hard to believe."

Princeton nudges me, arm still on my shoulders. "I thought you'd be happier."

"I am, I really am," I say, but the happiness hurts. This is supposed to be one of the best years of high school, but I'm not going to be here to enjoy it.

"Christina said we gotta meet her out back near the bleachers in front of the football field when the bell rings—homecoming business. So, you might wanna give Leroy a heads-up, since I know he gon' be waitin'.'" He shoulder-bumps me, grins.

I try to play it off because if I think about Leroy, everything we've been through and the fact that now I have to leave him behind, I'll probably start crying again.

On the football field in the back of the school, Christina body-rolls and shines with the majorettes in a green halter top and white short shorts. It's been fifteen minutes after the last bell rung, but I look around and still don't see Princeton anywhere.

"Whaddup, Skatedown," a voice says behind me.

I bro-nod, not sure how else to respond. I'd forgotten all about being named skatedown king with Jacob and Leroy. After the fire at the diner, nothing else seemed to matter. For a second, I can almost hear the cheers, see the dancing, feel Leroy's hands around my waist.

"Jay, wait up," Princeton calls from behind, jogging so fast that he's standing next to me by the time I turn toward the sound of his voice. "Ready?" He's not even winded.

"For what?"

"Hey, y'all!" Christina smiles and glistens. The other majorettes grin at us as she meets us halfway, then latches her elbows around ours.

"I just choreographed the best homecoming routine ever, but it's going to take all of us to pull it off."

"Routine?" we say in unison. I hope she's joking—not hope, pray with all my heart that she isn't serious.

"Yup, something people will never forget."

It doesn't take long for Christina to blow our minds with her plans for this year's homecoming performance, then a different noise catches everybody's attention.

Four cars—three Cadillacs and a Suburban—with rattling trunks vibrate and shake egos when they stop on the side of the football field. When everyone gets out, even the air blows in accordance to their will, sending a mixture of sweet smoke from a wine-flavored Black & Mild, cinnamon, and Egyptian musk, with a hint of peppermint and Cool Water cologne.

In Timberland boots, jeans, Dickie suits, and oversized plaid shirts and jackets, swagger is the armor of the Black Diamonds, the silent protectors of K-Town's Black neighborhoods from abuses of power and oppression, as well as the keepers of the peace, since most of the gangs are unified under them and adhere to a truce. They stand tall, for themselves and all they represent, pride shimmering in the sunlight.

Me, Princeton, and Christina walk over as Taj steps out of his Cadillac and sings, "Whaddup, Tina, baby?"

Leroy doesn't wait for me to get to him. He gets out of the car and walks toward us, winks at Christina, then swallows me in a bear hug.

"Let him breathe, Lee," Taj cackles as Christina hugs him.

Princeton and Leroy bro-hug, and I try to hide what feels like a body-sized blush, fully shaken. Outside of Leroy visiting each day while I was in the hospital, I haven't seen him in a couple of days. I forgot what it feels like to be touched by him.

As we walk back over to Taj, Leroy's arms wrap around my waist as he waddles behind me in large steps. I've never felt so embarrassed—and so safe.

"Whaddup, Jay? Lemme get some love." Taj wraps his arms around me, and I'm blushing even more.

It's my first time being hugged by Taj—and now that I have, suddenly I get why Jacob fell for him and why Leroy emulates his older brother, down to wearing the same cologne. Just standing next to him, you can feel his strength; he's only one person but feels like the unstoppable force of many.

"Blame Lee for us bein late. He wouldn't quit changin his clothes."

"Taj," Leroy grumbles, blushing.

"Don't Taj me, I'm tellin him so he don't get it twisted. I'm punctual."

"Did you hear the news?" Christina grins, changing the topic.

Suddenly I want to press another button and disappear before she says it. When she explains that I've been nominated for homecoming king, I can barely hear her because Taj and Leroy are bear-hugging me at the same time, whooping and hollering like their favorite football team scored a goal.

Christina didn't just tell them to brag; she told them so they'll make sure everybody they know will show up early at the game because she has a surprise for them, featuring me.

After more jokes and rabble-rousing, Christina and Princeton head back and Taj gives me and Leroy the rundown—we get an hour to hang, but we can't lose our BD escort. Taj barely finishes his sentence before Leroy grabs my hand and pulls me toward his car.

Once we're inside, he reaches for my hand and kisses the back of it. He holds it until we arrive, and I have to cross my legs to try and bury the heat causing parts of my body to rise.

"Somethin I wanna show you," Leroy says, pulling up to the steepleless church with the biggest smile on his face. He reaches for my hand, holds it as we walk through the field until I see a mini rock garden, a bench, and a porch swing. There are flower beds on each side, ranging from bright blue cornflowers to red, orange, and yellow chrysanthemums; it looks beautiful and enchanted.

"Did you do this?" I stop, blown away.

"Issa secret, you like it?" He walks behind me, wraps his arms around my waist, and leans in close. My heart races when he kisses the back of my neck and blows the wetness from his lips cool.

Leroy walks me backward to the swing, sits down, and then tries to lower me so I straddle him, sitting on top.

I pull back—I can't. I want to, but the memory of the shooting that happened the first time we got close stops me. And now it's only been a couple of days since both of us nearly died, again. I just want to be sure that there's no one else trying to end our lives. With Louis B's floral taunt arriving yesterday, we're hardly safer than we were the first time.

Then I see it: a flash of hurt and surprise in Leroy's eyes, before he can hide it.

"My bad . . ." He gets up, strokes his waves. "I thought . . ." His voice trails off, and all I can think about is that I don't want to lose him.

I pull him close, bury my head in the sweet spot between his chest and neck. "I didn't mean it like that, I'm just scared," I whisper, caring more that the words make it to his heart than his ears.

"Of me?"

"No. That because of me, because of us, you'll get hurt again. It's like we're cursed." Every time we touch, something bad happens, and I don't know if it's a sign that we shouldn't or a reason we should keep going. But even if we do get to that point, will it be enough? Will I be enough?

"It's okay." Leroy kisses me on the forehead, then on my lips. "I aint goin nowhere. You worth the wait. Imma show you we blessed, not cursed."

We hold each other until we get to catch up on the little things—what happened last night, how I'd been feeling, his recovery as well. Eventually, I tell him about Louis B's flowers, but I can't bring myself to mention my mom sending me to New York.

Not now, maybe later.

"You don't have to worry bout none of that," Leroy says as we walk back to the car. He signals to the Suburban for us to take ten more minutes. "Me, Taj, Auntie Rissa, Lady Tee, and the Black Diamonds can—"

"No." The word comes out stronger, more forceful than I mean for it to, but I try to explain why. "I can't go through that again: you trying to carry everything on your shoulders, making all the decisions, thinking you have to protect me."

"But ion want nothin bad to happen to you."

"And I don't want anything to happen to *you* either. Our fight with the Bainbridges, protecting the BDs, keeping our home safe, it involves me and my family, too. All I'm saying is don't do anything for me, let's do it together." He looks away, and suddenly, I'm no longer scared or shy. I turn his chin toward me. "Promise me you won't hide anything from me. That you'll tell me so we can figure it out together."

"Baby, iono if I can . . ." He catches me smiling. "What?"

"What did you call me?"

He remembers, then grins, looks down. "I mean . . . it's how I feel. I like you a lot."

"Hmm, is that so?" We sit in silence, allow his words to work on us.

"I promise. No mo secrets. But I got somethin else I need to ask you," Leroy says. "It's important." I freeze. Does he already know?

"Can I be yo boyfriend?"

"Huh?" I say, confused. Then I realize we never got to make it official back in the diner. I read his love letter, then everything else happened with Brown Brown's betrayal, unlocking the USB flash drive, and the fire. My smile melts the fear away.

"Yes, but only if you let me be yours." I kiss him with no fear, no doubt. I know it won't always feel this certain, but I mean it.

I promise myself to tell him the truth—soon.

2

Leroy

"The USB drive was damaged in the fire and much of the information is unretrievable," Lady Tee announces.

Her laptop got the USB flash drive plugged in, facin us. The folders still there, but when you click on em, especially the one wit the donor list me and Jay cracked the passcode fuh, nothin happens.

"How we get it back?" Ion care how desperate I sound.

"We can't. It's too damaged."

"But that's our key to takin down the Bainbridges! We had their network—errthang was right there! Jay and me nearly *died* gettin it fuh the BDs." What we gon do if errthang gone? Especially wit Louis B sendin flower pots threatenin Jay and his fam. This can't be happenin. I put my head in my hands, tryna think of somethin, anythin.

"Any leads on anythin else we could use?" Taj asks.

Auntie Rissa sighs. "Not yet. Right now, the binder that Brown Brown took has us doin all kinds of damage control."

"What was in it?" Lady Tee squints, the gears in her mind already workin.

"Normally, just some contacts and phone numbers of neighborhood leaders who work wit the BDs—nothin don't nobody already know."

"But we just had a meetin earlier that day wit Miss Rosalind, thinkin through how we could run interference at the upcomin city council meetin set to do some fucked-up redistrictin," Taj says, shakin his head. "The mayor in Louis B's pocket, but we had contact info of some of the heads of the crews and some names Miss Rosalind mentioned. City officials and allies willin to flip on the Bainbridges—and under what terms."

"We neva list names, only codes. But if Louis B is as diligent as we think he is, it won't take long," Auntie Rissa adds as she pinches the bridge of her nose.

"Sorry, Auntie," Taj says, smotherin his head in his hands. "I aint—"

"It's okay, Bittersweet. Aint nothin we can do bout it now."

"You find Brown Brown yet, Taj?" Iono if I wanna know the answer, but I'm askin cuz aint nobody heard nothin from him or PYT.

"Nah, but best believe, when I do—"

"One thing at a time," Auntie Rissa says. Taj grumbles but leaves it at that.

"Let's assume the Bainbridges know everything, all our current strategies to destroy their hold over Savannah. It's the only way to prepare for any and all contingencies." Lady

Tee looks at me. "Leroy, Rissa and Taj mentioned you know who's behind Brown Brown's betrayal."

"Yeah, Lyric. Based on what I heard and what Jay saw."

"As in Lyric Bryson at Providence Prep?"

"Yeah, he a Bainbridge. Louis B supposedly his pops, but don't nobody really know, and Louis B tryna keep it that way while he got Lyric doin all his dirty work."

"Have you shared this information with anyone else?" Her eyes sharpen.

"Aside from the people who told me. Nah, nobody."

"Good, it means we still have the element of surprise. When's the next time you all speak with Rosalind?"

"We got a meetin wit her lata today." Taj smooths ova his legs but keeps rockin em to settle his nerves. "But if Lyric flipped Brown Brown, it mean Frank and Myrrh the ones who set the fire. And if we right bout Louis B, he don't like failure. Maybe if we keep an eye out, we'll see what happens between Lyric and Frank and Myrrh. If they beefin, we might even be able to use it to our advantage."

"Taj, you think yall can keep an eye on that, and I'll make some calls to the OGs and some of the people on our list, so they kept in the loop," Auntie Rissa says.

Taj nods. "I'll let you know if I hear bout Brown Brown or PYT, too."

I can still rememba PYT's voice, his screams, befo the line went dead, back when I was pissed bout Lyric pullin the wool ova our eyes and tryna make Rouk his scapegoat.

Wait, Rouk—we still got Rouk.

"If Rouk mailed the drive to Lady Tee, what if me and him searched Faa's room to see if he left somethin behind? You knew Faa betta than errbody," I say, lookin at Taj, "and he aint eva had only one source. Rememba them notebooks he stayed writin in? What if one of em got clues bout what was on the flash drive or who he got it from?"

"That might work, but you sho you can do it wit Rouk?" Taj says. "I can—"

"It gotta be me. We still aint had a chance to come to peace wit errthang that happened. It's the only way."

Truth is tho, me and Rouk known fuh many things, but talkin shit out peacefully aint one of em. So, when I call him after the meetin ends, tell him bout the plan, a part of me is nervous he won't be down. But he agrees to meet me at Faa's and his old spot befo I even finish explainin.

On the way there, the sun begins to set. Out the window, the radio tower still looks like a metal ladder to heaven somebody gave up on buildin cuz it aint got no top and the steps too wide fuh any human.

Me and Rouk used to joke that Black folks from the hood gotta tightrope walk on the powerlines in order to get to the pearly gates. The only signal they leave behind to let those they love know they made it: shoes hangin from the powerlines. We knew betta, but in K-Town, sometimes you need lies to be able to deal wit the truth.

By the time I turn the corner in front of the Grayson 'n Daughters cleaners, it's almost time fuh the streetlights to flicker on and off, shinin like a makeshift flashlight against the white house. Surrounded by a black chain-link fence, it don't seem like much now, but back when me and Taj first visited Faa and Rouk, it was a one-story castle they was proud of.

As I get outta the car, Rouk come walkin from round a bush in the back of the house and lets me inside without a word.

Except fuh the wall of keys made by they granddad who was a key maker, the wood panelin, and the dark green sofa and mismatched recliner, it don't look like nobody been livin here. But if Rouk has, no wonder he be so depressed and lonely.

"If you gotta use the bathroom," Rouk says, lookin errwhere but at me, "just jiggle the handle and flush befohand." He stands barely in the livin room wit his hands in his pockets.

"You been livin here?" I ask. When Rouk just shrug and walk into the kitchen, I know it's true. But this place aint livable.

"You want somethin to eat?" I offer. "We could run round to Auntie Rissa's at the Bee to get a few plates. Prolly aint gon be here fuh no mo than a coupla hours, but she would want us to eat."

"I'm good," Rouk says. "Let's just get this shit ova wit." He

23

walks back into the kitchen, and I follow. If he knew he was gon act like this, why say I could come ova?

"So that's how you gon be?" I'm tryna keep my cool, but errtime Rouk look at me and say shit that couldn't be further away from an apology, I get pissed all ova again. "Is it really that hard to step up and say what need to be said?"

Rouk whips round. "Ion owe you shit."

Befo I can stop myself, I moosh his face so hard he trips and falls into the rack wit the pots and pans. The shelf breaks, sendin em crashin loudly to the ground.

He hops up, ready to scrap, when the front door slams open, makin us jump.

Thinkin it's Night, we go into the livin room, try to play off what just happened so he don't tell Taj we not gettin along, like I promised we would. But it aint him, it's Trish, standin in the middle of the room wit a bag of Flamin' Hot Cheetos, Blow Pops, and Now and Laters, eitha from the corner store or Edda Nae, the candy lady, can't tell.

"Trish?" we both say in unison, shocked to see her here. Rouk run up to her, all smiles, like he aint neva did nothin wrong. I shake my head.

"I aint knew you was comin," Rouk says to her. She grins cuz he don't know how to do nothin but be sweet on her.

"Taj called me, said Lee was comin, and that he might need some backup to get the job done," Trish says, handin the snacks to Rouk.

"Nah, we good," I say, grabbin whateva Rouk can't carry.

Trish looks long and hard at me and Rouk, then at the pots and pans scattered on the floor of the kitchen. "Right," she says.

She hooks her arm in mine and her otha arm in Rouk's to guide us to the back toward Faa's room, tiptoein round the mess, makin us promise to clean up when we done. When we get to the door, Rouk tries to pull back, as if he don't wanna go in no mo, but Trish got that magic touch.

Rouk trusts her, knowin she'll neva do him wrong. Me and Rouk talk wit our fists, so Trish always been our translator to help us hear one anotha. It takes me back to when it was just three of us, best friends fuh life.

That is, till she locks the door behind us.

"Trish, yo, quit playin," I say, knockin to make sho she hearin me. "Unlock the door."

Rouk shoves me outta the way so he can yell out, "Trish, open up—it's me."

"Whatchu mean, 'it's me'?" I say. "Like that mean somethin."

"It do—me and Trish always been able to see eye to eye. When yo blockheaded ass aint tryna listen to reason, she the one who make you see sense."

Iono who swing first. Maybe we both swing on each otha at the same time. All I know is we rollin on Faa's bed, tradin blow fuh blow. Neitha of us get in a real hit cuz we both got our guards still up, till we fall off the bed next to Faa's old-school box TV.

Rouk yells in pain, and all of a sudden, he flailin and scrappin, tellin me to let him go cuz I broke somethin.

Next to the TV, I see an old-school Super Nintendo. It's at his feet, and he keep pressin the gray Eject button in the center, but somethin aint workin right. The game cartridge is stuck. When he finally get it loose, he jumps up and tries to cut on the TV, but it won't work.

The Super Nintendo won't just a game. It was Faa's favorite thing, especially *Super Mario Bros.* No matta what happened, how rough shit got, nothin was mo important than that game—and the fact that they could play it togetha.

Rouk keeps tryin, blowin the bottom of the cartridge, placin the game in, and pullin the Reset buttons—nothin. The closer I get, the mo I notice he shakin.

"Aye . . . lemme see . . . maybe I can—" I try to help.

"Get the fuck away from me! You did this!" He cryin, doin the same thing ova and ova, knowin it aint gon work.

Blow. Click. Reset. Nothin.

Blow. Click. Wait. Reset. Nothin.

I stand, helpless. I aint mean to break it.

"Errthang you touch you break," Rouk growls, and his words hurt mo than I expect em to. He looks at the game console shut off wit no way to fix it. Then he rams me up against the closet doors hard enough that they break off the track, barely hangin on as somethin crashes behind em.

It must feel like Faa's death all ova again, and I aint tryna hurt Rouk no mo than I already have. So I stop blockin and let him choke me, till all I can see is black spots and my head feels like it's bout to explode.

The room slips away, crashes sideways, and crumbles outta sight. Then he lets go. We both fall to the ground, me coughin and him cryin.

That's when I feel my own tears fightin as they fall.

Our sobs seesaw us back and forth, pissed off that we just hurt boys, tryin our best not to grow up into hurt men who only know how to hurt each otha to win.

Iono how much time passes, but I eventually get up and silently pick up stuff that fell to the ground: CDs, pencils, pens, books. Rouk don't move, just watches. Ion mind cuz I want him to know I'm tryin.

I don't go near the Super Nintendo even tho I think I know how to fix it.

"I aint mean what I said." Rouk words are barely above a whisper. I stop cleanin but ion turn round cuz I want him to keep goin. "Ion think you break errthang you touch. Even if you did, you always been the one who knew how to put shit back togetha. Faa was the same way."

"I'm sorry." I turn round but look near him, not at him. "I aint mean to eitha. I know how much that game mean to you."

27

"I know—you one of the few people who do." He stands up, rubs his back where he landed. He starts pickin up the clothes and stuff that fell near the closet. As he cleans, we move round the room, keepin our distance. It's like we in the same boat, careful of our weight so it don't flip ova.

I take a step forward, hopin it's not a mistake.

"Why you stop comin round after they proved Taj was innocent? You aint come even when you found out it was the Bainbridges holdin the gun?" I say, tryna test my weight—our balance—in a different way.

"I aint know how."

"I kept tryin, tho. But you wouldn't even speak to me."

"Cuz it would neva be the same," Rouk says. I wanna tell him that me and Taj *was* here, but I get it—we aint Faa. "I wanted to, but after the shootin and Frank and Myrrh nearly killin you, iono, won't no goin back after that."

My throat hurts, and my eyes burnin cuz he stupid, all of this shit is stupid.

"I'm sorry, Lee," he says, makin sho I hear him. "If I woulda known, I woulda neva went—on God and errthang I love." I nod, cuz I know.

I slowly make my way ova to the Super Nintendo. When Rouk don't try to stop me, I unplug the TV, unplug errthang on that side of the room, and I count to fifteen, like Faa did. Then, I press the Eject button and pick up the console to hold it upside down so I can blow inside three times. I put the *Super Mario Bros.* cartridge in, plug errthang up, cut the TV on, and I press the Reset button one mo time.

Nothin happens. Nothin works.

I take the cartridge out, then I slap the console. Rouk whips round like he gon say somethin, but doesn't. Instead, he tries to pull the closet door out from the awkward angle it's jammed in, then somethin else falls in the closet.

I take a deep breath, say a lil prayer, and rattle the Reset button a few times. Then I try it one mo time. The music plays, and fuh a second, I swear I'm gon cry.

I turn round to show Rouk, but he's on his hands and knees pushin through clothes at the bottom of the closet. He pulls a handful of journals, all different colors.

"You found somethin?" I say, runnin ova to help. He rakes the clothes out on the floor, and I move all the ones on the hangers till the closet is clear, and we can both see somethin that look like a secret compartment—a slab of wood coverin a shelf.

We look fuh somethin to knock it loose. Rouk crawls into the closet and kicks at it. And when it gives way a lil, we both pull at it wit our fingers till it finally comes off and so do stacks of journals along wit it.

We stare at each otha, shocked. As we flip through the journals we see it's errthang we thought it would be, maybe mo.

"Aye, yall make up or—" Trish says, walkin through the

door. She runs to the stack of journals. "Yall found em?"

We each grab one, begin flippin through pages. As we get into it, errbody's face lights up. Iono if it's errthang from the flash drive, but Faa wrote out notes and drew sketches, connectin dots and names, newspaper clippins, and otha stuff. All togetha, it looks like the pieces of the Bainbridges' network—a puzzle we might be able to put togetha again and solve.

"Hol up!" Rouk turns one of em ova. "Look, they dated."

We line em up by dates till we find the last fifteen or so from the month or two befo he died, but there's still three times as many from befo then. The closer we read, the mo we realize it don't make sense.

It's like they written in a different language, but Rouk knows what it is. He tries to explain it to us, how he and Faa created it when they were young—pig Latin but Faa-level complicated.

My phone vibrates in my pocket. I look at the caller ID, but it's a blocked number. Don't nobody got this number who aint supposed to have it. And if they do, they know neva to call from a blocked number. I look at Rouk and Trish, wonderin if I should tell em. But what if it's Taj and he in trouble?

I answer it quickly, just in case.

"Lee, you there?" The voice on the other end is familiar, but I can't place it. Then it hits me—PYT.

I jump up. "Yeah! Where you at? Errbody lookin fuh you."

"I'll explain errthang, but we need to meet. Just you and me. Okay?"

"You okay? You in trouble?"

"I just texted you the address. I promise to explain when you get here," PYT says. His voice sounds mo hoarse than usual, like he might be in pain.

"Okay," I say. "I'm on my way."

I stand up, not sho what to do or say. I wanna keep PYT secret, but aint no way Taj gon be okay wit me goin nowhere by myself.

"Who was it?" Rouk and Trish ask, lookin at me.

I follow my gut, and I tell em the truth.

Night aint said nothin since he picked me up in the whip. It could be a good thing. After tellin him bout PYT's call, he coulda just called Taj, and that woulda been the end of it, but he didn't.

"Whatchu gon do if we headin into a trap?" Night breaks his silence.

"Iono . . ." His eyes say, *Wrong answer*, so I take a deep breath and ask, "That mean we turnin round, then?"

"Nah, if PYT hurt, we need to get him help now, and if he workin fuh the Bainbridges' DKs, we need to know so we can handle it befo it become anotha problem fuh Auntie Rissa and Taj."

Ion like how he said "handle it." Night aint known fuh his finesse, but at the same time, he aint no shoota who kill first and ask questions lata—is he?

"We here," Night announces. He pulls out a piece from the glove compartment, anotha from under his seat, and a smaller one from his armrest. I almost don't notice it, but the gray house on the block flips their lights on then off three times.

We walk to the otha side of the street to the house, and its front door opens—PYT steps out.

"So much fuh comin alone," he says, lightin a Black & Mild. He moves stiff, like one of his arms hurt.

The closer we get, the mo I see. PYT's got a busted lip, a bruise on his cheek, and big-ass bruises on his shoulders. He blows smoke that curls up in the porch light like a snake he charmin.

"PYT, you look like shit," Night says.

"Feel like it, too."

"Now, you know I gotta ask. Anybody in there I need to know bout?"

PYT takes a long drag, takes his time answerin. "Yup, which is why Imma need you to keep yo hands where I can see em."

"You know this shit only move at the speed of trust," Night says. "And let's just say we on some molasses drip right now."

"Why even call if you aint gon be honest?" I ask.

"Cuz errbody can't be trusted," a voice says from behind PYT. Fuh a second, I think I'm hearin things till he steps from behind the screen door and into the porch light.

It's Brown Brown.

Night moves fuh his piece so fast that all I see is him pointin a gun at Brown Brown, and PYT aimin his piece at Night. While them two stand off, Brown Brown waits wit his hands up.

"Night, I aint here to start no trouble," Brown Brown says. "Just wanted to talk to you and Lee. Hear me out, hear me out."

Night slowly lowers his piece, and PYT does the same.

"Let's get inside. Too many eyes and ears we can't see out here," Night says.

"I been meanin to—" Brown Brown begins, but then I hit him so hard he staggers and almost trips ova the livin room table.

"Damn, Lee! The fuck?" Brown Brown holds his face.

PYT sits down on the couch, don't even blink. "Glad we got that outta the way."

I only planned to hit him once, but the way I feel right now, once might not be enough. "The first one is a freebie." Brown Brown winces, readin my mind. "But best believe the second one gon cost you."

"What's he doin here?" I ask PYT.

"Look, I aint sayin what I did was right, but I had my

reasons," Brown Brown jumps in.

"Fuck yo reasons." I stand up, ready to rush at him again. "Aint no reason you could eva give to justify almost killin me and Jay, not to mention burnin down Auntie Rissa's diner."

"Lee, whatchu talm bout?" PYT calls back as he heads into the kitchen.

"You got him up in here, and you don't even know what he did? He burned down Auntie Rissa's wit me and Jay in there, after stealin the BDs' binder."

"Whatchu mean, you and Jay was in there?" Brown Brown says, shocked.

"When you was in there on the phone, me and Jay was hidin in the closet in the office after we heard somebody breakin in. Then I saw it was you. And we heard yo whole lil conversation wit Lyric."

"Lee, listen to me," Brown Brown says, desperate. "Yeah, I took the binder, cuz I couldn't go back empty-handed. But I would neva, eva hurt you or Jay—or burn down Auntie Rissa's."

"Whey yo proof? Cuz I'm runnin short on patience and even less on trust," Night says.

"You lookin at it," PYT says, returnin to the living room. He pops what looks like painkillers and chases em wit a glass of water. "Just as I left the skatedown to follow Brown Brown and Lyric, like Taj told me to, some wack-ass DKs jumped me befo I even made it out into the parkin lot." PYT winces as he sits back down. "Won't till Brown Brown was thrown into the same van that I even knew what was goin on."

"Right after I left wit the binder, the DKs held me at gunpoint, made me give em my keys and get in the van. That's when I saw PYT," Brown Brown says. "Then somebody else called one of the guys in the van, told em to finish it. I thought they was talm bout killin PYT cuz they already beat him so bad. So we waited till they let their guard down, and we jumped em wit what energy we had left."

"And how that turn out?" Night asks, sarcastic.

"Whatchu think?" PYT says. "After kickin our ass some mo, they stop and threw us outta the van in the middle of K-Heights. Turns out two against six is almost a fair fight."

"We aint even know bout nobody gettin hurt or Auntie Rissa's diner till yesterday. We been layin low," Brown Brown says. "We aint want the DKs tryna use us to get to Taj or the BDs."

I get up and pace cuz ioeno what to think. If what they sayin is true, then yeah, Brown Brown fucked up, but not as bad as I thought.

"I'm not sayin don't tell Taj eva," Brown Brown pleads. "I'm just sayin give me some time to figure out how I can make this right."

I look at Night, tryna read his face, and I can see he thinkin the same thing I am: *Can we trust em? And if so, what do we do?*

My mind racin so fast iono what to believe. But eitha way, it might be a real problem if anybody get hold of Brown Brown befo we get proof of what's true and what's not. Few people tryna hear anythin he got to say—and Taj out fuh blood—but what if none of this was by accident?

If the DKs really wanted to hurt Brown Brown and PYT, they woulda did it and we woulda neva heard from eitha of em again. But if they both alive, then it mean hurtin em don't fit into they plans—which mean anotha game bein played.

"Brown Brown, rememba when you was on the phone wit Lyric and he was talm bout makin yo pops the new chief of police and threatenin to kick out ya fam fuh corruption?" I ask.

"Yeah, that's what he said," Brown Brown says, deep in thought.

"What if it was all a bluff?"

Brown Brown don't respond, prolly cuz he aint sho, but Night and PYT start noddin they heads, like they pickin up what I'm puttin down.

"Just think bout it: yo pops is gon be chief cuz he aint dirty, errbody know that. And we all heard stories bout some of yo uncs and aunties bein crooked—they aint the only ones." I walk closer to Brown Brown, so he can see me real good. "What if they tryna act like they got mo power than they really do?"

"Iono . . . neva really thought bout it like that."

"You know who clean and who crooked on the force?" Night asks.

"Not errbody, but I got some ideas."

"Good. Who the cleanest, besides yo pops?" I say.

"Dane, my cousin. A lil too clean to the point the fam afraid it's gon get him hurt. My pops keep tryna send him away, but he won't go."

"I rememba him," PYT says. "He was the cop that Auntie Rissa was in touch wit tryna find Night and Taj when they went missin. I looked into him back then, when it seem like he won't gettin nowhere, but he legit."

"Then that's who we need to be tryna work wit," I say. Brown Brown seem to finally be catchin on. "Ion really think the DKs got it like they say they do, but we know one thing: they want you gone cuz they prolly already tryna control yo fam on the force, but they can't get they hands dirty, so they tryna make us do it."

"They wanted us to turn on Brown Brown and get rid of him so they could blame the BDs," Night says, shakin his head.

"And we already know how that would go down. The BDs would be numba one on the hit list wit the whole police department huntin us down till there aint nothin left," PYT says.

Don't none of us say nothin, we just take the truth in, thinkin bout how close we all got to fallin into they trap.

But, then again, we aint in the clear yet. There's still one thing that can blow all this up—Taj.

"Look, Brown Brown, I can't make no promises bout whether Taj will or won't find out, neitha can Night. Yall know Taj just like we do—aint bout *if* he gon find you, it's *when*."

"I know, I know," Brown Brown says, lookin ova at PYT.

"But if you can get Dane to agree to work witchu and, eventually, the BDs—maybe even get his help provin you aint burn down the diner—then we got our own connection wit the popos."

"I'm willin to try anythin. I'm on it."

"Bet. In the meantime, we aint gon say nothin on one condition: PYT, roll up on Auntie Rissa, let her know you aight. Errbody been worried." I look ova at Brown Brown. "When you lock in Dane, hit us up, and we'll figure out what to do next."

3

JAY

No matter how many times I use my inhaler, it still feels like there's a weight on my chest, hands around my neck. I know I shouldn't wait so long between uses, but how do you get used to needing something else to breathe?

"All set?" Jacob talks to me through minty foam before he spits and rinses. All that's left is for him to put on his baby-blue shirt that he likes to leave open.

Jacob begged me to color coordinate with him (don't ask me why), so I just put on a fitted white polo with small embroidered hyacinth blossoms he found while out thrifting. "You sure we should look this nice? We're just going to be in the house cooking."

"Always." He grins, scooping out some pomade from the jar. "Lee said they're doing the same thing . . . matching."

I sense the question coming before it even leaves his lips. I try to outrun it, but he asks before I can make it out of the bathroom door, "You gon' tell him today?"

There it is again. That invisible hand pressing down on my chest, making its way up to my neck. I can barely speak, so I shrug.

"I know it's hard, but don't drag it out." Jacob rubs his hands together to melt the pomade, firmly smooths down the top and sides of my hair, triggering the waves from the haircut he just gave me. Then Jacob carefully brushes from the hair circle out. My waves aren't as deep as his or Princeton's, but they are mine—and I'm proud of them.

When we're done, we jump down the stairs by twos and threes, Jacob first. Since Momma gave me the news a couple of days ago, I don't say much to her, try not to even be in the same room if I can help it.

Momma's in the kitchen making a pitcher of her sweet milk—the universal salve for any kind of pain. She pours us a glass, and Jacob immediately chugs his. I take mine to the table, quietly sit and sip.

"So what's on the breakfast menu?" She's trying to sound happier than she really is, throwing higher syllables at me, but I don't look up. I let Jacob answer, since he'll be doing most of the cooking anyway.

"An oldie but goodie," he says. "Your Frosted Flakes–covered fried chicken with waffles and a side of cheesy grits."

"And what dish are you gonna help with, Jay?" She adds my name, so I have to answer.

I shrug, still don't look at her, knowing the cost. Momma is kind, but she's far from patient; I've never gone this long without speaking to her.

"He's gonna—"

Momma puts up her finger, cutting Jacob off. I can feel his eyes pleading with me to make nice, so the day goes off smooth. It's our first time inviting Taj and Leroy over. But my heart won't let me—logic be damned.

"Jay, look at me." Momma pulls out a chair and sits next to me. "How long you gon' keep this up?"

"I don't know." I shake my head, look back down at my glass and the ice as it melts under the heat of her gaze.

She takes a deep breath, then sighs, "You don't have to like the decision, but it's been made. The quicker you accept it, the sooner you'll realize it's the best, the *only* way to keep you safe." I get it, but why does it hurt so bad?

The doorbell rings, but nobody moves. Momma just stares at me, waiting for a change because of her words. I lift my head but still avoid her eyes. I look at her eyebrows, her rose-colored lipstick, her earrings that dangle.

"I love you," she says.

"I love you, too," I mumble.

Seeing it as a temporary reprieve, Jacob opens the door, and we're bathed in the warmth of Taj's raspy voice. I walk over and stand between Jacob and Leroy. We look like competing teams because of our brother-based matching outfits. They wear white and black, even down to their shoes: Leroy a black fitted cap, white shirt, black jeans, and white and black Air Jordan 20s; Taj with a white fitted cap, black shirt, white jeans, and all-black Air Jordan 20s.

Leroy takes his chance to greet me with a half arm around my waist and a quick, tight hug. Suddenly, the weight disappears, and as I feel him hold on, I do the same.

"You gon stay fuh the festivities, Miss Julia?" Taj smiles as he rubs his hands together—the habit of only the best sweet-talkers.

"I wish I could, but I'm actually headed over to Lady Tee's."

"That's wassup, that's wassup. Auntie said 'hey,' and told me to let you know she's at the Holy Pente on Fridays and the May Street YMCA on Saturdays, teachin a cookin class till three p.m. She was hopin you'd come by and teach a lil somethin somethin."

"Okay, okay, I will," Momma sings as she gives out hugs to each of us, smelling of sugar vanilla wafers. Before she closes the door, she makes sure to catch my eyes. I smile, and she does, too.

When we head back into the kitchen and start cooking, Leroy and I stare in disbelief and amusement as Taj and Jacob go from flirting to fighting, back and forth, in a matter of seconds.

Every cabinet door Taj leaves open, Jacob closes. "I keep tellin' you, baked gon' be just as crispy, that's why I got the wire rack."

"Nah, we gotta fry this. Lee, what's that oil Auntie Rissa uses to fry her chicken?" Taj is almost fully inside the floor cabinet near the fridge, searching instead of just asking Jacob where it is.

"Are they always like this?" I ask, looking back at Leroy, whose eyes are so piercing they make me blush.

"Pritty much. Sometimes I wonder if they know how to do anythin but argue," he says. We watch Jacob pull Taj out of the cabinet, stand him up, and peck him on the lips.

"Lemme show you I'm right, lemme bake it, please," Jacob says.

"Wait fuh it," Leroy whispers next to me, his breath tickling my ear.

Taj is the hardest man I've ever seen, next to Dad, but the buckle starts in his eyes and then his body follows. He steps into Jacob's arms, gently pulling at his waist, eyes soft and glimmering, as Jacob leans in for another kiss. Then Taj smiles and yells over to me, "Jay, whey the oil at?"

Like a snap of fingers, unexpected teams are formed—me and Taj (Team Fried) against Jacob and Leroy (Team Baked). We split the portions of chicken, then get to work, until I realize that Taj is the full embodiment of confidence, but unfortunately, that doesn't mean he's ever actually fried chicken. So the frying is put on me. But because Taj's the best coach and cheerleader, we eventually make it through fine, after throwing two drumsticks into the trash (chicken's fault, not ours).

By the time we finish and switch to making waffles, the

rivalry gets even more heated as Taj tries to sabotage Leroy's waffle iron. Between making waffles and two types of chicken, while me and Jacob tackle the cheesy grits, Taj and Leroy still manage to provide updates about Faa's journals and their thoughts about what to do next.

"You think the journals gon' be enough to replace what couldn't be recovered from the flash drive?" Jacob asks, eyeing the chicken and saucepans. He puts his arm around me, and we lean with our backs on the sink as Leroy and Taj post up on the other side in front of the cabinets, working the waffle iron.

"From what I've seen already, maybe mo. In his notebooks, Faa laid out the 'why,' like how he found stuff bout the Bainbridges and what he was thinkin. In some ways, it's betta," Leroy says. "Won't know till we translate errthang."

"What if we put our heads together and write down whatever we remember of the donation list we saw on the flash drive? We could use that to try to connect the dots with what you find in the notebook," I say.

Taj nudges Leroy, and he blushes.

"What?" I ask, stirring the soft bubbles, smoothing the chunks of grits out with the whisk, as Jacob does the same.

"Lee knew you'd say that, told me he woulda neva cracked the password fuh the drive withoutchu."

"Really?" Jacob says, one eyebrow raised.

"He's exaggerating," I say, blushing.

"Mhmm." Jacob grins. "After we eat, y'all should kick it upstairs and put together your list to see what you find. You bring any of them witchu, Lee?"

Jacob's eyes meet mine. Then I realize he's giving us time alone so I can tell Leroy I'm moving, break it to him gently.

As far as anybody can tell, the competition between fried and baked ends in a tie. There are only bones and crispy Frosted Flake crumbs left as Taj and Jacob crunch the gristle and slurp the bone marrow.

Leroy and I eventually climb the stairs as we listen to the echo of Taj and Jacob fussing and flirting as they clean up the kitchen. I wonder how it is that love looks so easy for Jacob. Is it because of his confidence, his beauty? Is that what makes him so easy to love?

They look so much like how Momma and Dad were before everything changed. They fussed too but always seemed to reach their destination of hugs and kisses, even if tears were the highway that got them there.

With each step, I become more and more nervous about what lies in store for us. Are we like Taj and Jacob? Momma and Dad? Destined to fuss and flirt, always knowing we'll end up in each other's arms?

"Whatchu thinkin bout?" Leroy's hands guide my waist as I open the door to my room. *Whether or not we will survive what I need to tell you.* "Nothing," I say instead.

At first, I think Leroy's about to release me and look

around, but he holds me closer, tighter, and whispers, "Walk wit me."

I wonder what he's thinking. Most of the posters on the walls in my room are what Will left behind. But since then, Jacob pushed me to add more of my own. Posters of my favorite movies: *Love & Basketball*, *Bad Boys*, *The Fifth Element*, *The Best Man*. On the wall above my bed are the mini printouts of album cover art: Tupac, Toni Braxton, D'Angelo, Usher, Lauryn Hill.

I never really imagined Leroy would get to see my room, let alone us be in it together, but we're here. Maybe we can keep doing the impossible until it's just another word for us.

When he sees my calendar, he grins, reaching for the pen hanging by a string next to it. He circles a date in the next couple of weeks, writes his name between two hearts.

"What's that?" It can't be our anniversary, and it's too early to be his birthday.

"Reminda fuh you to send me some love. It's when I take the GED exam." Leroy softly guides me to the bed.

"Wow, time flies." I think back to when he asked me to help teach him how to write essays the first time we visited Auntie Rissa's. "You nervous?" I ask.

"A lil . . . just don't wanna let errbody down, especially Taj."

"You won't," I say.

"How you know?"

"Because I know you." My words trigger a slow smirk, the dimple in his right cheek.

I blush, imagine him whispering my name and "I'm yours."

He opens his arms as he lies back on the bed. I resist, but my body has a mind of its own. He pulls me on top of him, and suddenly the room is spinning again, and I can't breathe. It's not my throat this time or panic; it's my heart—and it feels like it's about to explode.

"I missed you," he whispers.

My face hovers over his, and even though I know I shouldn't, I kiss him. Because what else am I supposed to do when words aren't enough?

I want him to know how I feel, that when he's around, when he touches me, my mind goes blank and the world— no, time itself—stands still.

As he moves his hips beneath me, I do the same. My thoughts are clouded, hazy, but I focus on him. When Leroy moans, I want to hear it over and over, until he creates another language just for me, that belongs only to us.

"Touch me." The words surprise me when I realize they're mine. Leroy slides his hands beneath my shirt, around my waist, then past the band of my boxers, where his fingers light a spark.

Then I hear it . . . *Crack!*

The breaking of glass. The rough hands of smoke chafing the back of my throat. A burn I haven't felt since the shooting courses through my body—it hurts.

I try to fight back and follow the lighthouse of Leroy's touch, but the sounds only get louder, the pain only burrows deeper, until I'm shaking all over and suddenly crying.

"Baby, what's wrong?"

I know none of what I'm hearing is real, but I'm so scared.

Leroy squeezes me, shields me with his body like he did that night in the diner, as smoke and fire choked the oxygen out of the air and our lungs. I say in my head what I can't say out loud: *I'm sorry the only thing I seem to be able to say is "I'm sorry."*

When everything passes, Leroy still holds me tight. He kisses me on my forehead. I say it again, but for the first time out loud. "I'm sorry. I didn't mean to—" He moves my face and quickly kisses me on the lips. I feel relieved and sad at the same time. I need to tell him now. "Leroy—"

He softly puts his finger over my lips, preventing me from saying another word.

Leroy hops off the bed and jogs over to his bag. He pulls out a notebook and tosses it right in front of me as he crawls back on the bed, lying behind me so I can lean back on him, and I realize he's trying to give me a distraction.

"How many names you think we can rememba from the donor list, between the both of us?" Leroy adjusts so he can see my face more clearly.

"I don't know. I'm sure at least a few. Why?"

As he opens the notebook, I see that the pages are covered in sketches and handwriting, a mixture between cursive and print. I feel relieved, even though I shouldn't. I should just get it over with, say what needs to be said about my move. But maybe it's better if we focus on this first.

The donor list laid out *everyone* the Bainbridges had in their pockets, showing the scale of their power and their plan to force Black homeowners to sell their land well under market value or take it from them using tools like eminent domain, with one goal: to create a new downtown in their own image and get all the profits, while pushing Black communities out. When I think about what we stand to lose if we don't figure this out, this feels more important. I can tell him about my move later.

"Wow, it's so detailed," I say, flipping to the next page.

Leroy quickly explains Faa's code, pages that seemed unreadable now bloom with so much information, clues. I knew Faa was a brilliant investigative journalist, but I had no idea he'd done so much research and unearthed so many Bainbridge secrets.

"This, these names," I say, reaching for a pad and paper from the bottom drawer of my desk next to my bed. "They were on the list. You remember?"

Leroy shakes his head before he stops and points. "I rememba this one: Delroy."

"Isn't he in government?" I skim the other lines in Faa's

notebook until I find what I'm looking for. "Here, it says he's an alderman."

"Yup, he on the city council wit the mayor"—Leroy nods—"but word on the street is he mo than that, one of the main folks in the Bainbridge pockets. Let's keep skimmin and write down anythin that might look like a name, even if we don't know who they are. Got anotha pen?"

I reach into the drawer, hand him one. Instead of sitting up, he uses my hip as his personal table. "You sure you don't want to move to the desk?" I ask.

"Nah," he says, leaning in to kiss me on the cheek. "This perfect. I wanna stay close, so you can feel me now that I'm here."

I try to focus, build up my strength and confidence for what we'll eventually have to talk about after we finish this.

When we're done, we're staring at about fifteen potential names. Leroy keeps flipping, scribbling down more as they come to mind. "Hol up, I think I know somebody who might be able to help," he says, lying on top of me.

"It seems like the Bainbridges always a step ahead, from somehow convincin Lyric to lead the DKs to foolin Rouk and even blackmailin Brown Brown. But if we had somebody who could help us beat em at they own game, maybe create some high-tech shit that lets us listen in, we could flip the tables on em."

"And you know somebody who could do that?"

Leroy puckers his lips. I kiss him—quick and light.

"I do and he been under our nose this whole time. I'll tell you soon, if I can get him to say yes."

This is good. It's progress. The longer I stare at the names, though, I feel like there's a connection between them.

I ignore the first names and read over what seem to be the last names again and again in my head like a song. Then, it hits me, but I don't know if I'm sure enough to say what it is out loud. I reach for my phone and call Princeton.

"Wassup," he sings through the phone. "Miss me already?"

Leroy glares at me for interrupting our time alone together.

"Nope." I laugh. "Quick question: Leroy and I are trying to reconstruct the list we saw on the drive at the diner. Do these names sound familiar to you? Delroy, Macklebee, Sawyer, Timvee, Baxter . . ."

"Yeah, if you talkin' 'bout people our age, they either go to our school or Providence Prep."

"That's it!" I jump up. I try to crawl out from under Leroy, so he can hear better, but he just holds me tighter. I surrender and put the phone on speaker.

"Sound like you thinkin' ova there." Princeton giggles, greets some other people. There's one voice I recognize. "You on a date with Christina?" I joke.

Leroy sits up, mouths, *Furreal?*

"I'mma hang up if you keep talkin' crazy," Princeton says. "I'm volunteerin' at the Y. She's here, too." Christina does give me another idea, but I don't know how possible it is.

"Mmhmm . . . sure you are," I sing. "Remember a couple of weeks ago when she offered to help expand our love letter business to schools in exchange for me writing a breakup letter for her?"

Leroy looks up, locks eyes with me. Doesn't take long before he nods, understanding where I'm going.

"Yeah, whatchu thinkin'?" Princeton covers the phone, gives someone directions somewhere. "My bad, I'm back. You down to come out of love letter writin' retirement?"

I shake my head, even though he can't see me. *So dramatic.*

"I think it might be the easiest way to talk to some of the people on this list, put some faces to these names. We can use the love letters to do it."

"Okay, okay. Lemme chat with Christina real quick and hit you back. Maybe this might cheer her up. She been down lately, prolly got somethin' to do with Lyric." He hangs up.

I completely forgot about Christina and Lyric. With everything that happened, she never reached back out for the breakup letter she wanted me to write for her. Does that mean they're still together? Maybe I should bring it up the next time I see her at school?

Leroy uses the pause to his advantage, rolls us until I'm on top of him.

"Sho you aint tryna become a BD?" He grins.

I laugh at the thought.

"You know who else could help? Trish. She could use her connections at Providence Prep, and—"

I try to hide it, but he stops talking when he realizes why I'm upset. I know it shouldn't matter now that we're together, but him kissing Trish is burned into my memory. I don't think I'll ever be able to forget it.

"Hol up a sec." Leroy shifts until we're both lying on our sides. He leans in for another quick kiss and waits until my eyes find their way back to him. "What I did was fucked up, and I'm sorry. But you gotta believe me when I say me and Trish aint neva been like that. She only eva been my best friend."

I want to say I do, but I don't want to say it's okay, when I feel it's not.

"Can you tell me why you did it?" I ask.

"Back then, I thought you liked Princeton and you aint like me no mo." He plays with my fingers, holds my hand. "At least, that's where it started. You rememba how I dropped you off after we left Auntie Rissa's diner?"

I nod, shift so I can see his face more clearly.

"I went back to my place and Jacobee, I mean Jacob, was cookin fuh me and Taj. Things was good at first, till Taj joked round and told Jacob he liked him. Iono what went on between em, not at that point, but Jacob aint like it and straight up left. Taj ran after him, but when he came back, he went upstairs and cried.

"Seein that, I aint think I could handle it if you did somethin like that to me. So I got scared and wanted to end it cuz I thought I was the only one who had feelins. But when I found yo letter in the back seat, that's when I realized how bad I fucked up. Trish aint speak to me fuh weeks after she saw the letter, cuz she told me not to do what I did in the first place."

I remember wondering if Leroy thought I liked Princeton, even when I tried to tell him it wasn't like that. But I didn't know about Jacob and Taj, let alone that they went through a breakup. Jacob still hasn't told me anything about Taj—how they met or even their relationship. Today is really the first time I've been able to see them together.

Taj probably never did anything like kiss his best friend in order to make Jacob jealous, but I can understand what Leroy might have felt. I still don't like it, but at least now I know.

"That's why I fought so hard to get you back. Just tell me what I can do, so it don't hurt you no mo. Ion want you doubtin me."

I say how I feel instead of what might make him feel better. "I don't think there's anything you can do."

"Why not?" He lays his head on my chest.

"I don't know, but maybe time will heal it."

"How long that's gon take?" He's definitely pouting—and

I wish I could tell him it's the cutest thing I've ever seen.

I think more about everything he shared, especially about Trish. "I think it might be a good idea for me to at least meet her, get to know her based on more than just that one moment." Leroy wears the biggest smile. "You're that happy?"

"How can I not be? My baby gets to meet my best friend."

Leroy's eyes are doing it again, pulling me closer, making me feel safe.

Now I should tell him. It's the right thing to do. But is it wrong to hold it in just a little longer, so we can enjoy being together like this?

I feel his heart beating beneath my hands, the drum at my fingertips. I lay my head there to meet it, to listen as our heartbeats try to synchronize "like" growing into "love."

4

Leroy

"I want my best friend back, this shit is wack." I slam a box of canned goods, storm ova to the produce aisle where Trish is. But befo I can say anythin, she pointin fuh me to go back in Rouk's direction, just like Auntie Rissa. I can hear em in my head: *Quit runnin.*

"What the fuck you want me to say?" Rouk yells, arrangin stuff on the top shelf.

"Somethin. Anythin. Instead of walkin on eggshells like we aint neva been friends and you don't know how to talk to me."

Me and Rouk been tryna figure out how to find our way back to bein best friends, now that Ma and Taj asked him to live wit us, but it ain't easy.

I came to D&D's Grocery early to help Rouk and Trish during they shift, so we could talk some stuff through befo settin up fuh our meetin bout Operation Love Letter.

"Fuck it, then. You want some relationship advice, here you go." He slams a box of rice, like he gon throw it. *Do it, nigga. I dare you.* "Yo problem is you neva listen. The moment somethin don't go yo way, you eitha assume it's yo fault or you get mad and wanna fight. I betchu aint even think to ask Jay what he feelin. Cuz if you did, you would know why he scared to begin wit."

"Was that so hard?" I suck my teeth, pissed and grateful. That's my best friend.

When we done, me and Rouk roll our carts ova to the produce aisle to help Trish. We label-gun and stack apples, while Trish do the same wit bananas.

Wit her box braids pulled up in a bun, Trish remind me of Janet Jackson from *Poetic Justice*. Every now and then, I catch her smirkin. She feel it, too. Things gettin closer to how they used to be befo Faa was murdered.

"It sounds like those nightmares you kept havin after you got shot," Trish says.

"How I make em go away?"

"Aint somethin *you* can make go away." Rouk starts on the last box.

"What if it's me?" What if we can't make it past this and he break up wit me?

"Errthang aint boutchu," Rouk says.

I suck my teeth, mess up his side of apples cuz he right and ion like it.

"It aint *you* Jay is scared of." Trish shakes her head. "Just be patient."

When we finish, Rouk and Trish clock out, so we can set up the tables. Rouk bein a perfectionist, tryna make errthang perfect, but I know he nervous bout talkin to Jay. They aint said two words since he tried to bully Jay last spring.

Right when I turn round, Princeton and Jay walk through the automatic doors.

When Jay smiles, my heart beatboxes in my ears.

I dap Princeton and introduce him to Trish.

Befo I can say anythin else, Trish reaches out her hand to Jay. "I know we've met under the worst circumstances cuz of that knucklehead. But I'm glad we get to meet again—the right way." They both have a conversation without words.

Rouk slowly walks up, barely able to look Jay in the eyes.

Me and Princeton watch, wonderin how Jay gon react.

"I just wanted to say what I did to you was fucked up," Rouk begins. "I'm real sorry. Aint no excuse fuh what I did. I hope you accept my apology."

Jay looks at him. He don't rush neitha.

"I can't promise I'll forget—"

"Nah, neva that," Rouk says.

"But apology accepted," Jay adds. "Out of all the years we went to school together, I know you would have never done any of those things if Faa were still here." When Jay finishes, it's like all of us take a deep breath.

I dap Rouk, proud of him, and hook him in a headlock. But when Trish jump on Rouk's back and start talkin sweet to him, it's like she brings him back to life.

I wrap my arms round Jay, so he know I'm proud of him, too.

Trish squeals, hops off Rouk's back, and runs toward the

door. That's when I know our special guest done made it—PYT.

When Brown Brown called me a coupla days ago, said he met up wit Detective Dane—no promises but somethin we could work wit—it's like somethin clicked.

Since then, me and PYT been tryna put our heads togetha bout Operation Love Letter, figure out how Brown Brown could work his connections, get us some real evidence we can use. That way, we could break the news to Taj in a way that don't feel like a betrayal but a benefit.

"Why you wait so long to come see me?" Trish's happy squeals as she jumps on PYT shake me outta my thoughts. I laugh as she lands a few soft love taps.

I hug PYT and introduce him to Jay and Princeton.

"You were at Auntie Rissa's that day we learned about everything?" Jay says.

PYT nods, grins at how my arm finds its way back round Jay.

Wit errbody finally here, Trish's unc Derek get to whippin up a lil somethin fuh us to snack on while we get seated and finally get down to business. Me, Trish, and Rouk bring back the trays of sweet hush puppies and deviled eggs, and errbody go up to the counter to get they own bucket of D&D's famous spicy-hot boiled peanuts.

As we start eatin, me, Trish, and Rouk start wit a recap so errbody up to speed. I talk bout the damaged flash drive and me and Rouk discoverin Faa's journals. Rouk explains what he found out so far from the journals: Faa was workin on a huge story bout how the corruption of Savannah's top politicians and people in power were all linked to Louis B.

Jay talks bout the list of names me and him put togetha, mention some of the names we rememba, like Delroy, the one just bout errbody knows, and that's when Jay and Princeton explain the love letter business they run out of Daniel Lee.

"We know we could use love letters to connect with folks on the list, but I'm usually the one to make contact, get the background, handwritin' sample, and collect the moolah," Princeton explains. "As Jay work his magic, I do my thang paintin' the envelopes. But I ain't close enough with nobody at Providence to chat up love letters, not without attractin' too much attention."

"Any ideas, Trish?" Jay says. "Between me and Leroy's memories and the notebooks, we only got about fifteen names, but on the flash drive there were hundreds."

Trish holds up a greasy thumb. "I can help wit Providence Prep, since I go there. Plus, I know Christina too. Lee said yall already talked wit her, right?" Princeton and Jay nod. "What if the way to do this is tweakin how yall do the letters?"

"Like how we write 'em?" Princeton grabs the last cornbread hush puppy. Trish chuckles. He can't hide how good it taste.

"Not how you write em, the experience," Trish says. "Make it mo exclusive, where you do house visits to learn mo bout the person."

Jay's eyes light up. "We could do mini interviews, get the info directly."

"A Trojan horse," PYT says, noddin. "And while you in there and Jay's interviewin, Princeton can find a computer and plug in one of these."

PYT holds up somethin that looks like half the size of a flash drive, hands it to Princeton.

"What is it?" Jay asks.

"A remake of some spy tech and malware that's out on the market. When you plug it into the PC tower, it'll download a virus, where I can see and record errthang they do."

An idea hits me. "You sayin you could use that anywhere? Like even in a police station, if we was able to get somebody inside?"

Immediately, PYT get where I'm goin wit it—the last part we needed to figure out how to use Brown Brown. "Yup, we could hear whateva they talm bout, and I can control things from my end, if needed." PYT grins.

"You serious? You gon' bug a police station?" Princeton says, shocked and curious. "You a spy or somethin'?"

"We aint really allowed to talk much bout it," I say, proud. "But PYT's one of the biggest hackers in Georgia, prolly the whole South."

"Lee, quit exaggeratin." PYT blushes.

"I'm not. Yall rememba 'Black Night,' a few years ago?"

"Talm 'bout when the power was cut off to the police station and the person wired two hundred fifty thousand dollars from the police department payroll to the fam who son was put in a coma after bein' beat by the cops?" Princeton says.

"Yup, he did all that. And back then, PYT was only fifteen."

Suddenly, errbody lookin at PYT like he a superhero, wonderin if he was behind any otha hackin incidents that happened the past few years. Knowin PYT, he prolly was, but he could neva say, not even here.

"So all we do is use that?" Jay says, getting us back on track. "What happens after it's downloaded?"

"We just gotta set up somewhere we can listen in and record errthang we hear," PYT explains. "I wanted to run it by errbody here first to see if it'll work befo we took it to Taj furreal, furreal. Whatchyall think?"

Errbody nods, excited.

"We just gotta figure out who the first person gon be," I say, lookin at Jay and Princeton to see if they know yet.

"What bout Denise? Delroy's granddaughter," Trish says. "I've met her a few times, but Tina is really close wit her. Maybe she could make the connect."

"That could work," Princeton says, lookin at Jay, who also agrees.

"Can't nobody know bout this outside this table, tho." I

look errbody in the eye. "We can't even tell Tina the whole truth, especially not knowin if she still wit Lyric."

Errbody quiet, cuz they know what's at stake, till Night's voice rings through the automatic doors loud and worried, as he runs inside, "Aye, Lee, Rouk, PYT! You aint been pickin up any of yo phones. We gotta head out, somethin came up."

"Why? What's goin on?" I stand up, try to read the answer from his face.

"I'll tell you when we get there. Errbody else, yall go *straight* home."

Errbody hug and dap it out. I steal a kiss on the lips from Jay and laugh as he stands there frozen in shock while me, PYT, and Rouk run out to get in the whip.

I miss him already.

Night don't say why, but he drop Rouk off at Ma's before he tell me we goin to the mall. To fill the silence, me and PYT let him in on what we talked bout durin the Operation Love Letter meetin. Then he blows our mind when he explains how the BDs, if they backed it, could give us protection, boots on the ground, and a buildin if we needed.

I forgot the BDs aint just OGs and YGs—it's whole neighborhoods, even businesses, which mean all kinda ways of sharin and collectin info. And wit somethin like Operation Love Letter, the tech and the love letters gon help fill in the gaps as we translate the journals, but we gon need people out in the streets, keepin an eye on the people we trackin, seein who they meetin wit and how they movin, even eavesdroppin, cuz gossip gon help us confirm things documents won't.

When the mall is in sight, Night whole body starts tensin up. He pulls up right at the front entrance, behind Taj.

"Did they say where Frank and Myrrh were spotted?" Night asks Taj as he comes to the car.

"Right across from the shoe store and the barbershop in the food court," Taj says. "Already got a few crews in position, in case anythin pop off."

What Frank and Myrrh doin here? Errbody know this a BDs neutral zone.

PYT pulls out his bag, the one he carry fuh protection. Night arms himself and hands me one.

"Just in case," Taj says, makin sho I hear him.

We walk through the automatic doors, then we see Frank and Myrrh sittin at a table right in front of the shoe store. They rearranged the tables, creatin front-row seats just to prove a point. And they aint alone, a crew of bout twenty surroundin em. But the closer we get, we see anotha problem: we recognize some of the faces in they crew, folks who used to be BDs, which mean they flippin our own.

"Whaddup, whaddup? If I aint know no betta, I woulda thought you came all this way cuz you missed me." Taj is all smiles, but errbody who know him can feel the rage hidin underneath. And I bet him seein some of our crew on the wrong side of the BDs got even mo to do wit it. I just hope he can keep his cool.

"I was hopin you'd be done cryin bout yo diner," Frank says.

Taj smiles wider, a threat by a different name.

Frank narrows his eyes, sees me but focuses on PYT. "You aint change sides yet, now that we got yo boyfriend?"

PYT's eyes wanna tell the truth, make sho Taj know Brown Brown hidin so they can't use him against the BDs. But we can't tell Taj, not yet.

Taj walks closer, stands directly in front of Frank. "You know, I think I get how yo face could grow on somebody like a mutt, once you teach it how to sit and roll ova." He leans lower so they eye to eye. "Is that what Lyric make you do? Play fetch?"

Myrrh jumps up. When he does, most of the food court except a few families and they kids on the carousel stop what they doin.

All the DKs behind Frank and Myrrh rise up, like they gon do somethin. But we outnumber em, maybe eight to one—point proven.

Unfazed, Frank sips some lemonade and bites off a piece of cinnamon pretzel. He sits there chewin befo he licks his fingers clean. "I'm here fuh Rouk. Where he at?"

Taj look round at us, like he should be behind us. "Nonya. Next question."

Frank chuckles, stands up real slow. He takes a final bite out of his pretzel and watches Taj, as he chews slowly. He takes anotha sip, waits. "When you see him, give him a message fuh me: the BDs' days are numbered. So he betta think quick bout how he can make his lil tantrum up to me befo I lose my patience and he lose somethin he can't get back."

"Like what? Just curious, I wanna make sho I deliver yo message fully." Taj smiles, close enough to kiss.

"Tell him to ask his brotha."

It happens so quick, it's hard to know who did what till we hear the tables and chairs crash to the floor and see Frank and Myrrh on the ground. Taj punched Frank and kicked Myrrh in the chest just to make a point. The DKs jump up, but Frank lifts his hand, stops em.

Frank stands, strokes his jaw, laughs. Myrrh wobbles, still winded.

"I see why it was so easy to flip Brown Brown." Frank holds up a finger so errbody can see it. "One month to eitha give Rouk up or have him come to us. Otherwise, there aint gon be no BDs left to protect him."

"You promise?" Taj holds his gaze.

All of us watch Frank, Myrrh, and the DKs stroll outta the automatic doors.

"You good?" Night says, readin Taj face.

Taj don't answer. Instead, he chews on the inside of his cheek wit both hands on his hips, thinkin.

The first night I was in the hospital after the fire, I rememba Taj askin Auntie Rissa if me bein alive was a sign that he should do what she asked and step down from the

BDs to do somethin' else. He asked her, "Who gon respect somebody who can't protect they own?" If the DKs even flippin folks from K-Town, Frank's threat hits different.

"We need to go to Auntie Rissa's," Taj says. As we walk to the car, he tosses me the keys. "You drive."

Taj neva let me drive, eva since he got the Black Chevy Avalanche we nicknamed Da Lanche. When he gets in the car, Taj just leans his seat back, eyes closed.

Auntie Rissa's new spot in Avalon Park look much bigger than the place in K-Heights, but when you open the door, it feels just as homey. As we finally make our way inside, we hear Benji and Ma laughin in the kitchen, but there aint no sign of Auntie Rissa.

"Stop—put ya hands up and step away from the pot," Taj jokes as he pops his head in. He makes his way ova to Benji fuh a bro-hug befo bear-huggin Ma and pickin her up off the ground. I wonder if she knows, if she can feel him goin ova the top cuz he aint got nothin left.

"You not lettin her cook, are you?" I say, pretendin to protect the pot.

Ma laughs and holds the spoon up to Taj's lips. "Taste it."

She looks at him, waitin fuh his reaction as he finishes swallowin. When Taj nods wit approval, she lets the whole world know: "Aint I told you ya gurl could burn?" She high-fives Benji, the culinary miracle worker.

"Do I hear a victory dance?" Auntie Rissa comes in from the back. She glides across the room in a flowy gray dress with streaks of turquoise and blue as she loves on all of us, wavin errbody ova to the cherry-oak-colored dinner table. Benji brings the pot, and Ma comes right behind him wit the honey biscuits.

"You gotta work tonight?" Taj asks, since Ma got on her pink and blue flower scrubs.

"Yeah, we short-staffed but still gettin flooded wit patients."

Errbody look at each otha, feelin the tense silence. We know the increase in cases is cuz of the DKs and the BDs battlin it out in the streets.

When errbody clean they plates and soak up the dumplin sauce wit they biscuits, we proud and full twice ova. But it don't take long befo Ma's headin to the hospital. We kiss her and let her know we'll see her when she gets off in the mornin.

It's kinda hard to believe me and Taj chose to move in wit Ma and went this long without too many problems. Ma and Taj still argue, but it aint bout the same stuff—her leavin or choosin men ova us. It's her workin too hard and Taj wantin her to take betta care of herself.

"So who gon tell me the reason behind the long faces?" Auntie Rissa finally asks.

"Frank and Myrrh called us out," I start.

"Not just out," PYT says. "They was at the mall wit a

crew mo than twenty deep, and they got way mo than they showed us."

"Well, it wouldn't be the first time somebody tried to call the BDs out. Why is this any different?" Auntie Rissa waits, like she already knows but wants Taj to say it out loud.

"They been flippin BDs. Not a lot, but we recognized some of the faces," I say.

"And they want Rouk," PYT adds. "Gave us one month to give him up or get him to turn himself ova befo he said there wouldn't be no BDs left to protect him."

"A month?" Auntie Rissa interrupts wit a frown, stands to bring ova some papers she tucked away in the kitchen. She passes a few pamphlets to the center of the table and says, "We think this how they been recruitin and flippin people. Errbody, not just BDs."

"I've seen em posted up on bulletin boards and light poles, too," Benji says.

I open one of the pamphlets, PYT and Night come ova to see what it says. At the top, it reads:

CLAIM YOUR AMERICAN DREAM IN PROMISE HEIGHTS
**The home and community you've always
hoped for is waiting for you.
$6,000 cash vouchers if you sign before Oct. 31.
An additional $1,000 per referral that signs a new lease.
Funded by BPD Corp.**

"Look at the date—October thirty-first. Almost four weeks from now. The same as yo deadline to give up Rouk," Auntie Rissa says. "And it says funded by BPD, the same Bainbridge Promise Development Lee and Jay discovered on the drive. That's not all, tho, cuz look at the map," Auntie Rissa says, flippin the brochure ova on the back. "Do you see where it's located?"

"Putnam Parkway? That's thirty minutes away. They don't even have buses out there," Night says.

Auntie Rissa shakes her head. "I think that's the point."

"It's fucked up," Taj says. We all agree, whether silently or loudly.

"Then we know whateva it is they plannin gotta be some-how connected to this. We just gotta figure out what, befo it's too late," I say.

"We need to talk wit Rosalind. Lady Tee too," Auntie Rissa says.

If the Bainbridges can do all this, even if we translate all Faa's journals and get what we need through Operation Love Letter, will we be able to stop it?

5

JAY

I don't know if I'm going to make it to my front door alive. Christina may be the reigning homecoming queen since we were freshmen, but she's a tyrant bootcamp instructor when it comes to learning dance routines. Sometimes I wonder if she's pushing herself—and all of us—so hard for a different reason, as if she's waging a losing war with something else, while hiding everything behind her radiant smile.

All I want to do is go into the house, drop off my book bag, which is already heavier than it needs to be with my roller skates, and pass out. It's the only reason I'm glad Leroy said he couldn't make it today because he's trying to sort out some BD stuff.

When I finally walk in, Momma and Jacob are in the kitchen. But the look on Jacob's face means only one thing, bad news.

"Hey, baby, how was school?" Momma walks my way as I sit on the couch.

In my mind, I scream, *Just say it!*

But I know better. There's only one kind of a person

willing to raise his voice at Julia Baptiste-Dupresh—a (soon-to-be) dead one.

"Long but good." I offer the last part to remind her of how special this moment is in my life, just as special as it was in hers when she and Dad were nominated to be (and eventually became) homecoming king and queen. But I don't get my hopes up.

I sit on my hands to hide that they're shaking.

"I know it's never going to be a 'good' time to say this, so I'll just get to it: Lin and I have officially set up the paperwork for your transfer. Originally, I was planning for it to be sooner than later, but given homecoming, maybe even as homecoming king, I'm delaying it until the end of this month. So you will leave the week after, and that way, you can still experience it before moving to New York. You'll still have enough time to settle in before Will's school—your new school—goes on Thanksgiving break."

I know I should be relieved that I won't miss homecoming and that she only wants me to be safe. I get that, but what about what I want? Not want. What about what I *need*?

I pick up my book bag and walk toward the stairs. Just as the doorbell rings, I think about letting one of them get it. But what if it's Leroy?

I open the door and freeze. I can't speak, so I open the door wide enough for Jacob and Momma to see.

"J.D., what are you doing here?" Momma says. "I thought

we had an agreement?"

She comes toward the door but stops just short of me, crossing her arms—proof she's listening but not a promise she'll do much more than that.

"Julia, I get it. Y'all don't want me here. You made it clear, but I needed to know y'all were safe," Dad says. "You and I both know the kind of man Louis Bainbridge is. Did he really send you flowers?"

Momma sits in her right hip, frowns.

Dad folds his work hat in his hands and says, "If he sent you flowers, he sent them for a reason. Please, just tell me."

Outside of the last time I saw him in the living room, when I revealed what he did to me and Jacob, I've never seen him look this nervous.

Momma's face falters. It's too late for her to hide it now. She looks at us, then invites Dad in. We all sit across from Dad, like a tribunal of his past crimes.

"He did send me some flowers," Momma admits.

"Do you remember what kind?" Dad asks.

"Angel trumpets," I say.

I looked it up not long after Jacob showed me the card.

"Are you sure?" Dad's eyes glare then turn soft, caring.

I look away from him. I can't let my guard down and allow him to become my hero again.

Dad starts to say something but doesn't. Instead, he heads to the door until Momma suddenly calls him to her, asks him to sit at the barstool. I'm not sure what's happening, but I assume she sees it too. The way he folds his hat, clenches his jaw, like he's made up his mind to do something he shouldn't.

She pours him a glass of sweet milk. He looks at it, surprised. His hands cup the glass like a gift—a small one.

Jacob gets up, making a decision of his own, and disappears upstairs. I grab my bag, prepare to follow.

"What did you mean that there's always a reason?" The words come out without my permission, but I need to hear the answer just the same.

Dad doesn't respond right away, almost like he's choosing his words carefully.

"Louis wants what *he* wants. He's always been that way. It's how he was raised. Those who help him, he sees them as heroes; those who don't help him, he sees as villains. And no villain survives him."

"He wasn't always like that," Momma says to me, stirring a new pitcher after she's drizzled in honey and a pinch of more spices. "There was a time, if you could imagine, your father and Louis were pretty close."

Dad shakes his head. "He never saw it that way, though. It's complicated. I guess at some point we all have to choose who we are—who we want to become."

Like Jacob, Dad chugs the glass in seconds, then stands up to leave. "Thanks for helping me keep my head on straight," he says to Momma. Then he looks at me. "You may not want to hear it from me, given everything that's going on, but I hope you get to enjoy yourself up there in New York. Have you spoken to Will yet?"

I'm surprised by his question, even though I shouldn't be. If he didn't hear it from Momma, he heard it from Miss Rosalind—they are close friends, after all.

"No, I haven't spoken to him. Not since I was in the hospital."

At first, Will and I texted nonstop. It helped that I couldn't talk too often because it meant I could just text. It made it easier for me to tell him everything about the flash drive and about Lyric being the Bainbridge who was behind everything. I even got to tell him about Rouk and how Frank and Myrrh tricked him.

For the first couple of days, it was like we picked up where we left off, back when we were going on adventures all over Savannah. Then I asked him if he'd ever forgive me for what happened between us, and I haven't heard from him since.

"You should reach out," Dad says, walking toward the door. "You'd be surprised how much he might be waiting to hear from you."

Dad stops when he reaches the doorknob and sees Jacob sitting there on the steps. I thought he'd gone upstairs, but I guess even he wanted to know more.

"What did it mean? The flowers?" Jacob says, cautious.

Dad takes a deep breath. "It's a warning. Angel trumpets are pretty but deadly. All parts of the plant are poisonous if ingested, and even touching them can irritate your skin, without proper precautions."

"You saying he tried to poison Ma?"

"No, that's too simple for Louis. I think the flower choice means 'choose your friends wisely.'" Dad is about to reach for the door but turns and faces Jacob. "For Louis, everything is about power and nothing is ever what it seems. Edda Nae and the elders had a saying: 'The most dangerous snakes kiss long before they kill.' The Bainbridges are just like that—masters of the long game." Dad looks at Ma. "I'll keep my distance until y'all say otherwise, like I promised. Just know, regardless of how you feel about me now, I'll always protect you. Never forget that."

Dad closes the door softly behind him. And for a second, we stare at it, wondering if he was actually there or just a figment of our imagination, his last words echoing.

I head up to my room just to sit on my bed and continue to roam through my thoughts. I haven't wanted to see Dad for a long time, but I'd be lying if I said a part of me didn't feel safer with him present.

"Whatchu thinking so hard about?" Jacob leans in the doorway, half-in, half-out. He's changed into his favorite Daniel Lee Spartan shirt and muscle shorts.

I shrug, not sure what to say. He uses my lack of answer as

an excuse to come in—not that he ever needs one.

"C'mon, you can tell me." Jacob sits in the middle of the floor and begins stretching. I know what he wants me to say, *Can I join you?* But my thighs, back, and arms protest.

He taps the space in front of him anyway, a signal. I do what any other sane, sore, and sleepy person would do—I ignore him.

"Quit bein' lazy. Princeton told me you promised you'd stretch before bed and in the morning, so you aren't stiff tomorrow. And earlier, Lee was telling me how he been missing you like crazy."

I pull out my phone and prepare to send Princeton the most prolific rebuke in the history of our friendship, but Jacob jumps up and swipes my phone.

In my mind, I hold Jacob away with one arm, laughing as he tries to strong-arm me (you weakling!). In reality, he scoops me up like a fireman and lays me on the ground.

"Don't blame him for making sure you honor your promise. And don't get on Lee about him and his feelings. He's a lot more emotional than you think. Remember that."

Why does it feel like Jacob is closer to everyone that's supposed to be closest to me? If Princeton isn't calling and texting him, Leroy is. Princeton is *my* best friend, and Leroy is *my* boyfriend. It feels like his relationship with everyone is growing stronger the closer it gets to the time for me to leave—and I don't like it. The stitch of pain returns. I try to play it off, rub it away.

As if Jacob can feel it, too, he lines up the soles of our feet, so we can do his favorite stretch: a partner straddle, like we did when we were young after long skating sessions at Da Rink.

I'm sure Jacob does care about my soreness and the need for me to stretch to avoid injury. But I know it's not the real reason he's in here. It doesn't matter how big Jacob gets, he's still a Daddy's boy at heart, and seeing him must've shaken something loose.

It's easy staying mad at Dad, when he's gone, to bully the phantoms of him in our memory. But what do I do when a part of me wants to be saved by the very person who hurt me in the first place?

After two more rounds of stretches, we end, side by side, our legs propped up on the wall. I don't know if it's the after-stretch high or me being deliriously tired, but the question comes out: "Do you want me to go to New York?"

"No, I want you to stay here." He exhales like he's picking up another burden. "But I can't protect you."

I want to say it's not his job, he shouldn't worry about protecting me, but I know it would only make him feel worse, helpless. And Jacob doesn't do helpless very well.

"You know, me and Faa were the same year," Jacob says. "I know people called me the Golden Boy, but I ain't had nothin' on Faa. The way he could light up a room without even trying, he made you feel like your story, your pain, mattered. The more I think about it, you remind me of him—and I'm not the only one who thinks that. Taj said the same thing."

I look at him, surprised.

"Yeah, he brought it up when you and Lee were upstairs. I wasn't close to Taj back when Faa was murdered, but I still see the pain in his eyes. I don't think I'd be able to make it if something happened to you." He looks at me, pokes at me until he steals a chuckle out of me. "I want you to stay here, but if it's the difference between you being safe and alive, there's only one option: for you to leave."

Hearing Jacob's words doesn't make me feel better, but something in me settles. If it were my choice, I'd stay, even if it means being hurt or even something worse. But I've never been good at caring about me, so if it means Jacob, Momma, and everyone else won't be in pain, I'll do it— even if it hurts.

Tomorrow I'll find a way to tell Princeton, and I'm hoping he can give me advice on the best way to tell Leroy. As me and Jacob get up and shake out our sweaty clothes, I realize there's someone else I need to talk to.

After my shower, I dial Will's number. I'm ready to count the rings, so I can finally say something, anything. But he sends me straight to voice mail. Maybe it's an accident.

I call again. And then again. But each time, it rings once,

maybe twice, before it's clipped, leaving me on the other side, alone.

As soon as the last bell rings the next day, me and Princeton are out the green double doors so fast, you would think we are being chased. Once Christina canceled today's practice, we wanted to leave before she changed her mind.

I'd agreed to go over to Princeton's house, but when we arrive, I already regret it. After he's popped my favorite blueberry Toaster Strudels in the toaster and kicked off his shoes, spreading out in practiceless bliss on his living room sectional, it seems cruel for me to ruin it.

I have to break the news to him about my move, but every minute that passes screams for me to reconsider.

"My mom is sending me to New York." I blurt out the words so quickly, even I don't understand them, and I'm the one who said them.

I can't see Princeton's facial expressions because, in the buildup, I clenched my eyes shut and I'm still afraid to open them.

"What?" I hear him get up and feel him come closer. "Jay, whatchu just say?"

I don't want to say it again. If I do, the tears will start.

I open my eyes. Princeton is leaning over the kitchen island, chewing on his bottom lip, lost in thought, just shaking his head in disbelief.

"I don't want you to go." His words are a soft prayer begging for a miracle.

The Toaster Strudels pop up, and we jump, then smile, nervous. Princeton grabs one, draws his initials in sloppy icing, "BPB" for Brandon Princeton Baxter. I chuckle because he runs out of icing, so it looks like "BP3." Without thinking, I do the same: "JTD," Joseph Theodore Dupresh.

We offer our initialed pastries to each other—a sweet pact and promise—taking bites almost big enough to eat the strudels whole. Princeton looks at me so deeply that I can't help but run from his eyes, but he's bold in his sadness and doesn't apologize.

"You know you my best friend, right?" He finishes the strudel and sets his sights on the icing packet.

"You're my best friend, too," I say. "Really, my *only* friend."

"What about my boy Will—oh, my bad."

Princeton and I haven't talked about Will since the last time I saw him at the diner. I try to hide my disappointment about how things turned out.

"Wait." Princeton suddenly puts the pieces together. "Nah."

"What?"

"Man, don't tell me you . . . ?"

"Princeton, finish your sentence."

"You cheatin' on Leroy?"

I actually consider hitting him.

"No! Just no." I laugh, wishing I'd known we could be this way years ago.

Princeton catches me looking at him, and now he's the one running. "If we best friends, why we ain't neva do best friend things?"

"We run a love letter business together."

"Yeah, but . . ." He fights for the charming upper hand. "You know what I mean."

I do, and I'll never admit it.

"C'mon." He grabs his car keys.

"Where are we going?"

"To do what best friends do: shop and whatever else we can think of."

I follow him out the door because, on the other side of his smile, no is never an option. And within fifteen minutes, we're at the mall. Thirty minutes later, and I'm already exhausted.

Between stores and the growing number of bags of shoes and clothes he buys for both of us, we talk about what my leaving means, and if there's some way for me to still write the love letters, even from all the way in New York.

No matter what, the most important thing is for us to keep up appearances, because the love letter business is really the best way for us to get close enough to the potential people on our list and get the leads we need to reconstruct the donation list. If it means Princeton has to pretend he's taken over completely so he can keep doing interviews, and I write in New York, then so be it.

We don't have answers, but at least we're talking about it. That's when we begin talking about our futures beyond high school: my dream of going to Northwestern University, his dream of going to Morehouse. After undergrad, he wants to go to Harvard, like both of his moms. But instead of medical school like Dr. Eva and law school like Lady Tee, Princeton wants to go to business school.

Despite spending so much time together, we've never talked about our futures. He didn't even know me and Jacob wanted to go to Northwestern because, if he did, he would've connected us to his mom who went there as an undergraduate. He's promising to tell her so she can write a recommendation when I accidentally bump into someone on our way into Savannah Sweets, Princeton's favorite candy store.

"I'm sorry. I didn't see you." I pick up the other person's bag they dropped.

"It's all good."

My knees almost buckle. I'd recognize that voice anywhere— and the chills that follow it. It's Frank with Myrrh and a few DKs.

"Jay, you good?" Princeton asks, but he doesn't see what I see.

The DKs slowly surround us. I pull Princeton behind me.

"Yeah, Jay." Frank laughs. "Look like you done seen a ghost."

I remember what Dad said about snakes. But Frank is no snake, he's a hyena. Even now, his laugh lures us into false comfort before he goes in for the kill.

"What do you want, Frank?" I stand my ground. At the end of the day, Louis Bainbridge won't allow him to touch me—at least not for now.

It's a gamble, but I refuse to be terrorized.

"You tell Jacob I look forward to all of us—you, Leroy, and Taj—spending more time together. I promise it'll be something you'll never forget."

I look around, try to remember the faces, and I wait. But nothing happens, and just like that, his minions slowly leave the candy shop. Frank is the last to go, and I hold his gaze, refusing to show any sign of weakness.

Now all that's left is the sweet scent of pralines and candy apples—and danger. Princeton and I leave to walk out of the mall. My chest feels full and my body light, like I can fly if I spread my arms and face the wind. I'm proud I didn't need to be saved, because no matter what anyone might think, I'm not helpless. They don't have to protect me because I—

"Jay, look out!" Princeton yanks me back so hard, some of the clothes and boxes jerk from their bags.

Two cars race by, leaving tire marks in the asphalt—another threat. I stand up, wave off the people who come by to check on us and help us put some of the clothes back in our bags.

The stench of burned rubber forces its way into my nostrils. I feel a rush of hot and cold air on my skin. My stomach turns, my mouth waters.

No. Not here. Not now.

I break away from Princeton to try to find his car, but I can't remember where he parked. Everything is too bright, too loud.

Something claws up my stomach.

Stop, I tell my body. *I'm fine. Nothing is wrong with me.* If I just walk it off, breathe in and out deeply, smell the air—

I spit. But because I'm not a spitter, the excess saliva lands awkwardly on the asphalt, leaving an uncontrollable trail still clinging to my lips and chin.

"Jay, what's wrong? The car is that way." Princeton touches my shoulder, and I recoil by accident. I want him to help, to stop my body from ignoring what I want.

I growl, clench my jaws shut, so angry at myself that tears must be falling, because Princeton keeps asking what's wrong, as if him doing so will magically reveal an answer. I hunch over, near one of the spindly trees in the parking lot, as my Toaster Strudel lunch lunges out of me.

I can't stop crying, and I hate it.

Princeton helps me up, somehow gets me into the car along with our bags.

It feels like I'm being bitten all over my body by silver ants, setting my nerves on fire. My vision goes black, even though I know my eyes are wide open.

It's a panic attack, I know. But it's taking too long to pass.

"It's gon' be okay," Princeton says, pulling me out of the car.

I trip over a step or maybe a sidewalk, hear him tell me we're going through a door. "Don't take me to a hospital. Turn around. We have to leave," I plead, but he says this isn't a hospital.

I hear what sounds like wind chimes as we walk through a door.

"Ma, please help him." Princeton's words are desperate.

Then a voice that isn't Lady Tee's, softer but strong like water, says, "Hello, Jay, I'm Miss Eunyoung Kim, Princeton's mom, but you can call me Dr. Eva. Can you tell me what you're feeling?"

Slowly her face morphs from a high contrast silver and black with dots to a smooth light brown, like the blemishless bark of a camellia tree. She smells of almond oil and sweet oranges, her hair cascading in curly waves around her shoulders as she wraps it up into a quick bun, whispering, "Come with me."

If Lady Tee looks like she can command weather, Dr. Eva reigns over all matters of spirit. Princeton didn't take me to a hospital, after all. We're in what looks like a community center, equal parts spa, game room, and library.

"How you like it?" Princeton hands me a can of ginger ale. "It's called the Hugs, Hope, and Healing Center, H-Cubed for short."

"I've never seen anyplace like it, didn't even know it existed," I say.

"It's kinda new. My moms had it built maybe a year or two ago. If I'm not at your house or at a track meet, I'm usually here." Princeton beams.

I put the soda can down to try to find the best way to apologize. "I'm sorry to put you through all that."

Princeton grabs my hands, smothers them under his own. "You a badass, you know that? The way you stared down them DKs." He smiles with both rows of teeth.

Princeton looks over his shoulder out the window behind me. It's Leroy, Taj, Night, and PYT speed walking to the front door, after barely parking their cars. Before I can ask, he explains, "Figured you needed some reinforcements, but I ain't wanna sound the alarm to your mom or Jacob."

Leroy is first through the door. He grabs me and hugs me tight, never saying a word. Taj comes through next, followed by PYT and Night.

"Imma put it like this: ion see none of this; I aint even here," Taj says.

I zip my lips, so he knows I hear him loud and clear: don't get him in trouble with Jacob.

It doesn't take long to tell them what happened—at least the part about the run-in with Frank, Myrrh, and the DKs at Savannah Sweets. Neither Princeton nor I feel compelled to share why he had to bring me here. When our eyes meet, it's clear—it'll be our best friend secret.

Leroy is quiet with a permanent frown when Dr. Eva comes back in. I'm not surprised when she hugs Taj. Of course, she would know the BDs. Both of them believe in the same thing: protecting everyone's right to hope and heal together.

As Dr. Eva ropes Taj into a conversation about the BDs helping get more community members transportation and access to their community center, Princeton says it's time for him to start his shift at H-Cubed.

Taj suggests Leroy take me to Lake Willow Park so I can get some air before bringing me home. He says Jacob already knows I'm with him, so I don't need to worry. PYT and Night will be close, but far enough so Leroy and I can talk.

Before I leave, I hug Princeton, and Dr. Eva invites me to come back anytime. I promise I will—and mean it.

Leroy won't look over or talk to me as we get into his car. And as he drives, it feels like an invisible door is closing between us, and I can't take it. If we're going to be like this, I'd rather him just take me home.

Yes, that's what I'll say. "Leroy—"

"Can I hold you?" His words mix into mine, and like

paint, we create our own colors.

I nod, speechless.

We climb into the back seat, sit next to each other, awkwardly at first. My body is lost, but his hands find me and guide me home until I'm sitting on top of him.

Leroy kisses me, pulls me close, looks up at me, whispers, "I love you." And I swear his words summon the perfect storm, until the hurricane-force winds of my body collide with the steady coast of his hips. Even though we're fully clothed, all that can be heard between us is hot and cold fronts mixing.

I am scared and fearless, pushing and pulling, happy and sad. I don't know why the memories from the fire aren't crashing in, robbing me of this present. But I promise myself, I won't stop.

"Baby, slow down," Leroy pleads. I can't.

Suddenly, Leroy moans between kisses, squeezing me so tight that time stops, and for a second, neither of us breathe. Then time stutters and we remember.

I don't know exactly what happened, but then again, there's only one thing I know that rushes over a person like death, then brings them back to life.

"I swear this aint neva happened befo," Leroy mumbles, staring at the front of his jeans. "It's just . . . that thing you did witcho hips." He trembles from the aftershocks.

I wait for him to elaborate, but he doesn't.

"Don't be actin all innocent, now," he says.

I try to play it off, but Leroy sees it immediately.

"Wayment," he says, sitting up. "You a virgin?"

I want to say no because I don't want him to think of me as someone who can't be with him, but I'm sure he already knows, so I tell the truth.

"Yeah . . . sorry."

"Whatchu apologizin fuh?"

I can't tell him I'm afraid to make a mistake, that he'll get bored of me and leave me for someone with more experience.

"Jay, iono what's goin on in yo head, but I told you I love you. That mean I love errthang bout you. Besides, bein a virgin don't mean you can't teach me some things, clearly." He shudders again, then laughs.

I nod, try to replace his reassuring words with the voice that blares in my head, saying I'm not good enough. The truth of my move threatens to escape my lips and ruin everything.

But not today. Not now. Maybe tomorrow.

6

Leroy

Mistah Prez writes a question on the board in all caps: WHY DO WE HURT?

He reads it while he draws two lines beneath, his arm sharp and quick like a master swordsman. It's his Intro to Poetry class, but it feel like way mo than that, which is probably why it stays packed.

I'm lucky he got me a scholarship to take it after we met and chopped it up in the hallway when I got kicked outta class by my GED instructor. But cuz of the fire and me havin to be in the hospital fuh almost a week and Taj, Ma, and Auntie Rissa not wantin me to do too much, I missed a few classes.

I see Mistah Prez still got errbody speechless like always, folks lookin round at each otha fuh a clue cuz his questions aint neva really bout bein right or wrong but why and how you get to yo answer.

"Because life makes us," a classmate at the front of the class says, chewin on the tip of her pen.

"Forces us to protect those we love, self-defense," says a

guy in the back, who remind me of Jacobee—every word endin in a smile.

"Anyone else?" Mistah Prez asks.

"Jealousy, envy . . . wanting what others have, wishing it was yours."

"To control, keep ourselves safe."

"But what if you don't mean to?" anotha person says. "Is it the same hurt if it wasn't intentional?"

Iono bout that. Somethin bout the way he says it feel like a cop-out. Hurt aint based on the person doin the hurtin, it's based on the one bein hurt. Aint it?

"Mr. Leroy, glad you're back with us. You look like you have something to say."

Ion really know, but Mistah Prez aint tryna hear that, so I say what I'm thinkin, "It's kinda confusin cuz I feel like it's two questions in one."

Mistah Prez nods and says, "Keep going."

"So far, errbody who answer assume we doin the hurtin. But you could also read it as askin why we hurtin, as in why we in pain, what's hurtin us?"

It's hard to read Mistah Prez facial expression, but errbody noddin like I said somethin they aint think bout befo.

"I think you're on to something, Mr. Leroy. Regardless of the question you choose to answer, what's the opposite of hurting?"

"Healin?" I say.

He chuckles. "Say it again but like you know what you're talking about, more confidence."

"Healin."

"Perfect," he says, and draws a line on the board. He adds the following words:

HURT(ING) _____ HEAL(ING)

"Here's the assignment," Mistah Prez begins. "Write two poems thinking about what Mr. Leroy said, but about one situation from two different perspectives. Your goal is to explore what's needed for both situations to arrive on the other side, from hurting to healing."

A hand shoots up in the front and someone asks, "What's the definition you want us to use for healing?"

"That's going to be your job to figure out," he says. "See you all next class."

I walk down the stairs to the front.

"Mr. Leroy, how have you been?" I wanna hug Mistah Prez, but iono if I should. Do you hug professors in college? What if they feel less like a teacher and mo like family? Iono what's right or wrong, so I don't do nothin.

"I'm good, hangin in there and tryna figure why aint nobody else in my old school taught like you do. If they did, I feel like I woulda had a whole different vibe when it came to it."

He grabs his bag, starts packin up. "You're too kind. Why don't more teachers teach like this?"

"Aww, man, c'mon, Mistah Prez. You can't answer a question wit anotha question."

"Why not? Sometimes the best answers are questions." He grins, wavin fuh me to follow him as we head out of the classroom down the hall. "Would you believe me if I said I had a similar experience with teachers when I was growing up?"

"You? Nah, I bet you always was at the top like somebody else I know."

Mistah Prez's eye catch my words. "Is this the young man who writes love letters? The one you call pritty?"

I nod, tryna hide the smile growin across my face. I wanna tell him errthang bout Jay and how close we gettin, but aint enough time.

We weave in and out the busy halls wit Mistah Prez neva missin a beat. "By the look on your face, you gave the letter to him—and it went well?"

"For the most part, yeah. I think we tryna figure it out. Not just him, tho, me too. Got a lot goin on wit me, the fam, iono—just tryna make sense of it all."

"Well, if it means anything, I think you're doing a great job. I want you to really lean into this assignment, it's one of my favorites. It helped me when I was at one of my lowest points." He walks into the new classroom, starts settin up. "Oh, and good luck! I hear it won't be long before it's time for you to take the GED exam."

I aint think nobody knew besides Jay. "Thanks, iono how it's gon turn out, but Imma do my best."

"That's all I think anyone can expect. Just be prepared for when your best is a lot better than you might think."

I neva woulda thought somebody like Mistah Prez would know what it feels like to not know. Does that mean one day even I could be like him?

Up until now, I was kinda stressed out bout the GED exam, which is why I aint really tell nobody. It's not hard stayin off errbody's radar wit Taj and Auntie Rissa bein so busy wit the BDs. But knowin Mistah Prez's cheerin me on got me feelin like I could do well.

I chuckle at the thought, and how it don't feel as impossible as it sounds.

I say goodbye to Mistah Prez and walk to the lake behind the student center. I sit on that same bench me and Jacobee was on not long ago and think bout the last conversation we had. I shared my fear of hurtin Jay, and Jacobee had said it aint a matta of *if* I'll hurt but *when*.

My phone rings, and I see it's Taj. I thought Night was supposed to pick me up. Maybe he ridin wit him. "Whaddup—"

"Where you at?" Taj cuts me off. I can feel it—he's pissed.

"I'm at school. Why? What's goin—"

"I'm out front. Get here. Now." The line beeps.

Did somethin happen? I run through any and errthang I

coulda did to piss him off till I see him standin in front of Da Lanche wit Night next to him.

When me and Night lock eyes, I know it's bad.

"Did you know?" Taj yells. "Did you know where Brown Brown was this whole time?"

My mind goes blank fuh a second, feels like my heart stop. How he know? I look at Night, confused.

"So, both yall been lyin to my face this whole time?" Taj says.

"It won't like that. I just wanted to figure out—"

"How many times I gotta tell yo ass to quit doin shit that could getchu hurt?"

I wanna say somethin, but I know betta. He gets in the car, slams the door.

I get in, make sho not to slam it. "Where we goin?"

"Whey you think?" Taj says, lookin at me in the sideview. He don't say nothin, but I can see what's happenin: the rage takin ova. He aint thinkin straight.

Taj superpower is he know people, can feel deep down not just what they want, what they need. It's why he always say he loved me when he hit the streets, cuz he knew I needed to hear it, even if I couldn't say it back.

It's why he fought to unify the gangs, cuz he rememba Auntie Rissa when our pops went missin, how she lost her light and almost gave up when she was drownin in guilt. She needed a reason to fight, to feel like she was safe, too. Taj stuck close to her so she could see us—and be reminded of Pops. And when he was old enough, he made the gangs her muscle, her protection, so she could be herself—the queen nurturer and protecta fuh errbody else.

There's a Glock sittin on Taj's lap as we pull onto PYT's block. Taj aint the picture of a man ready to listen, to feel so he can make sho we all get what we need. Nah, it's someone else, someone who hurtin—and because of it—ready to hurt othas.

Iono if Night warned him, but PYT already sittin on the steps outside the house. He got a Black & Mild hangin from his bottom lip, and when he sees us gettin outta the car wit Taj, he takes a long pull. The closer we get, we see next to him on each side both of his pieces.

"Taj, you aint gon need that. Why dontchu put it up?" Night says, searchin fuh the Taj he know, not this angry imposter.

Taj don't say nothin, he just glarin.

PYT pulls on the Black & Mild, lettin the snake of smoke slither from his lips, up his cheek, and into the sky.

"So you just gon stand there lookin pritty?" PYT flicks the Black & Mild into the front yard, squints in Taj's direction.

"Depends on you. You plan on usin em?" Taj nods toward PYT's weapons.

"Nah, they aint fuh you. Neva fuh you."

Taj opens the gate, walks up to the stairs, and stands in

front of PYT. We follow behind Taj and wait to see how he wanna play this.

"You comin here to talk or to take?" PYT says.

Taj place his foot in the middle step between PYT's legs and leans in.

"Whatchu think?"

PYT slides ova and says, "You got five minutes, then we comin in. And rememba—you break it, you buy it."

"Heard, I only need three."

PYT reaches out his hand. "Imma need that piece, tho."

Taj look at PYT's hand and the Glock on his waist, like he considerin not givin it to him. "Fist or words, but aint gon be no killin."

Fuh a second, PYT's face is somethin different, too. Not a threat, a promise to bring Taj back if he lose himself, even if he gotta hurt Taj to do so. Taj pulls out his Glock, flips the safety back on, and places it in PYT's hand.

"He in the back room, waitin. We already moved all the furniture outta the room."

PYT pick up a bag of sunflower seeds as Taj steps behind him and opens the front door and closes it quietly. He offers the bag to Night, who takes it and shakes out a palmful befo offerin the bag to me.

"No matta whatchu hear, you can't cross these steps till five minutes up, unless one of us does," Night says.

At first, I'm bout to pass on the seeds, say ion want none.

98

Then I realize it aint bout food, it's bout nerves and havin somethin else to focus on. I take the bag, a verbal contract to the terms errbody just set. When I finish grabbin my share, I try to give it back to PYT, but he snatches my wrist instead and sits me down between his legs like he bout to braid some hair I don't have. Night squeezes next to us.

"When you get scared—or feel them emotions runnin through you—hold my hand, my leg, my arm, whateva," PYT says to me.

"What bout me?" Night grins.

"Whatchu think? Hold the banister, nigga."

We chuckle, longer than the joke makes us laugh fuh, cuz like the sunflower seeds, it aint bout whether the joke is funny, it's anotha moment to hope.

PYT leans in, reaches down in my hand fuh some of the seeds. He playin it off, but I know a hug when I feel one.

"I'm good . . . you aint gotta worry," I say.

"Nah you not—we aint eitha. Aint easy hearin someone you love turn into somethin you don't recognize. It's ugly, that kinda pain, but it gotta come out. At least this way, we can control it, so it aint as dangerous."

Wit that, I feel protected, and—even tho I aint in the house, none of us are—like we here to protect them, too.

Night checks his watch, don't say how much time we gotta wait prolly cuz he thinks it's gon make it feel longer, slower. But not knowin only make it worse, cuz Taj and

Brown Brown fightin sound like the house's heartbeat, fightin to stay alive.

Somethin crashes, and I jump. Then one of em lets out a sound that stuns all of us quiet, and I can feel PYT shakin behind me. He wraps his arms round me to steady himself, while Night leans his shoulder into both of us to touch.

Inside, somebody is cryin and breakin from the inside out. It feels like the house walls might cave in under the weight. I wonder if this is what PYT meant by pain that turns you into somethin else. Aint till it stops that I realize I'm holdin my breath.

"C'mon, we gotta get in there," Night says, jumpin up. But it's hard fuh me to stand, cuz it feels like my knees might buckle.

PYT hands me Taj's gun, and I put it in my waist strap.

"Don't fall apart, don't break down—no matta what, okay?" PYT says, lookin me straight in the eye. "They need us to be strong, so they know it's okay if they not."

PYT grips my shoulders, then follows Night inside. Just bout errthang in the livin room is broken, except the sofa and the TV. There's blood leadin down the hallway, and I can hear it: a growl, heavy breathin. No, not breathin—chokin.

I run to the back where I see Night and PYT grapplin wit Taj.

"C'mon nenh, let go. Taj, let go," Night shouts. He's behind Taj, tryna break his grip while PYT on the otha side of Brown Brown tryna do the same.

Brown Brown and Taj are both in a chokehold, refusin to let the otha go. They tanks ripped and bloodied, torsos covered in sweat, scratches, and bruises. Brown Brown is gruntin, veins bulgin all ova his body, and iono what to do, how to stop it. Brown Brown's eyes startin to roll in the back of his head, on the verge of passin out but he somehow breaks free.

Night gets in front of Brown Brown, and PYT in front of Taj. It's like both still see red, hyped up on whateva emotions been let loose ova the past few minutes they been locked in here togetha.

When it looks like Taj gon push through PYT, I step in front of him, hands up. "You had yo five minutes, now it's time fuh mine—and that means you gotta listen."

"Chill out," Night yells behind me, tryna calm Brown Brown down.

Befo I can say anythin else, PYT walks past Night and hugs Brown Brown tight.

"Don't look at him, look at me," PYT says ova and ova, his forehead touchin Brown Brown's.

Time is runnin out, so I try to calm Taj down by tellin him the plan, "I need Brown Brown."

"Fuck you mean you *need* him?" he yells.

"You remember how me and Jay wrote down some of the names we saw on the donation list, right? Well, in order to reconstruct the list we lost on the flash drive, we gon need mo than just the BDs, we gon need to be one step ahead."

"Lee . . . get to the fuckin point. I aint tryna hear all that."

"Brown Brown is our connection to the cops, specifically Detective Dane. If anythin happen to him, it could mess up errthang, cuz I think this whole blackmailin was a trap—"

"Right . . . cuz he a fuckin traitor," Taj spits.

"No . . . you aint listenin. It's bigger than that. I think the DKs, prolly Frank and Myrrh, tryna make us do what they couldn't—get rid of Brown Brown—cuz they knew if they did, the whole police department would be on em. But if we did, errbody would be after the BDs, which sound like a win-win fuh them and Louis B.

"I know you hurt, I know you mad, and I know that don't even compare to what we both know Auntie Rissa feelin," I say, "but Brown Brown say he aint burn down the diner."

Taj look at me like he bout to lunge at Brown Brown again, but I stop him. "I believe him."

"You really think I'm gon trust anythin comin outta that nigga's mouth?" Taj says.

"Then trust me," PYT says, "cuz you aint listenin first. You don't know that he saved my life and stopped em from doin much worse, maybe even killin me."

"He did that so you'd do this!" Taj yells.

"No, I didn't!" Brown Brown yells back.

"Didn't I say don't look at me?" Taj shouts, then lunges at Brown Brown again.

Night almost slips tryna keep him back while reasonin wit Taj. "What Auntie Rissa say? Find it: calm and cool."

"I aint tryna hear that. He fucked us. Ioeno how the BDs gon make it outta this. Nobody fuckin trusts us, cuz they know he flipped, and if ion make an example outta him, they gon think we weak in these streets."

"Who the fuck is they?" PYT shouts.

PYT's so mad, he's red. And when Brown Brown is calm enough where he can step away, he walks closer to Taj. "You aint get where you at from playin the code of the streets. It's cuz you didn't that you can stand up to errbody out there and demand somethin none of em could. Fuck you mean, *them?* Worry bout tryna figure out what we gon do bout *us.* We the ones who always gotcho back, ready to ride and handle whateva it is."

"He fuckin betrayed me!"

"Yeah, he did!" PYT yells ova Taj. "But he aint burn Auntie Rissa's spot down. You heard Frank, he said as much at the mall. So don't blame him fuh shit he aint do."

Taj scoffs, shakes his head.

"He took that binder, and he buckled. But did he eva try to shake down Lee or steal the drive, even tho he knew Lee had it on him round his neck? Did he take a shot at Rouk or tell the DKs where he was?" PYT counters.

"He aint know," Taj spits back.

"It. Don't. Matta. Dontchu see? He here. We both here. You know me, you know what I can do, but I didn't. And

103

I done saved yo life enough times that you owe me this—
you owe all of us, cuz you aint the only one who sacrificed
shit to get the gangs unified. Night can't even go back to his
old crew, the Black Rydas, cuz he chose you—even tho they
eventually joined the BDs," PYT says.

Taj still mad, but he aint buckin no mo. He tryna listen,
cuz PYT aint neva yelled at him. He always do what Taj say
do, just like Night.

"I know I can't get yo trust back, I aint stupid," Brown
Brown says behind me, his voice hoarse. He spits out blood.
"But on errthang I love—and you know that's errbody in this
room—lemme try to make it right. You aint gotta forgive
me, but I gotta do somethin, cuz it's the only thing I can do
to forgive myself."

We all stare at Taj, waitin. But his eyes won't let up.

Brown Brown stumbles past us, stands in front of Taj,
then gets on his knees and pleads, "Let me at least tell you
what happened, so you can tell me what you want me to do
next. If you want, I'll go to Frank and Myrrh myself."

Brown Brown tells Taj errthang he told me and Night the
first night PYT called me ova, wit PYT fillin in the gaps.
Then I tell Taj bout the rest of the plan me, PYT, and Jay
came up wit, especially Operation Love Letter.

After errbody leave the room to get outta each otha way
fuh a minute, we all eventually end up on the porch. Taj
aint say yes, aint said nothin yet, but he aint lungin at Brown

Brown no mo or starin at PYT like he don't know who he is.

Me and PYT help clean both Taj's and Brown Brown's wounds, puttin bandages and disinfectant on they cuts. Iono if it's the sound of the wind through the trees or the City Kitty bus hissin and dissin errtime it drops somebody off at the corner, but it's enough. The silence, the stillness—nothin gettin betta but at the same time not gettin worse eitha.

Taj stands up, then walks ova to Brown Brown, who still nursin his jaw.

"You said you willin to do anythin fuh a chance to make it right?" The heat is gone from Taj voice. Now he sounds like himself, my brotha, the peacemaker.

Brown Brown nods, sits up.

"Iono if I can forgive you, not till I know the truth bout whether you burned down the diner or the DKs did it. But Lee know—and you confessed—to one thing fuh sho: handin ova that binder."

"It was the only thing I could do to—"

"It don't matta. Because you aint think it through or tell nobody what was goin on, I had to call some of our top folks in the BDs and our community to explain why they gotta be in the streets watchin they back, sleepin wit one eye open, cuz info I promised to keep safe was handed ova. And we don't know when, but we know the Bainbridges and the DKs gon use it against us." Taj take a deep breath. "If you serious bout whatchu said, then there's only one option: you, Rouk, and Lee gon have to make it official by startin the initiation process to become BDs."

Me and Brown Brown look at each otha, shocked. That aint nothin you just do, it take real commitment. It's hard to become a BD even when errbody wanna support you. How we supposed to go through the process when Rouk and Brown Brown already betrayed folks? I aint do nothin like that, but when you initiate, you take on the weight and burdens of those you wit.

"I know whatchu thinkin, and you right: it's gon be hard. But it's the only way I can protect you and Rouk. And, Lee, havin you initiate wit em is prolly the only way we can get the BDs to back yo love letter operation, cuz you gon need errbody to make it work."

We all look at each otha and let it sink in. Taj aint wrong; Night said we was gon need the BDs too. It aint gon be easy, but if all three of us officially become BDs, we got protection, whether we need it or not.

"Aint gon be no mo hidin. Yall gotta be out in them streets cuz errbody gotta know we a unified front and that, even tho they tried, aint nothin they can do to break us. So, PYT, you responsible fuh Brown Brown, and, Lee, you responsible fuh Rouk."

Taj walks ova to Brown Brown, puts his hands on both arms of his chair, leans real close. "I love you like a brotha, but the next time you do some stupid shit like this and get somebody hurt, Imma handle you myself. Undastood?"

Brown Brown nods.

"PYT, who I send the money to fuh the house?" Taj says.

"Me and I'll pass it along."

"Once they get the money, Night, we gon have to see bout gettin em moved. Too many people done seen us all here, so it's time to switch it up."

Night nods. "I'm on it."

As me, Night, and Taj start to head to the car, I think bout what Mistah Prez said bout hurt(in) and heal(in). I aint got no answers, so I start my first poem wit a question, *Wit errthang that's goin on, why do I hurt? And after today, how do I heal?*

7

JAY

Princeton is standing in front of me in a pink "Vote 4 Jay" T-shirt in white letters, and I think I might just die of embarrassment.

"Nice," Jacob and Momma sing in unison as he turns in a circle to show the full fit—pink top, white jeans, and customized pink Air Force 1s.

"What's in the bag?" Jacob meets him in the front of the barstools.

"Gifts," Princeton proudly says. He hands them two other shirts perfectly tied with white ribbons as he refers to Jacob as "former homecoming king" and Momma as "former homecoming queen."

"Why, thank you, my dear Prince," Momma says, untying the white ribbon and swaying with her new shirt, proud. Jacob takes off his shirt and pulls on the T-shirt to see how it looks.

"When do they vote?" Jacob says, looking at me, then back at Princeton. Suddenly, I want to disappear, just for a minute.

"He ain't tell you? Today," Princeton says.

"Today?" Momma yells. "Jay, why didn't you say anything? It's voting day, which means you have to be dressed to impress."

"I'm fine with what I got on," I say.

Momma and Jacob look at me like I'm crazy.

"As the head of Vote4Jay campaign, I gotchu," Princeton says, holding up a glossy bag.

Princeton carefully pulls out a pink shirt, but it's different from the one they're wearing. This one is woven fabric, sleek but light. It feels soft and expensive—almost too nice to put on. Then he shows me fitted gray slacks with pink pinstripes and Belgian slippers with tassels the same shade of pink as the shirt.

All of us nod in approval. If there was a way to leave a good impression, this is it. Before I can say anything, Jacob whisks me upstairs to our bathroom, leaving Momma and Princeton clinking and clanking cabinet doors, pots, and pans.

In the bathroom, I sit on the closed toilet seat as Jacob begins giving me a line-up.

"Why you ain't tell me?"

How do I tell him I didn't want to get my hopes up? As corny as it sounds, yes, I want to dance with (and be danced on by) somebody. I want to be carried on the shoulders of the football team when they make the winning field goal (how? I don't know, just roll with it).

If being popular isn't possible, I want people to remember I was here, too—that I belonged.

"You know, one of these days I want you to get out of your head long enough to enjoy this," Jacob continues when I don't answer. "To at least believe, like errbody else, you deserve to without being afraid of what happens next."

"*Errbody*, huh?" *Got 'em!*

Jacob, the sweet-talking, multidialect champ, is finally absorbing the "err" of Taj and his crew. He doesn't have to say it; now I know he's in love.

"Whatever." He blushes. "Just remember what I said."

"But I don't know how to do that." I turn around so he can finish my line-up.

"I ain't say it was easy, just that you should try." He holds my head still, turns robot-steady with laser focus as the clippers buzz, both of us holding our breath.

"I take it you ain't tell Leroy either?"

"No, but only because I know he's officially started initiation as a BD and I didn't want to distract him," I say.

Jacob flips the clippers silent, steps back, and eyes his handiwork. He'll do this twenty more times, until it's perfect. "I'll give you a pass on that. Taj says the process is hard and long, so no distractions sound about right to me."

Jacob reaches out his hand, brings me in front of the mirror so I can see my lining and the new zigzag loop part. He hands me the second mirror so I can see the temp fade all around. "Want them slits in your eyebrows?"

I nod, excited.

When Jacob finishes and we head downstairs, Momma and Princeton got two boxes of over one hundred little bags of Momma's ginger snack cookie sandwiches with pink bows.

"When did you make all these?" I hold one in my palm, impressed that they could do this with so little time.

"I had some left over from a hotel order. The bags and ribbons I always have for special-occasion and last-minute orders—and what's more special than my baby becoming homecoming king?" Momma says.

"They're just voting. We don't know how it'll turn out." I know Jacob said hope—no, expect—things to work out, but baby steps.

"Looking like that, people gon' vote off principle," Princeton says.

Momma holds the door open as Princeton carries a box, and I fight with Jacob to give me the one he's carrying, so I can feel useful. "Good luck, baby." Momma kisses me on the forehead.

Princeton has to honk three times before Jacob lets me go. When we finally drive off, he stands in the driveway, proud.

When we get to school, the hallway is madness. The cookies are gone in less than ten minutes. Christina in her Vote4Jay shirt only makes it worse.

The bell rings, and we all make our way down the hallway.

Christina arm-hooks me and asks, "How do you like the shirt? It looks even better than I thought. She did a great job."

"Who?"

"Only the biggest upcoming men's clothing designer of Providence Prep—Trish."

"Wow, I didn't know. That was nice of her." I look at the shirt with new eyes, as if it's a chainmail of jewels.

"Can you meet me out front when the bell rings?" Christina says abruptly.

"We have practice today?"

"No, today is stressful enough with voting. There's something else I want to talk to you and Princeton about. So come find me before you leave. Okay?"

I agree, but my questions trail behind her like a fifteen-foot-long wedding dress train. Christina, our school's Aaliyah, is the heart of Daniel Lee High, who's always smiling, so why does she look so sad?

The whole school is so quiet during the announcement that I can almost hear my heartbeat as Principal Patterson announces, "Christina Chisholm and Joseph—"

The roar is so loud that I can barely hear my name. If I hadn't seen the board and known I was the only Joseph, I would have sat there clueless until he said it again. Princeton runs from his class next door into mine and tackle-hugs me in my desk.

When the final bell rings, he ups the best **friend antics to** the highest level possible, screaming, "The **king is here! The** king is here!"

The football players come chanting **down the hallway** past the lockers—surrounding me and Christina—**the Dan-** iel Lee High ritual of greeting the king and **queen. But this** year, they take it a step further: lift me **and Christina up** on their shoulders and chant as they walk **toward the green** double doors.

As the crowd disperses and the riotous **river of congrats** trickles to a murmur in front of the building, **Princeton,** Christina, and I walk past the clique of **hydrangea bushes** blushing blue and gossiping purple on the **way to the park-** ing lot.

"Did you drive?" Princeton asks Christina. **"We can give** you a ride if it's easier."

She thinks it over. "You did say that you **two are starting** a VIP package for writing love letters, **right?"**

I look at Princeton. I don't know how much **he's told her** about us looking to expand the business or if **he's hinted that** he might be taking over the operation completely. **With me** leaving in the next week or two, we planned **to ease him into** taking over interviews after we've done a **couple together.**

"Yeah, I was planning to tell you—how'd **you find out?"** he asks.

Instead of answering his question, she says, **"Let's test** that out—now. I live in K-Heights, near Kensington Park and Lake Willow."

We nod, aware of her change in topic, and don't bring it up again even while we drive over. After we arrive at her house and kick our shoes off to line them up near the door, Christina guides us to her room, tiptoeing past a lavender sofa and silver plastic plants as big as banana leaves.

Me and Princeton follow her and the faint aroma of amber. We find its source in a scented oil burner with black and gold designs tucked in the corner of the hallway. When we turn right, we see a long wall of framed histories: family portraits, medals, and certificates.

Christina never talks much about her family, but most everybody knows she's an only child. Her father is a well-known mailman of over twenty-five years, and her mom is a former beauty queen turned English professor at Savannah State. Their love story is a legend, and they've been together for twenty years, still known for their doting love and grace.

Christina's room is just as happy as we'd expect her to be. One wall has white shelves with all kinds of perfumes, purses, and makeup. In the middle, a body-length mirror with a pink border that glitters and a wreath of big pink plastic roses at the top.

A calendar and schedule corkboard on the wall with prac-tice reminders, assignments, deadlines, and a single photo held in the corner by a silver tack. I stare at it on accident but am a little surprised: it's her, Faa, and Trish.

"Jay, you remember what I asked you before the skate-down?" Christina slides down into her computer chair, pulls her legs under her, as she invites us to sit.

"You wanted me to write you a breakup letter for Lyric," I say.

"I'd love to help y'all expand your love letter business to other schools, as promised." She doesn't look up. "But, first, I still need your help with this. I love Lyric, I do—I did—but for years we've been on and off."

Princeton nods. "You mind if we take notes? It'll help with the letter." He grabs his pad, checks to see if I'm ready as well.

Even though we didn't know we'd be doing this today, we'll stick with our plan: after we're done listening to Christina, we'll compare notes so we have a format of note-taking to make sure he captures everything we need for me to write the love letters when he does interviews after I move to New York.

Christina takes a deep breath. "Lyric and I have known each other for as long as we can remember. Our moms are close; it's how we got so close, too. But last year, he started closing himself off for no reason. And when Faa was killed, it was like he lost it."

"Were you close? You and Faa?" I point to the photo on her corkboard.

"Yeah, close as anyone could be with Faa. I think everybody felt like they had a special connection to Faa. I had a crush on him for a while, too."

"So what changed between you and Lyric?" I ask.

"I did . . . maybe . . . or he did. But if I'm being honest, that's not the whole truth. Someone else, someone I'd been close to for years, confessed that they liked me this whole time. I thought I loved Lyric, but when I heard those words, I realized I didn't as much as I thought."

"Can I?" I point to the corkboard and notice a collage of photos near her bed.

"Sure, go ahead."

Princeton explores, too. For her to have been with Lyric for three years, there is only one photo of her and Lyric alone—and even that isn't in the center. It's off to the side of the collage.

In the center, there are photos of her, Faa, Trish—even some of her, Rouk, Taj, and Leroy. There are no fake or forced smiles, only joy. I look at her, and for the first time I feel like I see her, past the glimmer she turns on and off.

I believe she does love Lyric, but I wonder if she was ever in love with him. "What did you say to the person who confessed?"

"That I had a boyfriend and I loved him."

One photo stands out to me of Christina, Faa, Trish, and Rouk—with Christina and Trish racing piggyback on Faa's and Rouk's backs. "The person saw through you, didn't they?"

Christina doesn't say anything, but Princeton reads my face and comes to check out the collage.

She shakes her head, looks at the photo on her corkboard, helpless. "I don't know what to do. How do you tell someone that you love them and then say something you know will break their heart? But I have to tell him the truth, don't I?"

"What did Trish say?" I say the truth on purpose, so at least with us she can breathe and stop talking around it.

Princeton looks at me, then looks at Christina.

She doesn't answer, but the tears do. Surprisingly, she laughs. It sounds like one of relief.

"You're pretty good," she says, wiping her eyes with tissue. She wears a smile I don't think I've ever seen on her in person, except in the photo, one of freedom. "She said she'll wait until I'm ready."

"Then I guess it's time, huh? I'll do my best," I say, moving back to the bed. "I've never written a breakup letter before, but now that I know the context, I can't say no—not to you."

She nods, smiles. "Thank you. And I'll do my part to make y'all so much business, you'll need to teach me how to write love letters just to keep up."

"I'll have the letter for you in a couple of days—at least before the homecoming game. Would that be too late?"

"No, I can make that work. In the meantime, when do you

want me to start spreading the word?" Before I can answer, she stops me.

"Oh, I almost forgot. I've already reached out to Denise. Trish mentioned y'all wanted her to be your first client."

Princeton and I look at each other. "That's great."

"How soon did y'all want to meet with her?"

"Now," Princeton says, but I cover his mouth. I jump back when he licks my palm. Christina giggles.

"Okay, I'll lock it in as soon as I can. Denise said she'd call me soon. I think she's interested."

"Let's just get through homecoming first," I say.

The house is quiet, which means Momma must be at the kitchen she rents for baking and packaging large orders. But as I climb the stairs, I hear the shower running. It's Jacob, probably getting ready before he leaves for his shift at the O Lounge.

I sneak into my room, leave the light off, and crawl into the bed. I burrow beneath the sheets, huddle closer to the wall. Outside this bed, these sheets, the world is shit, and I'm over it.

Despite feeling happy for Christina and the nonstop laughter with Princeton as we reviewed our notes together, by the time we pulled up to my house, all I could think about is how bad I'm going to miss this.

"When you get back? I ain't hear you when you get in."

Jacob's voice shakes me awake.

"Not long ago." I keep the covers over my head (don't judge me). The bed shifts under Jacob's weight as he sits on the corner. "Rough day, huh? You ain't hid under the covers in a minute."

"I'm not hiding." My pride answers before I get to. "It's just better under here."

"Okay." He isn't convinced. "Is it that you talked to Leroy? Did he take the news that hard?"

"He doesn't know," I say, holding back my anger, trying to blame him—anybody. "I haven't told him yet."

I don't like it, his silence. I can tell he's judging me.

"Jay, I know it's hard, but the longer you wait, the harder it's gonna be. He has a right to—"

"What do you mean, 'he'? What about me? I'm the one who is having a hard time. You're my brother, not his." I slap the covers from over my face, furious. "Unless that's why you don't care about me leaving, because he'll be here, you'll be with Taj, and y'all get to be the family you always wanted. The one you created and never told me about until I had to find out on accident.

"Don't think I haven't noticed you call him Lee. Only family, special people get to call him that. I don't even call him that." I should stop, but I can't. Anger feels better than sadness, and I'm tired of crying.

"You feel better?" Jacob asks.

No, idiot. And since you still want to push me, I'll push back. "I don't know. Are you moving to New York with me? Momma said I didn't have to go alone."

When he doesn't answer right away, it hits me so hard I can't breathe. Now I want to hurt him.

"You're just like him, a liar," I say, knowing Jacob will know who *him* is. "You pretend to care, act like you love me, but deep down, you hate me. You wish you had somebody else as your brother, somebody like Leroy."

His eyes smolder, and I wait for it. Egg it on in my mind, *Hit me, go ahead. Do it. So we both can drown together.*

"You're a real asshole, you know that?" Jacob says.

"If it ain't the truth, why would you lie? Why would you keep it from me, until the only way I could find out is seeing you—"

Jacob jumps up, and I flinch, on accident. Something in him is breaking, too, and I instantly regret every word, as he storms out.

I went too far, I know it. The last thing Jacob would ever do is hit me, and if we know nothing else, we know every bruise isn't from a hand or a fist; some are so deep, they're invisible.

What I just did to Jacob was worse. I lashed out. I'm no better than Dad—*I'm* the one just like him.

I punch the bed, hear something fall near the foot of it. When I see the gift bag, my heart sinks. I open it and pull out two boxes, a crown paperweight that says "Jay the King," for my desk, and a smaller box with a necklace, a mini crown, that says "Love, Jacob." Now all I can do is cry.

My tears run dry by the time it's 3:00 a.m., and I hear Jacob walk through the front door, much later than he usually gets in.

I wait in Jacob's room, hoping him seeing me in here will let him know I'm sorry. Even if he told me to get out, I'd understand. I was wrong.

Jacob doesn't say anything when he finally makes it upstairs. He just drops his stuff in the corner of his room, rummages through his drawer with the light still out, and walks to the bathroom to shower. After what feels like an eternity, he returns.

I face the wall, so he'll think I'm asleep and to decrease the chances he'll kick me out (I hope). I feel him standing there, watching me.

He cuts the fan on high, slides under the sheet, and leaves me the blanket. I turn over, pretending I'm just waking up.

He lies there, staring at the ceiling.

"You really think I'm like him?" His voice is raspy, hoarse.

"I didn't mean it, I'm sorry."

I place my hand, palm up, between us and wait—a flag of surrender, of sorry, of tell me how I can make it better.

He play-slaps my hand. It's easier to play tough than be tender as he feels. I leave my hand there, stubborn for the both of us (more so me).

I flex my fingers, for an honest reply.

He slaps it again, but lets his hand linger as he turns to face me.

I smell the sweet of alcohol, can hear the sleepy slur of spirits on his breath. Did I hurt him so bad he had to drink to numb the pain?

"You were right. I should have told you 'bout Taj and Leroy. But I just wanted time to figure things out first."

"I know, I just think I'm jealous of any and everyone who gets to stay. I don't know how things will turn out when I'm in New York by myself, forced to start over."

We tread water in the truth, offering no false hope or answers.

"Part of why I got so close to Leroy was you." He plays itsy-bitsy spider (or his version of it) pressing each of my fingertips as he talks. "He was having a hard time being away from you. Even came to the O Lounge, got into a big fight with Rouk that I had to break up, too."

I didn't know Leroy had suffered as much as I did when we had been apart.

"I was keeping my distance from Taj, too. It shook me up that a shooting could happen over at his place. Eventually, when Leroy broke down in front of me, I began to tell him little things, so he'd know you were okay, even taught him how to cook a few things. But I think I did it to help me too, because I was scared of being in a relationship.

"All the relationships I've been in end the same: me

breaking their heart because I don't want to give them all of me. But I can't give what I don't have. That night when J.D. . . . ." He doesn't say the words, but I feel their weight. "It left a hole nobody could fill, and then I ran into Taj again." He chuckles softly. "And suddenly he needed me. These feelings came rushing out of nowhere and, before I knew it, I was in too deep."

I wish Jacob told me back when he met Taj and was trying to figure all of this out, that way I would have known I wasn't the only one who felt unlovable.

"I know it's hard to tell Lee." He almost corrects it but doesn't. He isn't ashamed of his closeness to Leroy. "But he can't choose you if you don't give him the choice. Taj taught me that.

"By the way, I do want to go with you to New York, but it won't look good if I leave school before applying to transfer. Our goal was to go to Northwestern together. I don't want to sacrifice that future dream unless you want me to." He knows I don't, I'd never want him to sacrifice something else for me—he's already done so much.

I hug him. Then he play-slaps me upside the head.

"What was that for?"

"For mouthing off and talking out the side of your neck. I'm the big brother. Don't forget."

I grumble, point taken.

"I can't promise I won't hurt you—I'm not perfect, but I'll

never hit you like Dad did."

I squeeze him back, a full-bodied agreement. "And I promise I won't try to push you over the edge. Instead, I'll just talk to you about what hurts," I say.

When Jacob falls asleep, in the moonlight, I write the start of Christina's letter, guided not by the sadness of something ending but the chance of something else beginning. Even if it hurts, I hope they both know, it's for the better, for both their sakes.

Writing Christina's breakup letter and hearing Jacob's advice reminds me I've done the one thing I've begged Leroy not to do, the reason we broke up in the first place. I was mad that he left me out and made the decisions without me.

So I make another promise, one I plan to keep. I'll tell Leroy in a couple of days, the night of homecoming. I'm afraid of what he'll say, but if I never tell him, I'll never get the chance to make sure he knows that if he chooses me, I'll do the same.

8

Leroy

It's day six of the BDs initiation, and iono if we gon make it. The first phase is service, which means we gotta cook round the clock each day fuh loved ones and harmed ones till we get six days of consecutive yeses. Today's menu is catfish fritters and hotcakes as the appetizer, red beans and rice, and honey-drizzled sweet and spicy cornbread fuh the entree, followed by lattice apple pie à la mode. The OG in charge is none otha than Auntie Rissa.

There is only one problem: the confirmation that the DKs' numbers are steadily risin as they convert mo people got her in a real bad mood. Not to mention, there's a rumor the DKs are tryna convince one of the gangs to break from the BDs, which got mo people signin up outta fear that the BDs aint as stable as we been sayin.

The BDs initiation process is already hard. You'd think cookin fuh folks would be easy, but not when errbody at the dinner table tryna make you lash out by sayin whateva they want to get under yo skin, knowin we can't speak unless somebody asks us a direct question. And even then, if we do respond, it gotta be calm and we can only answer the exact question. That aint easy when the people you servin think you a traitor and tryna do any and errthang to prove you aint got what it takes to become a BD.

We got five yeses so far, but each day, it feel like we barely make it. That aint sayin nothin bout how hard the cookin is and the fact that we gotta make whateva the lead person fuh the dinner wants. Plus, we gotta learn to make it from them or somebody they choose wit only one day's notice.

If we get that sixth yes, we move to the next phase: the action pitch. This is where we share a plan designed to expand and deepen the BDs' mission. Taj's action pitch was the unification of the gangs and crews. Ours is gonna be Operation Love Letter. And if the OGs approve it at the full BDs council meetin, we gon have access to the resources and advice of the full BD network. If we pull off Operation Love Letter, then we gon be able to move to the final step of swearin an oath of commitment, becomin full BDs and, in our case, YGs.

I wish we was happy and in high spirits. But we been up since 4:00 a.m. makin errthang from scratch. Errbody tired and keep makin lil mistakes like—

Crash!

Auntie Rissa's favorite baking dish, the one passed down from her grandma, explodes on the ground. I was just tryna move it, so we had mo room to work.

"Get out!" Auntie Rissa screams, so loud I freeze.

She pushes me outta the way and drops down to the floor, tryna pick up the pieces.

"I can't. That was it . . . the last thing I had after the diner, and you destroyed it. Yall just—"

Benji runs in, waves us outta the kitchen, and tells us to go upstairs fuh a couple of hours to sleep it off.

As we walk, I hear Auntie Rissa cryin, "Why did he have to break it? The one thing I can't replace. It's gone, it's gone. . . ."

She sobs, and all I know is she aint had to finish her sentence cuz it's the same thing Rouk said, and I'm startin to believe it: errthang I touch breaks.

After maybe thirty minutes, I been dozin on and off but aint really been able to sleep. I know Benji said to take a break, but I can't cuz Auntie Rissa's screams keep echoin in my head. Somethin bout it hurts deep in my chest, where she pushed me, like somethin shattered the same way the baking dish did. I wanna get outta here, but I can't do that to Brown Brown and Rouk, who doin errthang they can to make it through this.

I look ova at Rouk, who readin anotha one of Faa's journals even when he should be sleepin. "Find anythin new? Somethin we can use?"

He looks ova, shrugs. "Nothin we don't already know." Rouk sits up, rereads somethin, opens up anotha journal, looks confused.

"Wassup?"

He just stares quietly, then sighs. "We missin somethin when it come to these Promise Heights. Iono what it is yet, but Faa did. So, I'm readin through his otha journals wit notes from interviews he did wit different people."

"What kinda interviews?"

"People who been bullied by the cops and the DKs, even tho Faa aint know that's what they was called. Turns out they won't just threatenin folks in K-Town, they been harassin people on the border in K-Heights, too. I aint see no journal that summarized what he got outta all these, so I'm havin to read em one by one." He rubs his eyes, stares ova at me, exhausted.

"Go to sleep, you need it." I nudge his shoulders back as I stand, and he lets himself topple ova. "I'll be back soon."

I stand at the top of the stairs, listen fuh Auntie Rissa and Benji, but ion really hear nothin. I walk down the steps as quietly as I can to see who it is—Benji.

Iono if it's allowed, but I start pickin up the broken pieces on the otha side of the kitchen he aint get to yet. I avoid his eyes, so he don't ask me nothin. Even if he do, I aint got no words. All I got is my body, and I just wanna feel useful.

I move quick, cradlin all the pieces in the front of my shirt, which I hold like a makeshift basket. He don't say nothin, just let me keep pickin up pieces. When the floor is as clear as we can get it, I grab the broom and sweep up whateva been left behind.

Benji sits in a chair near the small table, then reaches into a toolbox next to his feet on the floor. He waves fuh me to come ova and sit across from him, as he unpacks tools and supplies on the table—stuff that looks like glue, small brushes, tubes of paint, and clamps.

"You alright?" he asks me.

I shrug cuz it feel like my words gone again and iono if they eva comin back. Feels like punishment fuh breakin Auntie Rissa's heart. I aint the only one.

Rouk and Brown Brown appear in the doorway. Benji waves em in, too. We make room so all of us can huddle tight and close round the small table.

"Let's start by puttin the pieces near each otha that look like they go togetha—big pieces first," Benji advises.

We start wit the base and two handles. It's a little easier cuz the base got flowers on the inside and out so people can see the art the mo food they eat.

"Don't take what she said personal, Lee. She's just been goin through a lot, which you know."

I put togetha anotha section, but some shards missin from the flower—chips of where there was mo color that are gone.

"She's been hidin it well, but she been havin a hard time findin a reason to smile these days. She almost aint even do this—planned to give it to anotha OG, even tho this used to be her favorite part of initiatin BDs."

Iono how I feel knowin this, that she wanted to give up and give us to somebody else, even tho I aint got no right.

"But she wanted to make sho yall got the full initiation experience, cuz it was always somethin she wanted to see eventually, tho under different circumstances." Benji pulls out otha pieces but don't seem to care they don't fit perfectly.

"I thought she hated doin it, especially cuz of us," I finally say.

Benji shakes his head, places a layer of glue on the biggest pieces, purses his lips while he presses and holds. "You know why Rissa and Tré, your pops, created this process fuh the BDs?"

"To test people loyalty," Rouk says.

"Make sho they can be trusted?" Brown Brown adds, thinkin bout the phases: service, action, commitment.

"That's part of it, but I rememba Rissa tellin Taj during his initiation it was to remind people of the process fuh findin their way back home when life throw em off track and they lose their way. It's so people learn what home can look and feel like.

"You notice how they have OGs and YGs, who been in charge and then they aren't anymore after being demoted? And then soon enough, they are back up there fuh much longer and wit even mo respect the second time. It's cuz diamonds are made ova time. As long as you don't give up, you can start ova, get centered by goin back to the basics.

"In the BDs, this process lets people know they will make mistakes, fuck up big-time. Rissa and Tré wanted to make sho, when it happened—not if—there was a process fuh workin through it and toward forgiveness—"

"Of self and othas." I whisper the words from Taj's commitment ceremony.

There are stories of OGs who had to go back through initiation after a certain amount of time. Some just choose to do it, like a ritual. Othas have to do it cuz they do somethin wrong. Regardless, they always do it togetha wit the people they initiated wit.

Benji releases the pressure from his hands, tests the hold.

"What we gon do bout these?" I point to the pieces too chipped to fit perfectly back togetha again.

"That's fuh us to figure out. Got any ideas?"

I'm bout to shrug, say iono, but I stop myself. I think bout Mistah Prez's words, bout askin the hard questions that scare me. Right now, I broke somethin that meant the world to Auntie Rissa, and I can't neva put it back togetha like it was. Ioeno why we tryna glue em back togetha.

But what if I'm lookin at it wrong? I can't make it what it was, but don't mean I can't fix it so it can be used, still hold the precious memories of Auntie Rissa's fam.

"What's that stuff you pulled out?" Rouk asks.

"Different types of glue, epoxy. Actually, everythin don't have to fit perfectly, because I can mix this togetha and fill

131

the gaps like cement. Won't be able to put it in the oven no mo, but could make it into somethin else of equal value and purpose."

I got an idea. I look ova at Rouk, and I can tell he already see what I see; it's crazy but maybe worth a shot.

"You good at makin stuff, right?" I ask.

"I manage. Why? Whatchu thinkin?" Benji says.

I point to the wall just above the oven, the backsplash. It's made of chips of different types that look like art, colorful and pritty. "What if we got some otha colors like that and put em togetha enough to keep the flower pieces but make somethin pritty wit the same colors? I can see it in my head, but iono how to describe it."

I run into the livin room, grab my notebook outta my bag, and sketch somethin, hopin he understand what I'm tryna say. I aint no professional, but maybe he'll get it, see what I see.

Benji nods as he looks at my sketch. "I see whatchu mean. We could get some of this from Freedom's Pottery Palace."

"The one ova near Liberty Street?" Brown Brown asks.

"Yeah, you know it?" Benji pauses.

"Freedom is my godmomma. She used to teach me pottery classes when I was younger. I can call her, if yall want me to."

"That would be great. Do yall know what you want to make? It doesn't have to be the same, since she could recast

132

it into somethin else."

"Whatchu think bout a cake dish?" Rouk looks at each of us. "If it can't go in the fire and bake no mo, what if it could stunt and show out on purpose? Auntie Rissa always say she was born twirlin, but not just cuz of who she is, cuz of who she come from too. This can be the most colorful, Auntie-Rissa-like cake dish that don't know how to do nothin but shine."

Brown Brown calls Freedom, and as he sweet-talks her into this favor, me and Rouk sketch some mo, try words, too.

Suddenly, they take on a life of they own: *Is it possible to make somethin you broke betta than it once was? And if I can, does it make all the hurt, tears, anger worth it?*

Iono if it's the same, but in this kitchen the past six days, I feel like we been doin just that, tryna fix what we broke, get to the point where it don't hurt so much, and eventually have the chance to turn this pain into somethin that make us betta. And if we do it right, make the BDs betta too.

When Brown Brown confirms his godmomma can do it, we do our best to explain to Freedom what we hopin to make. That feelin in my heart starts to change when I can feel her smilin and noddin on the otha side of the phone as she says, "I know just the thing."

Not long after we finish up with Freedom, Auntie Rissa comes back. But even tho she aint really talkin to us or fillin the room wit the joy we mighta hoped fuh, she teachin us why the dishes we cookin are so important.

The sweet meat of the fried catfish fritters and the sand-dollar-sized hotcakes as a helpin to keep hunger pangs away when errbody hungry, but it aint dinnertime. That when we eat red beans and rice, it aint just a plate of food. It's history, slow-cooked and simmered, perfected by the taste buds of family ova generations.

And even if we can't trace all our roots, our blood knows what we been through as a people, no matta where you come from. The trauma, the hurt, the heartbreak that was shut up in they blood and bones, and passed down to us to figure out how to use and create change wit. So, when we taste-test, sip the soup, chew the beans, stir the cornbread batter, and drizzle the honey, we servin mo than food. We sharin love and a little somethin somethin to get us through errthang that hurts.

When we make Auntie Rissa's spin on the Dutch apple pie, we learn what the Bookers did to turn every no into a yes, every obstacle into an opportunity. They found the power of "and" ova "or" to create the Bookers' Lattice and Dutch Crumble Apple Pie—chewy, crunchy, and just the right kinda sweet as it slow dances wit the salty vanilla and cinnamon ice cream.

When errbody arrives and settles fuh dinner, we see why the dishes mean so much in the silence they leave behind. Errbody chewin and chompin, don't matta if they like us or not, believe Brown Brown or not, trust Rouk or not. At the dinner table and on the plate, errbody can appreciate and relate, somethin we all need.

As we watch errbody eat, we hope they give us what we desperately need, too: a chance to show how good we can be fuh errbody else, if they let us.

After the plates are scraped clean and all that's left is streaks of vanilla and sweet crumbs, Auntie Rissa folds her hands like she prayin fuh somethin we don't know she need and begins, "I don't know how to feel cuz I'm hurt and disappointed, but I'm also proud and impressed. These past six days not once did yall complain or make excuses as we pushed you to yo breakin point. But I'm wonderin if that's enough. So befo errbody go round and give final thoughts, I gotta question fuh each of you.

"Rouk, yo pain and rage was used as a tool fuh hate that not only hurt the BDs but it almost destroyed my family. How we know the next time you won't be so easily manipulated?"

Rouk sits not lookin at nobody until he says, "I aint neva felt a pain like I did when Faa was murdered. Even now, just sayin that word, admittin it happened and he aint just away on a trip and will be back home soon, it's still hard. I also aint neva felt mo lonely, thinkin those I loved coulda hurt Faa or me like that. It felt betta to be angry and fight than hurt and cry.

"It's still hard fuh me, and ion really know how to look too far into the future, cuz it hurt too much. But I know what I wanna do now, make sho what happened to Faa and me don't happen to nobody else. I can't bring him back, and even when we bring the Bainbridges down, he still aint gon be back. All I know is I wanna work wit yall to keep movin forward, keep my head on straight—and learn from what I did in the past, so I can do it different now and in the future."

Auntie Rissa don't smile or cheer, she just nods. Then she looks at Brown Brown—who already locked eyes wit her—and says, "You made a decision, a wrong one that we have yet to see how much it's gon hurt us and the people we serve. How can we eva trust you again when you already proved to us that you aint trustworthy?"

"Cuz I know what it feel like to lose the one thing I neva thought I would—errbody's trust. Yall know my story and my fam. Half are heroes, the rest villains who would stab you in the back if it benefited em. I thought I was betta, stronger. I aint think nobody could flip me, cuz I aint had no price. But I did, and it was the lives and dreams of my loved ones. When it happened, I just wanted to be a hero, cuz eva since I known yall, that's whatchu been to me. Don't matta how bad the BDs got beaten, terrorized, discriminated against, yall neva bent. So I did what I thought would fix my situation.

"Now I know where I went wrong—thinkin yall was

heroes on yo own. I neva understood that yall heroes cuz you always work togetha, neva leanin on yo own understandin. I know some of yall neva gon let what I did ride, I'm okay wit that. It just mean Imma have to work hard to show you, cuz yall the only ones who helped me be the best version of me. I aint gon stop till I win yall trust back."

The room go silent as errbody look at me next. Auntie Rissa quiet, thinkin befo she turns to me. "Lee, you hotblooded, hardheaded, and you don't think things through. You not only keep secrets, you can be reckless, which could get you killed. The BDs aint in the business of buryin caskets or fuelin fools. How will you move and be different, so you don't get yoself and othas killed?"

I try to say how I feel it and hope they feel where I'm comin from. "My whole life, I watched you, Taj, and what stories I heard bout Pops headbuttin the world and neva apologizin. But I know now that it aint just headbuttin and doin the impossible, it's bout timin, bout gettin errbody involved— learnin to follow as much as I wanna lead. I already know I'm gon mess up sometimes. But Imma get to learn from you—and all yall. Cuz of that, Imma find the balance I need, as long as I got yall by my side."

As errbody else speak they beef and they piece, the only one I remeba is Auntie Rissa and how, in the firestorm of her eyes, there's somethin I aint seen in a long time, peace. Taj used to say that the only one she could get that from was

Pops. It's what she missed and loved bout him the most. She don't have to say it, cuz I can feel it—a chance in the makin.

After two hours of bein grilled, doubted, and picked apart, we finally get sent upstairs while they deliberate ova coffee and tea. We done already fallen asleep and woke up a few times. But when they finally do call us down, we think we bout to just go to the kitchen and hear the news, only to find at the foot of the stairs, errbody lined up from the front door all the way to the kitchen.

One by one, they each shake our hands till we end up in front of Taj and Auntie Rissa, who standin next to the kitchen table. They give each of us a black braided-rope bracelet, proof that we BD initiates. Then they say the words: "Welcome to the Black Diamonds, welcome home."

9

JAY

Thursday is the day of presents and broken (bestie) promises.

I roll my eyes at Princeton in my driveway. "You said I could walk to your place, so why did you bring your car?" I wait for his answer, ready to pounce.

"Because you never know what could happen."

"Princeton, we've been practicing hours each day after school, dancing nonstop, and I barely use my inhaler. I think I can walk fifteen minutes to your house."

I walk past him and his car, mind made up. He follows quietly but doesn't apologize.

"I wanted to cut out the unnecessary walkin', so yo body could rest and heal." He smiles and wraps his arm around me. "Besides, when was you gon' tell me?"

We bus-stop around chunks of sidewalk kicked up by a southern oak.

"Tell you what?"

"That homecoming is also your birthday." I try to avoid his prying eyes.

"It's not a big deal," I say, flustered by the attention.

"It is to me."

In my heart, the "me" echoes. Even though I should be, I'm still not used to hearing how Princeton feels toward me—and that he has no problem saying it.

"You know, you really make it hard for me to keep up my best friend duties," Princeton says.

"What about you? When is your birthday?"

"Not tellin'. Just know ya boy is an Aries." He chuckles. "Let's make a pit stop, I'm cravin' a thrill."

Up the block from Edda Nae's, Princeton and I see guys on low-rider bikes. I recognize the leader as Husani, Edda Nae's grandson, but none of the others. Princeton smiles, grabs my hand, and pulls me into a jog. We stomp up, just as Husani—who looks about Jacob's age and has cornrows down his back, tats, and a full mouth of gold—hops off his bike.

When he sees Princeton, his eyes turn to small slits of joy, and he pulls Princeton in for a bro hug. Princeton makes his way through the crew, giving hugs, daps, even play-sparring with the biggest guy, who goes by Khalif. They all wear purple and white jackets, with "LRC" in letters on the front, and on the back is a pimped-out low-rider graphic that looks more like a motorcycle than a bicycle.

"This Jay," Princeton says, presenting me to them.

"Jay over at Daniel Lee?" Khalif says.

I agree, then the guy smiles.

"Yo, you shut it down ova at Da Rink. When you goin back? People still aint stopped talm bout it."

"Aye, tell Dr. Eva we'll start transportin kids this weekend to all the way through the summer," Husani says.

"Bet," Princeton says, beaming. The LRCs must have been who Taj was mentioning to Dr. Eva about transportation when we were at H-Cubed.

Husani walks with us since Edda Nae's is only three houses down. Then a melody like a bird whistle rings out. As it echoes our way, Husani's face turns to stone.

Everyone looks the same direction as a trail of six tricked-out racing cars, some that look familiar from outside the mall, ride slow but growl and kick back as if the cars were alive. The first one, an all-black '68 Shelby Mustang with metallic trimmings, revs up and purrs with tinted windows so dark, you can't see inside.

Whoever it is stops right in front of Edda Nae's. The trunk rattles 50 Cent's "Wanksta" before it goes quiet. The doors open, and Frank and Myrrh step out. Behind them, guys step out of the other cars, line up hands crossed in front of them.

No one smiles but Frank. "Can't stay away, huh, Jay?"

Before he can get closer, four pimped-out Chevy vans swarm. The doors open, and people jump out wearing matching LRC letterman jackets.

"What's all that noise?" Edda Nae comes out, covered head to toe in a Starburst-yellow outfit.

"We got it," Husani says, sweet but firm.

"Boy, quit wit all that fussin." She sees me and Princeton, then looks at Frank and Myrrh.

Frank greets her. "Mrs. Edda Nae, nice to meetcha, I'm—"

"Don't matta, baby. You aint gon be round long enough to rememba. Whatchu want? All that noise means you aint here fuh no candy."

Frank grins, like a cat caught by a canary. "What happened to that Southern hospitality I hear so much about?"

Edda Nae's warm face turns weary, moves in his direction till she stands in front of us.

"Who yo people?" She looks him over.

"You lookin at em. But if you talkin bout fam, I got people in New York and Chicago," Frank says.

"That why you move like that. All threat like you aint got no good or God in you?"

Frank's smile twitches. He scans all of us, until his eyes land back on me. Whatever he was planning, with Edda Nae and the Low Rider Crew, it isn't happening—and he knows it. "How bout we consider this an introduction, and I can swing by when it aint so crowded."

Edda Nae doesn't answer, just shakes her head.

As soon as Frank and the DKs leave, Husani and his crew offer us a ride back to Princeton's in one of their tricked-out vans to make sure we are safe.

When we finally pull up to Princeton's house, I'm so

relieved that it's almost over.

"Fuh now, let's keep this between us." Husani turns around in the front seat. "Right now, don't want nothin to distract Taj or Auntie Rissa, now that Leroy has started the process of becomin a BD."

"Is it as hard as they say?" I ask. I haven't been able to speak with Leroy besides quick text messages here and there, him telling me he missed me.

"Harder," Husani says, looking at Khalif, who nods, remembering. Everyone nods silently in agreement. "But not fuh the reasons you might think."

"Fuh some crews, initiatin is bout breakin you, literally and figuratively, so you belong to them and only them," Khalif says. "But wit the BDs, it's different. They aint tryna control you, it's the opposite: they want you to know who you are and own it—fuh better or worse. Aint no brain-washin, but you def gon do some soul-searchin."

"You aint neva lied." Husani laughs.

But will he be okay?

"Don't look so scared," Husani says. "You neva initiate alone, so he wit people he trust, and they goin through the process togetha."

"Is there anything I can do to help?" I ask.

Everyone looks at each other, Khalif grins. "Just hit him up from time to time, talk sweet to him. It helps knowin somebody out here missin you, too!"

143

"In the meantime, if you see anythin that don't look right, call." Husani hands us his business card. "That's our direct line."

As soon as we get out of Husani's van, we beeline it to Princeton's and head to his kitchen. We eat all except one Toaster Strudel, then stretch out on the sectional, staring at the sunlight turning purple, teal, and green as it shines through a bejeweled wind chime.

"I'm really glad Husani and his crew were there," I say.

"Yeah . . ." Neither one of us wants to imagine what could have happened if they weren't. Although I don't think Frank, Myrrh, or the DKs are allowed to hurt us, it's scary not knowing at what point they will. I remember me and Will being chased and having to fight Frank and Myrrh last summer, until my dad and the BDs intervened.

For a second, we're both silent. Then, all of a sudden, Princeton shrieks and hides behind me, when he sees a moth fly over his head. I laugh so hard I cry, confused at how he can be so in touch with nature but terrified of something so gentle and beautiful.

He pours us both some mocktails, and we randomly break into laughter as we replay his scream and leap in our minds.

"When was the last time you spoke wit Leroy?"

"Maybe yesterday? He texted me really late, but I replied this morning."

"You ready to talk sweet to him." Princeton grins.

"I guess . . . I don't really know how to do that. . . ."

"Yes, you do. Just tell him how you feel, that you miss him." I nod, take notes in my head. "Just let it flow and don't overthink it. And when all else fails, you know, flirt a lil bit."

It's a little embarrassing, but I say it anyway. "I don't know how."

"Whatchu mean?" Princeton says, confused.

"Just what I said. . . . I don't know how to flirt. I've never really done it before."

"Yes, you have. You do it all the time."

"What?" Now it's my turn to be confused. "No, I don't."

"Yeah, you do." He chuckles. "You do the lil shy thing, then you look lovingly in a nigga's eyes, pull a Jacob on 'em. You even been usin' some of *my* tricks."

I'm flabbergasted—and convinced he's making all of this up.

"And what are those?"

"You know . . . my dance moves." Princeton proceeds to narrate his favorite dance moves, as always, every one of them ending in a body roll. I don't know whether to laugh or scream from embarrassment—I do both. It helps, takes the edge off.

We carry our glasses back to the sectional, but only after Princeton forces me to check to make sure there aren't any more moths.

As we enjoy the silence and the wind chime, I smile

because I've never really done this with anyone but Jacob. Princeton makes it feel easy and natural to just be me. I feel free, almost fearless. Maybe that's why the question comes out of my mouth, something I'd never have the guts to ask him any other time.

"What's it like?" My courage pitters away, shortens my sentence.

"What's what like?"

I don't answer, just look at him, hoping he'll read my mind. He almost chokes on his colorful straw. "You mean what I think you mean?"

Yep, he got it.

"What's it like to lose your virginity?"

The way Princeton looks at me, I can't tell if he's confused, curious, or entertained (maybe all three?). "Lemme think," he says.

"Wow, it's been that long since you lost your virginity?"

"Nah," he laughs, shaking his head. "I don't count my first time 'cuz I ain't like it." I expected him to brag, go on and on about his sexual prowess, how he got his name, Prince Ten, but he doesn't, he actually looks sad, disappointed.

"Why?" I want to tell him about the painful, illogical thoughts, my fear that getting too close, going all the way, might result in me and Leroy getting hurt. But I can't.

"Because it wasn't with somebody I really liked. I did it because people said I should. So it happened, and I didn't do it again for a long time until I met someone I did like. Then I did like it—a lot."

My face says it all: *So I'm told.*

"No, not like that." He laughs. "I'm just sayin' iono if it matters what you do as much as it bein' with somebody you trust. It might feel good regardless, but when I did it with somebody I liked furreal, furreal, there won't nothin' like it."

Is that why spending time with Leroy feels easier now? Because I trust him? Not just me; when we're close, I can literally feel it—that we trust each other.

We sip, giggle at the awkwardness that melts away between us.

"Have you told Leroy you leavin' yet?"

I hide from his eyes. "Not yet . . . but I will soon."

"Is that why you thinkin' of losin' your virginity? 'Cuz you leavin' soon?"

I don't answer at first. "No, at least, I don't think so."

He nods, doesn't say anything. "Just think on it—and don't do it unless you really, really want to."

So many questions run through my mind now. How do I know I'm ready? What if I'm not? Am I doing this for the right reasons?

"Leroy know you a virgin?" Princeton's question brings me back.

"Yeah, I told him." I take a longer sip, nervous all over again.

"Do you trust him?" he asks.

I nod.

"Then you ain't got nothin' to worry 'bout. If he cares about you and you care about him, you'll both figure it out togetha."

We talk and sip until the mocktail pitcher is empty, and the walls become a second home for the echoes of our laughter.

Princeton puts his glass down, grabs my hand, and waves me to his room. I follow, but when we get in the front of his room, I pull back, unsure.

"What are you doing?"

"Givin' you your birthday present." He opens the door to his room, and I almost gasp.

It's nothing like I expected. He has a floor-to-ceiling bookcase opposite a huge window to his backyard. He lets my hand go, and I immediately feel his drawings on the other side of the room pull at me when I spot them.

They look like photos, but they're drawings—sketches of different places and people in K-Town and K-Heights. A piece on the easel takes my breath away. Extending outside of a frame is a drawing with accents of paint of the day Leroy asked me to get in his car when he stopped Rouk.

In the drawing, I lock eyes with Princeton—or whoever is looking from the perspective of the piece. My face is beautiful, my eyes fierce, lingering. In the center of the frame are other sketches of recent moments we've shared: me on the first day of school in my new fit, me in my outfit at the skatedown, a silhouette of me and him under the sweetgum tree in front of the school when he helped me through my panic attack.

I'm drowning in emotions with no words to describe what it's like to be seen by him. I want to tell him I'm happy, sad, and angry that I just realized he could do this. I want to lie in the middle of the floor and refuse to move from this spot, this special moment so I can hold on to it forever.

I hug him and say everything all at once in two simple words: "Thank you."

When he releases me, I hold on longer. We need to stay like this, just a little longer, him as my shield against the sadness. He doesn't resist, doesn't even make one of his flirty jokes, which is worse.

Then I hear it. "I love you, Jay."

I pull back, make sure I look at him, and smile as I say, "I love you, too."

10

Leroy

After what feels like twenty-four hours of sleep, and wit Benji's help, me, Rouk, and Brown Brown knock on Auntie Rissa's door to surprise her. She opens it, brighter than she was the day befo in an all-white dress and her hair pulled back in a long ponytail. When I see the turquoise belt wit a pink flower in the center, I hide my smile, feelin mo proud to present our gift.

We all gotta head out to meet Taj, Night, and PYT at the stadium fuh the homecomin game, but we wanted to show this gift since I got plans wit Jay after.

"Yall aint say nothin bout no gifts." Auntie Rissa eyes the box and lets us lead her into the kitchen. "You know bout this?" she says to Benji, suspicious.

"Maybe." He grins.

"I know that dish I broke was really special and meant a lot. So, wit Benji's help—and wit us three chippin in and helpin Freedom make it—we wanted to present it to you as a present, hopin it'll stay in the fam fuh years and years to come."

Auntie Rissa opens the box and shrieks in joy. Her sprintin fuh the tissues is all the proof we need to know she likes it.

Instead of the original baking dish that was white porcelain wit a turquoise flower in the middle, it's been remade into a cake dish wit a turquoise flower at the base and a new flower made of old pieces. Outside of that, we made multiple rings and flowers wit each of our initials and Auntie Rissa's ma's and great-grandma's in the center. The glass cover got a turquoise knob as a flower, the final touch.

As she hugs us, she ends wit me, and that's when I feel it. Not just Auntie Rissa's light but her recipe fuh touch.

"I wish all YG initiates brought gifts like these," she says, marvelin at the handiwork.

When we all move toward the door, Auntie Rissa puts her hand round me, stealin one mo hug, and says, "Thank you."

If we aint leave when we did and asked Taj, PYT, and Night to save us some seats, we woulda been outta luck. I aint neva seen the stands so packed, and errwhere I look is mo and mo people walkin in. When I think bout Christina's sweet-talkin that made us promise to come, it look like we won't the only ones.

"Tina might have just as much pull as you." I shoulder-bump Taj and sit down.

"When she put her mind to it, aint nothin she can't do. I want you to bring that same kinda energy at the BDs council meetin next week," Taj says.

"It's official? Yall set the date," I say, excited and nervous at the same time.

"Yup, which is why I want you, me, Rouk, and Brown Brown to run through errthang togetha one mo time and try to pick out any weaknesses. Auntie Rissa said she down to help now that yall official BD initiates. Don't fuhget what I said, tho. Keep yo eyes peeled fuh anythin that don't seem right. The closer it gets to the meetin, the mo we wanna be prepared fuh any and errthang."

The Daniel Lee High band blares so loud, errbody stunned to silence as they play "Are We Cuttin'" by Pastor Troy, marchin into the entrance.

Taj waves ova Jacob and Miss Julia, and has em sit in the two seats next to him, Auntie Rissa, and Benji. After hugs and kisses, errbody lookin round as the majorettes and the band surround the stage out on the field. But when don't nobody see Jay or Christina, the music stops.

Princeton runs up onstage, frantic. Somethin aint right.

Me and Taj stand up. We bout to run downstairs to see what's happenin when "Don't Leave Me" by Blackstreet blasts ova the speakers. The drum majors and majorettes run onto the stage and get in formation behind Princeton as he starts to body-roll and pop-lock.

The beat drops, and Jay and Christina pop up from behind him. Tina's in a green and white majorette body suit fit that glitters, wit the knee-high boots. Jay's in a drum major fit that's styled like the majorette but different, covered in jewels wit a cape. Fuh a second, it look like they glidin till I realize they are.

The music changes, and Purple Ribbon All-Stars' "Kryptonite" plays, the same song from the skatedown suddenly, Jay and Christina lettin loose wit dance moves and body rolls I aint neva seen.

Miss Julia and Jacob both got tears in they eyes as the whole band rocks the stadium wit Cameo's "Candy," and Jay, Christina, and Princeton get errbody up so they can do the bus stop in front of they seats. And as I watch Jay dancin and rollin, all the faces laughin and waterin up, I can't describe how it feels.

All I know is, I wanna run down there and kiss him. But I do the next best thing: I dance and sing along, get a high-five in from Rouk standin next to me and try to soak it all in. I grapevine step to the right, to the left, rock back, and kick my leg forward, and start all ova again. While I do it, I aint neva felt so good or free.

After goin into overtime, Daniel Lee wins the homecomin game. Befo the swarm, I run ova to Jay to tell him the plan. Wit this bein one of the last warm days, I ask if he would be down fuh a date at the beach. And prittier than anythin I eva seen as he stands in his performance fit, we beeline fuh the parkin lot befo we get blocked in.

Twenty minutes lata, we at the shore and the weather is

perfect, just hot enough fuh the water to feel cool but not cold. We stare at the moon shinin in all her glory—feelin like she gettin bigger, close enough to touch.

After we test it, we realize the water is perfect. Me and Jay leave our towels on the sand and run back to the car. Jay changes into the trunks in the car befo hoppin out, ready.

Befo we run back, I stop him and ask, "Why you still got yo shirt on?"

I tug at it, but he shrugs, looks at my body. Fuh the first time I wonder if he feel self-conscious that his body don't look like mine.

"The salt water gon fuck it up. Leave it here."

"I don't know. I don't—"

"I wanna see you." I step closer, reach fuh the bottom of his shirt, and slowly help him pull it ova his head. He catch me starin even tho ion mean to. It's just, to me, every part of him is perfect. I reach fuh his hand and hold it as we walk to the water.

Slowly, the waves get bolder, greedier fuh mo attention. The mo the waves push Jay back, try to pull us apart, the closer we get as I guide him wit my hands round his waist.

"This water is too dark. I can't see what's rolling around my ankles. It could be seaweed, but what if it's something else?" he says, nervous.

I wanna tell him how cute he is scared, but I don't.

"Yeah, it could be—ah!" I yell, makin him jump. When

I laugh, he just stares at me, then pulls away and tries to leave. "Wait, wait, my fault! I aint know you was that scared furreal."

"There are over one million species that live in the ocean—that we know of! Anything could be in here, Leroy. Anything."

I swallow a laugh tryna make a fool of me and ruin this moment. Instead, I reach fuh his hand, just to hold it till he calm down, trust me again.

Jay edges closer to me. "This isn't me saying yes, but if I see a fin, you're on your own."

"Oh, you gon do me like that?" I move closer to him, put my arms around him. "We can walk like this wit me behind you. I'll be yo anchor. C'mon, one step at a time."

We go deeper, while we get pushed and pulled by the sand beneath our feet. As the water rises past our knees, the waves play harder, testin our balance. Each wave that splashes against him pushes him back into my chest.

"I gotchu," I whisper, but holdin him aint enough.

"Turn round, look at me." As he does, a wave shoves him into my arms, and I catch him. I feel us growin from both sides.

He pulls back and mumbles, "I'm sorry, I didn't mean to—"

I pull him closer, so shame aint got no room between us. I lean down, tilt Jay's chin toward me and wait fuh his answer.

He kisses me back, but it feel like mo than just a kiss. I feel it through my whole body, like every kiss is an answer to a question he aint gotta eva ask.

I kiss him harder, pull him into me, till he aint afraid to touch all of me and knows that every part of me is his to keep.

When the waves get too rough, the water too deep, I can feel him gettin nervous.

"C'mon, let's go back. I wanna show you somethin," I say.

On the shore, the water clings to my trunks, showin mo than I want anybody to see. But seein him wet, the water holdin on to his curves, don't make it no betta. When we get our towels, I grab mine, the biggest, and wrap it round both of us. Jay freezes when he feels me behind him.

"Don't move. Ion want nobody else to see unless you—"

Jay pulls the towel round us tighter, and I smile. We stand here a little longer till I'm calm enough to walk.

"So I heard it's yo birthday."

"How did you . . . ? Jacob," Jay accuses.

"You won't gon tell me?"

Jay shrugs and blushes at the same time.

"Then I'm glad I found out." I turn him round, take a deep breath, and go fuh it. "Want some room service?"

I turn him toward the hotel overlookin the water, wait fuh his eyes to see what I'm askin. My heart beatin so loud, tho, I wonder if he can hear it. I read his lips, pray he don't say no. I wait, feelin like my heart's bout to explode.

"Okay."

"Furreal?" My voice cracks. I clear my throat while Jay smiles, nods.

The hotel don't look like much from the outside, but when we finally get to the room and flick on the lights, it's perfect. Just enough space so we don't feel lost in it but much betta than some of the hotels me and Taj had to stay in after the shootin. As Jay walks in holdin his extra clothes close to his chest like they might get swallowed up if he places em on the bed, I know why this feels perfect—cuz he here, we here, togetha.

On the bed are three letters, "HBD," made of snack size Twix, Snickers, and Baby Ruth chocolate bars. Jay looks at it, chuckles. "Nice touch. I like all of them."

He picks up a Snickers, places his clothes on the desk area next to the TV. He looks out the window—the moon wavin back at us from the shore.

"Want to take a shower?" he asks.

If I already put a chocolate bar in my mouth, I woulda choked.

"Togetha?"

Jay shrugs. "Unless you wanted to—"

"Yeah, let's do that," I say.

Iono why this feels like it's my first time. I mean, I aint

neva got down in no hotel, always was at somebody house or in the car, if we couldn't wait. But this feels different, mo special. Maybe cuz ion want it to end like it did last time—I want it to last fuheva.

I put my book bag next to the bed, and I go to check it out but also to calm down. Watchin Jay chew the candy bar, the way it disappears between his lips got me thinkin bout stuff ion want to, at least not yet.

"This is really nice," he says, bringin me outta my trance. I cut on the shower, wait fuh the water to heat up, test it. Jay leans into me, reaches his hand in the space between the shower curtain and the water. He nods again, backs away.

Jay looks round, as if he waitin.

"Can I?" I step closer as the room fills wit steam. My fingertips find the bottom of his shirt, pull it over the top of his head. He does the same, rolls the bottom of my beater up and ova my head.

My arm gets caught, and I'm stuck. He helps, laughs.

I unbutton Jay's pants and untie the drawstring of his trunks. I feel him tremble beneath my touch. I lean in so he can feel me and slide the shorts past the smooth curves as they drop to his ankles and he steps out.

Next thing I know, I'm pullin him closer to me, my hands feelin his body fuh the first time, as Jay reaches to unbutton my shorts.

I pause his hands, not sho if he should, not yet. I'm too

excited, hard. But I can see him growin, too.

I pull him so close he barely has room to see. He undoes the drawstrings, slides em down, but they get caught.

I reach down, adjust myself, so the trunks can fall to the floor. I kick em away.

We stand, afraid to look down but ready to feel.

I'm usually proud to show all of me, but wit Jay it's different. I keep pullin him close cuz I'm scared he will see me and not want to.

Where I normally feel strong, proud, I feel nervous, like I'm hangin on the edge of a cliff afraid to fall. Jay wraps his arms round my waist, lays his head on my chest, and every fear disappears. It's just him and me, and our skin stickin togetha cuz of the wet heat.

I open the shower curtain and get in, wincin as my back gets used to the sting of the water. Jay steps in and, fuh a second, we're huddled togetha sideways, teeterin like we in a small boat and don't wanna flip ova.

The water aint the only heat I'm tryna get used to cuz the mo Jay bump into me tryin not to get hit by the hot water, the mo I feel his soft skin rubbin against me. And errtime he do, my nervousness gets replaced by somethin that aint scared but yearnin to do mo, feel every part of him as he touches every part of me.

"Close yo eyes," I say. When he does, I pull him back onto me, and I take on the water, feel the hot get hotter till it's whippin my back, tinglin all ova. As the water pours ova my head, I groan, then start to kiss him hard. But I underestimate the heat of the water and we both gotta rush to the otha side of the shower, gigglin so hard at ourselves and each otha.

After we wash up and towel off, Jay grabs anotha candy bar, sits on the bed. I sit next to him. I lean ova and kiss him. At first to taste the chocolate on his lips, but he kisses back and holds on to my neck, pullin me outta my towel. I put my hands round his waist as we move to the center of the bed.

It's hot. Wit our bodies touchin, I'm so hard it hurts and when he wraps his legs round my waist, it makes it worse. "Can I try to put it in?"

"Okay," he says, worried and suddenly tense.

"Hol up." I reach fuh my bag, pull out the box of condoms and lube, so I can reach em when it's time. "Turn ova," I say.

I lift up his waist and kiss down his back. He shudders. When it feels like he's relaxed again, I turn him on his back and put on the condom.

In the moonlight, Jay's body and legs moist wit sweat look like they glowin in the dark, mo pritty than I eva seen him. I put the lube on me, then start to put the lube on him.

And then Jay almost roundhouse kicks me off the bed.

11

JAY

It hurts! No matter what Leroy does, the pain is too much. I don't think I can do this. I don't know what I was thinking, but this isn't it.

As Leroy kisses my neck and chest, squeezes my waist, I wonder, *Can I really say no to someone with the moon as his halo?* The pain is a searing heat up my back.

Nope. Can't do it. Fuck his halo.

"Let's try one last thing." Leroy lies flat on the bed, his face turned toward me.

"I keep hurtin you when I do it. Maybe it feel betta if you in control." He leans up to meet me and hugs me from the front.

With his back to the window, the moon is bright enough to light the whole room. He looks up into my eyes, almost desperate, and all I can think of is how perfect everything is, except for this pain that won't allow us to continue.

Leroy shifts his hips. "One mo time," he says, applying more lubricant.

I relax my hips, try to brace myself, and try again. In a full fit of emotions and a body that feels like it's turning against me, I lean into his neck and bite him, but it lights a spark that unleashes a moan out of him and makes my heart skip. The pain is there but mostly as pressure, a tingling spreads throughout my body like wildfire.

Soon enough it feels like waves from a different kind of ocean flood over and submerge both of us. I hold Leroy's face, watch his eyes melt, feel him waver.

Our bodies are the drum beneath our song and the wind that carries us, as the moon and the waves thunderclap in celebration.

Leroy leans forward, till I fall on my back, welcoming him. In my mind, I imagine us immersed in a blue flame and each minute that passes, we burn brighter until we eventually burn out.

Leroy whispers, "I love you," over and over until his words melt into sounds, and all I can do is bite and kiss because I love him, too.

Now I know why Jacob said not to hold off, not to wait, because of this feeling piercing my chest like a jagged sword during a moment Leroy and I should be the happiest we've ever been. Now that we've been the closest we've ever been, I want to tell him everything about my move and, most of all, that I love him.

When Leroy gets up to go to the bathroom, I notice that I feel like I lost something. No, not lost, discovered—that another person could make me feel whole. But I'm worried because now I know what it feels like for Leroy to touch parts of me I didn't know existed, to feel parts of me I don't want anyone else to ever have. I'm consumed with fear; there's a secret that lies here between us—and now I can't stop crying.

I turn on my side, away from the bathroom. When Leroy comes back to bed, he cuddles me from behind. He whispers, "Happy birthday, baby."

Leroy must notice that something's wrong, because the next thing he says is, "Baby, you okay?" He strokes my shoulder, his fingers mimicking the wind. "I didn't mean to make you cry. Did I do somethin wrong?"

I shake my head.

"Did you have that feelin again? Afraid somethin might happen to us?"

I don't answer. I fight for my life—our lives—against the words that threaten to destroy this moment.

Leroy turns my face toward him, dives deep into my eyes. His face shifts, as if he knows. "Baby, what's wrong?"

He can't know, but the tears come, and I can't stop them. The words break through. "My mom is sending me to live in New York."

At first, Leroy smiles, thinking it's a joke, but the longer he stares, the more he realizes this isn't a joke. Nothing about this is funny. It's real.

"Wait . . . no . . . let's call Jacobee and Taj. Maybe even Auntie Rissa. If it's bout the diner, we can tell yo mom it won't happen again, or maybe if you moved somewhere else, like we did, you could . . ." His words trail off as if he realizes something else, the question I don't want him to ask.

"When you leavin?"

"In a couple of days."

"Why she tell you so late? Did somethin else happen? Is it Louis B? Did he threaten her again?" He sits up, waiting for an explanation I don't have.

The silence fills in the gaps. I don't look at him.

"Jay . . . ," Leroy asks, but it sounds more like him pleading. "When did you find out?"

I don't want to hurt you.

"Jay, why you aint answerin?"

I never meant to hurt you.

"When I got home from the hospital."

Leroy's face is wiped clear of emotion, slowly unfolding into a question mark. "What? But why would you . . ."

He backs away from me in shock, shakes his head in disbelief. "But we just—"

"I'm sorry. I meant to tell you. I almost told you so many times. I just couldn't . . ."

Leroy's eyes turn wet, and when tears start falling, something in me cracks. I reach for him, but he jumps back. Before I can say anything else, he runs to the bathroom, slams the door.

I can hear him as he sobs.

I knock, begging him to open it. I say the things I've been telling myself: "We can work through this together. We just have to figure it out. Please, Leroy. Don't do this, talk to me."

He won't open the door. He won't listen to me.

Leroy eventually comes out of the bathroom, eyes red. He says we should get dressed and head home. We do, but on the drive, he doesn't say anything else, won't even look at me. He just silently takes me home, and twenty minutes feel like a lifetime.

Every now and then, he wipes a rogue tear away, bites his trembling bottom lip. He won't let me talk to him or hold his hand.

We love each other.

He said he loved me, right?

In front of my house, we sit in silence long after parking. He won't tell me to leave, and I won't get out of the car until he makes me. No matter what, today can't end like this. I need proof that tomorrow will be different, better.

"Ion understand. We just . . . I just . . . I thought you loved me." His voice is hoarse, heartbreaking.

"I do."

"Then why? You made me promise to tell you errthang, then you . . ."

"I just couldn't—"

"Fuck you mean, *couldn't?* I did errthang you asked me to do! Wheneva somethin was goin down, I made sho you knew bout it, cuz I promised not to hurt you like I did in the past. I thought you loved me . . . but you just like errbody else. You say one thing and do anotha."

"Leroy, no, that's not what happened," I plead, but he won't listen to me.

"You neva fuhgave me, did you?" he says, looking at me, furious. "For breakin up witchu through that note. You did this cuz you wanted me to feel like you did."

What? No, no, no, I'd never do that. Why won't he believe me?

"Well, you win." *No, Leroy. Please.* "Iono if we can—"

"No!" I yell, tears in my eyes. "Please, Leroy. We just—"

I feel it: that ache, throb where he pushed through and told me he loved me.

"I can't, Jay."

"You *can*, just take some time."

"Ion trust you no mo." His words punch me in the stomach. "I'm sorry, I'm done. I gotta go."

I shake my head. If I can just think of the right words, like in one of my letters, he'll—

"Jay, I gotta go. Can you get out?" he says, without looking at me.

My body betrays me. It opens the door, steps out, and before I can say anything else, he peels away, leaving the scent of burned rubber.

Bad turns to worse as I throw up in the grass, cool needles

prickling my face. I walk, numb, to the front door and stand there, waiting for Leroy to turn around, to tell me he thought about it and changed his mind. But he doesn't.

I walk in, see Jacob waiting for me.

"Jay, what's wrong? What happened?"

I look at him and he knows. He just pulls me into him and holds me—does the one thing I wanted—no, I needed—Leroy to do.

"He hates me," I say.

"Jay, don't say that."

I pull away. "He broke up with me . . . again."

Momma comes downstairs. "Jay . . . what's wrong?"

Jacob must give her a signal, because she doesn't ask again, just puts her hand on my forehead and says, "You're burnin' up. Lemme get you some tea. I know we got some turmeric and ginger."

I want to tell her I don't want any, but I'm done talking, done crying. Done with—

The doorbell rings.

My heart skips. I knew it. I knew Leroy wouldn't just leave me like that without at least a hug or something. I run to the door, open it, and freeze.

It's Will, his eyes just as red as mine, with a book bag and a suitcase.

"Will?" Jacob says what I can't.

Momma hears him and runs to the door. "Will, what are

you doing here? Jay is supposed to fly to New York in—"

"Mum's been kidnapped." Will walks in while Jacob helps him with his suitcase.

"What? What do you mean?" Momma's face looks just as confused as ours. "Did y'all get into another fight? Did she send you—"

"No, somebody took her. I was on the phone with her when there was a crash. She sounded scared, like she was fightin'. Then the line went dead."

12

Leroy

I thought Jay was different.

He the one who made me promise to tell him errthang so we could make decisions togetha. But he been keepin secrets this whole time knowin he was movin, leavin me.

Fuck him.

Errthang you touch, you break.

Why he aint just tell me? What's so hard bout that? If you say you love somebody, aint you supposed to wanna tell the truth? That's love, aint it?

Errthang you touch, you break.

Did he eva love me in the first place? Or did he just wanna hurt me like I hurt him? Who fault is it if you hurt somebody who hurt you?

Errthang you touch, you break.

But we just made love, aint it? Why sleep wit me when he know he gon leave me? Is that the *only* thing he wanted?

You . . . you . . . you . . . break.

Dayum! I slap the steerin wheel.

I shouldn'ta broke up wit him befo he could tell me why.

Maybe there's a reason? Maybe we just gotta figure it out. Maybe . . .

No. Don't matta.

I can't shake that he knew but he kept it from me. Iono if I can eva trust him. I just want this pain in my chest to stop, to stop feelin, period. I can't deal wit it.

It's too much. Too many questions. Too many feelins. Not enough answers. And even the answers I get don't make me feel no betta.

I wanna go home, but I aint tryna be alone, cuz all that shit do is make it hurt worse.

I pull up at the O Lounge fuh the homecomin after-party. Ioeno why I'm here or if I'm in the mood, but it's betta than bein at home. But soon as I see Trish dancin on one of the blocks wit one of her homegirls, and PYT, Brown Brown, Night, Taj, and Rouk sittin on the couches nearby, I feel like if I try hard enough, I might even be able to forget, even if only fuh a few hours.

PYT see me, and befo I know it, I'm where he at, sippin on a flask. Fuh a second, the pain subsides. I see Taj lookin at me, and I know he know. He can always tell, whether I want him to or not, so I avoid him.

When "Hey Ya!" by Outkast plays, Trish dances in her sequined dress, shinin bright enough to chase all my cares away. It's enough to pull Rouk to his feet, and like old times, us be the trio that's the life of the party.

After a few mo songs and three orders of hot wings, it aint perfect, but it's betta than it was. But when Purple Ribbon All-Stars' "Kryptonite" starts shakin the club, I can't do it.

All I can see is Jay at the homecomin performance, at the skatedown, knees bent, dippin and risin as he rides the beat. All I can feel is me in his arms, his soft skin, smellin of chocolate, as he holds on to me like he neva gon let me go. All I can hear is heavy breathin, me tellin him I love him, him sayin, *I love you, too*.

I gotta get outta here. I hop down and go to anotha floor where they playin anotha song. Not to dance, but to find somewhere in the cut near the bar. Ion even order, just point.

Rouk shoulder-bumps me and, fuh a second, I think bout walkin away till he says, "Wanna talk bout it? I aint gotta say nothin. I can just listen."

The bartender hands me my drink.

"Aint nothin to say." I feel the tickle in my throat, the burnin in my eyes. I can't do nothin, just shake my head.

"Fuck him," Rouk say.

It aint perfect, it aint gentle, but in a way, it's what I need to hear. I smile, sip, and stir. I shoulder-bump him back, and we both laugh. He orders anotha trio of whateva he has, and I ask no questions, so neitha of us gotta tell no lies bout why our drinks taste stronger.

Trish walks ova to us, hangs her arms round our shoulders.

"He tell you what's wrong yet?" Trish sips outta Rouk's drink. His eyes light up like he done won the lottery.

"Nope, prolly brokenhearted, tho, least that's my take." Rouk guesses right.

Trish leans on me, keep leanin till I look up at her.

"Yeah, that's it," I say.

She sucks her teeth. "You aint gotta talk bout it, not now. But Imma tell you what you already know—we too fine to be sad, so c'mon. Let's flirt and eat till we can't no mo, and tomorrow, we can all cry togetha."

She puts her forehead on mine, gives me some of her strength, and then she shimmies. I wait fuh her to say somethin, but outta nowhere, she jerks me and Rouk back.

The music stops.

All of a sudden, we surrounded by people wit red masks, like the ones Jay said he seen the day of the shootin. Mo people in masks keep comin in like a Red Sea down the stairs.

Then they start stompin they feet, beatin on the bar, the walls, whereva they can to the same beat. But fuh every one of em, it's still two of us. The BDs crowd round me, Trish, and Rouk.

Taj, Night, PYT, and Brown Brown race into the room, lookin fuh us. We meet em and stand behind a wall of BDs as two men enter at the top of the stairs in black and white masks.

Errbody beats faster till it sounds like a drumroll. When

one guy raises his hand, it sounds like errbody hisses—like a kettle bout to whistle, explode. When he turns his hand into a fist, errbody go quiet.

The two people remove they masks, but we already know who it is, Frank and Myrrh. Anybody else woulda looked scared—like me, Trish, and Rouk—but not Taj. He grin like he got somethin up his sleeve only he know bout.

"I was waitin on you to show up, even tho you aint had no invitation." Taj angles his face, a challenge. "What's next? You got a song and dance fuh us? There's a room in the back if you want some one-on-one time."

Frank aint smilin wit his lips, just his eyes. He walks down, followed by Myrrh. He can't get no closer to Taj than the lines of BDs in front. Errbody is starin, ready to tear Frank and errbody wit a red and black mask on from limb to limb.

Did Taj already know they was gon show? That why so many BDs was at the homecomin game and even came here?

"Nah, Imma lil shy, I don't dance in front of people. Plus, aint nothin in this world for free, and I don't think you could afford me."

Frank looks at Taj. Nah, *look* aint the right word fuh it. More like stares so hard fuh a second you wonder if one of em gon burst into flames.

"You know, I can't figure it out." Frank finally grins.

"What's that?"

"Are you pretending, or are you really as weak as you

look?" Frank looks ova at Rouk, then Brown Brown. "Then again, I could be wrong. Maybe you brought me two snitches for the price of one."

"I think you pose an interesting question, Franklin Malachi. How do you suppose we find an answer?" Lady Tee says, standin at the top of the stairs, like a warrior queen overlookin her kingdom.

Next to her is Auntie Rissa, flanked by Benji and armed guards, his friends from the armed forces who look like they can take errbody and then some.

"You must be Lady Tee," Frank says, almost excited. "And . . . Auntie Rissa?" He sniffs the air. "Anybody smell that?"

"Smoke," errbody in masks chant. Frank hushes em silent.

"Forgive me. Sorry for ya loss. I'll make sure Brown Brown helps you rebuild it, brick by brick."

"Let that be yo first and last joke, if you plan on leavin here in one piece, any of you," Benji says, loud enough fuh errbody to feel it.

"I take it that means yall don't know yet. Well, that defeats the purpose. I was here hopin we could trade—two snitches for yo blue jay."

Blue jay? What he talm bout?

"The offer still stands, two mo weeks to make yo choice." He looks at Taj. "Befo it's too late and the BDs become a thing of the past."

"Is that a threat, Franklin?" Lady Tee smiles, and I wonder if it's scarier than Frank's.

"No, ma'am, wouldn't dream of it, especially not to you, since you gon be switchin sides soon too."

"Is that on your authority or Louis Bainbridge?"

Frank's smile breaks into a sneer. He don't respond, just slowly walks up the stairs toward her. The guards round her shift, but she puts her hand up, signals em to stay put.

Frank suddenly throws up a wad of cash, the bills rain down. "For the drinks."

Lady Tee doesn't even blink. "Feel free to pick them all up and take them with you, if you'd like. This is a Daniel Lee Homecoming Game celebration, which means all the drinks and food are on the house."

Frank disappears and the Red Sea along wit him.

We all head upstairs into Lady Tee's office. Her and Auntie Rissa look at each otha. They don't have to say nothin, cuz we all know: after tonight, nothin gon be the same.

As we file into the conference room full of chairs that look like thrones, errbody sit but Taj, who just keep pacin.

"Gimme three minutes wit that nigga, and I swear—" Taj clenches his fist and cusses under his breath.

"Focus. We need to figure out how we move forward," Lady Tee says. "Does anybody know what he meant by 'blue jay'?"

"No, but we gotta find out so we can figure out what the

DKs know that we don't," Night says.

"Could it be a distraction? Somethin meant to confuse us?" I ask.

"That's what I wondered, too," Auntie Rissa says. "But we all saw Frank. He's too strategic to do all of that fuh no reason."

"I know the reason," Rouk says. "There's only one: to declare war."

Part Two
Operation Love Letter

13

Will

Mum is cookin' her cinnamon French toast, dancin' in the mornin' light as she fans her silk pajamas like an evenin' gown. When she sees me, Mum shimmies a greetin' and invitation as "See-Line Woman" by Nina Simone hums through the speakers.

In her make-believe evenin' gown, she twirls, then footworks front and back, side to side, in make-believe stilettos made of crystal. I watch, an audience of one on behalf of the multitudes.

She reaches out her hand, and I join her. In the soft light of sunrise and the backdrop of the beat, we are the stomps, claps, and spells of Nina croonin'. We shake and sway till Mum hands me the spatula and we switch.

I flip the slices in the cast-iron skillet, smilin' at the golden brown. She almost levitates as she talks 'bout the few things that make her like this—her childhood growin' up in Savannah, chewin' on stems of Bahia grass, adventures to Edda Nae's, and Miss Julia—always Miss Julia.

There's a crash.

The sound of twisted metal. I jump, but Mum keeps talkin', keeps dancin'. I try to stop her, see if she hears it, but she doesn't listen.

Suddenly, the walls quake. Glass and dishes rain from the cabinets, shatterin' on the floor, but Mum keeps dancin', leavin' bloody footprints as the walls are engulfed in darkness and everythin' freezes, except me.

I look around for a way out before the darkness swallows me whole, but I don't see one. All I can do is hear my muffled scream for Mum.

Anotha crash. No, kickin' and slammin', glass explodin' as if smashed by a hammer.

Then, I hear his voice, and I'm choked by a chill.

"Hey, Blue Jay," he sings.

The dark swallows the light and me along with it, till I'm fallin', foreva in—

I wake up covered in sweat, my body achin' and ears ringin'. I reach for her, but Mum ain't here, and I have no idea where to look. Only thing I know is I gotta get outta here or I'm gonna scream.

I grab my bag with my trunks and goggles, and sneak downstairs while the house is still quiet. Just as Miss Julia's light cuts on and I hear Jacob's voice, I slip outta the front door, closin' it quietly behind me.

With the sun just beginnin' to rise, I got just enough light as I walk several blocks, tryna trace them from memory till

I'm starin' at the blue and white sign that reads Aquatic Center.

The scent of chlorine is a comfort. The shimmerin' blue is the only otha home away from home I can rememba, and I just wanna stop thinkin'.

After a quick change in the lockers, I find an empty lane at the lap pool and dive in and embrace the shock of the cool and begin. I focus on freestyle, but every stroke feels like a battle I can't win.

Lap one is hard, but I'm findin' my way, able to regulate my breathin' as my muscles wake up. Laps two and three, it's harder, and I can't quite find my balance. I swim a few more laps, finish up my two-hundred-yard warm-up.

I reach out of the pool and grab the kickboard I borrowed from the black baskets near the entrance, but it's stuck? How?

I look ova, and somebody's foot is standin' on it, refusin' to move.

My goggles are fogged up, so I flip them inside out, wipe the lenses with my thumbs till I can see, and follow the muscular leg up past the black Speedo to a wide smile tucked behind blue goggles and a black cap.

"You in my lane." His voice tries to be deeper than it really is.

Any otha time I'd laugh it off, play nice, but I ain't in the fuckin' mood. I look at the otha guys around him and notice that their jackets look similar. A swim team? I look around for a coach or a sign sayin' the swimmin' lanes are reserved—there ain't one.

His teammates smirk.

Now I get it. He's messin' with me, testin' whetha I'm a pushova. I'm not.

"Find a different one." I pull at the kickboard; he steps down harder.

"Race you for it," he says.

"For what? A free kickboard that's been used by everybody?"

"No, for something more fun than that. If I win, you never swim in here again." The way he smiles, it's like he wants me to knock his ass out.

I breathe, tryna take it easy and rememba what I promised Mum—no more fightin'.

"And if I win?" I ask.

"*If* you win, I'll let you take my spot as team captain."

Is he crazy or stupid—maybe both?

I agree, just for the chance to see his face when he loses. His team of groupies cheer him on as I climb out, then get on the startin' block.

"One lap, freestyle," he says, grinnin'.

When he gets up on the block, I wonder if he might be a betta swimmer than he gives off. He's tall, with even longer arms than I expected. If his arms are as powerful as they look, it won't be easy. But then again, I have a similar build with a longer torso and bigger hands.

"On your mark," one of his teammates says. We get in position. "Get set."

I grip the edge of the block with both hands even as I hear it—the crash of twisted metal, Mum's groan. My legs tremble.

"Go!" I push off, feel my body slice through the water.

I was off, I know it, but I keep my cool. I use my wide hands to pull more water, faster. I push, breathe out in a steady hum, pullin' in every three strokes. I see the marks at the bottom of the pool and that it's almost time so I flip turn, pushin' off strong.

I can see him to my right, we're neck and neck. I blitz, my signature finish, arms pullin' water so fast my torso's almost outta the water. I see him holdin' steady.

I push harder, give it everythin' I got, and slap the side. I look ova—he's here, too.

His teammates stare at him, confused.

"Who won?" he asks.

"It was a tie," a woman with a clipboard says. She's tall with long black hair pulled up into a topknot. A man stands to her right and someone more androgynous stands to her left—they are all shades of brown.

"Tied?" The guy almost spits but sucks the words back in and mumbles an apology. He takes off his cap and goggles, face flared in disappointment.

I'm no happier than he is. A tie is the furthest from what I expected, but I ain't lose, which means I can still swim here. Not that I wouldn't if I lost.

"Lyric, you're supposed to be heading stretches. Why are you even in the water, let alone racing?"

I hide from her eyes, like I'm on the team in trouble.

Wait . . . *Lyric?* As in Lyric Bryson? I look at him closer, and I can see it. I couldn't really tell when I was in the pool 'cuz he had the goggles and his cap on. But standin' there, body like a burnt sienna torpedo, he looks just like his photos.

Now it makes sense. I was surprised anyone would be able to tie with my time as one of the fastest swimmers in New York State. After Jay mentioned him, I saw his times when I looked him up—they're side by side with my own.

"Sorry, Coach," Lyric says.

"Not yet you aren't. Coach Deidre will take it from here."

The teammates grumble, and Lyric hangs his head. He looks at me, shoots icicles, but I thaw them out with my smile. "Sucks to be you."

"Hey, what's your name?" The lead coach walks closer to me.

I climb outta the water, grab my towel. "William, but you can call me Will."

"So what did you think of Lyric's offer?"

"To be banned from the pool?"

"No, to take over as captain or maybe become co-captains."

"I don't go to the same school," I say.

"You don't have to. It's a community team, no particular school required. Just a passion and talent for swimming."

Lyric looks ova at me as if he can hear her. For a second, he looks nervous, like he's 'bout to lose his pride. "Nah, I'm good."

"Don't give me an answer yet. Just consider training with us, then decide."

I shake my head. I'm nobody's leader, barely a team player. I tried it, but it always ends the same way. The team gets jealous, then comes the bullyin' till I knock somebody out, and I eitha get kicked off or quit.

Coaches always approach me, promisin' the same thing, but they neva got a handle on their swimmers, and I always have to suffer. I shake off the memory, beat it away with invisible fists. I'm just in Savannah to find Mum and take us both back to New York.

I won't even be here long. "I don't live around here, just visitin'."

"From where?" The way she tilts her head, I can tell she's an expert at turnin' every no into a yes.

"Triton."

There's a flash in her eyes. "Triton . . . in New York?"

I nod, wait for her to connect the dots. Few people don't know Triton, one of the top private schools in New York State, top five in the nation, especially for swimmin'.

"For swimming? That's impressive."

"No, for music. Swimmin' is just for fun, to release stress."

"Just come to our next practice, watch what we do. And if you say no, I'll leave you alone. Deal?"

"Okay, just one practice, no promises." She pulls a smile outta me with the strength of her own. I'm impressed—that neva happens.

I should get back before it's too late, so I climb out and walk to the showers. The water pulsin' from the showerhead has a mind of its own, holdin' me in its warm embrace. If I close my eyes just a little, I can feel my wish come true, even though I'll neva say it, of Jay standin' behind me, his arms wrapped around, whisperin', *Everything will be alright*.

I drown the images and his words outta my mind, try to numb the ache they leave behind. When I feel myself gettin' hard, I try to think of everythin' but him. The dull gray tiles, the pale blue walls—but the memory of Jay, the curve of his smile, the taste of his lips, makes tiles and walls breathe and come alive.

Too bad it doesn't stop time and allow me to travel back to when he just made my heart skip a beat, not stutter and feel foreva broken.

In the locker room, I dry off quickly, so I can step into my spare clothes and head back. I don't wanna be here when the swim team finishes.

"Aww, you been waiting for me?" It's Lyric.

I turn, show him the glory of my middle finger, and say, "Sit on it and rotate."

He walks toward me, stands too close. "You got a problem with me?"

But I rememba what Jay said and don't react. Lyric's a secret Bainbridge, the one who's been pullin' strings behind the scenes of the DKs. And if my suspicion is correct and I heard Frank on the phone when Mum was kidnapped, he's the only one who might know where she is or know how to get information on who does.

My only hope is that I'm not a big enough player in the Bainbridges' chess game for him to know my face. If Lyric recognizes who I am, my options on how to play him narrow down.

"You like me that much?" The false confidence in his voice makes my ears hurt.

"What?" I can't hide the truth; I can't stand him.

"You heard me. I know you came here to see me swim. You must know I'm on the Scholastic All-America Team."

Does he like the sound of his own voice? I roll my eyes. I ignore him like the gnat buzzin' around my ears he is. "Go somewhere with all that."

"If I give you what you want, how about you head on back to wherever you came from?" He pushes up behind me, rubs the front of my thighs as he does it.

I clench my fists, try my best to hold it in. "You might

187

wanna back up," I warn him.

"Maybe I'm not making myself clear." His face changes, wears a different kind of smile. He ain't charmin'.

No, this the face of the nigga nobody knows, the one capable of tryna to hurt Jay. "Don't come back. Otherwise, I'd hate to have to show you—"

I gut punch him so hard, his face turns every shade of red on the way to purple. Then I shove him ova the bench. He trips, barely breakin' his fall.

He glares like he's 'bout to get up, but I'm already next to him with a handful of his hair, pullin' his head back so far all he can do is try to prevent the tears from the shock of fallin'.

"Say that shit again," I growl. "G'on 'head, try me." I squeeze my fist till he whimpers.

I let him go, reach into my locker, and grab my bag. I walk out in my shorts and plan to dress in the hall near the double doors.

Lyric runs out with fear in his eyes, probably afraid I'll snitch. I beat him at his own game.

"Coach!" I yell ova.

Lyric almost goes pale.

"I don't need to watch practice. I'll join the team as a co-captain."

She smiles, and Lyric is so mad he looks like he's 'bout to pass out. I chuckle at him and wink.

I get dressed, then head outta the front doors, but standin' near one of the stone planters addin' somethin' to the soil is someone I neva thought I'd see, J.D.

I don't know what to say or do. I still feel some type of way after learnin' how bad he hurt Jay and Jacob. I can't stand the thought of it, and I got enough on my mind without thinkin' 'bout this. I have to come up with a plan of how to get Lyric to trust me, even though I prolly just made him want to kill me.

"You're never going to beat him swimming like that." J.D.'s voice snatches me around, and I don't know if I'm confused or insulted. "Your head position is too high, and you're overextending your pull, which creates gaps in your stroke rate. You're overkicking, and your breathing is a mess too."

"How did you . . ." The words come out before I can stop them. I walk ova to him, slowly. He pretty much the enemy, but I gotta know. "You used to swim?"

He doesn't look up at me, just focuses on the soil in the planter.

I move closer, make sure he hear me. "How you know all that if you ain't neva swim before?"

"I never said I didn't—that's your second assumption." He looks up at me. "Three assumptions, and you're out." But what's the first assumption?

It don't matta. If he could see all that, he knows more than most. "How you know all that, then?"

"Anybody watching you can see your head and heart

somewhere else, but they sure aren't in the pool. You start there, you can shave off at least a second, and it'll help with your pull rate and your breathing."

"Coach me." It takes a second for me to realize the words are mine.

"You don't mean that, because if you did, you wouldn't have tried to walk out of here without speaking."

I stand silent but not ashamed. If he lookin' for an apology, he ain't gettin' one.

J.D. continues massagin' the soil of the next stone planter. "I know you're close to Jacob and Jay. But remember Lin chose me and Julia as your godparents—both of us—so I expect you to at least be respectful enough to speak."

"Fair enough," I say. "Ain't mean to offend but, where I'm from, respect ain't somethin' I just give, it gotta be earned." I stand, still waitin' on an answer. Did I fuck up?

I shouldn't care; I should walk right outta here 'cuz of what he did to Jay and Jacob. But if the locker room showed me anythin', it's that Lyric's used to gettin' his way. Chasin' him won't work; I'll need to make him come to me. That's the only way I can flip what I did and use it to my advantage.

I need to beat Lyric to get anywhere with him, and J.D. may be the only person who can help me do it.

"You want me to coach you to beat him or to be a better swimmer?"

Trick question? "Both."

He stops, makes eye contact, and suddenly I avoid his eyes, realizin' what he expected me to say: beatin' Lyric is short-sighted. That's what Mum would've said. Beatin' myself to become the best swimmer should be the goal, 'cuz then I'll win against Lyric regardless. I stop hidin' from his eyes and stand tall.

"I'll coach you only under one condition. You do whatever I say, no exceptions."

I seal the deal with a nod. "I'll let you know when I get my schedule from the coach."

He barely makes any expression. "Get home safe."

On the way back, I try to think through my plan now that I know who Lyric is. If I work with J.D., how do I explain it to Jay or Jacob—or Miss Julia? Do I say anythin' at all?

Not till Mum is home safe, I decide. Then everyone will understand why we had to work togetha, even if they don't like the decision.

It's a secret—a burden I'll bear if it'll bring me one step closer to findin' Mum.

I walk in the house with a smile, but Miss Julia stands near the barstools on her phone, spatula in her hand. Her eyes lock on to me the same way Mum's do when she's 'bout to chew me out.

Jacob and Jay run down the stairs, their faces different stages of worry. Did somethin' happen? Do they have news 'bout Mum? Is she okay?

"I see him. I'll call you later." Miss Julia hangs up the phone, walks ova to me slowly, hand on her hip. "Where were you?"

"At the—"

"In what world do you think you can get up and leave this house without telling anybody where you are going? Huh? Answer me!" she yells, makin' all three of us jump.

"I didn't mean to—"

"Do you know how worried we were? How scared I was after hearing that Lin is missing, only to get up and see you gone, too? What were you thinking?"

All I can see is the spatula in her hand, all I can smell is somethin' I've been cravin' since my dream this mornin', cinnamon French toast.

How does she know how to . . . ? Mum said it was her favorite.

"Don't you hear me talking to you?"

I nod 'cuz I don't think I can do much else. Her and Mum are so similar—the way she talks, the way she yells. It only makes me miss Mum more.

I don't mean to. I try to stop it, but everythin' I was tryna push through since this mornin' pours out without me bein' able to stop it. I don't even realize I'm cryin' till Miss Julia hugs me.

14

Leroy

"Yo, Taj! Hurry up. We gotta be at the museum in less than an hour, and I still need to take a shower—you takin fuheva." Taj don't answer, just keeps rappin "California Love," by Tupac, the song blastin on repeat fuh the millionth time.

"Ma, tell Taj not to take the last of the hot water," I beg as she walks outta her closet in a light blue suit and skirt, her hair pritty all up in a bun.

She don't answer, just kisses me on the cheek as she heads toward the livin room leavin behind a trail of Chanel N°5.

Rouk pulls me into the room, nervous.

"You sho we gotta do the council meetin today? Somethin don't feel right."

"If we don't, it's gon take fuheva to get errbody togetha again."

"Just hear me out." Rouk pulls out a bunch of papers, his notepad, and one of Faa's journals. "I finished readin them journals full of interviews Faa had wit people who were gettin bullied by the cops, and Faa found a connection between Louis B, the district attorney, and the chief of police, so wheneva anybody complained, they just covered it up. Only time they couldn't was, you know . . ." It still hurt fuh him to say it: when that detective framed Taj fuh Faa's murder.

"But we knew that already. That's why the detective got kicked out the force."

"Not kicked out, paid off and transferred to anotha city, mo likely."

What? I thought . . . That can't be true.

"That was what they always did when somebody on the force got caught doin somethin wrong—no jail, just hush money and a new city accordin to Faa's journals, but he thought they mighta been plannin somethin bigger—a way to get rid of the BDs fuh good." Rouk flips through pages to find the exact words, but he can't read his own handwritin.

"Exactly like how Frank and Myrrh have been threatenin," I add.

Rouk don't usually get caught up unless he believe somethin true. Most of the time he right; the only time he eva really been wrong was wit the DKs and Lyric, and he won't really in his right mind then.

"Should we run it by Auntie Rissa?" I say, wonderin if Rouk might be onto somethin we just don't understand yet.

"Iono . . . Auntie been under so much stress. How bout you and I look into it some mo? And, after the council meetin, we can get their thoughts, assumin we get all the votes we need."

After almost a week of Auntie Rissa and Taj bein on they phones nonstop, they finally locked errbody in. Can't nothin go wrong today. This meetin gotta happen.

After barely havin long enough to get dressed, me, Ma, Taj, and Rouk pile into the car and drive to the Ralph Mark Gilbert Civil Rights Museum, Ma complainin bout Taj speedin the whole way.

Fuh a second, I think I left my notepad back at the apartment, but Rouk hands it to me as we jog back across the white stone gravel parkin lot befo they close the doors.

The museum is technically closed today, despite all the cars parked errwhere the eye can see. Members from different BD crews stand guard, makin sho aint no unexpected visitors.

Inside, the museum is just like I rememba from middle school and the high school tours. There are walls of history wit photos of some well-known civil rights heroes from Savannah like Reverend Ralph Mark Gilbert, Addie Byrd Byers, W. W. Law, Benjamin Van Clark, Bridie "Madame" Freeman, and the Original Nine, the city's first Black police officers. Even my favorite: pictures of people our age doin sit-ins at diners and wade-ins at the beach.

In the banquet hall on the back end of the museum, it's like a whole different buildin wit tall ceilins and open space wit the center a pentagon of long tables, like our own version of the United Nations wit colored chairs and tables gathered in a semicircle in front of an elevated stage.

At each table are different colors, like flags, reppin the one hundred crews, gangs, groups, and organizations, like the Pearls Crew, who protect any and all trans, gender noncon-formin, and nonbinary folx, and the Queen Onyx Gang that handle any and errthang related to Black women and girls.

Then you got otha crews united by blood, like Figya and Eight's crew, the Black Rydas, who mostly all family; or peo-ple united by diversity like the Four Elements, made up of all races, includin folks who identify as white usin they posi-tions and influence round the city to keep the BDs safe.

Taj wave me and Rouk up closer to the front, so we sit at the table next to him, Auntie Rissa, Night, PYT, and Brown Brown. In front of our seats are black tags wit "initiate" writ-ten in white letters, so errbody know who we are and why we here.

But it's almost like errbody disappear when I see him.

Jay sits next to Jacobee, Miss Julia, and Will, a couple rows back, in a section where invited guests of the BDs sit. He was supposed to have left already, but when Miss Julia called us and said Miss Rosalind been kidnapped, we realized she was the "blue jay" Frank was talm bout. He aint had to leave no mo, but we still aint seen each otha or talked since.

If we do manage to get Operation Love Letter approved, me and Jay gon have to not only see each otha all the time but talk to make sho errthang go smoothly. Iono how I feel bout it, but I shake the feelins off, try to just focus on what I gotta do right now.

Auntie Rissa brings the room to alert wit three taps of a black palm gavel. She sets the stage as president, callin each crew, who then responds so errbody is clear on who there and who not. Finally, she kicks it off and lets errbody know why we here—to welcome new initiates and a long-awaited guest at the end.

Errbody look round, tryna figure out who she means as the long-awaited guest.

"You know what's goin on?" I nudge Taj.

He shakes his head. "C'mon, it's time for us to go up."

I grab my notepad, follow Taj to the podium, and stand next to him, quiet. The whole room is watchin us, but Jay's eyes are the only ones I feel.

Taj takes to the mic and begins as we rehearsed. "Some of you may have already heard, but a new crew has been formed around town, and they go by the DKs, which stands for Diamond Kuttaz. There have been new crews befo, but the DKs are different. They were created by the Bainbridges to destroy the BDs.

"One of our biggest allies, Miss Rosalind, has been kid-napped by the DKs. Sources tell us that befo she was taken, a familiar voice called her Blue Jay. The same name was used by Frank and Myrrh, some leaders of the DKs, when they rolled through the O, proof that they the ones who took her."

"Who is this Miss Rosalind? And what exactly was she workin on to get kidnapped?" says anotha one of the OGs.

"It was only known to Rissa and myself that she was here followin a lead based on some documents we were gon release in a plan against the Bainbridges."

Anotha BD leader taps in, mic lights up. It's Bridgette of the Queen Onyx Gang. "Where was she last seen? Do we know who did it?"

"We traced her phone to K-Town, ova on the west side near the parkway."

Bridgette rolls her eyes. "That can't be nobody but Alderman Delroy."

"We don't know if he is the one behind it. But we know aint nobody gon be on that side of town without him knowin it."

Taj steps aside so I can better speak into the mic. "The DKs aint somebody who plannin to do somethin, they already started doin it. They shot at us and tried to burn us alive in Rissa's diner. Now they flippin our own community members against us, tryna make us doubt one anotha."

I let their outrage have its place, rememba what Taj told me: use it, don't be afraid of it. "We got a plan that will allow us to use tech to get inside information and identify sources that will help us uncover the Bainbridges' network and dismantle it, as well as locate Miss Rosalind."

"When did we start lettin snitches and proven traitors

make it through initiation?" an OG yells from the back, referrin to Brown Brown and Rouk.

Taj step back up to the mic wit fire in his eyes. "Let's hear yo idea, then, but only if you can deliver us the police force *and* somebody who can read Faa's coded journals written in a language only him and his younger brotha, Rouk, understand."

Errbody look round, quiet.

"I aint tellin you to fuhget what Rouk and Brown Brown did. I'm askin fuh what we need: resources and protection so we can all have a fightin chance, cuz we all know how dirty the Bainbridges play," Taj says.

After we answer more questions and Taj even get Rouk and Brown Brown to remind folks of they commitment and allegiance to the BDs, errbody got thirty minutes to vote.

Initiates don't get no vote. But when I sit back down, PYT comes ova to me and Rouk like he know somethin. "Neitha one of yall talked to Will, the boy next to Jay, right?"

"Nah, why?" I ask.

I look ova, see Will tryna get our attention as he walks to the bathrooms near the back of the museum.

After PYT casts his vote, me, him, and Rouk slip away into the crowd and follow Will to the bathroom. He waitin fuh us, washin his hands.

"You mean what you said up there 'bout findin' my mum?" Will asks, as he grabs a paper towel.

"She saved Taj, so she one of us. Why?"

A few BDs walk through the door, making all of us a lil nervous. PYT leads us out the bathroom but makes a right turn. He walks past the door wit the exit sign till we in a stairwell under an exhibit.

We can see errthang, errbody, but can't nobody see us.

Will explains him runnin into Lyric by accident at the Aquatic Center and how he managed to get on the team as a co-captain, just to piss Lyric off after knockin him on his ass.

I aint gon lie, I'm impressed. I aint know he had it in him.

"You think you could get Lyric to invite you into his house?" PYT asks. "We could give you some tech so you could bug his computer. If you did that, we could see and hear errthang that happens."

"We already know Lyric connected wit the DKs," I say. "If we got eyes and ears on him, the moment they whisper somethin bout Miss Rosalind, we can be on it. It's the kinda advantage we need."

Will's eyes light up. "Tell me what I gotta do."

PYT gets his number. "I'll hit you when the tech is ready," PYT says.

"What y'all gon' do 'bout Frank and Myrrh?" Will asks. "I ain't know they were out of jail. Lyric neva saw my face, and he doesn't seem to know who I am, but if Frank and Myrrh saw me, they could ID me right away."

"We can think bout that, come up wit a plan," I say. "The

real question is can you charm the most charmin nigga in the city, the one who got errbody but Louis B in the palm of his hand?"

"If it will get Mum back safe and sound, I'll do anythin'—no questions asked."

Exactly what I wanted to hear. "One mo thing, tho. Imma need you to keep this between us. I'm only gon loop in Taj, so he aint blindsided by it, but can't nobody else know."

"You mean don't tell Jay?"

"Nobody." I can't even say his name. He agrees.

On the way back to our tables, I bump into Miss Julia. Even wit errthang goin on, I can't turn down one of her hugs. Jay won't look at me, but I can tell he watchin me outta the corner of his eye. Jacobee shoulder-bumps me and smiles on his way back ova to Jay.

Me and PYT keep walkin to our table with Taj. I tap him on the shoulder, so I can fill him in on Will. And at first, he aint too happy bout it—I expected that much. It's hella risky, and aint no tellin if it can even work. But Taj makes me promise to keep him in the loop, and to let him know if anythin seem off.

When we hear Auntie Rissa tappin the palm gavel and see errbody takin they seats, we fall quiet.

"Thank you fuh votin, and after a chance to count, it's official. The BD initiates' plan has been approved," Auntie Rissa announces. "Taj will guide the initiates Leroy, Rouk, and Brown Brown toward the finish line, keepin errbody in the loop, and I'll help coordinate additional support through the OGs once the plan is in motion."

Me, Rouk, Brown Brown, and Taj clench our fists in quiet victory. It's the first big step we reached togetha as BDs. I'm glad we got Will, too, as our secret weapon.

Auntie Rissa stares out into the crowd, silent.

I look at Taj, and he looks back at me, wit no answer.

"Now on to our final matter. Six years ago, yall know I learned firsthand what hate could look like," Auntie Rissa says. "Not just any kind—the Bainbridge kind."

Where is this goin?

"Every day fuh six years, I mourned—we all did. And when Taj and Night were kidnapped by the DKs a few months ago, I felt the same feelin. But Rosalind came in on her chariot and protected them. She would neva speak of why or who she worked fuh, but I recently found out through some diggin, it was a company called Rah Enterprises."

Errbody start mumblin, their whispers grow into a soft roar.

I nudge Taj. "Aint that Pops's nickname?"

He don't answer, just sit there. Is she sayin what I think she sayin?

"Today, in front of all the BDs' top leadership—and his sons," Auntie Rissa looks at us, tears in her eyes. "I welcome back the co-founder of the BDs and my beloved brother, Tré

Booker. Thought to be missin, killed, he has been workin in the shadows, buildin his power and resources so he could return home and help us put an end to this fight wit the Bainbridges."

The double doors to the parkin lot fly open. People in dark suits pour into the auditorium, protectin somebody walkin through the center. They shift into a triangle wit him as the point. I can't see much, but I can feel him like a rushin wind shakin the trees—errthang and errbody in sight.

When he passes the row where Ma is, she nods, tears in her eyes as well, and that's when I realize what's happenin. Ma and Auntie Rissa knew Pops was alive, but iono how long they been knowin.

Errbody stand to they feet, the OGs shout and chant, as he walks toward the podium in what looks like a mix of tactical gear and a suit. His dark skin, like Taj, gleams in the light. He really here, our Pops, the fearless Haitian warrior.

Me and Taj stand—nah, mo like we brought to our feet by invisible hands. Pops reaches ova and pulls us into him, kisses each of us on the forehead.

He still smells the same, like Cool Water cologne and peppermints.

Pops walks up to Auntie Rissa, holds her, and togetha, they stand as the room roars wit applause.

Pops's voice thunders through the applause, even tho he barely speakin above a whisper in the mic. "It's good to be home. I've missed you. All of you."

The doors slam shut. Pops's soldiers and a handful of BDs still stand, guardin every exit.

"Let me lead wit I'm sorry," Pops says. "I'm sorry that I couldn't reveal the truth ova these past years, no matta how bad I wanted to. But I hope you know that I prayed fuh this day."

The floors sound out under stompin heels and calls from the OGs. Words of a chant that, up until now we only sang each year on Pops's birthday to rememba him, bellow and echo off the walls loud and from the soul. A combination of singin, stompin, clappin, and different phrases yelled out, it shakes the soul like protest marchin songs but electrifies any and errbody like a ring shout.

He looks ova at Ma, who nods with her hand clenched into a fist ova her heart. Taj still aint said nothin but looks like he doin errthang he can to stay still, look strong.

"Rosalind, one of the top fixers and strategists in the northeast, agreed to rep Rah Enterprises a few years ago to develop a lucrative but untraceable network that would allow me to track the Bainbridges' influence and wealth in order to sever it befo drivin em outta Savannah once and fuh all," Pops says.

Errbody in the room listen, spellbound. But why does this feel like a betrayal?

"Rosalind, wit her connection to Savannah, agreed to step

forward and monitor things mo closely. After savin Taj and Night, she put her own plan in motion, usin their same tactics against em. But when she disappeared, I knew it was time to not only work arm in arm to get her returned safe and sound but to reclaim my position as the head of the BDs."

What?! Taj's face mirrors mine.

We look at Auntie Rissa, confused. Did she agree to this? Nah, she couldn'ta, cuz hidden beneath her turquoise eye shadow and long eyelashes, she holds her body tight like a fist.

Taj just stares at Auntie Rissa standin at the podium, wit his jaw clenched and a vein gettin bigger on his temple.

"Rissa has done incredible wit my oldest, Taj," Pops says. "But now it's time to get our house in order so we are ready fuh what lies ahead."

The doors fly open again, but this time soldiers drag people in. Their hands are tied behind their backs.

Errbody jumps up. We see the colors and recognize who they are: members of the Low Rider Crew. Me and Taj look at each otha, cuz he was just negotiatin terms wit em to make sho they stayed on board wit bein part of the BDs. What are they doin in handcuffs like prisoners?

Pops takes the mic down and carries it wit him as he walks down the stage to the center where Husani and the Low Rider Crew been gathered.

"One thing bout watchin from the outside is you can see

how the enemy tries to sneak in and turn errbody against each otha, like this crew who thinks they can switch sides and join the DKs."

"That aint true. I keep fuckin tellin you." Husani spits blood from a bruised lip. He shakes his head at his crew in the audience, makin sho they stand down and let this play out.

"So you weren't negotiatin wit Taj, tryna to set terms so you *wouldn't* leave the BDs?"

"We needed mo manpower to protect our community when we got attacked by the DKs. Won't nobody tryna strong-arm Taj."

"Therein lies the problem, young blood," Pops says as his guards yank errbody to they feet. "I think you might be mistaken, but all is good cuz I'm here to correct it. You eitha wit the BDs as a member or you against us as our enemy."

"That's not what was promised. Taj and Rissa said we—"

"Ion care," he growls. "There aint no *you*, young blood. There's only *we*, the Black Diamonds. If there's a problem, we'll sit down and figure it out; there aint no switchin sides, no bargainin. Eitha you fight as a BD or we treat you like all our enemies. Cuz *that* is the BD way."

Many of the OGs cheer, stomp they feet. But they don't see what me and Taj see: in a matter of minutes, Pops just destroyed what it took Taj and Auntie Rissa the past few years to build.

Suddenly, errbody phones are eitha ringin or vibratin wit texts and phone calls.

"Yo, get the TV! Turn on the news!" someone yells.

"Yo, they raidin K-Town neighborhoods," anotha person shouts.

One of the YGs rolls in a TV on wheels that's been moved outta the way fuh the event. Plugs it back up and turns on the local news.

There stands the chief of police and the district attorney wit the followin title at the bottom of the screen:

NEW ANTI-GANG POLICY PROPOSED
FOR A SAFER SAVANNAH

The chief of police talks bout a rapid increase in gang activity, says Savannah is losin the war on drugs and crime cuz gangs are corruptin innocent children through criminal enterprises masqueradin as grassroots organizations wit ulterior motives.

They proposin a bill that allows em to call three or mo people between thirteen and seventeen years of age a gang, and if charged wit criminal activity, they will be tried as adults wit minimum sentences of five years, or mo at the judge's discretion.

We look at each otha, in shock, knowin what this mean. But befo any of it sets in, the news station shows photos and video of back when Taj was arrested and accused of killin Faa, even his mug shot and a video from Faa's vigil. They don't say nothin bout him bein set up.

The reporters then show the scene of cop cars errwhere on different streets of K-Town, as they line people up against walls of buildings and cop cars fuh no reason.

The cameraman zooms in on a YG cussin back at a cop fuh the way he was treatin him. Suddenly, half a dozen cops pile on top of him.

Otha YGs fight to protect him, yell at the cameras he aint armed as a few otha try to pull the cop tryna choke the YG out. But befo we can see what happen, the station cuts to a mob of people we don't recognize comin outta nowhere, surroundin some otha cops. Then we realize who they are— DKs.

We hear one of the men, Myrrh, scream into the camera, "Don't fuck wit the Black Diamonds," as they jump and stomp the cameraman till connection is lost.

The broadcasters look terrified as they try to reconnect wit the reporter.

Suddenly, Louis Bainbridge's face pops up on the screen. He's bein interviewed by a different reporter.

"What are your thoughts about what we've just seen, as one of the most respected Savannah natives and leaders responsible for so much of our city and its development?"

"I'm in shock, in awe, quite honestly," Louis B says. "That's not the Savannah I grew up in and far from the picture of peace and safety we deserve. I'm proud to have these brave officers on our side as they fight this never-ending war to keep us safe."

"Who he keepin safe? It damn sho aint us. I know you fuckin lyin!" a YG yells.

"Anything you'd like to say to the citizens of Savannah, who owe you and your family so much?" the reporter says, full of—neva mind.

"I believe in Savannah's future, which is why we, at the Bainbridge Promise Development, are proud to offer up to six thousand dollars per family for relocation to the new condos being built out in Putnam Parkway. Why? Because the only way to stand against crime, to guard against indoctrination of our children from criminal enterprises, is to join together and help those who can't help themselves—" Auntie Rissa turns off the TV.

Fuh a second, it's like errbody frozen, speechless.

"Did they just do what I think they did?" Rouk asks, confused.

"They just turned Savannah against us and made themselves the heroes," I say.

"You behind this, too, aintchu?" a YG screams, rushin toward Pops, but folks stop him. But the yellin and bickerin rises, all of it directed toward him.

"You tryna take us out, tryna hurt us like you did Sani and his crew," anotha YG yells. YGs get louda, and the OGs try to defend Pops as errthang falls into chaos.

"We aint got no time fuh this," Auntie Rissa blasts through the mic. "YGs, connect wit Taj and head to the neighborhoods to make sho errbody safe and off them streets. OGs, let's coordinate wit Lady Tee to get legal reps."

Errbody hops on they phones and run to they cars out front. Taj makes sense of the madness as the tide of YGs rush in and out.

Night escorts Jay, Jacobee, Will, and Miss Julia to her car. Taj gets Husani and his crew released, promises to somehow make this right.

As the auditorium clears out, we see Auntie Rissa wit Pops. All of us walk ova to join em now that most of the OGs and YGs are outside and the doors are closed, except fuh Pops's guards.

"You wanna explain what the hell that was? At no point did we discuss any of that!" Auntie Rissa shouts.

"The only way we can beat this—the Bainbridges *and* get rid of the DKs immediately—is if we stand togetha—" Pops attempts to argue.

"Wit you as the front, the lead. Am I understandin that correctly?"

"We can hash out the specifics lata, I just think—"

"What you did to the Low Rider Crew could destroy errthang," Auntie Rissa yells, frustrated. "Did you see their faces? All of the YGs?"

"I understand that, but it was a mistake fuh you to give so much power to the YGs," Pops says. "They still kids, this is a war, they not ready. Why else the DKs and the Bainbridges been able to shift their allegiances so easily?"

"Did you fuhget how old you were when you created the BDs? The same age as Taj," Auntie Rissa says.

He takes a deep breath, lets the real bomb of his intent fall. "I wasn't ready then eitha, which is why I'm movin to have full control and votin power restricted to only OGs."

"If you do that, the BDs may never recover from this," Auntie Rissa says.

"Let's calm down and at least see what's happenin first," Ma says, rubbin Pops shoulders, just like she used to. "Don't let this steal our joy, Rissa. We a family again. We can figure this out."

Taj is still silent in a way I aint neva know him to be. So I look Pops right in the eye and speak on both our behalf. "You wrong, and you know it." It comes out sharper than I mean but no less true.

"Excuse me?" Pops wears a smile, but I can feel the edge, the heat simmerin beneath.

"Shared power, shared understandin—*shared* responsibility. That's what Taj and Auntie Rissa promised all the YGs. You would know that if you aint choose to be gone."

I walk away and pull Taj behind me.

Back at Ma's, we in Taj's room after finally makin it home from the BDs council meetin, and he still aint said nothin bout what happened. I stare at him, try to get his attention, cuz I can't think straight and he the only one who can under-stand how I feel, even if he aint tryna feel.

Rouk wit Auntie Rissa, Lady Tee, and Trish's unc right now at D&D's Grocery as they try to figure out how to coordinate enough folks to stop the anti-gang bill, since Faa mentions somethin like it in his notes, which Rouk aint see till after the meetin. Ma gettin ready fuh work—aint really said much, just cooked and covered the food wit foil.

"How long you think they knew?" I ask Taj, movin from the foot of the bed to where he sittin wit his back to the wall.

"Don't matta," Taj finally answer, but don't even look up from his phone. "Fact is, they knew and they aint tell us."

I turn round, lean ova to see how far he got. Taj only play one game on his phone, *Snake*. I aint neva seen nobody betta at it than him. The snake is already one third the size of the screen gettin longer and longer, and Taj don't bat an eye.

"That why you answerin errbody calls but Auntie Rissa's?"

Taj don't say nothin, just props himself up on a pillow as he lays on his stomach.

"What we gon do?" I say, as his phone vibrates. Game ova.

"We move forward wit Operation Love Letter so yall can get some new leads wit Brown Brown, Trish . . . and Jay."

Just hearin his name is a punch in the chest. I breathe through it.

"And *anythin* Rouk say we need to pay attention to, we doin it from now on," Taj continues. "He sleep wit them journals so tight, it's almost like Faa speakin to him furreal. We can't be caught slippin again."

The doorbell rings.

"One of yall get it," Ma shouts from her bedroom. "Might be Rissa. I'm still changin."

I hop up and Taj follows, but he's headed to the kitchen to grab some of the spicy fried chicken, Spanish rice, and honey biscuits Ma cooked and left out fuh us. Ma walks in just as I open the door. She sees who it is befo I do.

"Tré, whatchu doin here?" She walks ova to him, happy but not fuh long, when she sees us givin him the cold shoulder.

Fuh a second, she lets it go, hugs Pops, kisses him.

Taj pushes himself from the table, grabs both our plates, and loudly empties them back into the bowl on the stove even tho we barely ate.

Ma stares at him one mo time, a second warnin befo she explode and bring the house down wit it.

"You plan on apologizin?" Taj turns round, adds fuel to the fire.

"You right," Pops says. "I do owe yall—"

"To Husani and his crew—"

"Taj!" Ma shouts. "You know disrespect will neva be allowed under my roof."

I wonder if she see it like I do—that even this feels like all the otha times, her choosin "men" ova us.

"Fine. Choose him, since he the only one you wanted

all these years anyway." Taj goes to the door, steps into his shoes. "Let's go, Lee."

I start putting on my shoes as well.

"Where yall goin?"

"Don't matta," Taj says, cold. "Me, Lee, and Rouk will move to Auntie Rissa's tomorrow, so you can move him right on in here, like he neva left."

I wait fuh Ma to explode, fuh her to throw somethin, slap him, try to make him feel the pain she do but she just stands there. When I look at Taj, I see why she hasn't. He fightin back tears. And it don't take long befo my eyes burnin, too— and all I want is fuh him to not leave me behind.

On the otha side of the door, in the hallway, we hear Ma breakin down, beggin Pops to bring us back. And as Taj walks faster, chokin back sobs, I realize that outta all these years, we neva heard Ma say that, choose *us*. It's the one thing we always wanted, but why does hearin it hurt so bad?

15

JAY

Momma turns the radio off. Now all we have to listen to is the soundtrack of the engine's complicated purr and the trunk rattle because of street potholes. She's been in a mood since we left the museum, her face pensive in a determined frown.

I stare out of my window as the space between me and Will in the second row of seats expands for no reason he'll explain. He still hasn't said more than a couple of words to me. I've started to get used to it all over again—feeling invisible.

Momma finally speaks. "I know a lot is going on, but I want y'all to promise me you won't go off and do something that could get you hurt."

There is silence where we'd expect.

"Will, did you hear me?" Momma speaks to him through the rearview mirror.

"I dunno if I can, Miss Julia."

"Excuse me?" Momma's eyes are hazard lights, a warning to watch out—do anything but what he's doing now.

"Would you just sit back and do nothin' if someone you loved was missin'?"

Momma almost answers on parent autopilot but probably considers her own shit-starter legacy Miss Rosalind has told stories about.

"If I'm being honest, I wouldn't," Momma says. "Especially if it was Lin."

Will nods.

"That's why we're going to follow the original plan, the one we made before you had to move back."

Will locks eyes with Momma. "You mean livin' here?"

"Yes, *and* I want you to enroll at Daniel Lee so you don't fall behind."

"What if I got all my credits already?" An honest question.

"You go to Daniel Lee anyway. An idle mind—"

"Is the devil's workshop," he finishes. "It's Mum's favorite phrase."

"Hers, too," I say on accident and on purpose.

Momma pulls into the driveway, cuts off the car, turns around in her seat, face gentle and honest. "Let me hear you promise with your words," she says.

Will is hesitant, but no one can withstand the pull of Momma's eyes, her love. "I promise."

When we enter the house, Will climbs the stairs to his room. And I follow Jacob into ours, but then he stops me and says the last thing I'd ever expect, "Jay, Leroy says he wants to talk."

Before I can say anything in response, we're headed downstairs, and Jacob has somehow convinced Momma to let us swing by Lake Willow Park. I follow his lead, both numb and hopeful.

When we arrive and I see the look on Leroy's face across the park as Taj lays out hamburger patties and hot dogs and buns on the wooden picnic table, I want to run the other way. He clearly doesn't want me here.

Taj forces out a smile, but Jacob sees through it, hugs him tight, kisses him.

Leroy and I look at them, aching in the silence. To the left of the wooden tables is an iron grill, where Leroy fumbles with the bag of charcoal, until Jacob takes it off his hands, layers them.

For a second, both Leroy and I hover in no-man's-land, not wanting to sit but not sure we should be standing.

"We got this." Taj tries to correct Jacob on how to layer the charcoal. "Yall got business to discuss, so come back when yall ready to eat." Taj motions and points toward the gravel path to a small but long pier at the lakefill. It's far enough of a walk that it might help with the awkwardness.

A few steps in, I speak first. "I know it's the last thing you want to hear from me, but I'm sorry." Nothing. I try a different angle. "Are you okay? It seemed like a lot . . . you finding out about your dad . . . then Louis B and the DKs . . ." Nothing still.

Is he really not going to speak to me at all?

"It is what it is," he says, kicking a rock down the path ahead of us.

"So what did you want to talk about?" I ask.

He abruptly stops and says, "Whatchu mean? You wanted to talk to me."

"No . . . Jacob said . . ." The truth slaps the back of our necks at the same time. We look at Jacob and Taj pretending to not watch us.

"Well, guess they got us." I keep walking, hoping he will, too.

We both need to figure this out. There's more at stake than our broken hearts.

"How are we going to do this?" I turn around, look him in the eyes. He stares at the ground. "Would you please look at me? This isn't easy for me either—"

"Easy for *you*?" he scoffs. That's not what I meant.

"You know what?" Leroy walks up to me, eyes burning, "Fuck you, Jay. How bout that?"

I can feel the tears coming, but I stop them. Now isn't the time. "Is that all you got?"

"What?" Leroy growls.

"Anything else you want to say to hurt me?" I stand my ground, even though my knees are shaking, and I just want to run back home and hide under the covers.

"Whatever it is, I'll deal with it. But Operation Love Letter won't succeed if we don't work together. I need you." I buckle at my words, what they really mean. "I can't do this without you, and you can't do this without me."

Leroy stares at the geese flying in a V, each higher than the one in front of them, to lessen the wind resistance for the rest of the group. They are stronger together than solo. He walks toward the piers, looks back to make sure I'm following.

Not a verbal invitation, but it's something—I hope.

It never gets easier, though. Leroy eventually talks but only about Operation Love Letter, what it means to have BD support, and what happens next as PYT finishes testing the tech, Rouk and Trish learn more from the journals, and Brown Brown cautiously connects with Detective Dane.

We talk about how we'll keep in touch: weekly calls with me, him, PYT, and Princeton—never just us two—maybe more when the love letters really pick up. In-person meetings only when necessary, when it's not safe to just talk over the phone.

He never says what I can feel beneath his words: that it hurts being in each other's presence, reminded of what we used to be. But what am I supposed to do with the parts of me reaching for him and, in the space between, his eyes returning the gesture?

Maybe it's all in my head because, as soon as we get clear on the details of Operation Love Letter, he leaves me for what feels like a third time. And it hurts just the same.

By the time Will, Princeton, and I make it to the traffic light up the street from Daniel Lee, I swear I'm already exhausted. After seeing Leroy at Lake Willow with Jacob, I barely slept the entire weekend.

I kept having nightmares of being stuck there with him, damned to silence for all eternity as he laughed and talked to everyone, even the geese and swans, but me. And with today being our meeting with our first Operation Love Letter client, Denise, I know I'll have to see Leroy again, but I'm just not ready. And on top of that, Will is still giving me the cold shoulder, leaves any room I enter like I'm the plague.

Maybe I should shut off my feelings like Will and Leroy or at least make it look like I don't care. Yeah, that's what I'll do.

As random people turn our trio into a small mob, with Will and Princeton at the center, I focus on the types of trees lining the block. I say their scientific names in my mind like Dad once taught me, as if I'm casting a spell, *Magnolia grandiflora* (southern magnolia), *Pinus palustris* (longleaf pine), *Liquidambar styraciflua* (sweetgum), and *Quercus virginiana* (southern live oak).

When we walk through the green double doors, it's like being in school with Jacob all over again—no, worse—as people push and pull to get Will's attention.

"Jay, you listenin'?" Princeton's words sideswipe my ear.

"Huh?" I say.

Princeton shakes his head and steers me over to my locker. Even there, my eyes are pulled toward the F5 tornado that's Will.

Princeton blocks my line of sight, and I sigh, grateful for him, my purple monochrome-wearing storm shelter.

"Y'all beefin' or somethin'?"

"No, we'd actually have to talk in order to do that." I slam and slap my books in frustration.

"Am I gon' have to file a restrainin' order on behalf of them books?"

Will walks by, glances at me for the first time all day, but looks away just as fast.

A rogue chuckle escapes my mouth as Princeton shimmies, shaking a pair of invisible maracas.

"See? That's mo' like it." He grins. "Furreal tho, I know you havin' a hard time, but give yoself some credit. Even tho you heartbroken, you ain't lettin' that stop you. Between helpin' me paint envelopes and the phone calls with Leroy and PYT ova the weekend to set today up, you makin' sho' Operation Love Letter is a success."

I blush, grateful. Then I do the only thing I can do in response to his bestie pep talk: I shimmy back with half the vigor, minus the maracas.

"Christina said to meet out front when the bell rings," Princeton says. "Then we can all head ova to Ronaldo's togetha."

When the last bell rings, I don't even try to make eye contact with Will anymore; he's made it clear that at Daniel Lee, we don't know each other.

I push through the double doors with my mean mug to the power of ten, wanting to shout, Magnolia grandiflora, *nigga—get thee behind me!*

An arm pulls me to the side; I assume it's Princeton, so I

don't protest. I'm shocked to see it's Will. "I'm headed this way. Catcha lata," he says.

Wait, what? "Where you going?"

"Why?" He pierces me with his hazel daggers.

"What do you mean? You heard my mom. She said we gotta stay together."

He looks right at me, unfazed.

"Don't tell me you expect me to lie for you." I hate that the words sound weak, whiny. I stand up straight, square my jaw to counter.

"You'll figure it out," he says.

"Why should I?"

He stops, turns around. "'Cuz you owe me." There's a crack in his façade, pain. I didn't even know he felt anything.

"You've been hurting me, too," I say, winded and wounded by his words.

"Don't matta. You broke my heart first."

I don't know what to say, so I don't. I just watch him pimp away. "Meet me at the convenience store by six p.m.," I yell in defeat, unsure if he hears me.

"Hey, Jay!" Christina walks up in a white top, a baby-blue skirt, and white knee-high boots, leaving broken hearts in her wake.

Princeton runs up, hooks his arm around our shoulders. "To Ronaldo's?"

"Yup, I just got a text from Trish and Denise." Christina

pulls away to head toward the driver's side of her car. "Get in, I'll drive."

I spot the powder-blue Cadillac behind Christina's car as soon as I slam my door. I prepare myself to see Leroy in person again the whole ride over. The planning phone calls have made it easier to talk to each other, but seeing him makes my heart race and break all over again.

When we arrive and all get out of the car, Leroy pimps over with Brown Brown.

"Sup, Jay." Leroy's voice is soft, like the hug I want from him but can't have.

Christina briefs him and Brown Brown, Leroy nods. He says they'll stay close but out of sight, in case anything pops off.

On the outside, Ronaldo's blends into the rough brick-faced buildings on Martin Luther King Jr. Blvd., who all feel like distant cousins, twice removed from the once glamorous West Broad, the Black Wall Street. But on the inside, Ronaldo's bursts free into music and colors, half coffee shop, half Cuban restaurant with flags of Caribbean countries.

A group of elders sit at a table nearly in the center playing dominoes, humming in Spanish. It sparks a chain reaction from who I assume is Denise. She's tall with a golden Afro shining like a halo against her ivory skin. Dancing while pulling the levers of the espresso machine as it hisses and rumbles, she sings in Spanish and English to a laughing Trish, who sits at the coffee bar in front of her.

"Having fun without us?" Christina says, her hips suddenly swaying to the soft drums and horns blaring from the old-school radio near the dominoes table. Whatever sadness rode Christina's shoulders on the way here has disappeared into thin air.

"What song is that?" I ask Princeton.

He's bobbing his head and shaking his shoulders, his feet stepping in the same cadence. "You don't know Celia?"

One of the elders turns the music louder, stands, and does his own version of whatever Princeton is doing with smaller steps but just as much heart and soul. Princeton moves in close, steps forward then back, pushing and pulling me with him.

"Just follow my lead," Princeton says, as he breaks it down in a way my body can understand. The weight on my heart flutters away, and suddenly I'm smiling.

The tempo picks up, and so does the room, as they chant the hook to "Quimbara" by Celia Cruz, a song I can only describe as joy, joy, and more joy.

The front doorbell chimes, and that joy evaporates.

Frank and Myrrh, and a few other DKs, strut in with prowling eyes.

"Don't stop on our account." Frank moves his shoulders and his hips, an invitation. But no one is foolish enough to reply.

The elders shuffle past him, staring him down and

mumbling in Spanish. He argues back in Spanish, his hands waving with his words.

"What a surprise," Frank says, walking toward us.

"We was thinkin the same thing." Leroy and Brown Brown appear behind them from the side entrance.

Their standoff is interrupted by a man pushing his way through the front door.

"What's going on in here?" He towers above all of us, and even though he's younger than the elders, his words dance the same, just deeper.

"Wassup, sir?" Frank says, shifting his attention. "Delroy in?"

"No, but I thought I made it clear you don't enter unless one of us is here."

Frank's eyes narrow.

"Wait for him outside," the man says.

Christina and Trish exchange looks with Denise as she presses buttons, turns knobs, and pours different shapes of latte art, some with whipped cream, others with steamed milk. "Here you go, on the house, since you're regulars."

Frank smirks. "That's better. 'Bout time we get some Southern hospitality."

"Let's go," Christina says. All of us head out, Frank's eyes trailing us.

"So what now?" Princeton blows hot air into the fall breeze.

As I stand next to Christina and Trish, their perfumes

swirl and mix with the wind, caramel and coconut.

"Denise says meet her at Forsyth Park, near the stone flower garden," Trish says, looking at her phone. "Yall go ahead. I'm gon grab us some snacks."

"We'll be nearby. Gotta run an errand to the precinct," Brown Brown says. "You see Frank and Myrrh again, text and we'll shut that shit down."

When Christina parks at Forsyth Park near the tennis courts, she starts walking past the statue of Mother Mathilda Beasley that replaced the Confederate monument. Soon we're facing two playgrounds, one with wood chips and the other sand. By the time we see Trish and Denise, we are cooling down at the rows of swings, enjoying the smell of wood chips and sweat.

"Sorry it took so long," Denise says, holding a big blanket.

We walk a little further and then we see it: a white-stone-enclosed aromatic garden. Once we walk through the cast-iron gate, it's like we enter another world as the hints of citrus from the Meyer lemon trees and the scent of roses blanket us.

After we settle down, Denise finally speaks. "Thanks for coming. I wanted to talk at the shop, but you know."

"Yeah, we do," Trish says. "Do Frank and the DKs always show up like that?"

"Depends. When Nate was around, it was different."

"Nate is the guy Denise wants you to write the letter to,

Jay," Christina says. "Oh, we got interrupted before I could introduce y'all. Denise, meet Jay and Princeton—y'all meet Denise."

We greet each other with tentative smiles.

"Tell us 'bout Nate, and why you want Jay to write a letter," Princeton says.

"We met when Nate was a BD initiate. He stopped a mob from trying to burn down my granddad's restaurant when people found out he was in the Bainbridge family's pockets. Nate stayed in front of our store all night.

"After that, even though Granddad never liked him, he always swung by with his digital camcorder, filmed me making drinks, even made a video to advertise our restaurant. When that lady was pulled from her car by the DKs earlier this week, Nate called over the BDs and recorded as they all jumped in to protect her."

I don't realize I've stopped writing until my pencil almost falls out of my hand. I can't stop thinking about Miss Rosalind, wondering if she's okay.

"That's when Frank and Myrrh and the other guys jumped them. I tried to get to Nate to help, but my dad locked the door, and my granddad yanked the landline out of the wall. He said to not even think about calling the police; this was the new order of things."

"What happened next? Did they ever stop?" Princeton asks, nervous.

"Only after the lady threw herself over Nate," Denise says.

"She what?" I ask.

"Yeah, she covered him. Frank and Myrrh's crew barely stopped one another from beating her too bad. They left Nate and rushed away with her."

If Alderman Delroy speaks to Frank and Myrrh frequently, there's a chance they'll bring up Miss Rosalind, since it all went down at Ronaldo's, which means we need tech installed ASAP.

But if Nate was filming, do the BDs know about this video? Have they seen it? Maybe it could be used to turn the tables somehow. We'll have to tell Leroy and Brown Brown as soon as we're done here.

"When's the last time you spoke to Nate?" I say.

"Almost a week . . . he said not to contact him anymore," Denise says, on the verge of tears. "He can't trust a Delroy who won't stand up for what's right."

We stop, let her breathe and calm down. I don't think any love letter I could write would fix this.

"What would you tell Nate if you could?" Princeton keeps hope alive, pulls out his own sketchbook, ready.

Denise wipes her face, and a softer sun rises behind her eyes. "I'd tell him I'm sorry and I'm willing to choose."

She plays with the ends of her sweater, pulling at the fabric until she finds confidence waiting for her in the tattered seams.

"I just want to hold him, tell him I know how scared he must have been. I don't want him to ever feel that way again." Denise tears up. "I want to finally say what I've been too scared to: I love him. I'd rather fight to figure this out together than be miserable apart."

Denise, Trish, and Christina wipe tears from their eyes, their smiles having conversations above our heads. Then they collapse into a three-way hug.

"I'll write it," I say, almost without thinking, overwhelmed and full of enough emotion to write multiple letters. "I can't promise forgiveness but maybe a chance to say you're sorry, and hopefully, that can be the start of something more."

Denise nods, and they smile again as a trio.

As Princeton and I get up, I can feel Denise still watching me.

"You're helping me, so is it my turn to help you?" she asks.

"What do you mean?" Did Trish or Christina tell her why we're really here?

"My granddad is Alderman Delroy. There's no one more paranoid or slick. You all need my help to find out about that lady? That's why you were asking all those questions," Denise says. "Do you know her?"

I don't know whether to hide the truth or tell it. Christina's and Trish's faces tell me to take the risk. "Yes, she's like family to me."

"What do you need?" Denise asks.

"We need to be able to listen in on your granddad," Princeton says. "A place he might take a call or talk about Miss Rosalind, the lady the DKs kidnapped."

"Okay, that would be the storage room in the back of the restaurant. He uses it as an office most of the time."

"Is there a computer?" I ask.

"Yes, and you won't have a hard time hearing him because he's loud and thinks no one is more clever than him."

We nod and hold space for the feeling that is hovering above her, above all of us, waiting for us to let it in.

"So, we really doin' this?" Princeton says.

Our eyes say yes.

I text PYT and ask what's next.

Not long after sharing what we learned with Leroy and Brown Brown—or should I say Brown Brown, since Leroy still wouldn't even look at me—and having to endure yet another silent walk home with Will from the convenience store, I can't take it anymore. I may not be able to thaw Leroy's cold shoulder, but if Will and I are going to live under the same roof, something has to change—and today.

I decide to storm down the hallway and into Will's room to force him to talk—or feel the "burn." At first, he doesn't notice me. His back is to the door as he bobs his head while doing his homework with headphones on.

When he finally sees me, his smile falters.

Is it that awful seeing me? Being in my presence?

Will doesn't say anything, just looks at me. I try to concentrate on his face, but the oversized white tank reveals his neck, his tattoo that says "Kiss me." And the shorts that fall away from his propped-up thighs make it hard to—I can't think.

It's suddenly hot, and I can't focus. But, regardless, I stand strong. If he won't speak to me, I won't speak to him. We'll just have a nonverbal conversation.

Will gets flustered, shakes his head, and tosses the books aside to get up to leave.

I close the door, blocking it. Will reaches behind me, but I won't move. He stares at me, and steps so close to me that I can smell the scent of the tangerines he's just eaten, the peels curled up on the desk next to the bed.

"Jay, move." A command, not a conversation.

I don't move. He looks down at me, eyes sharp, lips pink, eyelashes like peacock feathers, the light catching the peach fuzz on his chin and just above his lips.

Will reaches to move me, but I grab his forearms.

"Lemme go," he whispers.

But his hips are pushing into me when his arms should be pulling away. He leans closer and closer, our lips playing chicken run, him daring me to stop first.

I refuse to move, to obey.

I need him to see me and know I'm not going to run away.

Will grabs me, first with his lips, then follows with his tongue until my knees buckle and Will washes over me like a wave. My body betrays me, surrenders to his hands reaching under my shirt, down the back of my shorts, until we're walking backward toward the bed, me falling back as he falls on top of me.

I shouldn't, but his hands are hungry.

I can't, but my mouth is thirsty for his kisses.

I won't, but I do—my body misses him too.

My lips return to the tattoo on his neck that was made for them. I want him, no, I need him too. And as my lips and teeth attack the salty sweet of his skin, he buckles, letting me bear his full weight. He finds himself beneath his shorts and reaches through the bottom of mine.

For a second, I'm dizzy and I can't breathe. I can't think, I don't know, and the words shoot from my lips, a flare into the hot and humid air between us. "Wait!"

I crawl from under him and run to my room, trying to catch my breath.

I hear him smack the bed, whisper-yelling under his breath.

I went into Will's room to make things better, to clear up the bad feelings or at least talk so we can find a way forward, but I've just made everything worse.

16

Will

In the water, everythin' feels off, wrong—and it's all Jay's fault. In my mind, he is everywhere. I need Jay, even though I know I can't have him. When I finish my fourth lap, the last of my mornin' warm-up, I slap the water, cussin'.

"What's wrong?" J.D. comes to the edge of the pool.

"Everythin'," I say, almost chokin'.

He shakes his head.

"I know, I know," I say before he does. "Cut through the fire with the cool. I just feel slow, like I'm not movin', no matta how hard I try." It's been four sessions, and I still ain't shave no seconds off my time, and the meet is in two days.

"It's good you've finally hit that wall you feel you can't push past." J.D. leans back on the startin' block like it's a chair. "This is what I've been waiting for."

I don't get it. But if I don't find a way to pull my weight in the team relay with me as the last leg, Lyric won't have a reason to want to get close to me.

"Alright, listen, your swimming isn't the problem," J.D. says, crouchin' down closer to where I am on the side of the pool. "Come on out. I know just the thing."

I pull myself outta the pool, and he directs me to stand near the startin' block.

"As a swimmer, you might think you're competing against others, but every time you get on this, you're competing against yourself." He motions for me to touch the startin' block, to feel the base. "That means whatever you're carrying, whatever you're worried about, you bring it to the water. You offer it up, allowing the water to be a partner and help you through it."

My face must show what I'm thinkin', 'cuz he laughs.

"I know it may sound all woo-woo."

"Woo-woo?" I chuckle.

"You know what I mean." He laughs at himself. "Just remember, right now, we're not focusing on racing, it's about technique. And you can't focus on the fundamentals going fast. For that, you have to go slow so you know what to change, what to keep the same."

I think I get it, a little bit—enough to try it.

"When you're ready, get on the block and in starting position. Close your eyes. Then imagine whatever you're afraid of, then imagine yourself letting it go."

"Then what?"

"Nothing, wait three minutes and then dive. And when you touch that water, give me everything you got for one hundred yards. I'm talking about four laps of the best swimming you've ever done in your life."

"How will I know when the three minutes are up?"

"Feel your way through it."

"C'mon, man," I say under my breath.

"If you jump in before the three minutes are up, you're going to have to wait double and swim double, until I feel better."

That ain't an option, so I focus on the ripplin' blue, listen as it laps at the grates on the side. I get in position, fold my body till my chest and abs kiss the front of my thighs. Suddenly, my legs start shakin' and then the questions come roarin': *Why did I kiss Jay? What does it mean for him to kiss me back? Why can't I stop myself from fallin' for him every time I'm near him?*

The questions keep pilin' on top of me till I can't think and all I feel is a heavy, suffocatin' darkness.

I can't hold the startin' position anymore.

The pool blurs in and out. I wipe my eyes, fight back by stayin' still. I balance my weight across my feet, get ready to push off, and then I see Jay's face from back when we were younger, when all my feelings for him started.

There he is, in a big playground just like I remember it. Even though he missin' two front teeth, his smile is so bright.

Everythin' fades till all I can hear is the hypnotic lull of his laughter unleashin' the hilarious squeal of my own.

I push off the startin' block, my arms in perfect streamline for a smooth entry. Under water, I give six dolphin kicks till the red line, then the first pull with my left, the strongest for freestyle. I breathe on three, only 80 percent leg power, so I don't burn through my energy. Out of nowhere, somethin' throws me off rhythm.

I rememba what Jay said yesterday in my room: "Wait!" Him pullin' himself from under me.

I take in too much water. I panic.

Then I hear the crash, the twist of metal, Mum's groan.

I miss a breath, before it's time for me to turn underwater at the wall, and I take in too much water again. My nose burns, forehead aches from the discomfort. My body wants to quit, my mind says, *Let it.* I've done enough, I've tried, it's too hard.

I hear Mum's laugh. I fight to see the memory of all of us—Jay, Jacob, Miss Julia, Mum, and me—togetha. And even if it feels impossible, this is all that matters.

I push, give it all I got. I race to reach that memory till I slap the wall, finished.

I can barely breathe. I look at J.D., prayin' that what I just did was enough.

"Not bad," he says, grinnin' at the stop clock.

"Did I shave time off?"

"Yes and no. If you're asking if you swam faster than your fastest record competition time, yes—by half a second."

"That's good, right?" It's not a big difference, but races have been won by less.

"It is, which means now we have a new target time." J.D.

crouches down, holds up the pad with two times written on it. "What do you notice?"

"One second?"

"Exactly. If you shave two seconds off, it would mean you can beat Lyric's fastest time on record, which would be a game changer in any relay."

I pull myself outta the pool and get back on the startin' block. "Again, let's go again."

"You sure? You could take a few minutes to recover if you need it," he jokes.

"Nah, I know everythin' I need to know. If I can beat his time a few more times today and tomorrow, by the time we have the swim meet this weekend, I should be able to do it durin' the relay."

"Won't argue with that. Dive in three—and remember, offer it all to the water."

This time on the block, there's no shakin', no fear.

As we line up at the meet, our coaches give us good luck pats as our teammates give hype-man daps and slaps before they go to the other side to cheer us on.

A part of me wishes I could of invited Jay, Jacob, and Miss Julia, but I stretch my arms and legs, fight to stay centered.

My goal is simple. As the fourth leg of the medley relay and co-captain, I need to help our team crush the local record so Lyric's jaw will drop, and hopefully, his defenses along with it so I can gain his trust.

I see J.D. with his arms crossed near the entrance, leanin' on the side of the bleachers. I tell myself I don't need him here, but seein' him and his nod makes me feel like I can do anythin'.

Lyric gets in startin' position for the backstroke. His arms hold on to the bar in front of the startin' block. Then for a moment, he locks eyes with me. As he settles into position, calmin' his breathin', a warmth spreads in my chest, one that doesn't belong—at least, not to him.

He looks at me, gives me a thumbs-up, which surprises me—and our teammates. We've been fightin' and bickerin' nonstop since I joined, but I finally see it: beneath that shit-talkin' grin and his asshole demeanor, there's a boy like me, hidin' 'cuz he hurtin'.

When the start horn blares, he launches backward ova the water, his body a bow stretched at full length to launch an arrow, as he slices through, barely makin' a splash.

Now the real race begins as his arms flip fast like blades. I'd heard Lyric was a master at the backstroke, but seein' him pull so far ahead of everyone else at breakneck speed, there are no words for it. Well, maybe two—superhuman and effortless.

The next teammate is on the startin' block, as Lyric pushes even faster to go back to the end after swimmin' two laps. Then our teammate dives in, holds our lead in the breaststroke.

As Lyric pulls himself outta the pool, he walks back near

238

me, his eyes glued to the race. The next swimmer, Avery, one of the strongest we have in the butterfly, is already up on the startin' block, hips high and hands clenched at the front of the board.

I stretch my arms but nearly jump outta my skin when I feel hands on my shoulders.

"Hold still," Lyric says behind me. "This always helps me."

I don't know exactly what he does, but the way he massages my shoulders relaxes a stiff area I've been tryin' to reach. I nod a thank-you.

I get on the startin' block.

"You got this. Bring it home," Lyric says.

I look back, but he avoids my eyes, as if embarrassed. There it is again—the sheepish boy behind the eyes of a fierce wolf.

Avery fights to keep the lead on his last lap back. My heart races, my stomach churns. I grip the front of the board. I close my eyes, rememba that I may be the only person on the block, but I have the strength of all those I love.

I soar off the board as Avery returns. At once, I am dominatin' wit dolphin kicks so strong I can almost hear the whip sound underwater. Then just like Lyric, my arms are propellers, nearly liftin' me outta the water. I've hit my rhythm betta than I eva have, and I can feel it—the water like hands pushin' me faster till I'm tinglin' all ova.

I hear the voices of my teammates screamin' my name. All teams do it, but this feels different. It's as if their voices lock arms with the hands of the water, pullin' and pushin', till I'm possessed, like I'm flyin'.

After my last turn underwater, I can barely hear them, but I can feel the energy, the shouts, the electricity. And that's when it clicks, we must still be in the lead. Now is the time to give it everythin' else I got, till all I see is Mum in her sunflower dress, her smile charmin' the sun and her laugh ridin' the wind to my heart. I do it for her, I do it for me, I do it for us.

I slap the wall, almost dizzy from exhaustion.

I don't have time to look at the clock 'cuz a strong pair of arms almost pulls me completely outta the water, and next thing I know, I'm bein' hugged, slapped, and shaken by everyone, all at the same time.

Through the chaos, I hear Lyric's scream: "We did it. We broke the record!"

I look across the water, try to find J.D. He offers a solitary nod and a grin. And before I can say or do anythin', his face changes, and I see someone I least expect—Louis B. J.D. ignores him, leaves before Louis B can say a word.

Lyric appears at Louis B's side, giddy, talkin' a mile a minute.

"Want me to introduce you?" Avery puts his arm around my shoulder, still drippin' wet from the race.

"To who?" I ask, confused.

"Louis Bainbridge. He's one of the biggest backers of our swim team and Providence Prep. He's also Lyric's sponsor, since he's an Olympic hopeful. Between him and my dad, the head of the booster club, anythin' you need you got."

"Maybe some otha time, I gotta change." I jog to the locker room instead, try and get my head right for what's next: the team house party to celebrate our victory.

After the meet, I catch a ride with Avery, since the party is at his house, although most of our teammates are already there since he left the door unlocked for folks to let themselves in. When we pull up, Notorious B.I.G. echoes through the speakers near the backyard pool. Right when you enter the living room, Avery points out the minibar of drinks rangin' from liquor to soda.

Lyric, who has his arms around Saturday, the coach's daughter, suddenly steps away and walks upstairs as he answers a call. He wears a frown as he speaks, almost on the verge of cussin', which makes me wanna follow him. As Saturday waves everyone ova to the backyard pool, I slip outta view and climb the stairs instead, pretendin' I'm lookin' for the bathroom.

Down the hall, in a room with the door cracked, I can hear Lyric, pissed. I cut the light on in the bathroom and close the door, so it looks like someone is in there, and I try to get closer.

Lyric is pacin' with his back to the door, nearly growlin' into the phone even though it's on speaker. He holds a fancy silver pen in his other hand. I rememba him wearin' it in the top pocket of his collared shirt. He holds it tight between his hand and the phone.

"No, *you* don't run shit, Frank. The only person who orders me around is my father, Louis Bainbridge. Remember that," he yell-whispers. Weirdly, he repositions the pen up against the speaker of the phone.

"Nah, you rememba this, Daddy's boy. The only reason Louis B aint got rid of you is cuz you blood. But that's as long as don't nobody else find out you blood. Ya feel me?" Frank says. "So, do what the fuck I tell you to do, othawise you gon be the next one takin a swim in the marsh *after* everybody find out you a Bainbridge."

"You think so, Frank?" Lyric laughs, his voice rugged and guttural. "If I were you, I'd watch what I say and who I say it to. I don't just know where the skeletons are buried, I know who buried them. . . . Fuck around and find out."

Is that pen *recordin'* this?

"Lyric! You gon' taste some of this or what?" Avery yells from downstairs.

I slip into the bathroom in front of me, flush the toilet. I wait a little longer, till I hear Avery drag Lyric back downstairs.

Leroy and PYT were right about Lyric bein' involved, but there's definitely a power struggle in the DKs' camp.

Does that threat mean what I think it does? Wasn't Faa, that Black journalist, found in the marsh? Did Lyric have somethin' to do with his murder?

I splash water on my face and dry it with a towel. I need more answers, which is why I just have to get him to invite me ova to his place, then I'll be ready to use the USB bug PYT and Leroy gave me a couple of days ago.

I open the door and walk downstairs. Before I can look for him, Lyric jumps on me and shoves a red cup in my hand.

"Where you been?" he says, clearly feelin' good on the way to bein' drunk.

"Had to use the restroom."

"Why you ain't use that one right there at the foot of the stairs?" He points.

I lean in close so only he can hear. "'Cuz I had the BGs . . . the bubble guts."

Lyric nods, chuckles. I don't know if he believes me, so I take a long swig from my cup, liquid courage to win his trust.

Saturday dances toward us, rappin' the lyrics from Lauryn Hill's "Doo Wop (That Thing)." She puts her arm around each of our necks and drags us back outside where the party is loud and allurin'.

The more people arrive to Avery's celebratory party, the more drunk Lyric gets. And because everyone seems to know how needy and cranky he gets, as co-captain, I'm officially assigned with "Lyric Duty" by Avery. The only problem is that Lyric is a touchy-feely drunk. He speaks with his hands, holdin' my thighs, arms, and even lap hostage as he carries on conversations with others.

It turns out Lyric is usually the opposite of what he is now, neva happy and a relentless perfectionist, where no victory is big enough. But because we broke the record, everythin' is different, people say. So everyone enjoys Lyric's childish joy and stupor, assumin' he's drunk because he's happy.

I watch him, knowin' better. Whatever Frank said shook him, threatened to unravel all kinds of skeletons. Every now and then, he stares at me deeply or grabs my hand and just holds it, tellin' me randomly not to leave him.

Jay texts me, **Where are you?**

I reply, **Out.**

It's almost 6:30 p.m., and the food and liquor have already almost run dry, but Avery is screamin' 'bout an after-party at the beach with the football players, cheerleaders, and majorettes.

When Jay says he's at Princeton's, I know what to do next. I text Princeton.

Outside of Leroy and PYT, Princeton is the only person I told about my plan, and not 'cuz I wanted to. He found out through Saturday, who told him I was on the team when she was at his mom's community center. It didn't take long for Princeton to call me and not ask but tell me most of what he thought I was up to—a plan to get close to Lyric—even though he didn't know 'bout the Leroy connection.

Princeton said the fastest way to get invited ova to Lyric's place, so I can install the tech, is to wait till Lyric's drunk and neva leave his side. He's especially needy when he's drunk, and if I'm always there, he'll beg me to stay with him.

When I asked Princeton to keep my plan a secret, surprisingly, he agreed. He wouldn't say why, just that there was a history between him and Lyric that he neva wanted to talk 'bout—and it's easier if Jay doesn't know.

Turns out, Princeton was right, because a tipsy and exhausted Lyric has already said he wants to go home at least fifteen times and has begged me to be the person to walk with him, since he lives a few blocks from Avery's.

When Jay texts again, sayin' that he wants to talk, I ask him to make another excuse for why I won't be back yet. Thankfully, he agrees to tell Miss Julia I'm ova there with him and Princeton, which means I can stay with Lyric as long as I need to.

Five minutes and a few stumbles lata, we're in front of his house, which looks very similar to Avery's but has a red door. He drops his keys a third time, so I take ova and try to balance him on my shoulder as I maneuver the lock.

The door opens, and a lady I assume to be Lyric's mom stands there, surprised.

"Lyric?" she says, her next words going in and outta English and Portuguese as she leads us inside.

Lyric rambles loud in his home language, and from what I can tell, introduces me to his mom, Miss Camilah, who is already familiar with me from the swim meet. Then he asks if I can stay the night, a fact I don't realize till after I've managed to get him upstairs.

After he collapses on his bed, mumblin' somethin' I can't

245

quite understand, I spot his computer, which is not far from his bathroom. I make a mental note for lata. It shouldn't be too hard to install PYT's device without attractin' too much attention.

Suddenly my phone vibrates, but I don't have to read it. I know it's Jay probably demandin' an answer tomorrow mornin'. It's one that I don't plan on givin' him, 'cuz he hasn't given me an answer on why he kissed me back and then ran from me.

Having enough of thinkin' 'bout Jay and Lyric hangin' on to me, I try to create some distance, but Lyric pulls me back, clutches his arms around my waist, and begs me to lie down with him. At first, I say no.

Only Lyric won't let me go, and there's somethin' 'bout the way he holds on to me. He buries his head into my stomach and looks up at me, his eyes on the verge of lost and desperate.

Everythin' in me is screamin' to run, to leave—USB bug be damned—because he's a master manipulator. But what if I'm seein' a part of the real him, the side no one else sees? If I reject him now while he's vulnerable and tryin' so hard, how do I know he won't get mad at me and shut me out?

No matta how simple I want it to be, it's complicated. Each decision comes with its own risks, and although I could come back in the future, time is a luxury Mum doesn't have. I'm here right now.

I agree to stay, but only after puttin' him in a headlock and remindin' him what will happen if he touches me without my permission. When he taps out and says, "Uncle," I release him, and he sits on the bed starin' at me.

"So, if I ask this time, will you let me?" Lyric strokes his throat and jaw, tryna drum up sympathy that I'll neva let him know exists.

"Let you what?"

"Hold you."

"Why would I do that?"

Lyric moves closer, made bolder and fearless in the moonlight. I watch his shadow touch mine, even though he's too far away to actually touch. "Because you want somebody to hold you, too."

I don't mean to, but a crack appears in the mask I'm wearin'. I change my mind and eye the door, but he hooks his pinky around mine, and I swear it's like a lasso around my heart.

I pull away, flash heat behind my eyes, and remind him of my threat from earlier. I clench my fist, ready to make good on my promise.

"You got somebody else to hold you?" He moves closer. "That why you sayin' no?"

"How's that any of your business?" My voice cracks, and I wish it didn't.

My phone vibrates again.

"You need to answer that?"

We both look at it. I don't pick it up, which is an answer. Lyric doesn't say anythin' else, at least not with words. He doesn't have to. Instead, he pulls somethin' from one of his drawers in the dresser and places it softly next to me. It's a new ribbed tank and pair of silk boxers still in the package, unopened.

He walks to his bathroom, turns on the shower, and closes the door.

I see what I should do next. It plays in my mind ova and ova, me gettin' up and walkin' out, but I can't, no matter how hard I try. I don't want Lyric to be right; I don't want to go home to an empty bed, yearnin' for someone I know won't be there.

I don't want to, not tonight. So I watch the shadows of the trees sway in the throes of their own heartbreak, sliced into pieces by the window blinds. I pull up the blinds so the trees can sway whole in peace.

When Lyric opens the bathroom door, he emerges in white and navy-blue boxers, dryin' the remainin' droplets of water from his chest and back. His movements are still sleepy from the liquor. I don't say anythin', but I grab the clothes and walk into the bathroom. A steamy cloud of spices I've neva smelled togetha—notes of vanilla, dates, and herbs—washes ova me. I drown out the shouldn'ts, take a shower, and dry off, only puttin' on the silk boxers.

When I walk to the bed, Lyric is already asleep. At least,

I think he is. But when I get in on the otha side, his eyes are there to meet me. This time, he doesn't ask me, he doesn't have to 'cuz on my face he can see the answer.

I clarify, so he isn't mistaken. "Just this one time."

"Okay, this one time." He places his head on my chest.

Just this time, for him, for me.

Lyric falls asleep to the sound of my heartbeat, and for a second, I'm glad he's not starin' at me, 'cuz it means he can't see my stubborn tears, me wishin' he was Jay.

I wait till it's the middle of the night. Lyric is close but no longer usin' my chest as a pillow, and the house is quiet. I rememba PYT's words: *You don't have to do anythin', just plug the USB bug in and leave it for one minute till the light at the end turns green.*

Now is my only chance, but I don't know if Lyric is really sleepin'. So, after four false starts to test, I watch if his eyelids flutter. When they don't and I hear his steady snore remain uninterrupted, I slide outta the bed, pull the USB outta my pants folded up on the nightstand, and walk quietly toward the bathroom.

I leave the light on and the water runnin'. I pretend like I need to walk back to get somethin' as I slide the USB into his CPU tower without breakin' my stride. But suddenly his monitor cuts on, shines so bright I'm afraid it'll wake him up.

As I search for a way to turn off the monitor, I see the pen from earlier, but it's attached to a cord that is plugged into the CPU tower. He's definitely usin' that pen to—

The computer tower clicks and starts the fan, loud. I'm doin' everythin' I can to turn it off when Miss Camilah walks by the door.

There she stands, watchin' me.

I turn off the monitor. I want to say somethin', offer an excuse of why this isn't what it looks like, even though it is. Only there's no time because she disappears down the hall.

Frightened and unsure of what will happen next, I run back to the bathroom to cut off the faucet and turn off the light. When the USB bug glows green, I remove it and slip it back into my pocket, as if I'm just placin' my phone back inside.

When I'm back under the covers, I expect Lyric to stay where he is, but as if by muscle memory, he returns to my chest and intertwines his legs with mine.

I look down at him, watch his face stir slightly and settle. My hands have a mind of their own as they trace his thick eyebrows, the outline of his full lips. He pulls closer, nestles his face deeper into my neck, and adjusts his thighs so he lies more comfortably on me. Right now, even after installin' the tech, I wonder, *Which one is the real Lyric?*

There's the cold and calculatin' person who argued with Frank and then there's the swimmer doing everythin' he can to make the dad he can neva talk 'bout proud of him. More importantly, *Which one should I fear?*

17

Leroy

I wait fuh Mistah Prez after class and watch as he keep blowin people's minds wit answers in the form of questions.

"Mr. Leroy, just the man I wanted to see." Mistah Prez packs up his bag and nods fuh me to follow. "Every time you're in class, I'm reminded of how much we need your brilliance."

Mistah Prez's words drag a smile across my face, even tho smilin is the last thing I feel like doin right now. In the hallway, he talks in between waves to errbody he passes.

"I would've thought you would be beaming with joy right about now," he says.

"Whatchu mean?"

"I saw your GED scores. They are the highest we've seen in the history of our program. Didn't they tell you?"

I nod but don't really say much. I still don't know how I feel bout it.

We arrive at the front office and Mistah Prez turns to his secretary. "Hey, Mrs. Barbara, can you push my meetings back by forty-five minutes? I want to chat over a few things with C-Pote Tech's VIP."

Mistah Prez presses his hands down on my shoulders, then points me in the direction of his office. There are two comfy-lookin chairs, a table, and a couch, but they all look too nice to be used, like somebody's aunt or unc need to come wrap it in a plastic cover so it'll last forever.

Mistah Prez invites me to sit at the table next to the comfy chairs as he goes to one of his many bookshelves, pulls out a few books.

"Have you told your folks about your scores?"

"Nah, not yet."

"Why not? You should let them celebrate you. Those kinds of scores don't come easy, even for naturally brilliant students like yourself."

The truth trickles outta my lips. "What if they not happy?"

"Why wouldn't they be?" His eyes watch my hands. They keep tappin, fidgetin without my permission. "Said differently, why aren't *you* happy?"

I look down and try to find words, but I keep comin up blank.

"Do you ever feel like you have a problem with words sometimes—like they are gone when you need them the most?" Mistah Prez asks.

I nod. *All the time.*

"Me too. I find it's not because I don't have them, but perhaps, I have too many words running through my mind at one time, and as a result, I get overwhelmed. I want you to try something for me." Mistah Prez takes out a sheet of paper from the printer and hands me a pen that's heavy, looks like black marble lined wit gold. "Write whatever scares you about your high scores and maybe the opportunities or feelings that come with them. And when you're done, you can ball up the paper and throw it away or you can just use it as a point of reference if you feel comfortable telling me what's on your mind."

I take the paper and pen in my hands, unsure of what to write—or think. But befo I know it, my hand is scribblin on its own as words pour onto the page. My hand already aches, but I feel like I'm just gettin started.

When it all starts to slow down, I read back ova my words, tryna make sense of what they mean. It aint easy, but Mistah Prez was right, this helps. I say the first thing I started writin bout, "Ion really know what happens next, like, after these high scores. What am I supposed to do?"

"Whatever you want."

"But that's the thing. I'm only here cuz you said I should take yo class and I promised my brotha I would get my GED so he could finally be proud of me and not think all I know how to do is fuck up." I cover my mouth, aint mean to cuss like that.

Mistah Prez waves it off and just chuckles. "You sure that's how your brother feels about you, or is that how you see yourself?"

Aint nobody eva really described me as talented or smart, but that paper wit them scores say somethin different.

"Open this and read a few of the pieces." Mistah Prez hands me a book. It's slim wit a dope cover I can't help but stare at.

I read it fuh a coupla minutes, and I aint neva read no stuff like this. Not just poetry, but stories and essays. The way the words dance on the page hit me in the heart and make me feel things is wild.

"That's an anthology of a nationwide competition for young writers."

I rub the cover wit my hands fuh good luck, wonder if I could eva see my words in somethin like this.

"The editor, who selects all the authors and their pieces for the issues, is a good friend of mine. Remember when I asked if I could share one of your poems from the last assignment about harm and healing with a friend of mine? She's the one. After reading your work, she wanted me to ask if you'd be interested in being published in their next edition."

"In a book like this?" Ion think I heard him right.

"Not just the book. The editor runs a special program at a university in the Midwest, Wisconsin to be exact, where you could get a full ride to study creative writing as a college student. It's one of the top writing programs in the country. She would like for you to apply."

Ion mean to look at him like he crazy, it's just hard to believe.

"You don't have to answer now, but take that book and this." He hands me a white and red brochure. "Let me know if you, or your family, have any questions."

My phone vibrates—it's Taj.

"Duty calls?" Mistah Prez says.

"Yeah, my brotha here to pick me up." I fold the paper I wrote on and slide it into the pages of the book wit the brochure.

I wanna read em both lata. Iono what to do wit the pen, it's so nice. I give it back so he don't think I'm tryna steal it. That's the kind of pen you miss.

"How about you keep it?"

"You sho?" I rememba Rouk and Auntie Rissa. *Errthang you touch you break.*

"Every writer should have a special pen, so you are reminded of how valuable your words are."

Mrs. Barbara calls fuh Mistah Prez, and he walks me out to the front of the office and waves goodbye. I wander out the doors, lost in thought.

I neva thought any of this could happen—that I would get a chance to get my GED, go to college, maybe even move away. Ioeno if I want to, but wit errthang goin on, maybe change wouldn't be too bad. But I would only wanna do it if Taj down. If I told him, would he be proud? What if he think

I'm tryna leave him again and he get upset?

The closer I get to the parkin lot, I can hear Taj in the car singin at the top of his lungs to "Ex-Factor" by Lauryn Hill. People who walk by smilin, mumblin the words too.

"Whey Night at?" I hop in the passenger seat, stretch out my legs, mo excited than I thought to finally have enough legroom.

"He already at the spot wit PYT, Rouk, and Brown Brown. I wanted to get you myself since we aint really had much time fuh a one-on-one wit errthang that's been going on."

I aint really thought bout how little we been seein of each otha since we got into it wit Pops and stormed out the apartment. Between Operation Love Letter, us tryna keep tabs on the YGs, and mo clashes between the popos ova shit the DKs been doin usin the BDs' name, there aint been much time to sit still.

I've only gotten to see him these days when he kiss me on the forehead befo he leave, usually while I'm half sleep. Today's the first day he's lettin me in on what he's been workin on wit Auntie Rissa and Lady Tee, our new secret YGs headquarters just fuh us. It's where me, PYT, Brown Brown, Rouk, and every now and then Trish will monitor errthang we gettin from the tech fuh Operation Love Letter.

Princeton and Jay will learn about it too since they gon prolly have to visit time to time. But iono, tho, things have been awkward wit Jay. I'm gettin used to the phone calls, but when I see him in person, it hurts all ova again, and I can't think straight.

"How was class?" Taj pulls outta the parkin lot, drives toward downtown.

"It was cool."

He looks ova at me like he always do when he expectin me to use mo of my words. I won't plannin on it, but I decide to play a trick on him befo I give him the good news bout my GED test scores.

I let go of the smile on my face and look out the window, barely lookin at him.

"Whatchu do?" He grips the steerin wheel on the way to bein mad.

"Nothin."

"Lee, save that shit fuh somebody else. Get to it, and you betta make it quick."

I shrug, tryna feel out how far I can take it befo I let out the truth.

"You got kicked outta C-Pote? That instructor been fuckin witchu again?" He lookin fuh where he can flip a U-turn and go back up to the school.

"I'm playin. It's nothin like that."

"Don't lie." He look ova at me, clenchin his teeth, tryna calm down.

"I'm not, I aint get kicked out. Aint bad news at all. I got my GED scores."

"Okay." He takes a deep breath, prepare fuh somethin, even tho I already told him it won't bad news. "Whatchu waitin fuh, lay it on me."

I tell him the scores. I can see him calculatin based on when he took it. Then he yell so loud it makes me jump.

At the red light, he damn near climb ova the armrest to place a big, sloppy kiss on my forehead as he shakes me. The light turns green, and people honkin behind us cuz he still won't move. Even as they speed round, honkin mad, Taj don't care.

I laugh till I see him brush away tears.

He don't say nothin at first, just nods, tryna keep it togetha. Then he flips a U-turn at the next intersection and finds his smile again.

"Where we goin? I thought we was headed to the new YG spot?"

"Takin a quick detour. Can't miss this chance to celebrate, just me and you." Befo he say anythin else, I can tell by how he grinnin where we headed: BaBa's Seafood, home of one of the best low-country boils and Dungeness crabs in K-Town—maybe all of Savannah.

It's the first of the month, so luckily we at BaBa's early enough to avoid the rush as errbody and they momma get seafood rich as they swipe food stamp cards, buyin bushels of cooked crabs, spicy or garlic conch by the pint, and low-country boils by the tray.

At the counter, Guo take orders four and five at a time. He may be only a few years older than Taj, but he speaks multiple languages, includin Savannah K-Town slang, where our words sing and tilt sideways while our bodies back it up.

Guo's eyes light up while he flash pritty white teeth in two rows, shinin when he sees Taj. And twenty minutes lata, we headin back to the car wit our bags and cherry Fanta sodas. Aint long befo Taj pull up at Daffin Park near the water fountains, where we sit, eatin Dungeness crabs and sharin a low-country boil. Taj keep eatin up all the damn sausages. I aint mad, cuz he ordered extra jumbo shrimp just fuh me.

"So when you wanna tell Auntie Rissa and Ma? I can see em both gettin shirts made. Ma's sayin she gave birth to two geniuses and Auntie Rissa sayin she helped raise em," Taj says.

"Iono, maybe this weekend."

"What's on ya mind? C'mon, talk to me."

It takes one cluster of Dungeness crabs and just bout all the shrimp and sausages in the boil fuh me to do it, but I finally tell him bout my convo wit Mistah Prez, my work bein published, and the school up in the Midwest.

Taj hangs on every word, suckin, chewin, and crackin shells.

When I'm finished, he still aint said much. Instead, he asks me to walk wit him. We listen to the water droplets dance across the pond and feel the mist from the fountain carried our way by the breeze. We stop where it feels best, like tiny kisses on our foreheads.

"I think you should do it." Taj picks up a twig, breaks it into smaller pieces, and throws em as far into the water as he can, one by one. "I know you scared, but I think you gotta do it anyway. Whatchu givin me that look fuh?"

My eyes say it, not my lips: *Ion wanna leave you behind.*

Taj squints, pulls me in by my head, and my hands wrap round him. Iono why good news like this hurts.

"Quit makin it seem like you gon be up there all by yoself, all lonely and sad." Wait, what? He sayin what I think he sayin?

"You would leave here and come wit me?"

"You just gon have to see." He pauses before askin, "How you feel bout Pops bein back?"

The question catches me off guard. I can't bring myself to say the truth in case he might feel different.

"Right, I feel the same way." He chuckles. "All this really got me thinkin if it's time to do somethin else like Auntie Rissa said."

"You would leave the BDs?" Is *that* why he said I aint gotta go to college alone? He thinkin bout walkin away from it all? "But what bout all you sacrificed? Errthang you went through to unify the gangs."

"I did all that to keep us safe. Iono if it's worth it if I gotta fight Pops just to keep it. I'm just tired of trustin people and em breakin my heart."

He don't say it, but I know he talm bout what Auntie Rissa and Ma did. Taj actually looked up to Pops, missed him the most since he been gone. Them keepin the truth hidden from him feels like anotha betrayal on top of too many to begin wit.

Taj's phone rings, and he looks down at it, frowns. "We gotta head to the south side real quick. Sani and the Low Rider Crew wanna talk. This might be our only chance to keep em in the BDs, maybe even get em on board wit Operation Love Letter."

After pullin up at Edda Nae's, me and Taj let her hold our faces and tell us things bout ourselves only she knows. That I'm heartbroken but still got the face of a boy in love; that Taj gotta let go and let God if he gon eva get the answer to his questions.

When Husani and his crew roll up—the rims of their Skittles-colored tricked-out cars, vans, and bicycles glitter colors and shapes on the asphalt—she holds they faces as well, tells Husani he gotta trust, even when it hurts.

When we full on her love, Edda Nae sends us to walk and talk on the block while we eat thrills, each of us eatin the frozen sweet a different way. Taj waits fuh Husani and his right hand, Khalif, a redbone wit orange locs, to speak first. Some of Husani's people stand posted up, engines on, ready.

After what Pops did to Husani, aint no otha BDs been

allowed on they territory.

"Yo pops fulla shit, you know that, right?" Husani sucks, then chews, slow struttin like he bowlegged to prove a point. He aint rushin fuh nobody, especially now.

"Aint disagreein witchu on that. So how you gon play this?" Taj says, stoppin and facin him.

"You know I was the first one on board, same time as Night when he put it all on the line to convince the Black Rydas to join you. But where he had to beg, I told my niggas to fall back and get in line cuz we doin this."

"Yeah, and I hope you still trust and believe in me."

"But am I right, tho?" Husani says. "You willin to put yo life on the line to keep us safe? I aint talm bout dyin—"

"I know whatchu mean. I heard some of the YGs askin the same thing. If I'm willin to fight my pops to protect what I—we—created."

Taj aint said things was *this* bad.

"Good. Then lemme make it real clear: if yo pops try to take the BDs from you and Auntie Rissa, we gon see it fuh the only thing it is, war."

"You serious?" Taj looks just as shocked as I do, but Husani and Khalif just laugh, like he the one just cracked a joke.

"We followed you cuz you aint just talk. When shit went down, you was here, got fucked up right along wit us as the popos tried to raid our homes and slap us wit bogus charges," Husani continues. "Even how you kept Brown Brown and

Rouk safe, when they acted against you. You showed errbody what true respect look like. Yo pops aint the same—least not no mo."

Taj nods, takin it all in.

"Aight, I said my piece," Husani says. "Now, what's on yo mind?"

Taj's eyes tap me in, and Husani and Khalif motion fuh me to speak.

"We workin on the plan me, Taj, Auntie Rissa, and the BD council approved befo errthang went down. And we heard through the grapevine that one of yo crew members, Nate, mighta witnessed, maybe even filmed, the kidnappin of—"

"The Blue Jay," Khalif finishes my sentence. "How yall know bout that? Errbody I know lips is sealed—fuh a reason."

I promised Trish I wouldn't say no names. "We got eyes and ears in places we aint neva had befo. And cuz we still got Brown Brown in our corner, we made a connect in the police department who might see things our way, if we show some real evidence . . ."

"Sound like you askin fuh a favor." Khalif grins.

"That's what I heard." Husani laughs, tongue blue wit the Popsicle stick from the thrill danglin at the corner of his mouth. "When you need him?" Husani looks ova at me. "Tell me when and where, and he'll be there wit bells, camcorder and all."

Errbody hugs it out, signalin the meetin ova, and then we

all walk back to our cars. Befo Taj leave furreal this time, Husani salutes him, tell him to think real hard bout what he said, hit him up wit his answer in a few days. Taj agrees.

We hop in the car and head downtown to the new BD spot. When Taj pulls up near Lady Tee's building and walks to a beauty salon, I look at him, confused. "I thought we was goin to Lady Tee's? Aint the new spot in there?"

The way Taj smiles, I can tell I'm in fuh a real surprise. I follow him to the door wit a black and baby-blue sign in cursive that reads "Luscious Looks."

When Taj open the door, a wave of sweet smells rush ova us, argan oil and spices. Past the waitin lounge wit love seats that look mo like thrones is a long walkway wit salon chairs on both sides in front of mirrors lined in lights. I aint realize it till now that it's both a barbershop and a beauty salon.

"Yall takin fuheva, aint it?" PYT calls from across the room, near the shampoo stations. He got his hair out and the closer he walks to us, the mo I see it. Errbody swoon and shake, hearts stoppin and learnin to beat again.

PYT hugs Taj, then hooks his arm round my neck, guides me toward the back to walk down some stairs. After the third set, we turn left, and it's like we in a whole otha buildin.

At the end of the hallway, we enter anotha door, and suddenly we in a room that look like a legit headquarters wit computers linin a corner in the back. There's desks near tinted glass walls to the right of a big table where Brown Brown, Rouk, Night, and Trish sit, scannin through papers in mid-conversation.

Trish jumps up, adds her arm round my neck on top of PYT's. I sit down, and Brown Brown nods to say hello but finishes starin at some papers that look like copies of one of Faa's journals.

"Night said you were held up wit Husani and the Low Rider Crew. How'd it go?" Trish asks.

Errbody all eyes and ears, even Brown Brown. They listen to Taj explain just bout errthang we learned from Husani, except the question of whether Taj would lead the fight against the OGs. Keepin that part out mean we can just focus on the fact that Husani gave permission fuh Nate to talk to Detective Dane—and wit evidence even he can't deny.

Now we just gotta figure out when and where.

Auntie Rissa comes through the door wit Benji, carryin bags of goodies: fried catfish and collards, French fries, and some new desserts, prolly from Miss Julia. She goes round givin her hugs, but errbody notice that when she hug me and Taj, it's different.

There's tension.

It was hard enough tryna bounce back from Rouk's and Brown Brown's betrayals, but what Ma and Auntie Rissa did just hit different.

Taj repeats a lil bit of what he mentioned befo Auntie

Rissa arrived, then asks Brown Brown, "You think you can make it happen?"

"The meetin wit Detective Dane? Yeah. Where yall want it to be? I know he can't come here. . . ."

"Lady Tee's?" Taj says.

"How bout the Bee Baptist church?" Auntie Rissa says. "It's close to downtown, not far from the police station."

Taj agrees.

"Cool, lemme confirm wit Pastor Beatrice and First Lady Jeanine. But we should be good to meet round there, no problem," Auntie Rissa says.

"Bet, I'll call Dane and set it up," Brown Brown says.

"You think he suspicious bout you? Now might be yo chance to pay him a visit and plant the tech in his office," Taj says.

"No, we still good." Brown Brown shakes his head, talkin between French fry bites. "I'll head to the precinct tomorrow and get it done."

"It's prolly a good time fuh you to link up wit Jay and Princeton now that we got who our next big target is," Trish says to me.

"Uh . . . yeah, I'm on it," I say. Iono how I feel bout seein Jay again so soon. After last time at Ronaldo's, it hurt too much to even be round him, but I can't think bout that right now.

"Who is it?" Taj asks. "The target?"

"We all know the district attorney is crooked, so we

thinkin our way into the department is Risé, Assistant District Attorney Butler's younger siblin," Trish says.

"They work at H-Cubed sometimes, right? A year or two older than you too if I rememba correctly," Auntie Rissa says. "They are a part of the Pearl Crew. Most of the proceeds from Risé's parties go to their network supportin trans, nonbinary, and gender nonconforming folx."

"Yup, that's Risé, one of the biggest DJ and club promoters in Savannah right now, which means we gotta reach out quick because they're so famous," Trish explains. "I got class after school, but Lee and PYT, could yall make it to Daniel Lee lata this week and talk to Jay and Princeton?"

"Anythin else from the tech at Ronaldo's? Was Jay and Princeton able to connect wit anybody, get mo names?" Taj brings us back to the present.

"Actually, yeah. They been hustlin hard, I aint gon lie. Cuz of the tech we got at Ronaldo's, we got bout thirty names and companies. Between Tina's and my connections at Providence Prep and otha schools, we been able to link almost all of the names wit one of our classmates and sell em on the love letters. Jay and Princeton been able to upload the tech durin most visits wit the clients."

"I been able to track errthang from keystrokes to monitorin screens," PYT jumps in, "and sometimes even a lil audio."

"Dayum, all that from love letters?" Taj say, impressed.

267

"That's been part of it, but I gotta shout out Rouk," Trish says. "If he aint damn near had that codex and so many of those journals translated and almost memorized, we wouldn'ta known who important and who not when a name pop up. Cuz of him, we been able to track the money and find out *why* people tied up wit the Bainbridges."

"And since just bout errthang the Bainbridges do barely got a paper trail, we been able to track the favors done fuh and by the Bainbridges wit Faa's notes," Rouk adds.

"That gon be enough?" I ask. "We all saw it; Louis B got the DA, the chief of police, half the detectives."

"Depends on how we use it. But me and Trish mighta found somethin else, somethin important. Faa aint just get the flash drive from research, someone close to the Bainbridges gave it to him. Mentions the initials CB."

"Who is CB?" Taj says.

"Iono, but me and Trish lookin into it, combin through mo journals to see what we can find. Whoeva it is, they know mo than just the donation list. They may know where *all* the Bainbridges' secrets are buried."

Me, Taj, and Auntie Rissa look at each otha. This could give us errthang we need to end this once and fuh all.

"So we need to keep doing what we been doin, trackin down all these leads," Taj announces. "And if yall can connect wit Risé, we gon figure out what ADA Butler knows soon enough."

"And I can check wit Will today, too, and see if he got anythin on Lyric yet," I say. "But what's the long game? How we gon use all this information?"

The room go quiet. How you supposed to beat somebody who already got errthang they need and can crush you without even thinkin twice?

"Use it to break em," Taj says. "On one hand, it sounds like Louis B got it all, but there's a catch to doin all that dirt. Errbody he do a deal wit is a snake that could bite and poison him too. We figure out what we need to shake errbody up, then they gon get real honest."

"And who knows, maybe yo pops can go back up north wit Miss Rosalind when we rescue her, and this will all be ova," PYT mumbles under his breath.

"PYT . . . ," Auntie Rissa says, firm.

PYT apologizes fuh speakin outta turn but not fuh what he said. The eyes round the room show he aint the only one who feel that way, least of all me and Taj.

I can tell Auntie Rissa senses it, too. She been workin double time tryna clean up the mess Pops created, always on the phone puttin out fires. Right now, her and Ma are the only ones that keep in contact wit him. Me and Taj keep turnin her down errtime.

"Anythin else?" Auntie Rissa asks, pinchin the bridge of her nose and tappin her hot pink nails.

Taj gives me permission to talk bout what really needs

to be said: the YGs' revolt. "Cuz of what Pops did, the YGs aint just mad, they don't trust the OGs." Auntie Rissa sits up, leanin outta reach of Benji's hands. "If Pops try to force they hand and do anythin else like he did befo, it could start somethin bigger."

"A war between the OGs and the YGs," Taj says, lockin eyes wit Auntie Rissa.

"War? We can't afford to—"

"And if they do, Imma lead it," Taj says.

Errbody look shook just hearin Taj's words, even I aint expect that. I thought he was gon think bout it. Don't matta, guess he's made his decision.

"Taj," Auntie Rissa says. "Are you serious right now?"

"He aint got no otha choice," Night says. "If he don't step in—"

"The DKs could flip errbody who fall out and aint got no home." The words slip out my mouth.

"Is this yo theory, or you speakin cuz you know?" Benji asks.

"The Black Rydas done already made it known. Twenty otha crews have, too, if my count is correct—and that was as of last week. Prolly even mo now," Night says.

An uncomfortable silence falls ova all of us. If twenty of the crews already pledged their loyalty to Taj, that's already half of all the crews.

Auntie Rissa looks ova at Taj and says, "You sho bout this, Bittersweet?"

270

"I am, Auntie. You raised me to treat people we love—and even those we don't—wit respect. Pops violated that."

Auntie Rissa shakes her head and takes a deep breath. Benji massages mo strength into her. He aint gotta say what we all see workin its way through her mind and heart. Pops aint actin in hers, Taj's, or the BDs' best interest, not in the way they created it—only his own.

"Just gimme the day to process this," Auntie Rissa says. "I know what you sayin, and I know I can't stop you eitha, but lemme think. In the meantime, we can stay at it and move forward wit what yall already got in motion."

18

JAY

No matter how I try to talk myself up, today is just not a good day. I woke up feeling more alone than ever, I barely got any sleep, and when I did, I kept having nightmares of Leroy turning his back on me, disappearing from my life forever.

I know we have an in-person meeting with Leroy and PYT to talk about the next big person for Operation Love Letter, but I feel like I'm dangling by a thread, and I don't know why. All I can ask myself is, will I feel like this forever? Will it ever end?

After school, as we walk over to Leroy and PYT, Princeton keeps me grounded, but as soon as I see Leroy, I feel like I'd barrel toward him, a kamikaze of pain, until I disappeared into nothingness. I want—no, I need—him to save me.

"We're here as promised." Princeton breaks away to dap Leroy and PYT up, before he's back at my side. "Y'all got our next VIP client?"

"Word on the street is you connected to Risé." PYT looks at Princeton.

"Why? Ain't I cool enough?" He grins. But there's something he isn't saying.

"Who is Risé?" I say, trying to understand what's making Princeton, the master of cool, respond this way.

"They're one of the most popular DJs and promoters, known for throwing house parties you'll never forget," Princeton answers.

"And the younger sibling of Assistant District Attorney Butler," PYT says.

"Are you thinking that the ADA is crooked too?" I ask.

"No, we pritty sho she's clean after Brown Brown bugged Detective Dane's office a coupla days ago," Leroy says. "A call came in from her to Dane's personal phone, and she asked him to meet but wouldn't say nothin else. And we got to wonderin, why would the ADA be callin by-the-book Dane off the record on his personal line? Then we overheard the police chief cussin out Dane cuz both the BDs and DKs got arrest warrants. They only gave him the stack of the YGs, said somebody else was gon handle the 'otha' BDs, but Dane been grabbin the DKs anyway."

"And this after we connected Dane to Nate and got to show him the footage of Miss Rosalind gettin kidnapped," PYT says, jumping in. "He been suspicious bout the DKs, cuz he brought the police report, signed and closed out by the chief himself. He lookin into stuff on the side based on the video, so don't nobody find out. The moment we got some real evidence or her location, he said we can count on him."

"But the important part is that when he do bring a YG to

court, the case be gettin mysteriously dropped on a techni-cality," Leroy adds. "We thinkin the ADA and Dane runnin game on both the chief and the DA."

"If you're saying that ADA Butler's ordering the charges to be dropped, then why do we still need to bug her? You know she's already on our side, then, even if she doesn't know it," I say, rubbing my temples. My head is starting to hurt trying to follow all these twists and turns.

"Cuz the mo information we got, the mo options we got. It looks like Dane and the ADA know the difference between BDs and DKs cuz of how they movin, but we don't know fuh sho, and we still need eyes and ears in the district attorney's department," PYT says. "So like we said, you need to find a way to get into Risé's party this weekend."

"I can make that happen, but I'mma need Christina's help," Princeton answers.

"Why?" I ask. What isn't he saying?

"If we bring Risé on as a love letter client, I already know who they gon' wanna write a love letter to."

"Who?"

"Me. So she gotta be the one to make the connect." It's written all on Princeton's forehead: *Don't ask, it's complicated.*

Throwing him a lifeline, I get us back on topic. "Do we know where the party's going to be?" I ask, looking at Leroy. He motions back over to Princeton.

"Risé's spot," Princeton says. "Lemme make a few calls real quick then I'll be right back. I'll hit up Trish, too, 'cuz we'll def' need her help 'cuz there's a dress code."

As he walks out of earshot, I feel exposed, alone. I try to ignore the questions everyone else is also wondering about. *Why is Risé in love with Princeton? And does it mean they were ever together?*

I look off into the distance and get lost somewhere in the tops of the trees. I think about how trees have seen it all, so they too must know heartbreak.

"I'm gon take a call, too," PYT says, stepping back.

Leroy tries to order him back with his eyes, but anyone who has met PYT knows he is like Will, ordered around by no one.

Here me and Leroy stand, unwilling and uncertain.

"Will you ever forgive me?" The words jump out. It's been repeating in my mind over and over, and I just can't hold it in any longer.

"Iono," Leroy says. My chest aches.

"That's it?" Really?

"Jay, whatchu want me to say?" You know what I want you to say.

"I told you I was sorry." Forgive me. Please.

"So cuz you said you was sorry, it aint supposed to hurt no mo?"

"But I forgave you," I snap back. "Why can't you forgive me?"

"Did you?"

The words stuck in my throat grow claws and threaten to tear me apart from the inside out. Leroy refuses to even look at me—no, not look, see me, as if whatever I was, we were, it never even existed.

"Aye, we in!" Princeton jogs back, but I really wish he hadn't.

Princeton and Leroy swap words, but they just crash around my ears. My eyes start to burn. To save the little pride I have left, I walk away toward the promenade of trees, slow and deliberate, but when my knees feel like they're about to buckle, I run to keep from falling as the tears leap with abandon.

I don't hear him at first, not until I'm near the spot where Leroy first became my protector. It's Princeton, calling after me.

I just need to get around the corner, out of sight so I can finally break down. When I do, I stop, heaving. I can't catch my breath, but I at least try to wipe my face. Princeton sees me, and it's all on his face, pity or something like it.

I don't care. I'm no longer ashamed, I just can't keep putting on a brave face. I'm tired. I'm just so tired. That's why, when Princeton deliberately steps in front of me so the others walking by can't see me, I embrace the scent of Old Spice and Egyptian musk.

It's a quiet meltdown, more ache and tears than sound. Princeton finally lets me go, wipes my face, and just stands in silent solidarity.

Leroy's car pulls up to the corner, near the stop sign. I wait for him to hop out, run over to make sure I'm okay.

But he glances over at me, and then just like that, he drives away, never looking back.

"Aye, you don't look too good. You aight?" Princeton says, crouching down so he's looking up.

I shake my head, fight back the dizziness threatening to slap me horizontal.

"Want me to run you home?"

"No." The word shoots out louder than I mean it to. "I don't want to go home, not now."

"Then let's go to my spot instead."

Together, we walk to his car, me fighting back tears and him drying them.

One day has turned into one week at Princeton's. I didn't mean for it to happen but, after we got to his place, I kept breaking down over and over, to the point I had to have a long talk with Dr. Eva. She recommended I stay, take a break from everything, and use it as an opportunity to recover.

Now I feel better, stronger, and lighter. I don't know if it's because of Lady Tee's tonics or Dr. Eva's meals and meditation, but I'm no longer drowning in tears.

Momma was grateful to talk with Dr. Eva about some ideas on how to help all three of us process the trauma we've been through. Since then, I get daily calls or texts from her, and Jacob even calls to talk to me and Princeton on speakerphone.

Will . . . Well, nothing's changed with him or Leroy, for that matter.

No word. No call. No text.

I'd be lying if I said I didn't care, but I can be honest and say I'll be fine regardless. But standing in front of the mirror after Trish puts the finishing touches on our outfits for Risé's party, which officially starts in an hour, I'm getting cold feet.

The theme is gods and goddesses, and as I learned from Christina and Trish's talks about costume ideas, Risé's parties are like the Met Gala, invite-only, featuring outfits created by up-and-coming designers, which is why Trish agreed to do ours.

"Whatchu think?" Trish says as she adds the last pats of powder to my face. I'd like to run somewhere and hide, but when Princeton comes in from changing, it's too late. He whoops and hollers. I want to do the same for him, but I'm speechless, shook.

Around Princeton's forehead is a white silk fabric that flows down his back, and his shoulders are draped with a pearl chain-mail net that stops just above his abs. Off-white, low-riding leather shorts and knee-high sandal boots pop against his legs and thighs. Every part of him glows, shimmers. And when he smiles, both dimples come out to play. I want to say it out loud so everyone can hear: *That's my best friend!*

He beats me to the punch, turns me back toward the mirror. "Damn, Trish! I knew you was gon' do it, but you really did it."

"I didn't make it to fashion week fuh nothin." She grins, still adding final touches.

Standing next to me, Princeton admires the pearl-studded headpiece with a crystal birdcage veil that stops just above my nose. There are oversized pearls around my neck, and a sheer top embroidered with pearl beads around the midriff and my wrists. I'm in high-waisted shorts that stop halfway down my thigh and pearl-colored Belgian loafers.

Together, Princeton and I match. Our outfits worship our dark skin, which Trish now sprays with a mist that makes every part of us sparkle even more.

"Where's Christina?" Princeton says.

"She'll be here any minute now," Trish answers.

"Is that when you're going to reveal your outfit as well?" I say.

This whole time, Trish has been in a cloak, and under it is what seems like a firmly fitting one piece, but I think it's meant to conceal her actual outfit so she could just focus on us.

"Maybe." She grins.

An all-black stretch Hummer pulls up in front of Princeton's house, and I wonder if somebody accidentally chose us for MTV's *Super Sweet 16*. But Christina peeks her head out of the window, face shimmering with makeup that makes her shine like the goddess she's always been. On top of Christina's head now sits a golden tiara that looks like a spiked halo.

It perfectly hugs the top of her braided bun surrounded by hair ringlets shaped like roses.

Inside, Princeton and I sit on the other side, listening to Trish and Christina chat and giggle. He rarely drops his smile, but I know he's nervous. Not just about having to install tech in Risé's house, specifically ADA Butler's room, but to know I'll be writing a love letter (or some kind of letter), and he will be the recipient.

"How long have you known Risé, Princeton?" Christina asks.

"Since we were little, but apparently our families go way back. Their family is actually the reason my mom is where she is. They were one of her first clients when she was barely outta law school."

The gravity of the event finally settles in as we see a line of limos and black SUVs.

When we get out of the limousine, we marvel at the property, then follow a stone sidewalk to the sound of music and laughter. Everywhere around the paved path is beautifully wild, full of Russian sage swaying next to fountain grass and rubbing shoulders with black-eyed Susans. But the showstoppers are the pansies and violas blushing rich reds and deep oranges.

Past the winding road we grow closer to the flashes, and that's our cue.

"I'll take those," Trish says.

As we shed our protective silk cloaks, we emerge as embers in the setting sun. It's as if Trish planned our outfits to be seen at this time of the day.

Now we can finally see Christina's full outfit as she stands in a strapless bustier adorned in pearls that stop at her midriff. Riding the curve of her hips, the same golden fabric fans loose in layers, the same color of her bracelets and headpiece. She is magic and a melodic spell is cast every time she shifts her hips or wrists.

Next to her is Trish in a matching outfit that is all pearl-colored and white leather. When they stand next to each other, you don't have to ask if they belong as a pair. The only difference is Trish's long legs are made longer by pearl-studded heeled sandals.

At the entrance, an arch made of vines covering stone, we can feel the magnitude of the party as Ciara's "Promise" flirts over the top of the archway. As we walk in, without warning, cameras start flashing and we can literally hear people cheering and marveling. To add to the effect, there's a massive screen showing photographs after they are captured.

I panic. But I catch on quickly, as we pose in different variations.

On the other side, the courtyard explodes as Janet Jackson's "All Nite (Don't Stop)" blasts from the speakers and confetti rains from above.

Christina throws her hands up as we weave in and out of

the crowd until we are in the center of more people than we can count. All shapes and shades, some in colorful silk fabrics, others shining with the sheen of sweat.

Together, our bodies are proof that the walking wounded sure know how to dance, hands locked, hips popping, grinding to and fro, asking, *Will it—will we—ever be enough?*

Tonight, the answer is yes.

As the crowd sways side to side, Princeton taps me and points. We were so mesmerized by the song and the crowd, I never really noticed that off to the right, on an elevated platform, was a DJ booth with dancers and . . . Will? Will is the DJ?

So many questions short-circuit my mind as Will charms the crowd riding the beat, bare-chested in white angel wings; his shoulders are accentuated with white paint that makes his eyes and skin pop.

Next to him, dancers and people all around the elevated booth smile, swoon. Then, Kelis's "Milkshake" drips from the speakers. He looks in my direction, and suddenly his face tightens and the joy disappears.

Now I'm reminded of just how much everything hurts, even though the time away was helping. This sucks, and now all I want to do is leave. I turn around, try to head back to where we came from, anywhere but here.

Princeton stops me. "No."

I stare back at him, confused, then try to move around,

but he blocks me again. "No, Jay, no more runnin'."

"I'll be back, I just need to—"

"I said no." He steps closer, makes me look him in the eyes.

"I don't feel—"

"Jay, listen to me. Don't do that."

"Do what?" My words are louder than I mean for them to be, but I'm just tired of feeling like shit.

"Look, I know you feelin' all kinds of stuff, most of it right now might be bad. But look around. No, furreal, look." I do, since he's serious. "Do you see?"

Everywhere around us, people dance, some smile at me, others wink and blow kisses. Everywhere, someone is some version of free.

"Why don't I feel it? The joy they have . . . you have?" I ask him.

"Because it's a choice, Jay. One only you can make." He guides me back to the dance floor, embodying all the hope and energy I wish I had.

I try to free myself from the cage around my heart, but I can't.

Princeton playfully shakes my shoulders and hugs me, transferring some of his joy into me.

"Lemme let you in on a little secret," he says, swaying to the beat. "When it hurts too much to smile, dance harder."

I nod, overwhelmed in a good way. Sometimes I don't

have the words for how I feel when he does this, says the thing I need without me even knowing I need to hear it. "Thank you."

"It's what I'm here for."

Then I hear it: the tap of the drums on the cymbals and the tick of the clap of Nina Simone's "See-Line Woman." Instantly, I remember me and Will in his room during the summer, after our bike-riding adventure through K-Heights.

I take Princeton's advice. I follow the beat, tap my hips, shimmy my shoulders, and allow my face to flush warm with memory, a smile. I look up at the DJ booth and almost stumble back onto Princeton in shock.

There, dancing next to Will, one arm over his shoulder, is Lyric.

"Hey, hey, hey," a soft voice sings, smelling of grape candy and sweet things.

The person in front of us can only be Risé. They stand wrapped in silk strips of fabric along their arms like a majestic Cirque du Soleil performer. Against their dark skin, the Egyptian blue hugs curves, then swims down and out in layers just above their knees.

Christina and Trish fangirl proudly.

Risé's eyes float to Princeton, who reaches in for a side hug.

Taller than all of us, Risé reminds me of Lady Tee, beautiful, godlike, blessed.

I keep trying to focus on Risé, but my eyes pull to what's

happening behind them, as a girl joins Will and Lyric. Her hands gyrate behind Will as she nibbles on his ear, and I can see him blush all the way from here. The whole while, Lyric seems to watch them, entertained.

"And the one with the magic pen." Risé's voice lassos me back to the conversation. "You come very, very highly recommended."

Risé looks at my biggest cheerleaders, Christina and Princeton. I lean in for a half hug, overwhelmed by their confidence. I wonder if I'll ever be able to move like this—as love and light, instead of feeling destined to only chase it.

"I just write what you help me feel through you," I say.

Risé squints toward the DJ booth and waves at Will. "Y'all like the music? DJ Alexander comes highly recommended. Honestly, he saved me, since my other DJ got stuck in traffic and will be late."

"He's very talented." I look away when the girl kisses Will on the cheek and he laughs. It hurts because it's not the smile he gives everyone, the one that keeps them happy, it's the smile he used to give me.

"Should we try some of the food and drinks? There's a whole row of tables near the bonfire over there. Maybe we can then discuss business?" Risé says.

"Let's do it," Christina says, with Trish leading the way.

"Quick question, where's your restroom?" I ask.

"See the DJ booth? Past that into the house and down the

hallway to the left. There are some on the first floor and the second."

Princeton taps my arm and meaningfully glances toward the DJ booth. "They look like they switchin' out. Be careful, Lyric might realize we're here." I nod as Young Buck's "Shorty Wanna Ride" plays and jolts the crowd into a frenzy.

For a second, I almost forgot the reason we're here is to install tech and help bring the DKs and the Bainbridges to their knees. But doesn't Will know who Lyric is? I swear I told him when I was in the hospital.

I swerve in and out of the crowd toward the bathroom, making sure not to run into Lyric. I grab Will's hand as he comes down the stairs, and I pull him down the hall into the nearest room, closing the door behind us.

Will hasn't said anything. In fact, he doesn't even resist. But his eyes are far from warm or kind, his jaw tilted up. He's pissed.

Well, he ain't the only one.

"What are you doing here? And what was all that with Lyric?"

Again, he doesn't answer, just glares. I keep talking so I don't feel small or wrong, even if I might be. "He's dangerous. I told you what he did, about him leading the—"

"That's all you got to say to me?" Will's words burn like his eyes.

"Didn't you hear me? Lyric, he's—"

Will turns for the door, but I stop him.

"What the fuck do you want from me, Jay?" he yells.

"For you to listen!" I yell back.

"Well, I did, but you ain't talkin' 'bout nothin'."

My lips tremble, I'm so angry. Why would he put himself into Lyric's crosshairs?

"Why you here?" Will asks.

I can't tell him the real reason, so I lie. "Princeton and Christina."

"Whateva." Will pulls for the door, harder. He's serious, but I am, too. I don't want him to leave this room if he's going back to Lyric.

"Just wait for a minute, let me explain."

"You won't tell me the truth no way."

"Why are you saying that?"

When I feel his hand still on mine, there's that rush and the heat again. The only difference between us is he's not afraid of the burn.

"Please don't go out there to Lyric . . . or her." My voice cracks. I'm not proud of it.

"Why you care? You disappeared for a week, and I gotta hear from Jacob that you're at Princeton's. He doesn't even know when you're coming back."

"I didn't know what to . . . You wouldn't speak to me. *No one* was speaking to me," I say as Leroy's face pops into my mind. "I . . . I thought you still hated me. You wouldn't—"

"This look like hate to you?" His voice is loud, shaking, his eyes watering. "That what you want? Me to hate you?"

"No, please." My words fumble over themselves.

I can't get it together because he's standing so close. I can feel him hurting, and I don't know how to fix it. My lips rush into him, pulling his face to mine so quickly even he's taken off guard. He looks at me, lips quivering, trying to contain it. But is it really so bad if he lets go? If I do the same? Just tonight?

I kiss him again, even though I shouldn't. And when his tongue finds mine, between the curtain of our heartbroken lips, I'm dizzy on his moans and his hands around my waist.

Then he stops, a different fire behind his eyes.

"Do you love me?" He's shaking, I can feel it. "Or do you just not want anybody else to have me?"

I don't know what to say. I do love Will, but I also still love Leroy. "I—"

He cuts me off with a nod, coming to his own angry conclusion, and walks out the door. I stand still, stunned.

I go to run out the door, but standing there is Risé.

"I'm sorry. I was coming to find y'all soon, I just—" Risé puts their hand on my shoulder. "I actually need to speak with you alone. Is that okay?"

"Yeah, okay." I take a deep breath, realize we're in Risé's room based on the photos on an antique oak writing desk.

"Take a seat," Risé says. "Anywhere you want."

I sit at the writing desk, right in front of me, while Risé

288

sits on the bed. I pull out my small notepad. I hope Princeton will be able to find ADA Butler's room and install the tech. For now, I focus on doing my part.

"I have a special request." Risé's face grows heavy, weary. "Any chance you could write the letter now, after we chat for a bit? I know you don't usually write the letters during the visit, but I want to give it to Princeton tonight before he leaves the party. It's important."

"Is something wrong?" I ask. Risé motions toward the drawer in the writer's desk already stocked with textured paper and calligraphy pens of different colors.

"Have you ever let go of someone you weren't sure you could live without or, at least, you didn't want to?"

Risé stares off into space, then finds their way back, sadder yet again, pressing their thumbs in a rhythm. Are they counting?

I switch tactics, take the lead. "How long have you and Princeton known each other?"

Risé smiles, remembering, more relaxed. "For as long as I can remember, if I'm being honest. I used to call him peanut head, he hated it." Risé chuckles.

"I could see that."

"Him getting upset or why I called him peanut head?"

"Both." We laugh, relax into each other's presence.

"We didn't really start to get close until later. Middle school, I think."

"Why then?"

Risé gets up, walks to the bookshelf on the wall between the desk and the bed. It's small but packed to the brim with all kinds of books. They pull out a big photo album, flip to a specific page with a red silk ribbon, and hand it to me. On it are big and small photos of Risé and Princeton.

"I can't think of a time he ever said no to me when we were kids," Risé remembers. "Well, actually, I can. Once in the eighth grade, when I asked him out."

I'm surprised. Risé is not only beautiful, but someone Princeton clearly cares for. "Did he say why?"

Risé nods, a weak grin peeks through and then disappears. "He said he didn't want to lose me. He was afraid that if it didn't work out, we wouldn't be friends anymore. He even cried. . . ."

I'm moved to silence. I don't even know what to say.

"I know, right?" Risé reads my face. "My reason was much more simple. He'd gotten tall and was getting muscular. He was *fine*."

We chuckle at the man Princeton's becoming.

"I kid, I kid—well, a little. But it was also because we'd always needed each other. Me, reeling from the sadness and fear of losing my parents. Him, dealing with Lady Tee and his dad's divorce, which was around the same time—our seventh-grade year."

Princeton rarely talks about his father, just that he is a famous football player turned painter who Princeton never really felt close to because he was so sickly as a kid.

Risé flips the page. There is one photo from when they were younger, Princeton kissing Risé on the cheek, their head back in mid-laugh, as if in love.

"I used to think it was enough, Princeton just being here," Risé says, "but I realize it isn't. I want someone to look at me, to love me so much they risk losing me."

I never thought of it that way. "Did you ever ask Princeton again?"

"No, his health began to improve, and he finally made the track team and was pouring himself into that. I didn't want to get in the way of that, because track was the first time he could be the version of himself that in some way proved his father wrong."

Against the backdrop of the moon and the flashing lights, Risé looks even softer. I wonder if Princeton knows Risé feels this way. Or has Risé hidden it all behind their smile?

"What changed? Why a love letter now?"

Risé responds to my question with another. "How long should you wait for somebody to choose you?"

I can't think of an answer, because the question hurts so much.

"At first, I think I wanted you to write a love letter that might help Princeton change his mind. Or help him see I'm worth the chance, the risk. But now I don't think that's the right thing to do, because I know that out there is someone waiting on *me* to choose him right now, and I'm done making him wait. Tonight, I choose me, which means I choose him. So, can you do two things for me in the letter?"

I nod, listening.

"Let Princeton know how much I care, but don't tell him how much it hurts not being chosen. And most of all, tell him thank you for teaching me not only how to love others but myself."

It takes everything in me not to cry as the tears flow down Risé's face. I don't know if they are tears of sorrow, joy, or both, but I allow myself to feel them completely, and I keep guard over their hope and heart as I begin writing.

Somewhere, I once read that love isn't a one-word story. I wonder if that's why finding the right words, big and small enough to capture all the impossible feelings, is so hard. There are so many types of love, all sacred in their own right. And that's what I want to focus on in this letter to Princeton. That love, like energy, is neither lost nor destroyed, simply transferred or transformed. As a result, this isn't a love letter, but a record of all the ways Princeton has moved and defined love for Risé.

But I struggle with a competing truth: this record is also a goodbye to what once was and, perhaps one day, a new hello, once things have changed.

Risé shares with me a page of their handwriting. And when they finish reading the rewritten letter, they nod, overwhelmed but happy.

They hand me a special envelope and the photo of Princeton kissing them on the cheek. Risé kisses it, as if to return the affection before sliding it in the envelope as a parting gift. And when they are ready, we open the door. Together, we walk downstairs and across the courtyard to where everyone is waiting for us.

Risé brings Princeton to his feet, gives him the letter, and kisses him tenderly on the cheek before turning away to walk toward the dance floor.

The DJ plays Jesse Powell's "You" as Risé embraces a guy waiting for them on the sideline, but no more. Together, their bodies are a choice made, a decision to choose and be chosen, but most of all, a reminder that they are worthy, regardless.

In the stretch Hummer ride back, Princeton confirms what I've already assumed. He installed the tech with no problem in two rooms, so the mission was a success. And when Trish and Christina get out, they blow kisses as they go home together.

On the ride back to his house, Princeton opens the letter. And as he reads and looks at the photo, he cries. And as someone who knows all too well how much it hurts, I hold him—so that he, too, can be free.

19

Will

My legs were only supposed to get me outta the room with Jay before he ran away from me again, but they keep goin' till I'm at the entrance, where limos wait patiently foreva.

I kick at the gravel near a side stone garden. Maybe I shouldn't have run. Jay wanted to talk, but it's hard to listen when the words—well, the look on his face—are sayin' everythin' but *I love you*.

I slap my head. Why did I even say that? I don't know what came ova me. It was so clear that he was jealous. Isn't that proof enough that he likes me? I mean, we almost—

"So, when were you gonna tell me that you knew Jay?" Lyric drapes my jacket over my shoulders.

I don't look at him but answer quickly. "I wasn't."

This was also the point of tonight, what Leroy and PYT wanted me to prepare for. I have to admit a connection to Jay instead of fearin' it comes out some other way. It's risky because I don't know what he knows, but it's the only way I can remain in control—or at least figure out what he knows.

"I didn't know I needed to report everythin' I do and

everyone I know to you."

"Fair enough." He laughs, his eyes lingerin' like a lie detector. "Come on, let's go to my place."

"How do you know him? Is there a secret you're keepin' from me?" I ask as I stand to walk with him to his car.

"It's complicated, but let's just say we're connected by his love letters. Well, in my case, breakup letters. Because of him, I lost a three-year relationship and the girl I loved, thought I'd marry her one day and build a family. He's the reason why I'm heartbroken."

I scoff, shake my head.

"What? You don't believe me?" he asks.

"I do believe Jay wrote a breakup letter, but I know you aren't in love."

"How you figure?" There's a bark to his words.

I ignore it, dare him to bite. 'Cuz usually when someone is in love, they focus on the person they were with. You just said 'relationship' like you cared more about what she could be or do for you than actually bein' with her. That's not love."

Lyric is quiet, tense.

"I'm not sayin' you didn't like her, I'm sure you did . . . a lot. Just sayin' that somethin' might've changed and she could've felt what I mentioned."

He nods, still pissed but softenin'.

Silently, we climb into his car, and he pulls out into the road. Some time passes before he glances at me to ask, "What about you? How do you know Jay?"

"Just an old childhood love," I say. "Plus, I go to Daniel Lee with him. It's how I met Christina and Princeton."

"So he *is* the reason you're sad, heartbroken?"

"Among otha things," I say.

I look at him to see why he might be silent, but Lyric is starin' out the window, lost in thought—or maybe like me, lost period. By the time we get to his house and make it upstairs to his room, I'm so tired that I'm delirious. Plus, I feel a headache comin' on. A consequence of takin' shots at the request of Lyric and Saturday.

I yearn for the bed and can already feel the cool sheets callin' my name when suddenly Lyric bear-hugs me from behind. I wait for him to speak, for his arms to loosen, but he squeezes me tighter. "You gonna let me go, or do you plan on makin' us both sleep standin' up?"

"Not a bad idea," he jokes.

But when I feel his lips at the base of my neck, the heat of his breath caressin' my ear, the hairs all ova my body and other things stand up. A jolt of electricity shoots through me, and I feel like my knees are 'bout to buckle. "That's enough. Let me go."

"Is this how Saturday did it? This what made you blush in the DJ booth?"

"Lyric, come on. Quit playin'."

He nods and stands there, his forehead at the base of my

neck, before sighin' and finally lettin' me go. "Is that really what you want? To go to sleep? I know you feel it."

"Feel what?"

"As lonely as I do."

"And if I do, what does that have to do with you? There's nothin' you can do to fix it." I move to the otha side of the bed, grateful the lights are off.

The moon is naked and lazy in full sight without the blinds to hate. Lyric sits on his side of the bed, his back facin' me. "What if I could make you feel good and forget?"

"Just go to bed. The both of us will feel better in the mornin'."

"You promise?" He sings the words ova his shoulder, desperate.

"No, but I hope."

"Hope isn't enough. Every day I wake up hoping things will be different, and it never is. It just feels worse and worse, so heavy like I can't breathe, like I'm being smothered. I can't take it." He sounds small, fragile, like he's whisperin' to the wind, teeterin' on the edge. I know because I feel the same way, too—I have—for a while now.

I lie down and try to focus on the cool sheets, let them lull me to sleep and put an end to this conversation. Because for the first time, I'm scared I might be losin' my grip.

Lyric is the enemy. So why does every word that comes out of his mouth feel like he's a friend? No, not a friend, one of the only people I know who can give voice to everythin' I've been feelin'. You can't fake that, can you?

He finally lies down. I breathe in and out, welcomin' the sleep. But no matta how hard I shut my eyes, it won't come. Not even a little bit.

"I saw the way you looked at Jay tonight, like you were on the verge of crying."

He turns ova and I can feel him lookin' at me, but I won't turn to face him. I can't afford him to see what's happenin' on the inside of me, that I'm doin' everythin' I can not to fall apart.

Lyric moves closer till his body becomes water. First, a drip, his fingers glidin' ova my chest; then a trickle, him leadin' with his lips; and soon he becomes an ocean, made bold by the dizzyin' drum of our heartbeats. His hands become tides, pullin' at the shore of our clothes till we lie bare, and his mouth swallows me slowly, like footprints in the sand. He climbs on top of me, glowin', beautiful—and sad.

He reaches into the drawer next to the bed for a condom, places it on me without breakin' eye contact. He adds somethin' slick beneath him and on me till our bodies collide in sweat and moans.

"I don't love you," he says.

"I don't love you eitha."

I kiss him. He kisses me. I hold him. He holds me. And knowin' this could be the biggest mistake for the both of us, I follow through.

Like a flamin' train racin' toward its own destruction, we neva stop, even as we smother moans, tears fall, and in our own way, we fly till the impossible happens. Our lost bodies are found.

I wake up with Lyric asleep in my arms. When I wake him 'cuz I can hear his mom downstairs in the kitchen, he neva says a word. Instead, he climbs on top of me again, kissin' me. Before I can say anythin', my body does. He stares at me, grins, but I stop him.

A crash makes us both jump.

Without sayin' anythin', Lyric pulls on pants and races downstairs. I do the same, climbin' into a T-shirt and shorts. We see Miss Camilah's feet and run ova to her. She's unconscious, bleedin' from a wound on her head.

"Lyric, call 911!" I yell ova my shoulder as I make sure she's breathin'. I check her pulse, it's faint but there. "Lyric, did you—"

He's standin' right where I last saw him, face frozen wit fear, tears streamin'. But he's lookin' at the TV. On the screen, a news headline scrolls across in terrifyin' letters:

ILLEGITIMATE SON OF LOUIS BAINBRIDGE EXPOSED

He's shakin' his head, tryna convince himself it ain't real as images of him at swim meets and otha events with his mother are spliced with images of Louis Bainbridge and his family, and otha older images of Miss Camilah and Louis Bainbridge, suspiciously happy—maybe even in love.

I rememba what Jay said about the deal Miss Camilah has with Louis Bainbridge to keep the connection a secret or lose everythin'.

Lyric's face is pale with shock. I wanna scream, run up to him, and shake him outta it. His mom is in danger and needs help.

I look around for the landline. I see it on the wall behind me. I grab it, dial 911, and talk to the operator. Slowly, Miss Camilah comes to and speaks just as the paramedics arrive. Her words slur as they whisk her away.

When Lyric and I arrive at the waitin' room seconds behind the ambulance, we are stone sculptures. Even though Miss Camilah is okay, I can't help but rememba the blood. Next to me, Lyric goes back and forth, from noddin' on my shoulder to starin' off into space at *Jerry Springer* on the TV, too soft to be heard, too loud to be quiet.

I think 'bout Mum, if she has someone near her to do like I did for Miss Camilah and help her if she's hurt. I slap away the fears of her bein' tortured or, worse, dead. I tell myself Mum is okay because she has to be.

I reach for my phone but realize I left it at Lyric's. I hope no one has called, because I don't have an excuse to tell them. I can see Miss Julia's eyes, me fried like chicken in her cast-iron skillet as she turns up the heat. I wanna ask Lyric if I can use his, but I don't know if it's a good idea.

He knows I'm connected to Jay but not that I live with him. Besides, his phone has been ringin' off the hook, but he won't answer it. The way he looks at it as it vibrates, I imagine one of two people, Frank or Louis Bainbridge. Eitha way, I'm sure he doesn't wanna talk.

His phone vibrates again, and he doesn't even check. Just lets it buzz in his lap.

"You gon' get that? Maybe it's important," I say.

"They wanna be in charge. Let them figure it out," he mumbles, half-asleep, movin' his head closer up my shoulder. His breathin' is like fingers strokin' my neck and chin.

"Who are you talkin' 'bout?" I say, tracin' the freckles on the back of his hand still holdin' on to mine. "You know what? Not important."

We sit here, tryna compete in the swim meet of our thoughts. I hope he's winnin', 'cuz my heart and mind feel dead in the water.

"Why did I do that?" Lyric whispers.

"Do what?" I ask.

"I froze. She was lying there on the ground, bleeding and . . ." His voice is shattered by the kick of someone at the vendin' machine and a hush by a parent, threatenin' their kid into silence.

"It's okay, it worked out."

"No, *I* was supposed to protect her."

A doctor comes out to get us and explains that Miss Camilah's okay, but they are still runnin' tests. She'll need to be kept overnight, but they say it's okay for us to go in and see her.

As we enter the room, I feel outta place, like only Lyric and her should be togetha. I'm sure they have more private matters to discuss, but Lyric pulls me in with him.

Miss Camilah's hair frames her face, thick and almost swallowin' her small shoulders. But with it out, she looks years younger, even more beautiful.

Lyric hugs and kisses her. He lays his head in her palms, and she frees one hand to rub his back. I don't look her in the eyes, I can't. I just focus on the power of that hand, the fact that it has life with her magic still intact.

She whispers to him in Portuguese. I can feel her watchin' me, and when I finally look at her, I'm speechless. She reminds me of Mum, how her face, eyes, and small frame can feel larger than life but still have room enough for you to feel at home. She calls me ova to her, holds one of my hands, and says thank you.

Without releasin' my hand, she asks Lyric to grab her a snack from the vendin' machine and, while he's out there, to splash some water on his face because his eyes are a little swollen.

After he closes the door behind him, Miss Camilah asks

me to sit but still doesn't speak, just keeps rubbin' my hand.

"Thank you for helping me and being there for Lyric. It's better for him that you were there."

"No problem, are you okay? You don't seem surprised by what happened."

"I'm not," she says, smilin' weakly. "But there's nothing I can do about it, because the doctors still don't know what it is. I've been secretly battling these fainting spells since Lyric was in middle school, but the episodes and dizziness seem to be getting worse. That's something to discuss later. We don't have much time before Lyric returns."

"Ma'am?"

"I saw you in Lyric's room that night."

I avoid her eyes. I don't wanna lie, but I can't tell her the truth.

"Are you here to help or hurt him?" Her voice is like a wind chime, soft and melodic but strong so that it echoes.

I answer honestly. "I dunno."

Her eyes soften, the beginnin' of a smile. "I believe you, and since you didn't lie, I think there's hope that you might be able to actually help him, save him from himself."

She pauses and looks out the window filled to the brim with blue sky and light.

"Since you've been around, Lyric's started to be like he used to be, all smiles, laughs, and jokes. Before, he was just moody, always trying to one-up others, be the best, even though I told him he had nothing to prove. He's been trying to cozy up with Louis, and I know he's the reason behind it. I bet he made a promise to Lyric and told him what he could do for me. But Louis's promises always come with a price, and they're never worth it."

She faces me. "I knew you were special the moment I saw you at the swim meet and then again at our house. I want you to know that I also know what you're looking for."

I almost fall outta my chair. "What do you—"

"The evidence on the Bainbridges, the donation list and city plans, right?"

How does she know? I barely know much 'bout the donation list—only bits and pieces after Jay mentioned it and what Leroy has been down to share.

"You remind me of that young man from a year ago."

"Was his name Faa?"

She sits up, but her eyes look down. "If I would have known what would happen to him, I would have never given him the list. I would have held on to it, but he'd already figured out so much on his own. Since he was going to go public anyway, I wanted to give him the best chance he had at winning."

"Do you know who killed him?" Was it your son?

"I don't know, but I don't put anything past Louis. There's nothing he wouldn't do to protect his legacy. The only reason we're alive is because of what I know from my days working with him, and Louis still needs me for my expertise. That, and I think he's always had plans to use Lyric.

"After Faa died, I promised to never endanger another person. But I know Lyric is getting into Louis's clutches, even keeping secrets from me. I'll give you the original donation list—and even more—but only under one condition: you save Lyric from the Bainbridges."

I want to say I can, I will, but it wouldn't be fair to her. "I can't promise that because, at the end of the day, it's up to Lyric. But I'll do everythin' I can to convince him."

I don't know if it's good enough, but it's the truth.

"That'll do. For now, please stay by his side until I'm able to be discharged. I need to make sure he doesn't do anything reckless before I'm out. Then I'll just need a couple of days to get everything together for you."

I almost forgot the news report. I wonder if that's why so many people were starin' at Lyric in the waitin' room.

"Please, just keep an eye on him. With the news out, Louis is sure to show up with some kind of scheme, but we can't allow him to. You're the only one Lyric listens to," Miss Camilah says.

"Me? Are you sure? I didn't think he listened to anybody but himself."

A chuckle breaks free from her lips. "He's hardheaded, that's for sure. But he's so much softer, more gentle than he wants people to know. I have a feeling you already know."

Lyric bursts through the door with way more food than she asked for. It's as if he cleaned out half the snacks from the vendin' machine. He dumps most of it on the food tray near the recliner, and after we eat little pieces of this and that, Miss Camilah shoos us out.

As soon as we make it into the house, I nudge Lyric upstairs to hop in the shower. I check my phone and see the number of missed calls from Jay. I read his text sayin' he told Miss Julia we are at Princeton's but to text him back when I'm ready. Miss Julia asked him to be home by 6:00 p.m., but I beg him to see if she would let him stay there one more day, that there's somethin' important I gotta handle. He says he'll let me know, no questions asked.

Even though I neva told him 'bout my plan with Lyric, I wonder if he knows. Did Princeton tell him? Outside of Leroy and PYT, he's the only one who would know, but Jay was too surprised at the party. Princeton couldn't have told him, at least not before.

I cook the only real food I know how, Mum's French toast and eggs. I hear Lyric comin' down the stairs when I'm almost done. He looks different again. No longer cold or distant, he wears a soft grin, not necessarily happy but at least warm. It's enough, considerin' everythin' he's been through today.

I scramble one more egg in the dippin' batter, another splash of cream, cinnamon, and nutmeg—enough for three more slices.

Lyric hugs me from behind as I dip each of the slices and listen to them sizzle. He tightens his arms, and I'm surprised by how used to him touchin' me I am already. What does it mean? Why do I even care? No, I don't. I can't, and I won't.

"Thank you, for everything," Lyric mumbles. He kisses the back of my neck, and my face grows warm.

"No problem," I say, movin' to wash a dish at the sink, an excuse to break free from his embrace. It's the only way I know to keep my heart from racin'. It keeps doin' that, even though it shouldn't. Every time he touches me, it takes longer for me to settle down.

I hear him before I see the tears. Lyric fights them, smears them before they get the chance to fall. I want to hold him, tell him I know what it feels like to crack and have to do everythin' you can to hold togetha the pieces.

When his lips find mine, every wall I've built up brick by brick in preparation to do this—knowin' who he is and what he might have done or could still do—cracks and moans as it crumbles.

My body is taken ova. Feelings that still don't make sense pull him close to me and kiss back. And none of it mattas because here, we are mirrors fearin' our own reflection, lookin' for a way outta what hurts.

Right now, I wanna do anythin' to stop feelin' helpless that I could save Miss Camilah but haven't been able to save Mum. I can kiss, hug, and experience every part of Lyric, but

I can't even take it to the next level with Jay, someone I love more than I can eva explain.

Lyric kisses me hard and looks into my eyes as he speaks.

"I don't think I've ever felt this way with anyone before," he says. "I really like you, Will . . . which is why I want to give you the chance to tell the truth."

He caresses my cheeks with his thumbs.

"What do you—" I stop and step back when the smirk crawls across his face.

My stomach hurts, feels like I'm goin' to throw up. Lyric chuckles, then walks to the otha side where his plate is and begins to eat.

"How long have you known?" I ask.

"The whole time." He chews the food I've made for him happily. But the glare in his eyes is clear: he's sizin' me up, dangerous.

"Frank and Myrrh mentioned a pretty boy with green eyes who seemed close to the BDs when they got arrested for being stupid and falling into your trap. I figured that was that, but then I saw you in the pool—and I couldn't resist."

"So what now?" I wait, ready for any move he might make. If I have to, I'll end him right here. I won't let anythin' get in the way of savin' Mum.

"What would you do to see your mother again?" A rush of anger and relief washes ova me, but I won't let him see me falter.

"Anythin'," I say, defiant, "but betray my friends."

There's a flash behind his eyes. "Don't make me sound like the bad guy."

I send him a look the equivalent of the gut punch I gave him in the locker room when we first met.

"The French toast is really good. Sure you don't want any?" he asks.

Wait a minute. If he's this calm, did he call the DKs while I was talkin' to Miss Camilah? Are they on their way? Did she trick me, too? This doesn't make sense.

I look at Lyric, the window, and the door. Maybe I should make a run for it.

"I'm not going to hurt you, and no, I didn't call anybody, so you can stop looking at me like I'm going to snap my fingers and kidnap you."

I wouldn't be surprised if he did. "I don't trust you."

"Likewise. How do I know you didn't call the BDs?"

"You don't," I say, frontin'.

"So you didn't. They must not really know what you're up to," he says out loud.

I let him think what he wants. "You gon' tell me what you want or you just gon' stare at me?"

"Not a bad idea." He gets up, sucks syrup from his fingers, and walks ova to me. "Wanna pick up where we left off? I wanna feel—"

I shove him so hard, he knocks his plate and glass off

the table, tryna stop himself from fallin'. The crash is loud, echoin'.

He throws his hands up, surrenderin'.

"Don't fuckin' touch me," I growl.

"My bad, some other time, then, when you've calmed down." He takes a few more steps back, lowers his hands as he avoids the shards and chips of broken glass, and sits on the steps behind him, facin' me. "What about a favor?"

"What kind of favor?"

"I don't know yet. Think of it as a debt you owe me in the future, no questions asked."

"And if I say yes, and then I don't?"

"You won't."

"How you figure?"

"Because if you do, somethin' will happen to Jay, and we won't stop at kidnappin'."

My whole body is shakin'. If I didn't know any better, I'd do somethin' I'll regret and enjoy every minute of it.

"No snitchin', no info 'bout the BDs, nothin' that could get me or anyone I know and love put in jail."

"Yes to the first two. No promises on the third."

What does he have up his sleeve? "And you'll give me my mum?"

"Not quite," he says. "The address to where they're holding her and a tip for how you can rescue her."

"Address now, so we can confirm what you sayin' is true, then I'll agree."

"What if my favor is for you to fall in love and stay with me forever, as my boyfriend?" He grins, and for a second, I think I might actually hate him now more than I did a second ago.

"You won't."

"You sure?"

"Yup, 'cuz you only like things you can control, and you know betta than to think you'll eva have control ova me."

His smile twitches. He's pissed, but he's hidin' it well. "Call Leroy. I know you have his number, and I'll tell you the address so you can tell him."

"I need to be there, see for myself."

He shakes his head. "You have to stay here, where I can see you."

"What if it's a trap?"

"I'm sure they can handle it." What do I do? If I say no, I might lose this chance. If I say yes, it could put Leroy and the BDs in danger.

I don't have a choice. I don't want anybody to get hurt, but Lyric neva said I couldn't be honest about the threat of it bein' a trap. That's not exactly perfect odds, but it's all I got.

I read his face, searchin' for even the slightest proof that he's 'bout to trick me, but there's nothin'. I still don't know what he's schemin' or why he's tellin' me everythin' he knows now when he could have easily told me this mornin'—better yet, last night *before* we had sex. It's not like he thought I'd fall for him just 'cuz we slept togetha.

"You've got one minute to say yes or no," Lyric says.

"If I say no?"

"Your business. No harm will come to her." I still don't trust him, but trust ain't required.

I pick up the phone and dial, hopin' Leroy will pick up. Mum's life depends on it.

20

Leroy

The way Taj and Auntie Rissa look, they might just burn down the Ralph Mark Gilbert Civil Rights Museum—and all the OGs wit it. Can't nobody believe this is happenin as they motion fuh a no-confidence vote in Taj and Auntie Rissa as the leaders of the BDs, and to have Pops reinstated as the sole leader.

"It's simple, the YGs need to spend time learnin how to lead. They still too impressionable," an OG says. "You gotta be a soldier befo you try to be a general. That's just how it is."

I wanna say somethin, but this aint no democracy.

This a hostile takeova, and the only thing that matta aint yo words, it's votes.

Our best bet is to hold out and wait till errbody else get here. Even tho they called the meetin, they still gotta wait on a quorum, the minimum numba of folks present to pass a motion. And until the motion get passed, YGs still have the power to vote.

My phone vibrates, but I ignore it—this is mo important. But when it rings again, and again, I pull it out and see that it's Will. I tap Taj on the shoulder to let him know I gotta run to the bathroom. He tells me to hurry back.

"Yo, why you blowin me up?" I say.

"I know where Mum is."

"Whatchu say?" I switch ears. Don't think I heard him right.

"I have the address where my mum is bein' held."

"Furreal? You sho?"

"I think so. Only thing is they 'bout to move her in less than two hours. I just found out."

That aint enough time to get errbody togetha, especially not wit errthang that's goin on here. "How you find out?"

"Lyric."

"Tha fuck? Lyric just up and told you where Miss Rosalind at?"

"I'm skeptical, too. But he gave me the address as proof. Can you send somebody to check? Ain't gotta be you, just somebody."

Why Lyric decide to do somethin like this? What he plannin? "Lyric witchu right now? He know you callin?"

"Yeah to both."

"Put me on speaker."

Will presses buttons, and I can hear him put the phone down. "Okay, you on speaker."

"Hey, Leroy," Lyric says, soundin too confident fuh comfort.

"Whatchu plottin? Aint no way you just gon give this up fuh no reason."

"Who said I was? The deal's already been made. I'm just holding up my end of the bargain." My stomach drops. What did Will trade fuh this? "I agreed to show proof of life and help get Will's mom free from under the DKs. No more, no less. You the one wasting time you don't have."

The bathroom door opens—it's Rouk. "Yo, Lee, Taj say hurry up. Errbody almost here, but the OGs gettin antsy. Once they get some OGs to call in, they gonna try to push through the vote without lettin anybody else in."

"That Rouk?" Lyric says, loud enough to make sho he hear.

"Lyric?!" Rouk whisper-shouts. "Lee, the fuck you on the phone wit that snake fuh?"

"That's a little harsh, don't you think, Rouk? I thought we were friends—at least, we used to be."

"Yeah, how bout you come say that shit to my face."

"Rouk, chill," I say. "What's the address, Will?"

As he says it, I get Rouk to type it in his phone.

"Aight, Imma make a call and put eyes on it, and letchu know. But, Will, anythin you need to tell me?" I ask.

"It's not a trap, and no he didn't snitch," Lyric says, mockin me.

"You keep runnin yo mouth when I aint talkin to you, and Imma come visit you my damn self. Say somethin else."

"Just check, please," Will says. "I can't take not knowin'."

315

"Aight, stay by yo phone. And, Lyric . . ." He don't answer. "Now you hard of hearin?"

"Make up your mind, Leroy. Do you want me to ignore you or do you want me to pay attention?"

I breathe in and breathe out. I do errthang I can to find some calm, cuz if I don't, I swear Imma kill him. "If anythin go down or seem off, hear me, nenh, hear me good. I promise you I'm gon find you, undastood?"

"No need to waste it on idle threats. Besides, if I wanted to hurt you, I would've done it already. You know that more than any—"

The line goes dead. I look at it, but my phone is fine, fully charged.

I get a text from Will: **Hung up to nip drama. Call soon.**

I wanna call back and cuss Lyric clean out, but Will's right—no time fuh that.

"Rouk, who spot near that address? It's on the south side, right?"

"It's the Low Rider Crew. Want me to call Husani or Khalil?"

"Yeah, let em know we need eyes on it now and to call us when he do."

Rouk calls right away while I dial Brown Brown, who at the BDs' spot wit PYT. I ask him if Detective Dane still in his office based on what they hear in the tech. When he says he is, that it sound like he in a meetin, I tell him to keep an ear out and I'll hit him up soon.

If this what I think it is, we gon need him—and not just him, he gon have to join forces wit our crews to make it happen togetha.

"They got eyes," Rouk calls back minutes later. "Husani said the neighbors saw a woman goin in a coupla weeks ago, and aint nobody eva seen her come out. On top of that, the DKs stay ridin through the neighborhood. So they think it might be Miss Rosalind. What should we do?"

"Tell em to quietly get the word out that the Blue Jay's nest in the Windsor Forest between Woods and Deer." A code fuh the neighborhood and cross streets. "But keep it only wit the LRC and let em know Dane, who Nate spoke to, gon be down. We don't need em buckin when they see the popos. Tell em we workin togetha."

"Rouk and Lee!" Taj damn near kick the bathroom door down. "What's takin you so long?"

I explain what's goin on. When me and Rouk done tellin him errthang we know, he finally speak. "You fuckin reckless, Lee. I said keep me in the loop. Why you makin all these calls and aint bother tellin me?"

"I just found out myself. I aint know till now, I promise."

"You betta not be lyin," he says, glaring. "Let's just get Miss Rosalind back safe and sound, and then we can worry bout the rest."

"What bout all that's goin on out there? We aint got

enough time to do both," I say.

"We quittin." He don't even flinch and just walks toward the door.

"Whatchu mean, quittin?" I run after him.

"You hear that?" He leads us closer to the auditorium and waves me ova.

There's arguin, bickerin, and somebody kickin and hittin on the outside doors. "Pops's men won't let no YGs enter, and we havin a hard time makin it so they can call in. Look like the OGs gon steal the vote."

"They can't do that, can they?" I say.

"Don't matta. If Pops want to be the new leader, Imma let him."

Taj walks ova to Auntie Rissa and whispers in her ear.

She takes a deep breath and nods. They both walk up to the podium and use the mic to cut through all the noise.

Taj speak first. "Yall wanna do it yo way, even if it means stealin a vote? Don't worry bout it, cuz I've seen errthang I need to."

Auntie Rissa taps in. "If you willin to go this far, you willin to do worse. So, in acknowledgment of our different priorities and values: we both will step down from our positions."

"And I speak on behalf of the YGs," Taj says, "when I say we will no longer operate as part of the BDs. Effective immediately, all YG chapters, crews, and collectives withdraw."

Taj and Auntie Rissa drop the mic and walk off the podium toward the doors.

"Hold on, let's be reasonable and talk this out," Pops says, joggin ova to us. "We can figure out a path forward that's best fuh errbody."

My phone vibrates.

A few texts from Brown Brown: **Dane on ground. Preppin wit Sani and LRC. Otha crews on way. 15 mins out.**

I give Taj the signal. We gotta go, so we there when they strike and rescue Miss Rosalind.

Pops watches me. "Somethin wrong?" He looks at Auntie Rissa.

She ignores his question. "You think the only way to do this is *for* the younger generation, our future. But the difference between me and you is that Imma do it *wit* em. You want the BDs that bad, you got em. Good luck," Auntie Rissa says.

We leave the Ralph Mark Gilbert Civil Rights Museum togetha and go to find Miss Rosalind. When we're a few blocks from where she's bein held, we hear shots fired, tires screechin, and then a crash.

"Floor it!" Taj screams. My heart stops and kick-starts again.

We see tons of police cars wit their lights flashin. There are some guys we don't know bein handcuffed next to a car crashed into a tree. Errbody runs toward it, cuz somebody screamin bout the people in the car needin help and gas leakin as the car starts to smoke. Somebody shatters the windows on the driver and passenger sides too.

Errbody tryna do errthang they can to get the people out in time. Me and Taj are helpin wit the back seat when we see it's Miss Rosalind. She unconscious, wit blood all ova. We help lay her down as Auntie Rissa comes up behind us to make sho she breathin.

Dane runs to us and crouches down to help, as otha YGs carry out the DKs in the car who unconscious as well.

We hear the sirens of the ambulance and the fire truck. Don't take long befo the firefighters clearin the area and the paramedics put those from the car crash on stretchers.

Soon as the ambulance pulls off, Auntie Rissa calls Ma at the hospital to let her know Miss Rosalind is on her way in.

"We got Myrrh and a few others, but Frank is nowhere to be found." Dane signals fuh us to follow him, talk in private. "Just wanted to give you a heads-up that our chief is throwing a fit, asking who approved the operation and why he wasn't notified. We may not be able to hold them for long, but I'll do what I can."

My phone rings, and I see it's Trish. I step aside so I can answer.

"Yall get her? Is she okay?" Trish asks. "Rouk called to let me know what was goin down."

"She's on the way to the hospital. Auntie Rissa followin

behind. Iono how bad it is, but she aint conscious. Should know soon."

"Good, good, cuz we got anotha problem. Hold on, lemme put you on speaker."

"It's crazy ova at the police station," Brown Brown's voice says through the speaker.

"I know, Dane told us, said the chief is pissed, but he got it under control."

"No, he don't," Trish says. "We been listenin in, and the chief aint just pissed. They tryna set Dane up and get rid of him. They in his office wit boxes, packin up papers and everythin."

"What? Hol up, hol up, lemme get Taj. He need to hear this." I flag him and Rouk ova, give them a rundown on what I just heard.

We move farther away, near an alley so I can put Trish and Brown Brown on speaker, and we can listen without bein overheard.

"Aight, Taj and Rouk here and up to speed," I say. "How yall know they tryna set Dane up? Any proof?"

"They was real slick wit it," PYT says. "Befo they stormed his office wit boxes, somebody snuck in and uploaded some files on his computer." I can hear PYT punchin keys, findin answers. "From what I could see, it's records to make it look like he was takin bribes from Auntie Rissa, Lady Tee, and Miss Rosalind, and stealin money from the force to fund the BDs."

"PYT say he can wipe the whole drive so they can't find nothin, but he can only do it while it's plugged up to a power source. Should he wipe it befo they unplug and take Dane computer?" Trish asks.

Think. Think. Think. "PYT, if they search the computer, will they find yo tech?"

"Nah, I handled that already. Plus, they prolly aint gon be lookin fuh nothin else, cuz they already know what they gon find."

"Delete it, then?" Brown Brown says again, nervous.

"Whatchu think, Taj?" I ask.

"If somebody put it there, they prolly already got this set in motion," Taj replies.

"So, if they don't find it, it could work against Dane too. It could even reveal what we got going on, makin errthang worse."

"What if we told Dane?" Brown Brown says. "If he get kicked off the force, it could ruin errthang too."

"Ion think that's gon work. He barely trust us as it is. If we tell him, even if he figure out what to do to handle the chief, we aint neva gon be able to work wit him again," I say.

"Yall think this mighta been what Frank was talm bout when he gave us that wack-ass deadline?" PYT asks.

"Could be. Or it's somethin bigger, somethin still aint happen yet," I say.

Taj looks around, then has us huddle in closer as more fire trucks arrive.

"PYT, you seen exactly what they put on the computer, the files?" Taj asks.

"Yeah, a lil bit. Iono how they put it all togetha so fast or how long they been thinkin of doin this, but it's a lot. A lot of hands had to touch this."

"What if we figure out the original source, then, PYT?" Trish asks. "Maybe we can trace it back to the chief and errbody else workin fuh him, too. Then it'll show that Dane's bein framed."

"Yeah, but I'll need at least forty-eight hours."

"That's not gonna help Dane now," Brown Brown says.

We look up, see Dane workin wit some of the popos to secure the scene now that the fire been put out. He looks our way.

"Could we tip him off . . . let him know without letting him know?" Brown Brown says.

"I feel where you comin from, Brown Brown, but iono if we can risk it," Taj says.

If this go the way I think it will, Dane might get some heat from the popos, but if PYT can find the source, we gon have the dagger he need to take down the chief and anybody else corrupt at the force. Maybe even shake up some stuff fuh Louis Bainbridge.

"He could stay outta jail if ADA Butler takes up fuh him. We think they workin togetha, right?" PYT says.

"It could work," I say, lookin at Taj. "We could give PYT forty-eight hours, maybe mo, let Dane handle it, and then

323

when we hear ADA Butler gettin ready to strike, we give her the files anonymously. ADA Butler can take the chief and the DA down and clear Dane's name, cuz after that wave of BDs warrants, we all know the DA connected somehow in all this.

"What if our timin is off?" I ask. "And Lady Tee, Miss Rosalind, Auntie Rissa, and you get arrested fuh bribin befo our plan can play out?"

"It's a risk we gotta take," Taj says. "But one we should prepare fuh too. I'll talk it ova wit Auntie Rissa and Lady Tee." Taj looks up, motions to me and Rouk. "Aye, yall, we gotta wrap it up. Dane headed our way."

"Imma call yall back," I say to Trish and Brown Brown.

Errbody says goodbye, and I hang up.

As Dane walks ova, he says, "Hey, we've secured the scene, and we're ready to roll."

We all nod, knowin that our hands are tied fuh now, but hopin we'll be able help prove Dane's innocence when the time comes.

At the hospital, the waitin room is packed wit YGs. Errbody waitin fuh Taj to tell em what to do, so they stay put at least to keep Miss Rosalind safe from the DKs if they roll through. The only people missin is Auntie Rissa and Benji.

Night is up, waitin to talk to us the moment we walk in. He fills us in on what we missed. The otha DKs in the car are awake and gettin questioned by Dane on a different floor, and the doctor said Miss Rosalind should wake up in a coupla hours, maybe longer.

Night also explains that Pops might be rollin through any minute now that Auntie Rissa officially told em Miss Rosalind has been rescued, says we should dip befo then.

When we turn the corner, he shows us to the door and heads back to the front to keep a lookout. We can see Auntie Rissa, Benji, Jacobee, Miss Julia, and Will, but I don't see—

Jay opens the door, surprised. He slides by and walks into the hall. Taj and Rouk go in while I hang outside and follow him to the vendin machines. I stand beside him.

Ion say nothin, just wait. Only one Snickers bar left—our favorite. I quickly put in a dolla, get it, and pretend I'm gon eat it. When he look ova at me, I give it to him.

I expect him to leave, but he sits down in the mini waitin room next to Miss Rosalind's room. Jay takes a bite, folds the rest in the wrapper, and chews quietly.

"She doin aight?" I say, pretendin ion already know.

"Doctors say she's stable. They're waiting for her to wake up."

I rememba the last time I saw him back at the school, right befo he ran from me and cried in Princeton's arms.

He offers me some of the Snickers. I take it, bite the same side he did.

"I'm sorry, I never meant to hurt you by not telling you about New York. Part of me thought I could fix it, change my mom's mind, but I couldn't. And then there's the other part of me that didn't want to ruin our time together—I wanted us to *finally* be able to enjoy being in love, being together . . ." He pauses. "I want you to know that I know I was wrong, and I'm sorry for the pain it caused you."

Since that night, so much has happened that I just been tryna fuhget bout it, bout us, even tho I can't. Hearin his words release somethin in me like a cramp I aint been able to shake out. The pain is still there a lil, but it don't hurt like it used to.

"I'm sorry too."

"But you didn't do anything wrong."

"I did, tho. I kinda feel like a hypocrite."

Jay's eyes ask why, not his lips.

"Last summer, back when errthang happened and after I sent you that note, Auntie Rissa told me and Taj she thought we should move wit her to open up a franchise of her diner in Chicago," I say.

"Chicago?"

"Yeah, I was so pissed that I ran to Jacobee cryin. Begged him to try to talk to Taj and get him to have Auntie Rissa change her mind. That's part of why I fought so hard to crack the password on the drive, so I could figure it all out and we aint have to leave."

Jay just listens. He aint mad like I thought he would be.

"Back then, I kept it to myself, tried to do whateva I could to make sho it aint happen," I confess. "I neva told you, but when I think bout it, I also know it was cuz I aint wanna hurt you. If I had stopped to think bout that when you told me the truth, I woulda realized I knew exactly how you felt."

I give Jay the last part of the Snickers. He pops it into his mouth, chews, and lays his head on my shoulder. Iono what it really means till he says the words so soft, I think my heart might be playin tricks on me: "I missed you."

I reach fuh his hand, weave my fingers into his, and say, "I missed you, too."

Suddenly, there's screamin and shoutin at the front waitin room where we entered, and our hands fall apart in surprise. All that noise can only mean that Pops and the OGs are here.

"Stand down," Taj says to the YGs, who listen to him and only him. Taj jumps in front of Husani and pulls him back befo he gets any words out at Pops.

Pops side-eyes Husani and then looks at us.

"What they say? She safe?" Pops asks us, but I can tell he's mainly lookin at Auntie Rissa.

"Room 205," she says. "Tanya is the nurse takin care of her, and Dr. Eva, Lady Tee's wife, should be comin by fuh anotha check-up. She in good hands, but you should hear the news yoself."

Auntie Rissa moves round him, but he stops her.

"Is this how it's going to be?" Pops says. "We're family. We gotta stick togetha."

"Iono, is it?" Auntie Rissa asks. "What did you and the council decide?"

Pops don't say nothin at first, just sighs. "Well, wit both of you resignin, we didn't have a choice but to name me as the new president of the BDs. But what I said still stands—"

Taj aint havin it. "You heard us, we out—*both* of us."

"Son, listen," Pops says.

"No, you listen. Aint gon be none of that playin house shit neitha. You made yo choice!" Taj yells.

"This is business. We family, no matta what goes on in the BDs," Pops says.

"Correction, this *was* a family business, rooted in community. You killed it when you called that secret council meetin today and tried to steal it from us," Taj says. "When you disappeared, it almost destroyed us. Auntie Rissa made a miracle happen and found a way to keep our family *and* the BDs all togetha. Neva thought you comin back would hurt just as much."

Pops tries to stop him, but I grab Taj and walk ahead.

"I hope when you beat the Bainbridges and the DKs, it's worth it," Auntie Rissa says to Pops. "You won't have much of a family to come back to if this is how you plan to do it."

21

Will

"Will . . . Will . . ." Mum shakes me softly.

I wake up confused. Is this . . . anotha dream? But it can't be, 'cuz she's sittin' in her hospital gown.

I ask her ova and ova, "This really real? Are you awake? Are you okay?"

Mum reaches out her arms, and I crawl into them.

Miss Julia comes back in the room. When she sees me and Mum, she makes a noise I can only describe as a happy sigh of relief as she hugs both of us. Jacob and Jay arrive lata on, and I swear I'm happier than I've eva been.

After hugs that almost neva end and Mum tellin' us how she feels, the nurses check her vitals. She seems to be in good spirits, although there's somethin' on her mind she ain't sayin'; I can tell.

After Dr. Eva says everythin' looks good and that she'll be back down to check how she's feelin' in a few hours, Miss Julia says her, Jay, and Jacob are gonna run down to the cafeteria to grab us somethin' to eat. She asks what we want, then hurries Jay and Jacob out and whispers to them, "They need time alone."

My face hurts from smilin' so hard, but I can't stop.

"You been okay?" Mum pats the spot next to her.

I wanna tell her I'm fine, but she sees through me.

"Talk to me."

I answer with a hand ova my heart, rubbin' it in circles. She understands without me havin' to say a word.

Mum hugs my face, kisses me on the forehead. "I'm sorry, baby."

"What if someone you like is a bad person?" I ask.

Mum's eyebrows become two upside-down check marks. "Is it Jay?"

"No, somebody else." Her face relaxes as she takes a deep breath.

"You can love—"

I frown—a hell nah!

"Or *like* somebody and still not agree with their choices."

"But these ain't just *any* choices. There's some stuff I don't know I can eva forgive."

"That's your head thinking, not your heart. Sometimes I think the heart is simpler. It feels what it feels."

But is that really okay? To like Lyric? "What 'bout my feelings for Jay?"

"Do you feel any different about Jay?"

I shake my head, but still take the time to really think 'bout it.

"Then that's that. If you feel it, feel it. You just have to make sure you know how much you love yourself, and that you never compromise that *because* you like someone else. What's our motto?"

We say it togetha: "Shine brighter, even if it hurts."

Miss Julia, Jay, and Jacob come back with burgers and fries. Mum gives her burger to Jacob and puts her fries on my plate. I move from the bed to the chair next to her as we all catch up. We neva talk 'bout what's really on our minds, what happened to Mum while she was with the DKs.

Next time, I think, *next time*.

If I knew J.D. was gonna call me to the pool this mornin' outta nowhere, I wouldn't have stayed up all night with Miss Julia, Jay, and Jacob watchin' *Bad Boys* and *Bad Boys II* till we all fell asleep on the couches in the livin' room.

The pool is pretty much empty, so it's easy to spot J.D. sittin' on the startin' block, his feet touchin' the water. Once I make it ova to him, we dap and I get ready to dive in.

I get on the startin' block and pause, in my mind, to offer up everythin' to the water. When my legs, hands, and body feel free, I dive in.

It's been a little while since we practiced, more than a week.

Somethin' 'bout this warm-up feels different. I even notice colorful rings reflectin' off the bottom of the pool floor, like stars glimmerin' in their own sky.

After my last lap, I wait at the side of the pool with my kickboard.

"How are you feeling?"

Is he serious? He rarely asks this unless . . . I grin. He must've spoke to Mum. "I'm hangin' in there."

"Did you notice anything different as you swam?"

"Rings? I think I saw some at the bottom of the pool, different colors."

"Exactly. Today, you're going to get all of them, then we'll work on a few strokes before you're done for the day."

What kind of trainin' is this?

"Competition isn't enough," he says, readin' my face. "You've been carrying a lot lately, and now that Lin is safe, it's time to recalibrate with play."

"But where's the fun?" I joke.

His smile is a knock-knock joke. "The fun is in how you get them. Each time you have to get out of the water and dive in, but however you want. It could be a cannonball, for all I care. All that's required is that you accomplish the goal in the window of time—and have as much fun as possible."

I stare at him, skeptical, but I get outta the pool ready to test this out.

"Five minutes on the clock," he says. "Get as many as you can."

When he says go, I cannonball as high and hard as I can. In the cool blue, I find a yellow ring and bring it back.

"That all you got?" he says.

It's on! I jackknife and get the purple; Air Jordan and find the orange; I dance, then do the thinkin' man fuh pink. I can't stop laughin'. And when he asks me to swim a 100-yard freestyle as fast as I can, twice, by the time I slap the side of the wall and look up, he's wearin' a frown.

"What?" I ask, pullin' myself outta the pool. "Was it that bad?"

He shows me the time as his face explodes into the biggest smile. And before I can think 'bout it, I'm jumpin' up and huggin' him with happy tears fallin' down my face, 'cuz not only did I smash Lyric's record, I beat the state record without even tryin'.

After we finish a few more laps, I get dressed. On the bleachers near the double doors, J.D. sits so lost in thought that he doesn't hear me.

"You good?" I say, jokin'.

He brushes off my question, but it's clear somethin' is botherin' him. He was in a good mood earlier—did somethin' happen?

Then I realize I ain't see it 'cuz I been so focused on beatin' Lyric to win him ova. It's gotta be 'bout J.D.'s family—Miss Julia, Jacob, and Jay. Does he miss them?

J.D. leads me to the front of the buildin', then makes a left like he walkin' behind the Aquatic Center. I follow him, curious.

I stop, overwhelmed—there is a massive garden I ain't know was here. One thing catches my eye more: sunflowers. He reaches for his tools to clip two and wrap them in some newspaper.

"Give these to Lin. You headed to the hospital, right?" I nod.

I take them, blown away by their size and height. I don't know if I eva seen a sunflower in real life, at least not like these—they are huge.

"Why don't you just give them to her yourself?" The reason dawns on me as the words dive off the startin' block of my lips.

"Julia and the boys will be there. I don't want to stir anything up."

"So, you ain't neva gon' visit Miss Julia, Jacob, and Jay?" He looks at me, as if surprised I ain't let it go. "Ain't you gon' make it right?"

"It's not that simple. I agreed to not be around until—"

"They've forgiven you?" I finish his sentence. "But how long that's gon' take?"

J.D. ain't mad, but he don't seem to be happy eitha.

"How about you let me worry about that and you just focus on keeping your time where it is—or even lower?" He grins.

"In a way, I am. I need my coach to get what you need, your family."

He watches me, chuckling.

"What?"

"Nothing. If it makes you feel better, Lin said the same thing." J.D. looks at his watch and guides me back toward the front of the buildin'. "Today might be a hard one, so I'm hopin' these will help, since they're her favorite."

"Why would it be a hard one?" I frown, but he doesn't answer, just tells me to get to the hospital. I say what I been meanin' to say for a long time. "Apologize . . . like, furreal. Not just 'I'm sorry,' but why it happened and how you gonna make sure it neva happens again."

J.D. just stares at me, almost like he neva thought of it.

"It's what I would wanna hear, if my father eva came back." I leave before he can see how red my face is.

As I walk to the hospital, I wonder if we all got somebody we want to forgive us. But I stuff them feelings 'bout my father back down where they belong.

Mum is safe. To me, that's all that matters.

I hold the sunflowers close till I arrive at the hospital. When I enter her room, Mum has her glow back, but her face is serious, heavy with somethin' important.

"Happy birthday," I say.

The sunflowers in my hand are the perfect gift. She chuckles because we both know it's not her birthday.

"I don't know where you picked up this habit of pretend birthdays, but it cracks me up every time." She receives the bouquet, smilin'.

Mum neva said why sunflowers were her favorite, but she

always responds to them in the same way, in a trance.

"They come bright and beautiful by J.D. and yours truly." I grin.

"Tell him I said thank you. I take it you're coming from the pool?" Her eyes flash, revealin' her hand.

"J.D. said I have you to thank for my early mornin' workout," I say.

Mum's smile fades as quickly as it came. "Is there anything else you haven't told me that I should know?"

"No," I say, a reflex. Her eyes are waitin', sendin' a reminda that Mum neva asks questions she don't already know the answer to. "Maybe?"

I try to think my way outta it. I thought the truth would be easier to say, but it's not. It ain't just Mum I gotta worry 'bout; it's Miss Julia, too.

"How about I help you remember?" She narrows her eyes. "J.D. explained that you've been taking swimming lessons, that you even joined a swimming team. And on that team happens to be someone I didn't expect."

"Lyric," I finish, givin' up any thought I had of hidin' it.

"I'm assuming you didn't join the team out of your undying love for the sport."

I shake my head, caught. "You promise not to be mad?"

"Too late. You should have led with the truth. You know better."

"I ain't have no otha choice. It was the only thing I could do to help."

Mum's eyes leave me pissed and come back disappointed. "Does Miss Julia know?"

"No," I say quickly.

"Okay, anything else?"

Wait, what? Mum findin' out I kept somethin' like this from Miss Julia, somethin' she considers dangerous—no matta the reason—at least would result in me gettin' yelled at.

"Want me to call the doctor?" I try to check her temperature by puttin' my hand on her forehead. "You not dyin' and ain't tellin' me, are you?"

I stare at her from the side, even poke her in her arms till she slaps my hand away, makin' sure this ain't anotha dream 'bout to turn into a nightmare.

"No, nothing like that, I'm fine. It's just . . . I need you to know that everything I do is because I love you, and I don't ever want you to doubt that."

"Okay . . ." I plot how I can find Dr. Eva and Mum's charts.

There's a knock at the door, and it's not only Miss Julia, Jacob, and Jay, but Miss Rissa, Taj, and Leroy—and their mom, Miss Tanya, in her work uniform. Mum smiles at Miss Tanya as she checks her vitals and gestures for Leroy to close the door after they all finish fillin' the room.

Once greetings and small talk are ova, I can see Mum gearin' up to say somethin'.

"I'll start with what you probably already know after what Tré must have shared with y'all, but I was here setting up an operation to infiltrate the DKs and, in doing so, map the Bainbridges' network of corruption."

"When you say infiltrated, do you mean—" Taj says.

"Yes, I had a few of my own people in the DKs."

Everyone looks at each otha, speechless.

"The problem is that Frank and Myrrh had grown suspicious of them. And to save their lives, I had to act quickly."

Miss Julia shakes her head and clenches her jaw.

"I set up a meeting with Alderman Delroy at Ronaldo's, under the guise of representing potential investors. I had my men leak my location and identity. And when they arrived, they led the charge to kidnap me."

Mum *knew* this would happen? And she let it?

"But things got complicated when a young man with the BDs tried to intervene."

"Nate from the Low Rider Crew," Taj says.

Mum nods in agreement. "I did my best to warn him, but he was so focused on protecting me, he wouldn't listen. That's when Frank and Myrrh attacked him and the other BDs with him. Frank was beating Nate badly. Then I noticed he was filming, so I covered him with my own body, took some of the blows myself, to stop them from killing him, hoping he can use the footage somehow later."

They . . . beat . . . Mum? The room feels like it's shakin'.

"Nate shared the tape wit us and our contact at the police department that was workin on a way to arrest errbody involved. Things are a lil complicated now, cuz the chief is tryna throw him outta the force, but we still workin on the perfect timin so we can hit em all at once just like they did us," Leroy says, his eyes runnin' from mine.

The fuck? He knew they did this to my mum, and he neva told me!

"How could you?" Miss Julia asks, almost on the verge of a growl. "After everything, how could you still be this selfish?" Miss Julia almost crumbles. Her eyes fill with angry tears and her angrier hands become sharp knives ready to cut. She gets up to leave.

"I did it for you," Mum says.

"What?" Miss Julia turns around, furious. "Don't you dare justify doing something so reckless and dangerous for me."

"Ever since I left, I have been trying to find a way to make it clear to you that I'm sorry. That although I don't regret leaving and having Will, I've felt helpless all this time, because I know I made a mistake. When Tré approached me, I saw a chance to try to make things right, to play my part in something bigger, and figure out a way to be more—"

"No!" Miss Julia yells. "No, I won't hear another word. You took it too far."

Miss Julia's words melt into pure hurt and sadness. Mum sees it, too.

"And if it means that you and Jay, Jacob, J.D.—all of us could have a fighting chance—I would go further."

"Even if it means us losing you?" The question slaps Mum silent.

Miss Julia walks out. Jacob looks at me, then follows, sayin' he'll be back once he checks on her.

After hearin' everythin', I dunno how to feel.

"The two people who were on the inside. Who were they?" Leroy asks.

"They were the ones protecting me when you found us."

"But they tried to run," Leroy says.

"We thought Frank and Myrrh had caught us, so they were trying to get me out of there safely. But knowing that you were BDs will help avoid attracting too much suspicion, since now it looks like they were trying to get away from y'all."

"We get what's goin on *now*, but we aint know nothin besides what you shared wit us befo you were taken," Taj says. "How we know can we trust you?"

"Why wouldn't you be able to trust Mum, after all she did for y'all?" My words are rough, on purpose. "It's your pops that's the problem!"

Mum's eyes hush me quiet, but I want an answer. How could they doubt her?

"We aint arguin witchu on that, Will," Leroy says before he turns his eyes to Mum. "It's just things are a lil complicated between us and Pops, Miss Rosalind."

Mum nods slowly, lookin at Miss Rissa. "Right, I'm sure

it's been hard for you. Quite a shock after all these years, but I don't understand how you didn't already know the full—"

"Rosalind, you . . . you *do* know that Tré stole the BDs from us—" Miss Rissa begins to say.

"Excuse me?"

"You didn't know?" Miss Rissa asks.

"What do you mean?"

Miss Rissa, Taj, and Leroy exchange looks. They look at me, too.

"We thought you knew," Leroy says.

Taj, Miss Rissa, and Leroy explain what happened when Tré came to the BD's council meetin' and 'bout the new anti-gang bill proposed targetin' the BDs, mainly the YGs. Then they reveal stuff I ain't even know: the fight between the OGs and the YGs and Tré officially becomin' the new leader of the BDs. The whole time, Mum just listens. I had no idea any of this was goin' on, that it had got this bad.

"That's why Tré isn't here with you?" Mum asks.

"So you sayin this won't no plan of yours at all?" Taj says.

"No, because it won't work," Mum says. "Now is the worst time for this kind of power grab. The BDs have to be united. Otherwise—"

"The DKs will use it to their advantage." Jay finishes Mum's sentence, no longer quiet.

"Right," she says.

"So who you wit? Us or Pops?" Taj asks.

Mum don't say nothin' at first, but the look on Taj's, Leroy's, and Miss Rissa's faces says that this the only way they gon' say or do anythin' else. She gotta pick a side.

"If you're asking whether I agree with his actions, I don't. But if you're expecting me to choose you over him, I won't."

Taj frowns. "Why not?"

"Because this is much bigger than you think."

"Did you find somethin out while you were behind enemy lines?" Miss Rissa says, shiftin' Taj's focus. It's like she cracks open whateva invisible door Taj was 'bout to close.

"Not as much as I hoped, since Frank and Myrrh don't talk to anyone but Louis. I did get to confirm something me and Lady Tee had been suspicious about for a long time. Louis has his sights set on more than Savannah, more than Georgia—he wants to become president."

"President? How he gon do that?" Taj says.

"He's not running tomorrow, but he's about to take the first step and run for governor. I almost didn't know myself until one of my DK contacts revealed Myrrh said he hadn't heard anything from Louis since he left to visit OGEP."

"What does that even mean?"

"It's code for Oglethorpe Mansion, where the top king-makers and queenmakers meet potential candidates. Their blessing comes with a super PAC of tens of millions of dollars of support and connections as an initial investment, almost a guaranteed win, depending on the seat of office and state."

"That's why he had them propose that bill." Miss Rissa shakes her head. "Up there talm bout the Bainbridge Promise. That's a campaign slogan if I've eva heard one."

"And it's why, if he pulls off these plans we've unearthed, he won't just be considered successful, he will have won the favor of some powerful people," Mum says. "They'll fund him to dream bigger, backed by their interests."

"So how do we stop it? Is it even possible?" Jay says, scared.

"We need to figure out what Louis's full plan is now. We have his endgame, and I have part of his network uncovered."

"We have mo than that," Leroy says. "We've been hackin Louis B's network on our end too. We've got access to dozens of their computers and ears in both the police and District Attorney departments."

"Togetha we might actually have nearly his complete network, but I'm not convinced it's the entire picture yet," Miss Rissa says. "This is all relyin on the success of Bainbridge Promise, and that's dependent on dismantlin the BDs. If the bill goes through, it'll hit us hard, but it's not a sure win—they gotta have somethin else in the works."

"Whateva it is, it must be happenin soon," Taj says. "We can't fuhget that the DKs been passin round flyers tryna get people to sell they property in K-Town so they can sign up fuh this new housin development. Only thing is, Miss Rosalind, this aint no property downtown. It's all the way in the outskirts, Putnam Parkway."

Mum repeats the name to herself.

"It glitters real bright, but it aint nothin but a dressed-up land grab," Leroy says.

"Most of the folks in K-Town are still holdin out," Taj adds. "But after weeks of cop harassment, DKs doing any and err-thang, and the DA threatenin wit all kinds of warrants, we don't know how long folks gon be able to take, especially after the news coverage on the new bill, framin the BDs as a criminal enterprise."

"And what Pops did to Husani and the Low Rider Crew, don't—" Leroy stops halfway through as we all turn to hear the noise of stompin' feet comin' from outside Mum's room.

Miss Julia rushes in with Jacob, Night, and PYT, and a few otha people I don't recognize, and slams Mum's door closed behind them.

"The police are here," Miss Julia says, outta breath. "And they are storming the place looking for you, Lin—but also Rissa and Taj."

There's all kinds of shoutin' comin' from the hallway.

"Should we—" PYT says, but Taj stops him in his tracks with a look. Taj nods at Leroy and Miss Rissa.

"They're makin their move," Taj says. "Rememba the plan: PYT, hit up Brown Brown, let em know. Lee, text Trish, put her uncs on alert, and let em know we headed to the station."

"Julia, take this," Mum says, reachin' for a notepad next to her bed and scribblin' somethin' as fast as she can before handin' it over. "Call the names on this list and let them know who's been arrested. I think I can get out on health reasons, but just in case, let them know the moment you leave this room."

I'm 'bout to explode, 'cuz ain't nobody tellin' me nothin'. "What do we do?"

"It's gonna be okay. Will . . . Will . . . look at me," Mum says.

Jay's phone vibrates, and he pulls it out to read the text.

"It's Princeton," he announces. "The police stormed his house looking for Lady Tee."

There's bangin' on the door. Someone yells for us to open up.

"It's the chief," Miss Rissa says. "When I open this door, nobody move. Last thing we need is Chief and his men gettin trigger-happy and claimin self-defense." She opens the door slowly.

Everyone puts their hands up as Chief Laynor walks in and stares at Miss Rissa. He's a Black man, tall, with a full head of gray and a crooked smile.

"LaRissa Booker, Taj Booker, and Rosalind Alexander, you are all under arrest," Chief Laynor says.

"What are the charges, Officer?" Mum asks, her voice soft and calm.

Chief Laynor pauses as if he's thinkin' of not sayin' anythin' at all and takin' them by force just 'cuz he wants to.

I clench my fist. *Over my dead body.*

"Conspiracy and racketeering."

"And who's the judge who signed off on your warrant?" Mum asks.

"Cuff 'em," he says.

The cops move toward Mum. "Get the fuck away from her," I growl.

"William," Mum shouts, her voice yankin' me in her direction. "So help me God, if you say anything else."

I'm shakin' with the words she's trapped inside me.

"Chief, can anyone who wasn't listed leave first?" Mum asks.

He grumbles but agrees.

I feel like somebody's put a plastic bag ova my head, and dared me to breathe. I storm past the cops, wishin' I could get rid of them myself.

I turn down the hall and try to slip into a waitin' room where there ain't no people. I expect everyone else to keep walkin', but Jay comes in.

"Hey, Will. Are you—"

"Get the fuck away from me!" I'm tryna to keep it down, but I'm 'bout to explode.

He stares at me in disbelief.

"Who the fuck you think you talkin to?" Leroy says, jumpin' in front of him.

"Bitch, who you think?!" I shove him outta my way, but

Jacob catches me and pulls me back. "Chill, what's wrong witchu?"

"Fuck you mean? He knew what they did to Mum and ain't say shit. Did you?" I ask Jay.

When he don't say anythin', it feels like my heart is bein' stabbed ova and ova, and I'm bleedin' out.

"Y'all both betta get away from me . . . fuckin' liars." I narrow my eyes, lock on to Jay. "I shouldn't be surprised. You neva gave a fuck 'bout me. You just played with my heart, and now that Leroy's here again, you ain't gon' do nothin' but choose him all ova, again."

"How could you say that?" Jay yells back. "I never meant to—"

I laugh. Not 'cuz it's funny, but 'cuz it hurts.

"That's enough," Jacob says, movin' me further away from them and into a corner. He tryna make me look at him so he can cool the heat that got me ready to swing on Leroy if he keep starin' at me like he gon' do somethin'.

Only I gotta make sure they not doin' nothin' to Mum. I try to push past Jacob, but he won't budge. "Lemme out! I gotta . . . I need to—"

"No, Will . . . no," Jacob says.

I rush at him, but he backs me farther into the corner.

"I can't lose her." The words come out softer than I want them to.

"You won't." But he can't know for sure. Nobody can.

Why am I so weak? Why can't I do somethin'? If they hurt her . . . if they kill her . . . The questions suffocate me.

Somebody gotta pay. Since I can't protect her, I hurt myself.

I slap and punch myself till I bleed, till all I see is red as my body starts to shake against my will, tinglin' all over till it's almost like I'm full of electricity.

Jacob traps my arms in a bear hug, but as I fight to get free on the floor, I slam my head into the wall next to us.

Suddenly I hear Jacob, the strongest person I know, cryin', beggin' me to stop as Leroy yells for help. Jay breaks down, sobbin', barely holdin' it togetha.

Then everythin', all the pain, all the noise, all the tears just stop. And all I can think of is Mum's golden sunflowers, covered in blood.

Part Three
Freedom Festival

22

Leroy

By the time I make it to the police station, it's been almost two hours. Miss Rosalind was allowed to stay at the hospital, since she won't be discharged fuh a coupla days. But Auntie Rissa, Taj, and Lady Tee are still sittin, forced to wait, and the whole station might go up in flames any minute.

Errbody else is already here. I nod at Miss Julia and J.D., who sit right next to Dr. Eva and Lady Tee, talm bout somethin I can't really hear. But whateva it is, Auntie Rissa, Benji, and Ma noddin. Taj is sittin by em, busy on his phone.

Our plan mostly worked. Thanks to our calls to Brown Brown and Trish, we quickly and anonymously sent the ADA the evidence she needed to provide the chief's corruption, as well as clear Dane's and errbody else's name. But we don't know how long it's gon take to get the charges dropped, so we stuck here, havin the popos ignore us.

I sit in the seat right next to Benji, who got his arm round Auntie Rissa. I get a text from Rouk, lettin me know Night, Rouk, PYT, and Brown Brown still at the YGs' spot combin through Faa's journals fuh anythin we mighta missed and listenin in on the tech, especially connected to ADA Butler,

Lyric's room, and Ronaldo's fuh anythin we could use or need to know.

"Jacobee said him and Jay are okay, they still at the hospital wit Will, who sleepin it off. The docs gave em somethin to calm down." Taj reads through mo texts from the otha YGs to see if the DKs might be plottin somethin else that aint come through our tech. Nothin, not yet.

Out of the corner of my eye, I see Miss Julia stand up, J.D. quickly moves in front of her. When we see why, all of us stand up, too, in shock and anger, as Louis B walks through the front doors, followed by a team in suits.

He nods at Miss Julia and J.D., specifically, then calls fuh the chief of police. Errbody keep they guard up to see what he do next.

The chief almost runs ova. "Mr. Bainbridge, what brings—"

"Release them," Louis B says. I look at Taj, all the way confused.

"If you have no evidence and flimsy warrants, then it's unlawful and unconscionable to hold them. Is that what we're doing now? Terrorizing our citizens? If this is the type of police department you're running, I'm not sure you need to remain chief."

Lady Tee shakes her head, looks ova at Miss Julia and J.D. They eyes say it all, *Ain't that callin the kettle black.* Benji squeezes Auntie Rissa's shoulder, as we both see the anger in her risin.

"Louis, why are you here?" Miss Julia's voice shoots through like an arrow.

"I'm just doing my part, Julia, as a concerned citizen. Trying to rectify whatever misunderstandings might have occurred here against the leadership of the Black Diamonds, one of Savannah's most impactful grassroots community organizations."

"And what do you mean by that, exactly?" Lady Tee asks. "I know you and your office have been getting calls from congressmen, business leaders, and others the past two hours, notifying you we were here and withdrawing initial support for your insidious proposal that would *target* members of the Black Diamonds, after your men dragged me out of a call with the state attorney general."

Louis B winces, caught. "I'm not sure what you're implying by 'my men,' but like I've said to you personally, I'm committed to K-Town and its residents getting what they deserve—"

"While you strip em of their property rights? Or should they be grateful fuh that six-thousand-dollar 'gift' fuh relocation when you already trickin and intimidatin em to sell far under market value?" Auntie Rissa says.

"I understand that emotions might be running high, given your treatment today. But I welcome any feedback or recommendations you might have."

"When are you going to stop?" Miss Julia's voice is a one-hitta-quitta.

"I don't know what you mean, Julia. I'm just here to—"

"Help? Is that why you keep looking at J.D., no matter who you're supposedly talking to? Why won't you leave him be?" Miss Julia pushes toward Louis B, but J.D. pulls her back, keeps distance between em. "Haven't you done enough? You've stolen years from him, attacked our family, and left scars on every person here. Leave!"

Louis B tries to speak, but J.D. stands so close he can't see anybody else but him.

"Lou . . . you heard her. Go, while you still can," J.D. says. "If I hit you this time, I won't stop."

Louis B smirks as his eyes grow cold and he walks away.

After we finally finish up at the station, we all head ova to Auntie Rissa's, pickin up Night, Rouk, Brown Brown, and PYT from the YGs' spot on the way. Jacobee calls Taj, says he wants to come too, but that it might be lata, cuz things are lookin rough on they end. Fuh a second, I wonder if me and Jay was officially togetha again, would he do the same thing? Would he always know when I need him most befo I have to say the words?

In the livin room, we all chop it up and try to lift our spirits while Auntie Rissa's in the kitchen takin a call.

It aint errday that you can walk away from an interaction with Louis B after givin just as good as you got.

But just when I think we can finally take a breath, there's

a crash and scream in the kitchen.

Errbody jumps up and run in to find Auntie Rissa standin near the sink, so mad she's shakin. Benji moves quick, holds her tight, tells her to breathe. Eventually, she breaks down.

We all look at each otha, confused.

But Ma rushes ova and helps get Auntie Rissa to the seat closest to her at the dinin room table, while Night and Brown Brown sweep up the glass on the floor and Rouk makes some peppermint tea.

Errbody else sits round the table in silence and solidarity.

When the tea's ready, Rouk makes Auntie Rissa a glass. She whispers thanks, sips quietly wit her eyes closed, and softly says, "It's like when we take a step forward, we get kicked six steps back—and asked to be thankful fuh the chance."

"Did somethin happen?" Ma asks.

"The investors . . . talm bout pullin the franchise, all of it." Auntie Rissa shakes her head.

"What? They can't do that! Did they say why?" Ma says.

"Somebody flagged the warrant from today and said the insurance company wants to investigate again fuh foul play."

"But the insurance folks aint find nothin the first time," I say.

"Don't matta," Auntie Rissa says. "The threat was enough to spook the investors, and now all of a sudden, they don't want the bad press."

"So that's it? Aint nothin else we can do to change they mind?" Night asks.

Errbody is quiet—out of ideas, out of hope.

"You said they afraid of the bad press, that it would hurt the franchise, right?" Rouk asks, slowly pullin out one of the journals he keeps wit him at all times.

Auntie Rissa nods, defeated.

"When all you wanna do is cry, laugh instead," Rouk says, rubbin his finger over somethin written in the journal befo lookin up at us. "It's somethin our grandpop used to say. What if, instead of tryna outdo Louis B, we focused on the one thing we always had: the community?"

"What do you have in mind?" Benji says, rubbin Auntie Rissa's shoulders.

"I need mo time to think it through, but Faa had somethin in his journal bout K-Town owners' current property values versus what the lands gon be worth after the development. The difference between the two is wild. I think errbody in here know, but how many folks actually seen these numbers?

"So what if we focused on that? Laid it out, iono, like an investment opportunity where people see the numbers fuh themselves—the cost of stayin versus leavin. We let em make whateva decision is best fuh them. And maybe, fuh those who wanna leave, we find a way to buy em out, at the price they deserve. But we put it all out on front street, so errbody know."

"Like at a BD council meetin?" Auntie Rissa asks.

"Nah, in a way that only the BDs know how to get down, and in a way that will get you the publicity you need so errbody can be reminded of just how special you are to K-Town—a block party."

Errbody nods, sits up in their seats a lil different.

"Dayum, I aint think of that," Taj says. "It's like doin both at the same time: wowin the investors but upliftin community. The block party can be how we show errbody how we can do this togetha, instead of just tellin folks what they should and shouldn't do."

"And if we make the point of the block party be Auntie Rissa, errbody and they momma gon come through, drawin an even bigger crowd. Whateva people might feel about the BDs now wit all the DKs have done tryna destroy our reputation, errbody still got love fuh Auntie Rissa," Brown Brown says.

"Iono, yall," Auntie Rissa says. "This event should be bout errbody's right to freedom, not me or the diner. I can try to figure somethin out anotha way."

"Whatchu think yo diner is to errbody?" Ma says. "Been the one thing outta all this that kept our family togetha. It aint just boutchu, it's what you represent—the joy you been bringin into this world fuh ova twenty years. I think Rouk and Brown Brown right, if we do it this way, it's gon hit different. Plus, the joy of seein you back up there cookin and servin wit Benji and Jacob, even me and Julia helpin?"

Errbody look at each otha and grins, a silent joke bout whetha Ma should be cookin.

"Don't hate! Benji already gave me my props. Ya gurl can officially burn," Ma says.

"I second that. I stand by my student," Benji says.

"I third it. My taste buds have tasted the glory," Auntie Rissa adds.

Ma smiles wider than she has in a long time.

"So, whatchu say, baby?" Benji looks down at Auntie Rissa.

"Come on, Auntie," Taj say, cheesin wit both rows of teeth.

"Yall think we can really do it?" Errbody can see Auntie Rissa's waverin.

"It's time we showed em what the YGs know is worth protectin—you," Taj says.

When Auntie Rissa nods, breakin into the smile we been needin mo than anythin else, all our spirits are lifted.

I wake to the sound of laughter. Not just gigglin, but a lotta voices.

After washin up and brushin my teeth, I run downstairs to see who here, and that's when I realize errbody: PYT, Brown Brown, Night, Rouk, and Trish. But not just them, almost errbody—YGs from wall to wall.

In the kitchen, Ma and Jacobee switch places, shimmyin and shakin to the soundtrack of people talkin ova one anotha.

On the stove, they usin all the burners and the oven to fry sausages and cook pancakes.

In between bites of breakfast, errbody is workin to plan the Freedom Festival. Whateva one of us can't figure out on our own, Auntie Rissa, Ma, and Benji lend a helpin hand—or Lady Tee, Miss Rosalind, and Miss Julia on speed dial as we reach out to vendors, partners, sponsors, and errbody else we can think of. And when Christina arrives wit all the majorettes of Daniel Lee, plannin kicks into high gear, especially when she say Risé is callin in favors, too.

"Aye, Lee, somebody here fuh you!" Rouk yells from the livin room.

It don't take long fuh me to see who it is, and when I do, iono what to do wit myself. It's Mistah Prez in regular clothes, if you can call a linen suit regular. He walks into the kitchen wit a small gift bag and does a presidential nod to errbody who makes eye contact, but his eyes linger when he sees Jacobee. It don't take long befo they hug, too. Taj comes round, pulls him in, and does a special handshake.

"Wait, yall know each otha?" I ask Taj.

"Do I?" Mistah Prez says. "This one gave me a run for my money when I was dean a few years ago."

"Dean Henry—my bad, President Henry—used to be in charge of the GED program," Taj says.

I look at him, surprised. I neva woulda thought he knew Taj.

"I should've made the connection of your last names but I didn't put two and two together. You and your brother are so alike, brilliant and you have a knack for pushing people," he says.

Auntie Rissa and Ma find they way ova to Mistah Prez, lookin both like cartoons wit hearts in they eyes.

"I take it you two lovely ladies are Taj and Leroy's sisters?" He grins, turnin em into blushin schoolgirls.

"So, you the Mistah Prez Leroy's been goin on about?" Ma says. "It's a pleasure to finally meet you. What brings you to visit us?"

Mistah Prez looks at me, as if he askin permission, and I realize he's here cuz of the magazine and the scholarship. Wit errthang that's been goin on, I still aint told nobody but Taj bout my GED scores or the scholarship program in poetry.

"It's cool, Mistah Prez," Taj says, usin my name for him. "You can tell em."

I look at Taj and see that smirk that comes out when he been doin somethin behind my back. He the one who invited Mistah Prez?

Auntie Rissa calls to Trish in the livin room, askin her to turn the music down.

Mistah Prez begins to say errthang I couldn't. "Well, Leroy has become the man of the hour. Not just because he scored the highest on the GED than anyone, but he's attracted the attention of a few publishers because of his poetry."

"Lee been writin poetry?" Ma says, not sho she hearin him right. She says it again to Auntie Rissa, who face showin all kinds of emotions at once, just like Ma's.

"Tell us mo, Mistah Prez, we aint know Lee was a poet. He been keepin all this goodness a secret it would seem," Auntie Rissa says.

My face feels hot.

"Okay, I figured. There's nothing wrong with being shy." Mistah Prez winks at me. "Just in case you hadn't heard anything, I thought I'd bring a few copies of the anthology Leroy was published in with copies of his poems. I'd like to share them with you as long as Leroy is comfortable with it."

"He is, thank you." Ma's hands are out, purple nails flutterin toward the bag.

Iono why I expected Ma to want to read it lata, but as soon as she gets the bag, she pulls out the three books—all shiny, black, and new—and passes one to Taj and one to Auntie Rissa. Trish, PYT, Brown Brown, and Rouk sneak behind us to see what all the commotion is bout, readin ova Taj's shoulder.

If I could run to anotha room, I would. But errbody crowds round me, and there aint no way I can leave. It's weird watchin people read somethin I wrote, and seein they faces change through shades of emotions, some I can understand, most I can't. But when Ma's eyes start fillin up and Auntie Rissa's doin the same, iono what to do or say.

"I take it y'all feel the same way I do about Leroy's work," Mistah Prez says.

I feel grips and pats on my shoulder behind me, approval. As the books find they way in hands of errbody else, mo smiles, oohs, and ahhs sneak near my ears.

"I mentioned this to Leroy but wanted to formally tell him in person that his work has attracted the attention of a college in the Midwest that has one of the best creative writing programs I know for undergraduates. A good friend and former colleague runs it. She would like for Leroy to apply for their program and, if he's accepted, he would get a full-ride scholarship, including room and board and a modest stipend for all four years so he wouldn't have to take out any loans."

I rememba Mistah Prez sayin this to me in his office, but somethin bout him sayin it right here, right now, in front of errbody, makes it feel mo real.

"So you sayin Lee could go to college fuh poetry?" Rouk says.

"He would still need to apply, but I think he has a very high chance of getting in, and he wouldn't only need to apply to this school."

"What he gotta do? You need him to write somethin now? Taj, go get Lee a notebook and a pen. We gon get this handled today." Ma steps ova to the dinin table. "Yall move on ova. One of my babies a poet, give em some space to write so he can—"

"Not just yet," Mistah Prez says, smilin at Ma's pride. "I'm already working with him on some pieces for his midterm. But I just wanted to drop these off, since I told him they would be coming out soon. I thought they might give him a boost of confidence as he considers whether he wants to apply.

"We have a few weeks, so how about we meet soon and just look through the application questions together," Mistah Prez continues. "Jacob, I know you're also in the process of applying to Northwestern, perhaps you can help too. Plus, if you want, Leroy, Northwestern is just a two-and-a-half-hour bus ride from this school."

"Wait, Northwestern? Aint that where—" Taj squeezes my shoulder and smirks, stoppin me in my tracks.

Suddenly, it all feels different cuz it aint just bout a chance to go to college, but a whole notha future I aint considered, one where I'm near Jay, too. Is that why Taj said I should do it scared? Was that why he was considerin a change from the BDs? He already knew Jacobee might be leavin too.

Ion say nothin, but my head get to noddin and, again, my body feelin warm all ova, but this time, it's fuh a different reason. After Mistah Prez makes his goodbyes, I know who I need to go see.

As Jacobee pulls up in front of his house, I aint ready to get out of the car. I stare at the gift bag from Mistah Prez wit the slick black anthology and my poems bookmarked.

Befo leavin Auntie Rissa's, Jacobee said I should share it wit Jay and offered me a ride to their house. But somethin done changed between me leavin the house and makin it here.

I still wanna turn round, but I guess my heart wanna go forward mo than my mind wanna go back, cuz I grab the bag and head to the front door wit Jacobee.

He leads me by my shoulders to the stairs, gives me the strength I need to climb. From the hallway, I can hear Jay gigglin. In the doorway to his room, I see why. He's lyin on his back, wit his legs up on the wall as he reads a book.

When I knock on the open door to get his attention, my heart drops when his eyes meet mine. When he stands up, I scoop down and give him a tight hug.

Fuh some reason, my words aint workin like I need em to, so I pull out the anthology and open it to my section of poems and hand it to him.

"What's this?" he says, but when he sees my name and gives me that Kool-Aid smile, I realize why I wanted—nah, needed—to be here. Can't nobody see me like Jay.

He doesn't say anythin while I stand there on the edge of fuheva, but ion wanna be no otha place as he pulls me down to sit next to him on the bed. He reads, finger strokin the words, lips whisperin their sounds back like a spell. And by the time he reads the last poem and looks up at me, ion really know what to do, cuz his eyes are waterin, too.

"I'm sorry," he says. "It's just . . . really beautiful."

"I want you to have it, the book," I say. I try to keep my hands busy, cuz they don't wanna do nothin but touch and hold him, even tho I know we aint really talked bout us since the hospital.

"Will you sign it for me?" Jay hops up and grabs a pen from his desk, stands in front of me, a breath of sugar and vanilla.

"Sign it?"

"Yeah, I want your autograph. You're going to be a famous poet someday, so I want the first copy of them signed."

Really? My chest is so full it hurts.

"Leroy . . . you okay?" Jay asks.

"Oh, yeah. My bad. I'm good." I sign the page and tell him Mistah Prez's words bout the school, the scholarship, and where it's located. And then it's like I can't stop talkin as I share how scared I am of failin, not bein good enough to get in. But Jay just grabs my hand and holds it. Without sayin a word, it's like the worries disappear and he leaves somethin warm and unspoken in their place.

We don't notice anyone else has come inside the house until the front door slams shut so loud downstairs that we both jump up.

"J.D.'s in trouble!" Will yells, pantin in the entryway. "We have to help him—"

"Will, slow down. What did you say?" Jacobee says, runnin in from the kitchen.

He takes a deep breath, explains. "I was supposed to have a swimmin' lesson this mornin', like I always do. But when I got there, I saw Frank and Myrrh rollin' up, too, headed into the Aquatic Center, askin' fuh J.D. He was workin' outside in his garden, so when I saw him, I ran and tried to warn him, but he told me to run instead. Hurry, we gotta help him!"

Errbody grab they stuff and run to the car. I call Taj and Husani and his crew; Jay and Will make some calls, too.

I watch Jay in the back, his face frozen and confused.

"Do you have Lady Tee's number?" Will asks Jacobee.

"Yeah, I already gave her a heads-up, Ma too," Jacobee says, shakin his left leg, nervous. "She ain't know you was takin swimmin' lessons wit J.D., did she?"

Will shakes his head. He looks ova at Jay, avoids his eyes.

"I'm sorry . . . for keepin' it from y'all, especially Miss Julia," Will says. "I was gonna tell y'all eventually . . . after everythin'." His words get lost on the way to their ears.

"This got anything to do with what you said in the hospital about you getting close with Lyric?" Jay asks.

Will nods.

"So, Leroy, I suppose that means you knew, too?" Jay looks at me wit hurt in his eyes.

"Not the details, but yeah." I try to soften the blow. "Me, Rouk, and Taj been workin wit Will to see if he could get some intel from Lyric on the DKs and Louis B that could lead us to Miss Rosalind."

Iono if it help or hurt, maybe both, but Will fills in the gaps fuh all of us, explains how he met Lyric at the pool by accident and runnin into J.D. who told him exactly how he could beat Lyric, which is where he got the idea.

Will apologizes to Jacobee, especially Jay, explains how it was the only way he could do somethin to help. And even tho Jay don't look happy, by the time both of us talk bout the call, when Lyric gave me the address, and I explain how we got Miss Rosalind free cuz of it, he seem to at least understand.

Right as we pull up, Jacobee gets a call from Miss Julia and Will from Miss Rosalind. When the Aquatic Center in sight, Jay lookin errwhere, tryna see what's goin on when we see a crowd of people ova near Treat's BBQ.

He don't say nothin, don't have to, as all of us hold our breath, hopin the cost of Louis B's revenge fuh Miss Julia callin him out at the precinct won't paid wit J.D.'s life.

23

JAY

"He at Treat's BBQ across the street. I can see Husani and the Low Rider Crew," Leroy says, as Jacob parks behind tricked-out vans.

Everyone hops out of the car quickly, jogs toward Treat's BBQ's neon-blue-painted shack in the center of the corner block, but whatever adrenaline I had is gone, and suddenly I don't want to be here. I'm glad Dad's okay, but I take my time walking behind the matching brick building with tents, tables, and chairs.

I see Dad holding ice to his forehead, sitting in a foldable chair next to Husani and other people I'm assuming are YGs, followed by the six-foot-five pitmaster demigod that is Treat, who emerges from the shack and pulls up a chair next to Dad. All of us grab a seat around the table.

Dad looks across the table at me, Jacob, and Will, nods. We nod back, at a loss for words but grateful he's okay.

I don't know why, but seeing Dad smile at everyone hurts.

"Whaddup, Lee?" Treat says, his voice so deep, you can feel it vibrate through the air. He pulls Leroy into a tight bro hug.

Husani and the YGs do the same, making room for us.

"Yall missed it," Treat says, cheesing with two rows of teeth. "Sani and the LRC made the YGs proud, had the DKs runnin back to their cars."

"By the time you called," Husani says, "we was already on whoopin they ass the moment we saw em run up on Lavender Man."

I haven't heard Dad's nickname said like that in a long time. Not as a backhanded compliment of who he once was but with pride.

"I appreciate all your help," Dad says. "I knew something was coming, just didn't know when."

"You knew?" I ask out loud on accident.

"After Julia called Louis out, I knew there would be consequences. Let's just say his hurt feelings always come with a price." Dad looks at me, and I look down.

"J.D. is their pops," Leroy says to Husani and his crew.

"Werd? I aint know yo pops was Lavender Man!" Husani says to me, shocked. "But the mo I look, the mo it make sense. Yall look just like him."

With a wave, Treat asks one of his guys to bring out platters of ribs, wings, and more for the table, with the infamous thirty-sauce spread for us to dip and choose from.

"Yo, Lavender Man, sound like you know Louis B mo than you lettin on," Husani says.

"Weren't you and Louis best friends at Providence Prep?" Treat says.

369

"Long time ago, yeah."

"Then what happened?" Leroy says, listening but not missing the chance to slurp sauce and meat from the ribs almost perfectly. All of us hang on Dad's every word, waiting.

"I found out why: Louis wanted to use me to get rid of the BDs so he could win favor with his father." Dad is suddenly lost in thought. "If Tré and your auntie Rissa succeeded, the Bainbridges were going to lose a lot of money. So Louis made me an offer he thought I couldn't refuse: a six-figure contract with the city and a promise to triple it each year."

"Dayum." Husani shakes his head. "That's a lotta money."

"What was the catch?" Leroy asks.

"Get the location of the upcoming BDs' meeting. But I wouldn't. In fact, when I realized he found out anyway, I called Tré and Rissa, told them it was a trap."

"You were the reason they called the meetin off at the last minute?" Leroy asks. "If you didn't—"

"It would've been a bloodbath." Dad finishes his sentence. "By the time I got to them, Rissa was unconscious. But after she was taken away in an ambulance, I found Tré beaten and bloodied, passed out between two buildings."

"You what?" Leroy sits up, confused. "You knew Pops was alive?"

"If you would have seen the shape he was in, you wouldn't call that alive." Dad's voice falls away, leaving us to imagine the worst. "I helped him get to safety, and that was that. I never knew if he made it or not, much like the rest of you. I didn't have time to think about it either, because Louis quickly discovered I was the one who tipped them off, so he ran me out of business, turned everyone against me, and even attacked my family. I couldn't handle it, so I turned to drinking until one day I broke. I hurt those I cared about, and I couldn't live with myself, so I attacked Louis, knowing he would try to lock me up and throw away the key."

Everyone goes quiet. Me and Jacob look down at our plates.

"I didn't know," Leroy says, lost in thought.

Treat squeezes Dad's shoulder, says something without words only men their age can understand. And after a mountain of to-go plates and a sea of daps, we're all about to leave when Dad walks up to us quietly. He wraps his arms quickly and gently around me and Jacob, kisses us both on our foreheads, whispers, "I love you." But he's gone before we can answer. Jacob and I stare at each other, speechless and warm all over.

I can't sleep no matter what I try to do.

I feel too much. Frustrated that Will kept his contact with my dad a secret. Sad because I understand why he did it. Quietly angry at Leroy for keeping it from me but not knowing how he would have told me after such a bad breakup. And I can't even begin to put words to how confused I am about Dad—and the strange fact that I miss him.

I crawl out of bed and go downstairs to get a glass of water and swipe some fruit snacks. As I climb the stairs, I hear a muffled whimper coming from Will's room. The door is cracked, so I lean in closer to hear. The sound stops, but just as I'm about to walk away, I hear it again.

I open the door, and Will is tossing and turning. The comforter and sheets are a ball on the floor next to his bed. With the way the moonlight slides down his back and legs, it's almost as if he could levitate, glowing with magic.

I tell myself to stay out of it. I remember his angry words at the hospital, the wet hurt of his eyes. But his whimper turns into a slow groan. He's hurting, I feel it.

I'll just ask him if he's okay. "Will . . . Will . . . ," I say.

He sits up, startled. Even in low light, I can see the evidence that he's been crying.

"My bad, I ain't mean to wake you." He lies back down and curls the pillow around his arm with his back to me. "I'm good now. I'll be quiet."

If I were thinking straight, I would take his words for what they are: an arm up, saying, *Stay back, don't come any closer*. But the ache in my body can't ignore the pain in his.

"Which one?" I ask, drunk on moonlight or maybe my own pain. "Are you good now or will you just be quiet but still hurt?"

"Whatchu doin'?" Will turns, facing me.

I'm confused by the question, because his eyes say no, but his hands are almost reaching for me. "What do you mean?"

"Jay, you know how I feel 'bout you, that ain't change."

I watch his hands reach for mine, shadow upon shadow.

"I just want to help. I don't like seeing you like this."

"Every time you give me hope"—he grabs my hand, holds it to his chest—"it's like somethin' here breaks, I dunno if I can fix it. Jay. I don't just like you, I love you. If there's any part of you that doesn't feel the same or you're not sure, stop reachin' for me. 'Cuz when you give me hope, it hurts."

Before I can say anything else, Will kisses me on the lips and turns away, but it feels too much like a door closing forever. I stand up and whisper, "I love you, too," loud enough for him to feel it but not to hear it.

Not instead of. Not more than. Not less than. And because I do, I can't hurt him anymore because of what I don't know, even if walking out the door means hurting me.

I woke up this morning, and Will had already left for school. I wasn't sure if he got Leroy's urgent text this morning about all of us needing to meet at the new YGs' building, that he and Taj would swing by to pick us up right after school.

The whole time me and Princeton walked to school, I dreaded me and Will would be going back to the same routine of him ignoring me whenever and treating me like the black hole of joy. But when he taps me on the shoulder after

373

the last bell, I wonder, maybe we're okay after last night?

"You see Leroy's text?" Will asks.

"Yeah," I say. "Did you?"

"Just did . . . but I think I might have to come catch up with y'all lata."

"Why? Something wrong?"

Princeton and Christina join us as a motorcade led by Taj's Avalanche and Leroy's powder-blue Cadillac roll up.

"Yall ready?" Leroy stands with his door half open, his eyes never leaving mine.

"Y'all go ahead, I'll catch up," Will says to the whole group.

"Why? We need you there, too," Leroy says.

"My coach won't lemme skip, 'cuz we got a meet this Saturday with college scouts. I gotta swing by, at least for an hour."

"Dayum," Princeton says. "Gotta do whatchu gotta do when scouts involved."

"That's my cue to leave, then," Christina says. "I need to send more to-do lists for the Freedom Festival."

Taj waves her toward his car, steals a hug and some of her laughter.

"It's cool," Leroy says. "We'll take you and then scoop you. We already planned on chattin wit Husani and Khalif ova at Treat's across the street."

By the time we've dropped Will off at the Aquatic Center, an hour comes and goes. Leroy and Taj chat with Husani and his crew, then with me and Princeton as we share what letters we've finished, and they mention some new potential clients.

Will texts me he's ready. When we arrive at the Aquatic Center, I offer to run in and get Will, but Princeton says he's coming with me.

As we walk toward the bleachers in front of the lap pool lanes, a voice calls my name. I assume it's Will, but it's Lyric.

We walk toward him because we have to, not because either of us want to. Lyric skips down the steps of the bleachers in a baby-blue parka and white Speedo, goggles hanging around his neck.

I naturally step in front of Princeton, become his shield. Lyric's smile may irritate me, but Princeton's clenched fists are begging for a reason to swing.

"Adding swimming to your list of activities?" Lyric says.

"Not quite," I say. I don't hide how little interest I have in speaking to him.

"Wassup, Princeton? Long time no see."

"Let's keep it that way." Princeton won't even look at him.

"Aww, I'm hurt. We were once best friends, now we can't even be cordial?"

Best friends?

"Nigga, you don't have friends. You have toys you control and throw away when they break or you get bored."

"It was a misunderstanding, Princeton," Lyric says, grinning.

"Besides, you didn't break, and with you, I was never bored."

The way Princeton's head snaps back at Lyric with fire in his eyes, I'm reminded of Leroy and Rouk, the kind of heart-break that only fists try to fix.

"Where's Will?" I say, trying to calm Princeton down with my eyes.

Lyric points to a lane not far from us. I don't recognize Will at first, but when he's swimming back in our direction, it's like time stands still (or moves according to his will). I've never seen anything more—

"Beautiful." Lyric's words cannonball mine, even though they're only a whisper.

I hate it, hearing him admire Will.

"I've never seen anyone move in the water the way he does. It kinda makes me jealous. Because of him, we broke a state record in the medley relay."

"What?" I try to swallow my surprise. I don't want Lyric thinking he's special and that there are things he knows about Will that I don't.

"He didn't tell you?"

I keep my eyes on Will. *Don't answer.*

"Why'd you do it?" I ask. "Give Will the location to Miss Rosalind?"

I want to show him I know and that me and Will have no secrets, even though I know we do.

"Why do you think?"

I let my silence speak for itself.

"So, how much would it cost . . . if I wanted you to write a love letter for me?" He grins, makes sure I know it'll be from him to Will.

In my mind, I drag Lyric by the back of his parka up and down each step until that cocky grin on his face is gone and he begs for my forgiveness.

"Jay!" Will's voice sails over the screaming rage in my head. "Meet me in the lobby. I'm comin' now."

Will jogs with a towel wrapped around his waist into the locker room. Princeton and I walk down the bleachers without saying anything to Lyric. He follows behind, but I ignore him.

Taj is at the check-in counter, and the older lady, a spitting image of Edda Nae but taller, laughs loud at whatever he must have said to her.

Taj turns in our direction, narrows his eyes, and grins with Lyric in his sights.

"Whaddup, whaddup?" Taj sings, pimping toward us, eyes locked on Lyric.

"Hey, Taj, how's it going?" Lyric's voice is soft, sweeter.

Taj doesn't respond at first, just chuckles, amused. "You real bold, rollin up smilin like you aint did nothin bad enough to get beat to sleep."

Lyric's smile buckles. He looks at us, nervous.

Taj inches closer, smile gone, face hard like an executioner.

"Look, Taj—"

"Nah, keep that. Aint shit you can say. The only reason I aint draggin yo ass outta here and handlin you myself is cuz you helped us find Miss Rosalind. But lemme give you a piece of advice: quit befo I run outta patience."

"Can I go now?" Lyric says, smileless.

"Of course. . . . Let's not run into each otha too soon." Taj's smile is sharp, dangerous.

Will runs through the door, stops. "Why you out here?" he says to Lyric. "Coach been lookin' for you. See you Saturday."

Lyric nods, and it's like seeing Will wipes away everything he just felt—the nervousness, fear, and suspicion.

"Let's roll." Taj blows a kiss to the older lady at the counter.

When we get outside, Princeton puts his arm around my shoulder.

"It's okay," he says.

I don't know if it's for me, but I know I need to hear it.

When we first pull up at the salon, me, Princeton, and Will think it's a joke. But once we make it through the back door to the actual YGs' headquarters, we try to catch our breath as we sit down next to Night, PYT, Brown Brown, Rouk, and Trish.

After being caught up on everything that happened at Treat's BBQ, Will's face is as focused as Miss Rosalind's when she's planning something. He nods, listening.

"Aight, now that errbody caught up, what's the big news? Whatchu find out?" Taj asks.

"Know how you said Louis B showed up at the police station yesterday? Well, he went from there to Ronaldo's. And let's just say, he won't smilin," PYT says. "One of our folks was playin back and listenin to the tapes from yesterday, and we found out the chief must have slipped out of the precinct to meet him there.

"We'll play a snippet of it, but looks like we were able to find out all the promises Louis B was makin and how he managed to have such a tight hold ova the chief. Louis B promised him that he'll become the new head of the police academy they buildin. We also got confirmation he's announcin his campaign to run fuh governor on the same day as the Freedom Festival."

"What? You furreal?" I say. "Why would he do that?"

PYT plays the tape, so we can hear it from his mouth, says it starts in the middle of a conversation. After promising the chief the new position, Louis B asks him for a favor: "I'm going to need one thing from you."

The chief stirs uncomfortably. "What do you need me to do?"

"I need you to resign, claiming responsibility for your precinct's misuse of power that led to the detainment of LaRissa, Taj, and Rosalind. With our plans to oust Dane shot and Butler building a case, we can't have this falling apart because of one lousy ADA who can't be bought. There needs to be someone to blame, and that's you. No one will question the DA wanting to keep things quiet and internal—Butler will lose momentum.

"You'll need to do a quick press conference and say that you're taking some time to be with your family. Then your name will stay clean to the public, and when the new chief is in place, I want you to contact Frank and Myrrh and tell them all systems are go and that they have permission to make a special appearance at the Freedom Festival." Everyone looks at each other, shocked. "Remind them to use their masks, so they aren't implicated. They need to do just like they did for the news coverage and say they are the Black Diamonds before attacking."

"How'd you like us to . . . contain . . . the situation?"

"Injuries so people remember, but no casualties. It needs to look like it could have been a massacre, not actually be one."

"What's the difference?"

"Death leads to outrage, the burning of the city. The other, simply protests, a list of demands, which we'll use to bring you back as the captain of the academy—one to *restore* order."

"And a future governor. That's why you're announcing on the same day as the festival? Don't answer that."

Both of them chuckle.

"You still want Frank and Myrrh to pull in your son?"

Louis B scoffs, almost like he's about to spit in his face.

"Nice job tipping off the media about him."

"Better to control the narrative than to be controlled by it. Call Lyric one of the ring leaders, then lock him up with the rest of them. He needs to learn his place. And when this is done, Chief, I'll clean your record, and you'll be hailed a hero—the person who pursued justice at all costs. Who knows, maybe there's even a future mayor in you yet, depending on how well you lead us out of the dark and into the light."

The recording stops, and no one speaks. We all just stare, baffled by what we heard.

"So, he's gon use the Freedom Festival as a tool fuh becomin governor," Taj says, struggling to hold back the anger that is slowly taking all of us over.

"No, that's only part of it. I've been lookin into more of Faa's writin, not just his journals," Rouk says, starting to hand out a few printouts of different articles from what seems like are different years. Some look old, some look more recent. "And rememba Faa's research on that new youth detention center they was tryna build?"

"Yeah, but aint Faa pass that stuff to a newspaper and they squashed it?" Taj says.

"It aint die. BPD won the contract, they just aint build it."

"That's a good thing, ain't it?" Will says, confused.

"Not when that aint the whole story," Trish explains. "He aint just win the contract to the youth detention center but also a state-of-the-art adult prison too. Supposed to be one of the biggest in Georgia." Trish locks eyes with Rouk so he'll continue right where she leaves off.

"Put em all togetha: the youth detention center, the new adult prison, and the new police academy and all you gotta ask is one last important question: Where they gon be built?"

Rouk pulls out a bigger map of Savannah. On it are areas highlighted with stickies and notes to represent K-Town and the extension of downtown like where me and Leroy showed them based on our memory. He also highlighted where Promise Heights is supposed to be. Next to it, there's a massive plot of land also near Putnam Parkway.

"This is the part that's missin from the flyers. See?" Trish opens up to the page and shows the similarity from the brochures, and she's right.

Rouk points to the land. "That's where they gon build it—behind Promise Heights."

Taj folds two pieces of gum into his mouth, wearing the same face Momma used to make back when she smoked cigarettes. All of us stand up to get a better view.

"It would make sense, if you really think bout it . . ." Night takes a breath before continuing, "They been floodin errbody wit warrants, makin all kinda threats, pullin YGs into police cars just cuz they can, especially if they have a record. It even makes sense why the DKs showed up almost two years ago, if you really check when errthang started to go downhill."

"They had us out here thinkin they was tryna start a gang war in the beginnin," Taj says. "We won't thinkin big enough, aint see the whole forest from the trees, cuz we neva even knew Louis B was a player then."

"And now we runnin outta time," Leroy says, rubbing his waves. "The Freedom Festival is days away and we aint figured out how to stop the Bainbridges in all this time.

"We could send what we have—the recordin, Faa's records, and whateva otha YGs and OGs got—to the news. They may not work in legal court, but enough to hit em from all the angles at once out in public. Not a one-hitta-quitta, but strong enough," Leroy suggests.

"I know we aint got no leads on findin CB, but if we could just get anotha copy of the drive they gave Faa, that could be exactly what we need," Rouk says. "Whoeva that person is, they know where the bodies are buried. We release it, all of it, and bam."

"If we aint found nothin on CB yet, what's gonna change in a few days?" Leroy asks.

Beside me, Will is shifting in his seat. I can feel something rising out of him before he finally lets the words out. "I know already," he says. "It's Camilah Bryson."

"Lyric's momma?" Princeton's eyes grow wide. "She used to be Louis B secretary, aint she? You sayin she—"

"Gave Faa the donation list and the drive," Will confirms.

"Wait, how you know?" Princeton frowns so hard, his eyebrows touch at the center of his face.

"Because she told me."

Leroy almost spits out the soda he's drinking.

"I was gonna tell you that day when I called, but everythin' happened so fast. His mom fainted and had to go to the hospital after hittin' her head when it was leaked 'bout Lyric bein' Louis B's son. When she came to, she sent Lyric out the room, and that's when she told me she was the one who sent the information to Faa."

Rouk stands up, crosses his arms, and posts up on the wall. Trish rubs his shoulder, whispers something.

"I haven't spoken to her since then, but she told me it would take a few days to get the donation list and whateva we needed. Just one catch: we gotta protect Lyric from the DKs."

"I know you fuckin lyin!" Rouk screams. "No way in hell."

Just about everyone else either scoffs, sucks their teeth, or cusses, slamming their hands on the table. Everyone except Taj and Night, who look at each other, then Leroy.

"I know it don't sound good, but this gon' get us the stuff we need to ruin Louis B's chances of runnin' for governor. This ain't nothin'—it's the evidence that Faa sacrificed his life for—and more," Will explains. "And . . . and I think I can flip Lyric, which means we'll have another advantage."

"Iono bout that," Taj says. "Yo cover blown, he knows who you are. How you gon pull that off?"

"His mom is his Achilles heel—and he is Louis B's weakness."

"Did he sound like a weakness to you? He exposed his own son and is settin him up to go to prison. Don't sound like he care to me," Brown Brown says.

"'Cuz he don't know. I think part of Lyric hasn't trusted Louis B from the start," Will says. "I think he has evidence that he could use against him as insurance."

"Like what?" Brown Brown asks. "It would have to be somethin big."

"I think he has proof that Frank, Myrrh, and Louis B had something to do with Faa's death."

There's a chill in the room, riding on the heels of the truth he just shared. I almost can't believe it.

"You not fuckin wit us, are you?" Rouk demands.

"No, at a party, Frank called him. And based on the convo I overheard, Frank threatened him and said that if he didn't fall in line, he would be the next person swimmin' in the marsh. That's when Lyric threatened him back, said he knew where the skeletons were buried and who buried them."

The air is sucked out of the room. Rouk looks like he's either about to jump across the table and choke the life out of Will himself or literally explode into a million pieces.

"I saw him usin' a silver pen. The way he was holdin' it looked weird, like he wanted to make sure the pen caught the audio of the phone. And when I installed the tech, I saw it plugged into the computer. I didn't get a good look, but it—"

"That's a Spytech pen. It records audio, some of em even record video." PYT jumps up. "If he had it plugged into the CPU, Will could be right!"

Everyone looks at each other, thinks about what it could mean—not just for taking down Louis B, but getting justice for Faa.

"When can you do it?" Rouk interrupts.

"I can roll up on him today, see if him and Miss Camilah will be home."

"You do it, then. I mean it." Rouk looks at him, eyes sharp and voice firm. "I'll do anythin to protect Faa's legacy, so I aint gon stand in the way, but as far as *I'm* concerned, I aint doin shit fuh Lyric—don't eva ask me to."

For a second, no one says anything, everyone is lost in their heads. Trish just hugs Rouk. Taj pulls Leroy over as they both wipe tears from their eyes, considering something that seemed impossible.

"What do we do bout the festival?" Trish asks, softly. Not wanting to say out loud what I'm sure everyone else is thinking—canceling the festival to keep everyone safe.

"We gotta make the Freedom Festival so big, so loud, anythin done to hurt us will be captured so that, regardless, we win—whether our attack on Louis B works or not. With that and errthang we'll send to the media, we gon turn the court of public opinion in our favor and kill Louis B's dream of becomin president befo it even starts," Taj says.

I think everyone starts to get it, as they nod their heads.

"How we gon do that, in less than a week?" Brown Brown's got a good point. "There's only so much we can do, without the Bainbridges gettin a whiff of what we plannin."

"There is a way." Taj sighs. "And lemme just say, ion like it eitha."

"Pops . . . You talm bout Pops, aintchu?" Leroy reads his face. "You think it could work? Cuz Pops still aint apologized fuh what he did to Sani and the crew, and we gon need them, too."

"Iono, but I know if I could unify most of the gangs and get em to join the BDs, I can find a way to get Pops on our side—and not take no fuh an answer."

"So we doin this? Like, furreal, furreal?" Princeton scans everyone's faces.

"Furreal, furreal," I say.

"Then we need to split up, and focus on different things," Taj says. "Rouk and Trish, yall can keep tacklin Faa's journals, see if there's anythin new we can use. PYT, you can work wit em, too, and when yall ready, we could chat wit

Lady Tee and Miss Rosalind, since they know campaigns. Brown Brown and Night, yall can get the YGs togetha, see what errbody got, from Nate's camcorders to Sani's transportation."

Everyone gets out paper, pens, whatever we can to keep track because it's going to take all of us to make this work.

"Jay and Princeton, yall can work wit Tina to get errbody on the ground fuh the entertainment. You, too, Will—but only after you handle flippin Lyric and gettin all the info you can from Miss Camilah." Taj takes a moment to look at each of us in the eye, determined and strong. "But first things first, it's time to call an emergency meetin, but *this* time, it's gon be on our terms."

24

Will

I stand in front of Lyric's front door, and in my head, I practice my greetin' twenty different ways: a nod, a smile, a grin, a wave, a mean mug. But nothin' feels good enough.

I knock before I lose my nerve. I clench my phone in my pocket, which now has the recordin' of the chief and Louis B. Maybe hearin' the words will be enough to—

Miss Camilah opens the door in a purple linen outfit that flows free, smiles.

"Will, come on in—happy you could join us." She waves me in, and I'm greeted a second time by the smell of beans, meat, and somethin' sweet.

In the kitchen, Lyric stands in an apron, slicin' plantains. The moment he sees me, his smile is bullied into a frown.

"Are you hungry? I just finished making some feijoada, and Lyric's about to fry some sweet plantains, since we've both been craving them."

As soon as I'm close to him, Lyric turns his back and dumps some of the plantains into the grease, refusin' to speak. Miss Camilah sees it, rubs her fingers through his hair, and says somethin' to him I can't quite hear.

Reluctantly, he hands her the spatula, plops down near one of the barstools, and grumbles, "Hey."

"You both look like you have something on your minds. How about y'all take it upstairs, and when you're ready to discuss it with me, you bring it back down?"

Lyric pouts, draggin' his feet.

Miss Camilah speaks to him in Portuguese, and like Miss Julia and Mum, she wins with the last word, a reminder of who is really in charge.

Lyric leads me inside his room, whether he wants to talk or not. He belly-flops on the bed, while I sit on the corner just out of reach.

When he turns toward me, I won't look at him, not yet, so he rolls closer, softly crashes into me. After I don't respond, he folds around me, slippin' his hand up my shirt.

I punch him in his thigh, hard. "Quit bein' an asshole."

"You first." He still doesn't move. "Jay say anything to you?"

I snap back at him. "Why? You say somethin'?"

"Yup, told him to make me one of his love letter clients."

"Why?"

"You know why—and he did, too. That's why he got all pissed."

Is that why Jay was actin' like that when we left the pool?

"I'm out." I try to get up, knowin' that my words will pull

him back in. "It was a mistake to come here."

"Wait . . . wait . . ." He scrambles after me, latches on to me from behind. "I got a better idea." He tries to kiss me, but I dodge him.

"Stop, you know you wrong. So get yo' ass whooped so we can move on."

"I'm not wrong. I was telling Jay the truth."

"What truth? Stop messin' with him."

"He won't let you go. What else am I supposed to do?"

I think 'bout headbuttin' him. "You can quit frontin'. I ain't gon' let you manipulate me. I know you don't care 'bout me. You just wanna use me. You knew where my mum was, and you kept it from me."

"If I would've told you, I know you would have left—or maybe did something else that could have got you killed. Plus, she wasn't in danger. I wouldn't have let that happen. You know me."

"No, I don't." I hit him because I don't hate him as much as I want to.

We struggle for control ova each otha. He regains it, but I'm almost free. Now I'm gonna make him regret it.

"You love him?" he asks, darin' me to lash out.

"Why do you care? You don't love me. You don't even like me."

His façade buckles, then I feel it in his body, the tension. He pretends, tryna recover. "No, I don't, and I never will."

Liar. I kiss him so hard that it throws him off guard and he melts. I stir somethin' up so deep in him, he can't deny it. Then I pull away, staggerin' from the haze and heat from his touch.

"I'll see you downstairs." I walk out the door and wobble at the top of the stairs.

I hear him scream into his pillow. Mission accomplished.

"Did you figure out what you needed to?" Miss Camilah studies me as I walk to the kitchen island and sit at the barstool across from freshly fried and glistenin' plantains.

"Miss Camilah—"

"Unh-unh . . . eat first. Then we'll all hear what you need to say."

I nod.

Lyric comes down, still fumin' but not rollin' his eyes at me so much that Miss Camilah has to step in. When we're done eatin' dinner, Miss Camilah hands us forks, and we enjoy the sweet plantains.

"Here's everything you will need on Louis." Miss Camilah reaches under a drawer and hands me an envelope-sized zipped bag that seems to have documents in it. "With the jump drive of the donation list and his plan in its three phases."

"Ma! What are you—" Lyric says, stares at her, betrayed. "What did you say to her?" he spits at me, jumpin' up like he's ready to fight furreal this time.

"Lyric, sit down!" she yells.

He looks so angry, he could cry. He pleads with her in Portuguese, but she shushes him in both languages. "This is my decision to make, Lyric."

"It's dangerous. You know what Dad will do if he finds out."

"What? Kill me? Kill you? How is that any different from the string he's dangled us from all these years?"

Lyric doesn't respond, just stares at the rack of plantains, silent.

"I need you to promise me you won't try to take this on by yourself like Faa. Had I known, I wouldn't have given him this, but I know you have more people behind you. And remember my second condition about Lyric."

"Before I can agree, I need to tell you the truth 'bout Louis B and then ask you a question." I look at Lyric. "It was him who leaked that you are his son, not Frank and Myrrh, not the BDs, or anyone else you might be blamin'."

"Like I would believe you," Lyric says.

I pull out my phone, pull up the recordin', and play it. By the time it's done, Miss Camilah has turned all kinds of colors and Lyric is so still and quiet, he doesn't even look like he's breathin'.

"He admitted to it, but you knew what he was capable of all along. I know the reason you did all this and gave me the address to where my mum was being held. You wanted somethin' too. That's why you made me promise to do you a favor. Well, now I want to know what it is."

"Too bad. I ain't in the mood to tell."

"You don't have to, 'cuz I already know. You do want protection, don'tchu?"

"I don't want your protection, and I don't need it." Lyric's eyes widen, then turn sharp like daggers. "This is why I can't trust you or anyone else, because y'all will do anything to win. Dad was right—"

"Stop it!" Miss Camilah yells at him. "Just stop it!"

Tears fall from her eyes. Suddenly, all of the anger and denial on Lyric's face collapses into worry.

"You know this isn't a trick, Lyric. You've heard Louis say that kind of hateful stuff to my face. I know because you cried whenever he did."

Lyric looks away, embarrassed.

"What is it going to take for you to see him for the liar he is and always has been?" Miss Camilah says. "You heard it! He leaked your identity as our son when he was the one who threatened to take everything from us if anybody found out."

Lyric submits, a little-boy version of himself. But he still seems on the fence. But I need him to choose, and I need him to do it now.

"You're the biggest asshole I've eva met," I say louder than I mean to as I put away the recordin'. "But the more I think 'bout it, the more I realize it's because you're scared of the truth. So, since you won't say it, I'll say it for you, you love me. And whetha you want to admit it or not, you *do* trust me.

"And I refuse to sit here and watch Louis B ruin your life. If you're scared because you don't trust the BDs, trust me, 'cuz I already know you have evidence that you're not talkin' 'bout—audio recordin's from that silver pen you carry around with you all the time." Lyric looks up at me, for a second, shocked.

"You listened to my recordings?" he asks.

"No, I haven't, and you don't have to give me anythin' if you don't want to," I say, prayin' that my plan will work, for everyone's sake. "But I need to ask you one last thing 'cuz our lives and the lives of people I love are in danger. Yours are too, so tell me the truth."

Lyric stares at me, speechless. Miss Camilah does too, but her face softens into a grin. I dunno what she's thinkin', but I know she has her answer. I will protect him, as long as he protects us.

My question comes out, whether he's ready for it or not: "Did you kill Faa?"

Miss Camilah gasps, "Lyric?"

"The fuck? No!" he yells, genuinely surprised. He's just as shocked as she is. Then, somethin' settles, maybe a memory he wishes he could forget, and he looks down, tortured.

"Tell me, Lyric." I lean in.

He jumps up, walks away, and stands near the door to the sunroom.

"Just give me a minute. I don't know what to do," he mumbles.

Miss Camilah whispers to him in Portuguese, and even though he's away from her, it's like her words become arms that wrap around him.

"Okay," Lyric says, like a confession, "Dad reached out to me maybe a year ago. He said I was going to be eighteen soon, which meant I needed to think about my future. He was the one who told me about Mom's condition—and that the doctors didn't know what it was. He showed me a trust fund statement for over five million dollars and said it could be mine. He said I'm his only son, so—"

"Filho da puta," Miss Camilah shouts, shakin' her head. Her hand tremors start to take ova.

She reaches ova to me and grabs my hand to steady hers. Even now, she wants to hide her symptoms, so she doesn't burden Lyric. But it doesn't change the fact that he already knows.

"Ma, you okay?" Lyric walks ova to her and sits on the floor at her feet. He hugs her calves as he leans his head near her lap. "I'm sorry . . . desculpe."

"I'm not mad at you. It's your father. He just doesn't care who he hurts, as long as he gets what he wants." Miss Camilah pulls at Lyric, so he gets up and sits on the chair next to her.

"Keep going. We need to know everything." She smears the tears from her cheeks and lends him her strength, even a little of her rage.

"He said I'm his only son, a potential heir to the family business, which means I need to learn how to lead. The next day, Frank and Myrrh were waiting for me when I got out of school. They took me to practice, and on the way, they gave me a phone, telling me to keep it safe and take it straight home. They said not to look at it or I'd regret it, so I didn't. I kept it, but eventually, I couldn't help it, so I bought a charger for it. When I opened it and was finally able to cut it on, I looked through the call log and texts. That's when I realized it was Faa's. Later that day or the next day, Frank and Myrrh came and got it. Next thing I know, the cops arrested Taj, saying he did it."

"They must have planted the phone on Taj so that Louis B's crooked cops could use it as evidence against him," I realize.

"Part of me was scared of that too, so I asked Dad one time if he had anything to do with it. He said he didn't, but that sometimes you have to remove barriers on the path to greatness. He told me about the BDs, that they needed to be stopped, and the only way to do it was for me to befriend Rouk."

"At no point you thought to talk to me? To ask me before you got dragged into this?"

"I wanted to handle it on my own."

"But I keep telling you, Lyric. It's not your job to take care of me. You need to focus on—"

"If I don't protect you, who will? It was the only way I could get the kind of money you need for your treatments. I need—" Lyric's voice breaks. He turns away, swallowin' his words till he can try again, steadier.

Now his hands are shakin' as he takes his turn tryna hide from her. "I need you to be here, Ma . . . to see what I can do . . . how I can repay you for all the torture you had to put up with because of him, them. It's not worth it if you're not here with me."

Miss Camilah freezes and holds her hands togetha, starin' at them. Mum has also done this before when she wants to make a promise she doesn't know she can keep, even when hearin' the words will make me feel betta.

Mum says false hope is more dangerous than any type of violence because where violence can injure the body, false hope injures the soul.

"You are right," she says softly. "We're gonna figure this out. Okay?" She gets up, walks ova to us, and sits down so she can reach for his hands. But he beats her to it, hugs her.

"Listen to me." She pulls him back. "Did he have you do anything else? What about Rouk? You befriended him, right?" Lyric leans forward, balances his weight over his hands on both of his knees.

"Yeah, Dad wanted me to so Frank and Myrrh could meet him. He said something about a plan to break up the BDs."

"So you weren't behind the shootin'?" I say.

"No, Frank and Myrrh barely listened to me and kept more secrets than they told. And that's after Dad forced them to only speak to him through me. He wanted me to prove my leadership, show I was worthy of the Bainbridge name. After that happened, though, things changed."

"How?" Miss Camilah asks. "Did they hurt you?"

"No. I just had to be different. It's the only way they would respect me."

"You were the one who flipped Brown Brown and made him betray the BDs after you blackmailed him."

He nods. "And Frank and Myrrh came up with the idea of the DKs, based it off of where they're from and what they've done in their own cities, masks and all."

"Which means, you're the—"

"Scapegoat." Lyric nods. "I know. That's why I've been recording all of my convos with Dad, Frank, and Myrrh—tracking everything just in case."

Miss Camilah sits up, surprised.

"I didn't plan on using it. I wanted it in case Dad tried to lie or go back on his word."

"I don't know if that's enough to get him in jail or to keep you out of it . . . ," I say, thinkin' out loud.

"Louis will never see the inside of a jail cell. The Bainbridges are too powerful. But there's only one thing they care about more than Louis—their company—and his reputation is the only power they have. When that's gone, they're vulnerable."

I remember Mum's words about her own plan. "Would you be okay with talkin' to my mum and Lady Tee? They will likely have the kind of connections that can help if we get your recordins and the stuff from being Louis B's secretary."

Miss Camilah chuckles.

"Did I say something wrong?"

"Secretary?" she asks. "I wasn't his secretary. I was his chief strategy officer. I'm the one who helped him build his empire. At least the vision of it, before he distorted it and made it into something that hurts people, not helps them. Connect me with your mother and Lady Tee—I'll help them with whatever they need."

"Will you share your recordin's?" I turn to Lyric.

He doesn't answer at first. "I need to think about it. If it's the right thing to—"

"You want to strike a deal, don'tchu?" I cut him off. My eyes burn, and my face hurts. But that don't have nothin' on the sharp pains in my chest, like I'm breakin'. "This isn't 'bout gettin' rid of Louis B, is it? You just want what he promised. You could care less 'bout any of us."

Lyric looks like he's 'bout to say somethin' but doesn't.

I guess everyone was right; my plan was neva gonna work. I can't convince him.

"I'll let you know when I talk to my mum," I say, lookin' at Miss Camilah and ignorin' him.

I stand up and take the bag she gave me. Before leavin', I turn to Lyric and see the resistance in his eyes meltin'. He doesn't have to say it, I can feel his desire to protect his mom, to protect himself.

Now I just hope that's enough to make sure he protects us, too.

25

Leroy

After a twenty-minute drive, the parkway turns into a fortress of trees and marshland that I only eva really seen as part of history field trips bout Gullah Geechee heritage at the Pin Point Heritage Museum.

We make a few mo turns and the trees replaced wit houses so close to each otha they family. We park on the ground covered in white oyster shells and walk ova to the all-white buildin, past the thin but strong trees covered in blue upside-down bottles like glass leaves. We follow the sidewalk made of tabby concrete, the same material mixed wit seashells, till we at the open mouth of the buildin near the pier.

Standin on the edge of the bank near wooden tables and chairs is Pops wit errbody else, Ma, Auntie Rissa, Lady Tee, Miss Rosalind, Miss Julia, Benji, and the rest of our crew. Errbody find a seat and keep they greetins short and polite.

The smell of mud and water mixes wit the scent of salt and sweet incense. Pops move like he gon speak, but he stops himself. He looks at Auntie Rissa, follows her lead by listenin first.

Taj starts by tellin errbody what we know. Fuh a second, especially when he describes what the recordin said, the adults look at each otha, shocked and pissed. They can barely hold it in. So, Taj stop, hear what they gotta say.

"I take it you didn't bring us here to only say that." Lady Tee crosses her arms, waitin fuh what Taj is holdin back.

"Nah, I didn't. We decided we gon have the Freedom Festival anyway."

"Whatchu mean yall *decided*? We can't just let yall walk into somethin we know could get you hurt. Outta the question." Ma aint tryna hear nothin else.

"I know y'all want to help, and that you care a lot, but I'm inclined to agree with Tanya, we can't let this continue if we know it's dangerous." Miss Julia shakes her head.

"We have to," I say. "If we don't, Louis B not only gon announce he runnin fuh governor, but he gon have errthang he need to get rid of all of us."

I explain the plan. Each of us go through the key points, reasons why we have to do this, why we aint got no choice.

"I get the goal; I understand it completely. But it's too big for yall to handle on your own," Pops says.

"That's why we need yo help," Taj says. All of us nod in agreement, so errbody know we on the same accord. "Between errbody's connections here, we can all join togetha and make it happen."

"Why wontchu listen?" Pops says, gettin pissed.

Auntie Rissa pulls him back wit her eyes, he tries to say it different. "This aint our first time goin up against the Bainbridges—and those who support him. We don't want yall to have the same scars we have, some that may neva heal."

"And if we don't do this, if we don't fight back wit errthang we got, you think it's gon be easier to live? Or you think yall the only ones who got the right to decide if you live or if you die?"

"Taj, nobody's sayin that." Auntie Rissa's eyes are sad and mad and hopeless—but her trust in us shines through. "Keep goin, Bittersweet, I'm listenin. We *all* should be."

"There's a reason why I chose this place. Cuz it's where they taught us the story of Igbo Landing, where the Africans who refused to be anybody's slave walked into the river," Taj explains.

"We the ones who taught you that story, so what's your point?" Pops replies.

"That is my point! Yall were also the ones who taught us that, at first, the NAACP said no to people our age doin nonviolent sit-ins and boycotts," Taj explains. "Auntie Rissa, you told us they preferred Black folks just fight wit the law. But they aint let that ride, people our age pushed on anyway, got trained, organized—they didn't do it alone. They asked fuh help when they needed it and cuz of it, they were able to even go deep into Mississippi and Alabama, two of the most dangerous places fuh us, to prove a point. Our freedom aint a suggestion, and our silence can't be bought—or bullied into submission."

"Togetha, we can win this. Not just fuh us, but Faa and errbody else we lost in this fight," Rouk says. "Faa already paid the ultimate price. And we don't eva want anybody else to have to go through what I did—what yall did. Cuz, you right." He looks ova at Pops. "Yall got scars. But at least yall alive."

"We down to do whateva we gotta do to make this happen. So, are yall in? Cuz we only got a week befo Louis B announces he runnin fuh governor," Taj says.

"Alright." Auntie Rissa nods. "Tell me whatchu need, and I can get some calls started."

"Rissa . . . ," Pops says.

"Tré, rememba what we talked about. We do it *wit* them, not *for* them."

"Well said." Lady Tee nods. "I'll do everything I can and then some."

"I'm in, too," Miss Rosalind says. "We stand a better chance of success if we all work together. I know firsthand that y'all are more capable than we've given you credit for." She looks at errbody, but her eyes linger on Miss Julia, who don't say nothin but nods.

Slowly but surely, Taj do it again—the impossible. All the adults, even Pops, eventually agree.

After mo plannin, it's time fuh errbody to head out, at least fuh today. Me and Taj walk back to the car wit Night, Rouk, Brown Brown, and PYT, but Pops stops us.

"Can I get a minute?" he says, wavin us ova, near the pier overlookin the marshlands. We walk ova, unsure of what he gon say.

"Look, I'm not good at the small talk, so I'll just say it: you were right. I thought as long as everythin turned out a certain way and we beat the Bainbridges, it would be fine. But I miscalculated. No, to be honest, I fucked this up. No otha way to put it. I just wanted yall to know."

Me and Taj look at each otha, speechless. Is Pops apologizin?

"I've already spoken to Rissa and the OGs, and I've stepped down from being the president. I'll leave it to yall to figure out what's—"

"You leavin, aintchu?" Taj says, face hard and tryna hold back whateva emotions on the otha side. Pops don't deny it, just looks out at the water.

"What else am I supposed to do?" Pops face look different than I've eva seen it, soft and desperate. "I gave you back the BDs."

"Did we ask fuh that? Did you even ask us what we wanted or how we felt?" Taj bout to walk off, I can feel it. But then he looks Pops right in the eye. No mo runnin—fuh none of us. "Don't try to make this bout me or bout us. It's boutchu, cuz if it won't, you woulda neva left."

"You may not agree with the choice I made," Pops says. "But, to me, it was my only option. I'm supposed to be able to protect you. To die—"

"You keep talm bout how you willin to die to protect us. But that's just anotha way of runnin, of leavin us behind again," I say. Taj looks at me like I read his mind. Pops just stares, like he don't understand what I mean. "You asked what we want, what we need? Fuh you to fight to live—not *fuh* us, *wit* us."

Pops don't say nothin, just stares at us, our words errwhere but where he need em. But it's okay cuz we all feel errthang in full, togetha, even if it's only in silence.

I fall off the church pew, where I'd been sleepin, and onto the red carpet. Since we got errbody on board fuh the Freedom Festival, none of us been sleepin much wit all the plannin we got left to do.

Feelin the soft red carpet under me, I wonder if the altar still holy when errbody gone, and even if it aint and I pray, whetha God will make an exception.

"Lee! You okay?" Auntie Rissa shouts, stompin up from the stairway and glarin at me from a mile away. She musta heard me fall. I nod, tell her I'm fine, but Auntie Rissa look in my eyes, see somethin aint right. "Unh-unh, sit down fuh a second. When was the last time you ate?"

"Maybe this mornin?" I can't rememba. "We gotta make enough handouts, flyers, and parts of the exhibit—"

She interrupts me. "Lee, I know the festival is important, but it's almost five o'clock. No wonder you walkin round here on the verge of faintin. You starvin yoself. Now, you and me gon go downstairs, and you gon eat somethin, where I can watch. And when you finish, you gon be done fuh the night."

We walk downstairs to the basement and into the kitchen, where I eat some of the rotisserie chicken and vegetables wit a side of her bourbon bread puddin.

"Why dontchu go visit Jay?" she asks. I aint think bout it, aint thought I had time, but it's a good idea. She gets me a couple plastic containers. "For Jay, Jacob, and Julia."

After gettin errthang togetha, I'm out the door and headed to him. When I pull up, I realize I aint get to check to see if he was home, prolly shoulda texted. But after I knock and Jay opens the door, it takes errthang in me not to scoop him up in my arms.

There is so much I wanna say, that I want him to know, but all I can do is stare.

Iono why, but it's almost like Jay is glowin, at least err-where there's skin showin. I wanna touch errwhere I can see, his face, his neck, his shoulders where his white tank almost hangs off.

Maybe he was dancin? Practicin fuh his performance wit Tina?

"You good?" I say, wonderin.

"Me? Oh, yeah . . . I was just running over some of the choreography before everybody got back. Do you want to come in?"

Jay steps back, leavin room fuh me to walk inside. My legs pull me forward without me even havin time to think.

"Want something to drink?" he says, snappin me outta my train of thought.

"Yeah, thanks . . ." Errtime I try to say somethin mo, my words get stuck in my throat. I wonder if Jay can still do what he used to do. The slightest touch of his fingertips and, just like that, he make my pain go away.

"Leroy, did you hear me?"

"Oh, nah . . . My bad, whatchu say?"

"You okay?" Jay reaches up, puts his hand on my forehead.

I hold my breath, tryna keep it togetha.

Iono if I should, but my body move on its own, and I put my arms round his waist, pullin him up into me. I don't kiss him, even tho I want to.

Then he kisses me, and it's like somethin inside me breaks free. I pick him up and sit him on top of the back of the couch so we're eye to eye. He's breathin me like oxygen as if he's afraid of drownin.

I let him hold my face in his hands and guide my lips where he wants em, where they belong. When I reach behind him, under his shorts, he freezes.

"Wait . . ." I can barely hear him ova the sound of my heartbeat drummin in my ears.

Jay softly pushes me back a few steps, grabs my hand, and tells me to follow him upstairs to his room.

He closes the door behind us and locks it. He pulls his shirt ova his head and slides his shorts down his thighs till all that's left is light blue boxers fightin to control his excitement.

I'm so caught up in watchin him that I don't do nothin. Not till I feel his hands pullin at my white beater and then my shorts. He stops when he feels all of me pushin from beneath my clothes.

"I'll be back. I need to . . ." He unlocks the door and slips out into the hallway.

Iono where he went till I hear the faucet runnin. Soon, he's lockin the door behind him again and pullin me toward him on the bed. He reaches into the nightstand and pulls out a small box of condoms and lube. When he reaches fuh one of the condoms, I stop him.

"You sho?" I ask.

He nods. "You don't want to?"

I don't answer. I just think bout errthang we been through these past few months, the hurt, the distance, the—

"Lee . . . ," Jay says, squeezin me.

I look at him, like really look at him, realize this the first time he called me by my nickname.

"Are you okay?" he asks again. I shake my head.

"Baby, ion wanna fuck this up again. I'm scared Imma hurt you in the future, that I might not get it right, and you end up hatin me."

"I'm scared, too," Jay says, wraps his arms round me. "Neither of us know the future, but I know that if you want to try this again with me, I'm willing because I love you."

My body responds first, then my words. I say, "I love you, too," ova and ova, so he neva fuhgets it. So he knows how much he means to me.

Ion leave no part of him untouched, but it aint just me, Jay tryna make it so I neva fuhget eitha, cuz errwhere I kiss him, he kisses me. Our bodies are new words bein spoken where every sound is just as important as the silence.

My body trembles under his softness. When Jay holds my face, kisses me, it's like I finally realize we here. He's in my arms, tellin me he love me and he wanna be wit me after errthang we been through, and my heart feels so good that I start to cry.

Between my tears and his touch, I hear anotha poem . . . well, a set of poems. Ones that are bout not only why I hurt, but what comes after heartbreak: us.

26

JAY

My body aches, but my heart feels full. I load the sheets into the dryer, then head back upstairs to make up the bed with new ones. I'm pulled into my old room—Will's current room. And there, in front of me, a set of memories I should forget but still can't plays: the first time Will and I played his records, and he taught me how to make a song of our own.

I don't know what comes first, me thinking about Will or me reaching for the paper and pen in the bottom drawer of the desk. It doesn't matter because I'm wading—no, struggling to tread—through my own ocean of feelings with Will's name on it.

I love Leroy; he loves me. I want to be with him. But at the same time, my heart and mind are still remembering my feelings for Will. As I write, the memories I don't feel I can do without ripple, and like the waves of his own ocean, they pull at me, ask questions, and demand answers I don't have.

If I love Leroy, how can I love Will, too? If I choose Leroy over Will again, would I lose Will—and his love—forever? I know I shouldn't, but I want Will to stay. And each time I try to argue, explain that my feelings for Leroy are stronger and deeper, my feelings for Will lash back at me, leaving new scars.

I want someone to tell me how to break a heart without breaking my own or hating the empty space it leaves behind. Even if it might be confusing for him, in this letter, I fight for the right to love him, too, differently.

But what do I do when *I'm* the one hurting him?

Eventually, when my hand is shaking so bad and the tears falling so fast that I can't write or see straight, I finally get it. I haven't been keeping Will next to me solely because I love him, but because I'm more afraid of the emptiness he'd leave behind.

Through the tears, the fear of his answer, and the reality that he, too, has a right to choose, I promise him I'll respect whatever decision he makes. Even if I'm not strong enough now, I'll grow stronger, learn to love him more than the fear of his absence.

As I fold the confusing pages into an envelope and scribble his name as beautiful as I can, I say thank you and I'm sorry. I take a deep breath and brace myself for a new beginning and the end.

The day of the Freedom Festival is finally here. I know our plan backward and forward. I know what to do when the performance officially starts through to what happens when the DKs finally show themselves.

Last night, me, Rouk, Leroy, Jacob, Princeton, and Taj were on a never-ending conference call with Night, PYT, Brown Brown, Trish, and Christina, who we finally looped in all the way, so she could help us brainstorm every possible scenario, even Taj's fear that Tré might sabotage it all.

I put on my outfit by Trish and, as always, she doesn't disappoint.

The baby-blue top is fitted, worshipping my shoulders as it turns into long beaded white strings that reveal my abs and waist, right before the fitted white jeans. I'm surprised and grateful. Where I might have felt nervous seeing my body, the curves I did everything to hide, I'm proud of how I look. Everything from the perfect haircut with the slits in my eyebrows, to the two necklaces that glitter.

For the first time, I can't wipe the smile off my face because I like the boy I see in the mirror. I'm ready.

Jacob and I, yet again, look like outfit twins as we finish getting ready in the bathroom, applying scented oils in layers. He's wearing white fitted, high-waisted pants that make me want to tie a jacket around his hips since he's got too many curves. The woven, sheer baby-blue top that looks like a net is sure to drive everyone wild.

Just as we're running down the stairs, the doorbell rings. Momma, Miss Rosalind, and Will already left early to get things set up with Auntie Rissa. Leroy and Taj shouldn't be here to pick us up for another hour.

On the other side of the door, Dad stands in an all-white outfit of his own, a short-sleeve collared shirt with matching slacks.

In his hands are two small potted lavender plants.

"Momma, Miss Lin, and Will already left. You just missed them," I say.

"I know, I'm actually here to talk with you two." Jacob and I look at him, as if he started levitating before our very eyes. "I just got off the phone with Julia. She said Leroy and Taj would be over to get you soon, right?"

We nod and slide to the side, so he can come in.

Momma told him to come? I ask Jacob with my eyes. He shrugs, just as clueless.

Dad places the pots on the living room table and motions for us to sit, like we're the guests visiting.

I rub my hands on my knees to make sure this is real, not some dream about to turn into another nightmare.

"For years, I've thought about the perfect words to say so you know how sorry I am for what I did to you, how I broke your trust. But no matter how hard I think or wait, the perfect words haven't come. So I'm bringing these instead." He points at the pots.

"Lavender? You want us to garden?" Jacob says, less angry, more genuinely confused.

"Yes and no," Dad says. "People think of lavender as one of

the most difficult plants to grow well, but the truth is simple: it takes time, patience." He reaches for the two pots and slides each of them toward us, barely making a sound. "The key is if you pot it, you have to choose one with as much space as you're willing to let it grow.

"That's why I'm here, to apologize from the bottom of my heart for hurting you both. Jay, for hitting you for no reason, calling you a word my own father used to cut me down, leaving me with wounds here that still haven't healed," he says, pointing at his chest. "It's because of you those scars began to heal at all. I love you, because of who you are, and I'm proud of who you are becoming.

"And, Jacob, I'm sorry for breaking the rule I always said you should abide by—to protect, to love, to do no harm. Thank you for not letting my mistake strip your power to still be kind, protective, and loving. You're stronger than I ever was and living up to a standard I failed to reach. And I want you both to know, that if you let me, I'll be here by your side, to learn with you and from you—and most of all, I'll never stop trying, because I love you."

Me and Jacob sit in silence. I can feel Dad wanting an answer, proof that there's a chance for us to be a family again, but instead he turns the pots so we can see that on the side are instructions on how to grow the lavender year-round. "When you're ready, let me know what I can do to repair the trust I've broken."

Wiping the slate clean feels too far out of reach, but as Jacob and I look at each other, it finally feels like we're moving closer to whatever healing could look like. Dad reads our eyes, as if he knows, too.

Jacob says something I don't expect. "If you're headed to the festival now, can we ride witchu?"

Dad doesn't respond, just stares at him.

"If you don't want, we can just—"

"No . . . umm . . . I'd love to! I just have to clean out my truck real quick. Come on out in three—no, maybe five minutes." I haven't seen Dad's face light up like this in a long time.

When Dad leaves his keys and has to come back but tries to play it off, both me and Jacob chuckle at the awkward warmth filling both our faces.

"You sure you okay with this?" I say.

Jacob rubs his waves, deep in thought. "Nah, you?"

"I don't know. If you aren't sure either, why did you offer?"

He shrugs. "It felt like he needed some proof things could be different. Maybe I needed it too."

We let his words wash over us and wipe us clean of the worry that this might be a mistake. If it is one, it feels like one we have to make regardless, for each other.

When Dad honks the horn, Jacob and I head out and climb into Dad's ashy blue truck that gurgles steady. I get in the back and on the dried-out and cracked pleather seats are a few more lavender pots. When I see the names, I can't help but ask.

"You have lavender plants for Leroy and Taj?" I ask.

Jacob looks back at me like I must be mistaken, but he sees them, too.

"I thought they'd be a nice gesture, something to help them with their relationship with Tré."

Jacob shakes his head. "Taj couldn't keep dirt alive."

For some reason, the joke hits so hard, we all burst into laughter, probably because we know it's true, no matter how crazy it sounds.

"I don't think Leroy is any better," I add.

"That's alright. I have hope, since they both have you two, they'll learn."

Jacob tries to hide it, but I see him blushing.

When I look at the rearview mirror and see Dad's eyes, the blush finds me too. It feels different knowing that he knows so much but pretends to know so little.

The Freedom Festival, which is covering three blocks between the Bee Baptist church and the May Street YMCA, is not scheduled to start for another hour or two, but it's already crowded with volunteers and dozens upon dozens of people who came early to help.

The YGs are erecting multicolored tents and art exhibit displays that create a three-dimensional maze showing average property value per house, per block, per neighborhood, with statistics and activities to help people understand their options and potential investments. They also provide a clear breakdown of the Bainbridge Promise Development, including sketches of the proposed adult prison, youth detention center, and the police academy, as well as the statistics of how high arrest rates will be in comparison to what they are already.

The farther down the exhibit goes, it weaves between a massive platform where the performance will be held, with voting boxes and even games that help people determine the types of action they want to take with this information, individually and collectively.

I'm so lost in the beautiful graffiti-esque letters and numbers that I almost forget I need to meet Christina in the auditorium at the YMCA to practice one more time before the band arrives. As I walk in that direction, I see Auntie Rissa, Miss Rosalind, and Momma, who I can tell is trying to see if I'm okay.

When I smile and give her a thumbs-up, I can literally see her exhale in relief and Miss Rosalind doing the same. Together, they are all smiles near the booth already sweet with the aroma of Momma's ginger snap cookie sandwiches, cinnamon rolls, and cotton candy, and Treat's BBQ cooking sweet meat not far from them.

I look around but see Jacob back helping Dad, who is now talking to Taj and Tré about the lavender plants. Funny enough, with all of the times I've seen Tré look like a general ready to lead his soldiers into war, he stands in front of Jacob and Dad a different version. He's nodding and attentive as Jacob reads the sides of the plants and asks questions, like he's trying to remember everything so he can help Taj if he needs it. Watching them, I'm reminded of how Tré looks like Taj but feels like Leroy in the way he focuses, grows softer and more approachable, the longer you look.

I get a text from Leroy, **BABY OMW. B THERE IN 20.**

A smile skates across my face. I can't wait to see him.

As I walk into the gym, I expect to see Christina, maybe even with Trish, but no one's here. Then I hear Will call my name from the side of the bleachers.

I haven't seen much of him lately, outside of the planning for music for the event. He hasn't said much since I left the letter in his room on his pillow. No text. No letting me know he got it.

I even checked his room a few times to see if he might have thrown it away. I see he didn't, since he's holding the letter in his hand as he walks over to me.

Will is in an all-white outfit like Jacob, but where Jacob's top was sheer, his is more wrapped around him like white silk ribbons that hang long at his sides. In the white, his eyes feel sharper like he could read my thoughts if he wanted to.

My heart races as he gets closer, but instead of running from the feelings, I face them—and him.

I brace myself for his answer, even if it hurts.

"I read your letter," he says. His voice is almost hoarse, but he doesn't look like he's been crying. I wait for him to keep going.

"At first, I ain't gon' lie, it pissed me off and it hurt. It would be easier if you just told me you ain't like me."

"I know, but I didn't want to lie," I whisper. "You deserve the truth, even if it's complicated."

"I get it." He looks at the paper, as if his answer lies trapped somewhere on the pages. "I think I finally understand how you feel."

"You do?"

"Kinda. I like Lyric, even though I love you—and I hate it."

His name is like a punch in the chest. I breathe through it. But the truth is heavy-handed as it slaps me around. "So . . . I was right? You're with him now?"

He doesn't answer, just watches me squirm.

"You cute, you know that?" His hand grazes my cheek. I stare at him, wondering. "But, nah, I'm not with him—we not good for each otha. Too much has happened, but I realize I can like him, even if I don't like what he does."

"So what does that mean about us?"

"I dunno . . . I mean that. I'm gon' always have more feelings than friendship for you, but I also know it don't mean I can't have feelings for otha people too. Let's just say I'm gonna need some time to figure it all out."

"Does that mean when this is over, you're leaving again?"

"Nah, I'mma finish the year out here. Keep trainin' wit J.D., and Mum said she gon' hang around a little longer to just be still for a minute. But make me a promise."

He stares into my eyes, then at my lips.

"Can you be happy so I don't have any regrets? And if you see me strugglin', ask before you do anythin' like try to help, so you don't make it harder for me."

I nod as he kisses me on my forehead instead.

After Will leaves, I put my skates on, rub the ache in my chest.

This whole time, my worst fear was that those I love would one day leave me and never come back. That they would stop loving me, then that would be it. I'd never love again. But as I dance, I realize I had it all wrong. There's only one person required to love me, and it's me. And as long as I promise to never forget, to always love on and be there for me, I'll be fine.

Right when I finish my first pass through the routine, I see Leroy standing at the entrance of the gym in a white tank like the one he wore at the skatedown. It's mesh with just a strap on one shoulder and a section missing on the other side revealing his tats, which almost glimmer underneath.

He stands there as if he's nervous. He looks behind me and I turn around, but no one is there. He jogs over to me quickly, doesn't say anything, just folds me into him.

"You okay?" I ask.

Leroy kisses me, then presses his forehead into mine so we're connected, as a smile finds its way across his face.

"Baby, I missed you," he says.

"I missed you, too . . . Hold on." I change out of my skates, leaving them where Princeton and Christina will know to get them when they arrive.

I pull Leroy, arm-hook and drag him toward the door. We stand in front of the YMCA where the street is even more packed. Without even having to say anything, we wander over to Jacob and Taj, standing next to Dad's truck.

"See? He was right where I said he was," Taj says, grinning.

"You mean where I said he would be," Jacob corrects him.

"Same thing. For that, you officially on Lavender Duty," Taj says to Leroy.

"Taj, the only thing I know bout lavender is that it smell good. How Imma take care of it?"

"Easy, read the directions. They on the side." Jacob chuckles, knowing.

Leroy nods and looks at Taj. Like clockwork, their hands find each of us.

Taj wraps his arms around Jacob's waist, as he makes bedroom eyes at him; Leroy pulls at me from behind, whispering softly into my ear. They both say the same thing, first with their bodies, then with their words. *Don't you want to help us out? Take care of our plants as you take care of yours?*

423

Jacob and I look at each other, then we say our answer in the softest, most seductive way possible, *Nope.*

We pull ourselves free, high-five each other, and wish them luck.

As the Freedom Festival officially begins, so many of us look around in awe, both nervous and ecstatic. We were hoping a lot of people would come, but I don't think anyone was prepared for this. What looks like thousands, enough to fill the homecoming game stadium several times over, pour into the streets. It's a good thing they made two mirrored sides of the exhibit so more people could experience it without having to crowd together.

Christina almost makes Auntie Rissa cry when she and Lady Tee bring her to the stage supposedly to kick off the festival with a speech but surprise her with some news. We raised over five hundred thousand dollars to put toward renovating the diner and launching it in a new location.

The news not only makes the crowd go wild, it fills the streets with a level of music and joy I've rarely seen. Auntie Rissa says her words about how we are not only each other's medicine we are also each other's freedom, the reason all of us from every culture, race, and community must stand together and fight for what we all deserve, as if on cue. And to kick off the block party, Will mixes the record until the echo of "Shorty Wanna Ride" blends with YoungBloodZ's "Presidential," and they both sweep through the crowd like a cool breeze.

I look for Christina and see her near the YMCA side entrance where the band is lined up, ready to make their entrance. I jog in their direction but have to take the longer way around due to the crowd.

I accidentally bump into someone.

Before I can say anything, the band blasts Outkast's "Morris Brown." As the music rolls over the crowd, I come face-to-face with Myrrh.

I see the sea of DK faces try to surround me, but Princeton barrels through the group. He grabs my hand, and suddenly we're running toward the other entrance of the YMCA.

Night waves us down, propping open the door.

As soon as we make it through, he slams the door shut, locks it, and looks for something to hold them off a little longer as they begin to kick at the door.

"Don't get tired yet," Princeton says, looking at me. "We gotta get to the band on the other side of the building, or the plan won't work."

"Plan? What part of this is the plan, we only talked about—"

"This way is the fastest," Night says, leading the way. But at the opposite entrance, the DKs start flooding in ahead of us, just as they break open the door behind us, too.

The groups now wear red masks so we can't see their faces, but Night tells us to run faster behind him, and as we do, he takes down as many as he can. He yells for us to keep running, just to get to the double doors.

When we rush through them, we realize why. A crowd of YGs are waiting. They see us and run past us to go help Night. In the wake of their absence, the bass players are prepping—every time they strike, my heartbeat surges, electrifying the blood in my veins. I should be scared, I should be worried, but with Princeton at my side, I feel like I can do anything.

Christina sees us and waves us over. She stands in an all-white majorette outfit with a baby-blue lightning strike down her torso that blushes into a sparkly skirt the color of the bolt. The majorettes and Princeton help me change into my skates.

The song shifts, and it's our second cue that it's almost time to go out. More BDs file in around us to keep an eye out, this time OGs on the perimeter.

Based on the plan, nothing is allowed to stop us from performing. In fact, it is the performance that sets up the biggest moment of the festival, and it's why we pitched the story to every reporter and news station nearby. The only way to cut the DKs off at the knees and dismantle Louis B's plan is to do so publicly, as we're sure he's probably started his own gathering to make his announcement.

Once Christina and I have on our skates, the majorettes give us and Princeton the final part of our outfits, capes that glitter.

"Where is—" I start to ask, until Night runs up. Aside

from a few scratches, he's fine, just a little winded. He gives us the signal to go—phase two.

The skatedown favorite, "Kryptonite" morphs into another song I don't recognize, but it's almost like the ground beneath us quakes.

"You ready?" Christina says, winking at me.

"Are you?" I laugh.

She motions for me to stand in front, followed by her and Princeton. Once the intro by the band is done, Will flips the switch and plays a remixed version of "All Nite (Don't Stop)" by Janet Jackson to the backbeat with so much bass it threatens to possess us all.

We huddle behind the drum majors and a circle of majorettes. The drum line around us starts moving into formation toward the stairs.

The closer we get, the more people yell and scream along, and as me, Christina, and Princeton climb the stairs, the band switches to "Presidential" by YoungBloodZ.

As the beat blasts, we are a trio popping, locking, dropping, and rolling until we're a sea of hips. And with Princeton as the other base, we pull off partnering moves, turns, and even a flip that summons deafening screams, as people dance along. We ignore what keeps approaching in plain sight as people blend into the crowd.

Right on cue, Princeton backs away while Christina and I show off, a distraction as he motions toward Will and helps him give the signal to all those watching in the crowd. Then, taking center stage, Princeton pops and rolls with the drum majors and majorettes, giving me and Christina just enough time to change out of our skates and into boots.

When we're done, the three of us carve through the crowd in a phalanx of the drum line and majorettes, an arrow headed to the street corner. As we dance, I see Tré, Dad, and Night, but I don't see Leroy, Jacob, or Taj.

I shake off the fear and panic building, and dance harder.

Cops line up, mean-mugging, as more reporters and cameramen creep closer. Will cuts the music, and we hear the DKs before we see them chanting, "We the Black Diamonds."

The crowd parts, revealing more DKs than I could have ever imagined with two white-and-black masks leading the way. It doesn't take much guesswork to figure who two of them are: Frank and a newly out-on-bail Myrrh.

A different song builds, as the band and us get closer. The crowd reconnects, but it isn't who I thought. A chain of elders led by Edda Nae, Momma, Miss Rosalind, Dr. Eva, Lady Tee, Miss Tanya, Dad, and every adult we know sings the words to "Ain't Gonna Let Nobody Turn Me Around," arm in arm.

For a while, the songs collide, fighting to overwhelm each other, until one side swells so loud and wide that it drowns out the DKs, but not before they switch tactics.

The DKs scream, "Don't fuck wit us. Don't fuck wit us.

We the Black Diamonds!"

They get louder and louder until they are shouting on the verge of growling, an encroaching army of intimidation. Just when they are about to strike and push themselves into the crowd, our side does the unthinkable.

Like a ripple of dominoes as far as the eyes can see, all the YGs, OGs, and the community of K-Town present flip coverings like the ones we are wearing. Except theirs are all black with white letters, reading WE ARE THE *BLACK DIAMONDS*.

As the crowd on our end turns into a sea of black, the old-school chant we heard at the BD's council meeting layered by the different sounds of each crew begins. Together, they are the backbeat to the protest song as it rises louder, drowning out the DKs until they have no choice but to stand silent, overshadowed, with one final choice to make. They can do what they came to do—try to ravage and fight innocent people—or they could turn back.

At first, I think they are pausing because they are intimidated by the song of the crowd, but as I look around, I see what they see: the front line, our elders, mothers, fathers, friends, family, and even strangers, hand in hand, arm in arm, hoping for peace.

But behind us is another reality: every BD is armed, waiting and ready.

For every peaceful bystander singing, there are five more

armed—pistols, shotguns, and other firearms with their permits hanging around their necks, proof they have a right to own and protect us, if need be. Machetes are strapped to their waists, with bats and crowbars, their fingers glittering with brass knuckles itching for the chance to kiss.

If the DKs dare touch those we love, they are guaranteed one thing above all else, annihilation. And whether it be the DKs or crooked members of the police, if there must be blood in the streets, it will be theirs. No one will turn us around, no one will take what's ours, no one will threaten those we love without paying the ultimate cost.

Rouk, Leroy, PYT, and Brown Brown appear beside us, armed, creating a row in front of us, prepping for things to get ugly. Some cops encroach further, as if they will incite a response, help things along. But they underestimated us, too.

Tré's and Benji's forces arrive from the sides of houses, backed by even more crews than I've ever seen, as all of them pour onto the streets from every direction. There aren't enough cops in this city to even think of stopping us—and they know it.

There's chatter and clamor, then a clip of the mic as a news story plays behind us on the platform. The headline:

GUBERNATORIAL CANDIDATE LOUIS BAINBRIDGE SUSPECTED IN MURDER OF YOUNG BLACK JOURNALIST FAA MITCHELL

As the news story continues, it reveals a recording of Louis B we never heard but that clearly ties him to commissioning Frank and Myrrh to make Faa disappear. It sprawls into connected stories of corruption, Louis B seen in handcuffs.

Before Frank and Myrrh can lift a finger, the red masks behind them—most likely former BDs—beat them into submission and hold them so Detective Dane, newly reinstated this morning, thanks to ADA Butler, can arrest them.

As soon as Frank and Myrrh are carried away, those who helped apprehend them take off their masks, eyes red with tears, regretful of turning their back on the BDs. Regardless of what might have convinced some folks to become DKs, everyone has one thing in common. They've been touched at some point by the joy and warmth of Faa's light.

A long line of others, the DKs who tried to attack us in the school, are escorted by BDs in another direction. No cuffs are needed, because it shows on their faces, proof that the DKs and the leadership backing them are no more.

Over the speakers, the broadcaster finishes, and Auntie Rissa walks onstage.

"Today our community mourns the loss of Faa Mitchell." She fights back the tears but loses. "And now, as Louis Bainbridge and all those allegedly responsible wait to stand trial, may our community and Faa's family receive justice."

Rouk stands on the other side of Leroy, lips trembling. Then he bolts away, hard and fast. Leroy and Taj run after him—we all do. And as if everything that has hurt is finally released, a wail that can only be described as pain being purged ricochets like waves across all of us, until you cry whether you knew Faa or not, overwhelmed by the unbearable burden of Rouk's sadness.

Leroy and Taj hold him so tight, I wonder if he can breathe, but then I realize crying is its own form of breathing, of pulling in what hurts and releasing it, hoping that healing—or something like it—will find you.

Everyone crowds around Rouk all on one accord, and as we do so, those who can't hold him hold each other, whispering, "It's okay. It's over. May justice be served."

Epilogue

Leroy

Six Months Later

"Yall ready?" Taj says, lookin back at me and Rouk as we sit in the car parked at the beach. But Rouk can't answer, and I can't neitha. It's like time has stopped, and iono if it's a good thing or a bad thing.

If Rouk say he don't wanna go no mo, it don't matta who waitin or how many, I aint leavin this car or his side.

"We aint gotta go nowhere or do nothin till you ready," Taj says, reachin fuh Rouk's hands and holdin em tight.

After some time, Rouk turns, opens the car door, and on the otha side is Trish in a white camisole and a long dress that blows and flows. Next to her is Christina wearin somethin similar, just as angelic and perfect. PYT and Brown Brown are in matchin linen suits, and Night and Taj are already out and on the otha side of the car waitin.

Trish reaches out her hand, and when she whispers somethin I can't hear, Rouk finally steps out and stands wit em. All of us join arms—fuh him, fuh us—as we walk through the parkin lot, then the sand dunes, lettin ourselves rememba.

Even tho it seems like the Freedom Festival was just yesterday, it's almost been six months. We finished school, while givin Detective Dane and ADA Butler all the evidence we had of Faa's journals, the rest of our recordins, and Miss Camilah's drive and documents.

When the trial started, fuh a while it felt like all hope would be lost, especially when the judge threw out the recordins we got from Lyric fuh the festival. But when he showed up as a star witness, even tho he went ghost and aint nobody had heard or seen him in months, his testimony flipped it in our favor—Faa's favor—wit way mo records, even his own journal, which he kept while workin wit Louis B. Errbody finally heard the truth of how Louis B threatened and emotionally abused Lyric, and tricked him wit false promises that he would get his inheritance to take care of his ma's medical bills.

We thought that was that, but it won't enough. There still won't no proof that Louis B actually ordered the murder of Faa. Just when it seemed like he was gon wiggle his way out, Frank and Myrrh ended up bein the nail in his coffin, sharin some recordins of they own after he played his hand and tried to put errthang on em. His attorneys and testimony painted em as deranged criminals tryna blackmail him. Even Louis B won't ready fuh all the evidence they used to choke him out in court and back it up wit errthang from the payment logs to the plans he greenlit.

Errthang dragged ova our heads, even past graduation, till a coupla days ago when the jury, after deliberatin fuh almost two weeks, came out wit a guilty verdict fuh Frank, Myrrh, and Louis B. But when it came to Louis B, it won't just that. ADA Butler and Lady Tee led the charge, filin a wave of civil suits fuh damages to landowners and businesses—not to mention OGs and YGs targeted, harassed, and discriminated against.

Now we here, finally, togetha to rememba Faa. Cuz of the bogus charges by that detective who tried to frame Taj back when Faa was first killed, we neva got to attend Faa's funeral. But now we can, as a family. But not just that—as a community.

At the base of the sand dunes, we see Auntie Rissa, Ma, Miss Rosalind, Miss Julia, Jay, Jacobee, J.D., Pops, Princeton, Lady Tee, and Dr. Eva. They all stand waitin wit Faa's favorite flower, white and blue stargazer lilies, in they hands. Behind em, it's so many people lined up all the way to the pier that they look they own kind of wave. Arm in arm, we lead the way so Rouk don't have to do this alone.

In the DJ booth at the pier, Will plays Faa's favorite song, "Killing Me Softly" by the Fugees. And as Lauryn Hill's voice fills the sky, we keep walkin. As we pass the lines of people, they file behind us, errbody takin the time to rememba the good times, the arguments, the sleepless nights, and every life Faa touched by the light of his existence.

At the top of the pier, as Lauryn Hill breaks out into the iconic whoas and la-las at the end of the song, we sing and cry along, tossin our flowers into the sea, wonderin why any of this had to be. When Rouk loses his voice and can barely stand, we hold him.

Just when it all becomes too much, Will switches to Faa's second favorite song, one of the few that could get him up to dance—Strafe's "Set It Off." And through the tears, we bus-stop and electric slide, surrounded by the faint vanilla scent of the flowers ridin the salty breeze till it seems like even the seagulls bobbin to the beat.

Eventually Trish and Christina have Rouk laughin, and I finally get to take it all in: Auntie Rissa and Benji danc-ing; Miss Rosalind, Miss Julia, and J.D. two-steppin as a trio; Lady Tee and Dr. Eva becomin the smooth breeze; and Edda Nae and the Low Rider Crew, along wit PYT, Brown Brown, Princeton, Will, and Night, showin off moves aint nobody knew they had. I even see Ma wit Pops, smilin in each otha's arms, in love.

Jay's arms wrap round my waist from behind, and even tho I can still feel the pain of Faa's death gnawin at me along wit Rouk's grief, it's okay cuz, even tho it hurts, there's so much to look forward to.

Jacobee and Jay got into Northwestern. Auntie Rissa and Taj made a deal that Ma and Pops would stay and run Auntie

Rissa's diner in its new location on River Street, while they would go to Chicago fuh a new start. Taj's crew is comin right along wit em—a decision that only got easier once I got my acceptance letter to the school in Wisconsin. And wit Will also goin to Northwestern, it feels like a new beginnin fuh all of us.

"Whatchu thinkin bout?" I ask, bringin Jay to the front, so I can put my arms round his waist, too.

"How often we'll get to see each other, now that we'll be two hours away."

"Howeva often you wanna see me," I say.

"Not possible."

"Aww, you tryna say you don't wanna see me?" I joke.

Jay kisses me soft and sweet, makin it hard fuh me to keep my hands where Jacobee can see em. He's makin I-see-you eyes at me even while Taj is in his arms.

"I wanna see you every day, but that's way too much driving. Plus, I know we have a lot to get used to. College isn't easy, and with you being a star poet, you might need even more time to focus."

"Well, if it's bout poetry, I gotta see you as much as I can, cuz you my muse. If it won't fuh you and yo love letter, iono if I would eva found out I had a way wit words, too."

He blushes, and I wonder how we could be so lucky to find each otha.

"Matta of fact, I'm workin on a new poem as we speak."

"Is that so? What's it about?"

"Iono yet. You gotta spend some mo time wit me and find out."

As we continue to dance, errbody findin they way from hurt to healin, and I'm glad that my love fuh him—our love fuh each otha—was strong enough to get us here.

Iono what the future holds, all I know is I love Jay. He loves me. And whateva happens, we'll handle it togetha.

Acknowledgments

In my first book, I listed the many people who believed in me and have been such a powerful part of this journey.

For this book, I want to do it a little differently—just as honest, but reflecting something I learned that changed my life because of this book.

I've always struggled with forgiveness. From as early as I can remember, I built myself up tough and strong, like an impenetrable fist. When I was hurt, I hit back—and hard—so I would be remembered one way or another. To me, the only thing that has mattered, that has kept me safe, is remembering. Or perhaps, to never forget. That those who claim to love you can hurt you far deeper than those who claim to hate.

I've always struggled with love. From as early as I can remember, even when I didn't know it (or what it would cost me), love was something I trained myself to chase—in others. And when I found it, I did everything possible to keep it. Even if it meant losing myself. Because to me, the only thing that mattered, the only proof of love, was the number of people who chose to stay. But no matter how good you are at chasing, at the end of the day, it's just running. And none of it matters if you don't know what it feels like to be chosen.

Togetha has taught me that when it comes to forgiveness and love, rarely are we told that both start with you. We can grow so comfortable making ourselves smaller so that others feel big, dimmer so that others feel bright. But true love, true forgiveness, I believe requires us to do two things: 1) choose yourself first, so you remember who you are, and 2) shine brighter, even if it hurts.

At the end of the day, we are not only precious but we are worthy of protection. But we can't protect what we don't see. And we can't appreciate what we don't feel. So, above all, I'm grateful to each and every person who, by existing, proves that I'm not alone. And because of it, we will always find each other. Because we are each other's medicine.

Extra thanks to the world's best literary agent, Ellen Goff, and my oh-so-very-awesome editor, Carolina Mancheno Ortiz. Couldn't do this withoutcha!